Coping with Death and Destruction

By Arrison Kirby

El Deth Publications
Knoxville, Tennessee USA

Cover illustration by
Aaron Shugart-Brown

2016, a year that adds to nine, removed some of the brightest sources of light from earth, as we knew it at the time. Huge swaths of comfort and culture were noticeably stripped away from the population as if by some unseen, alien force. David Bowie, Prince, Muhammad Ali, Leonard Cohen and Carrie Fisher all stepped behind the veil in 2016, just to name a few. Even the circus was calling it quits after that season. Don't get me started on politics.

Most importantly, we lost our own personal loved ones. For our author, that included the beloved dog shown on the cover, the entity to whom this book is dedicated. A few months prior, our illustrator also lost his dog, Beta, upon whose death one of these stories (the true one) was based. His support given to this work is in her memory.

ISBN-13 : 978-0-692-84696-4
ISBN-10 : 0-692-84696-4

Contact the author at: **arrisonkirby@gmail.com**
Contact the illustrator at: **aaron@shugartbrown.com**

To Remy.

"For life and death are one, even as the river and the sea are one." – Kahlil Gibran

Selections
(in astrological order)

Myth

I

With a single, concussive pulse, darkness filled the earth. The entire Internet was erased in a blink. Along with it went the world's banking records, digital communication systems and social security databases. Entire industries were abandoned in almost as little time. The electrical grid ceased function for only about two months before people began purposely destroying it's components out of frustration. This anger soon spread into the domains of the wealthy and middle classes, no longer protected by conventional, electrical, alarm systems. Some were able to defend their homes by sheer force, while others were beaten and robbed, sometimes murdered, and occasionally torn apart by a mob. Law had become a dicey concept and order even more so. Some people fled for more remote areas to disappear from what was left of society. Others took their chances in the worlds they had already known, however different the tone had become. No matter fight or flight, every man became responsible for himself and his family.

Small communities in search of isolation came to populate the National Park system in America. These were prime locations for hunting and gathering once all the stores were pillaged of their resources. One such community, taking claim to a remote, off road, corner of the Badlands National Park, worked together to erect a small makeshift village nestled deep between the intimidating, rising rocks. All friends, family and coworkers of varying degrees prior to The Fall, they pooled their abilities to build simple, private homes, with a shared bathroom and kitchen. Within a matter of months, the community had even installed a basic plumbing system, carrying water to these facilities all the way from the Cheyenne River.

Each citizen fell into a ritual around whatever amenity they could provide to benefit the sustainability of the community. For Chloe Vallejo, this meant educating the children (as well as boiling water to store for future use – a task shared by all of the citizens who did not leave the village to work). Chloe had been a third grade teacher, prior to The Fall, so her role within the community was natural. A part of her deeply appreciated the environment she had found herself working in. The mighty vibrations of the rocks were more conducive to learning than a squared-in classroom, and the light breeze through the pavilion where she taught was the most reaffirming evidence she could find that God was still with them.

All of her students were aged below thirteen. Children above that age graduated to mentoring alongside adults and assisting them with their daily tasks. The youngest child was five and any child below that age was relegated to the full care and control of his mother or father. This range of age five through twelve was ideal for openness to exploration, unconventional thought, and an eagerness to learn. Coupling this with the new world still being built from scratch, lessons often veered into more philosophical and esoteric realms – sometimes to the point of pure, childlike, ridiculousness.

"When we feel anger, we are not thinking straight," she told the class one afternoon in autumn. "If we focus on our anger too deeply, or for too long, then that anger can make us do things that, later, we see were mistakes. These mistakes can embarrass us, or even hurt us or someone else."

"Like when I punched Tommy in the mouth because I thought he hid my shoes?" spoke Max, age seven, from the back. The children all laughed – including Tommy.

"Exactly like that," continued Chloe. "You were angry because your shoes were missing. Instead of stopping and thinking to solve your problem, you let anger take over and that anger made you blame your friend – and not just blame your friend, but also yell at your friend and hit your friend. And what happened after that, Max?"

"Tommy's parents talked to my parents and I got in trouble."

"That's right. And what happened to your shoes?"

"I put them in the wrong cubby hole," spoke Max and the children laughed again.

"Exactly! So you see that you had one simple problem, Max. You could not find your shoes. Instead of using your brain to think about where you put them, you used your heart, which was full of frustration and anger. And by doing that, you created lots of new, more difficult problems for yourself, didn't you?

"Yes, ma'am."

"You see, class, most problems start very small and then grow larger and larger as you feed them more of your emotions." The class was captivated. "One moment you are Anakin Skywalker, training to be a Jedi, and the next you are Darth Vader, trying to control the entire galaxy."

The class fell silent as the collective countenance of the children turned from jovial to confused. Finally, Josie, a louder, larger student aged to nine, spoke up, "Who is Dark Vader?" The rest of the class, seeing an opportunity to speak out of turn by noting their own ignorance on the topic, followed Josie's question with scattered variations of their own.

"His name is Darth," spoke Chloe, "Darth Vader. I guess it was before your time." Even six years after The Fall, she was still getting used to the fact that all access to cinematic culture prior to it had been lost. *Star Wars* was released three years before she was born; yet she had grown to be just as intimately familiar with it as her parents before her. During her first two and half decades of existence, culture permeated between generations as technology allowed for not only the preservation of film and sound over time, but the enhancement and improvement of it as well. Now, however, she found herself facing the first generation of children who would be completely cut off from all of it, with no concrete way to identify with the film-stock mythology of their ancestors.

The entire discussion could have ended there, but for its salvation at the voice of Samuel, age twelve. "I remember Darth Vader," he spoke, "I remember *Star Wars*. It was a movie, right?"

Chloe felt a glimmer of pure joy in Samuel's recognition. "Yes! It was a movie!"

"My dad showed it to me back when I was almost a baby," explained Samuel. "I only remember a little bit, but he's told me about movies a lot."

"What's a movie?" asked Tommy.

"It's like a story that you see happen," replied Samuel.

"Yeah. That's basically it," corroborated Chloe. "Kind of like a play in a box of light. They were very popular before The Fall, but now that there is no electricity, we can't watch them anymore."

"So what is the story of Darth Vader?" asked Max.

"Well his story was called *Star Wars*," spoke Chloe.

"Tell us!" implored Max.

"Tell us! Tell us!" joined the rest of the class.

And so Chloe told them. She told them about the Rebel Alliance and the Death Star. She told them about the droids and the Jawas, about Luke and Leia, Obi-Wan and Han Solo. She told them about the Millennium Falcon, the TIE fighters, and of course, Darth Vader. In as much detail as she could remember, she gleefully served the children the entire narrative of *Star Wars Episode IV: A New Hope*. The children remained silent and engaged through the entire delivery of the film's story.

After ending with the destruction of the Death Star and the subsequent homecoming of the heroes, Max was the first to speak, of course. "So did Darth Vader die in the Death Star?"

"No he actually lived," she replied.

"So there's more?" asked Shelby, another student, age nine.

"Yes. The Star Wars universe is very large," explained Chloe.

"Tell us more!" started one disembodied voice from the back. "Tell us more! Tell us more!" The children continued their clamor.

"Not today, I'm afraid," she said, though Chloe was ecstatic to find them interested in a piece of lost history that she held so closely. "We can continue with the next episode tomorrow." She dismissed the class and the children scattered.

The students were eager to accomplish the lessons of the following day so they could continue their journey through the *Star Wars* cannon. When that point was finally reached, they put away their slates and chalk and Chloe began to summarize *The Empire Strikes Back* in as great of detail as she could recall. She was most uncertain about the story's events that occurred on Hoth, but was mindful to cover the interactions between Obi-Wan's ghost and Luke, opening the door for the Yoda character. She told the students of the bounty hunter, Boba Fett, and the Imperial Fleet's retaliation against the Rebels. She spoke rather pointedly of Lando Calrissian's betrayal, tossing in the adage that "what goes around comes around." The children were stunned to learn of the family ties between Darth Vader and Luke and an audible gasp swept the room when Chloe climaxed a description of their saber battle. As she spoke the narrative of Han Solo being frozen in carbonite, the children grew loud and agitated – slapping their palms on their large table and hopelessly protesting the events of the story they were hearing.

"What is going on with this stuff?" shouted Josie over the clamor.

"We will continue with Star Wars tomorrow," spoke Chloe.

"We won't be here tomorrow," reminded Samuel.

"Oh, you're right." Chloe had forgotten that their break was beginning the following day. Having gradually returned to a lunar-based calendar, the idea of a seven-day workweek had become obsolete in the village. School was in session for six days, beginning when the new moon was completely obscured. This was followed by a four-day break, and then four more days of classes. In the second half of each cycle, starting at the full moon, the students were given a six-day break. This was followed by four more days in class and a final four-day break before their lunar month began again at the new moon. "We will continue with Star Wars in six days," she amended.

The children groaned.

"That will be plenty of time for you to think about what could happen next in the story and we can all talk about that when we return. If any of you can't wait and decide to ask your parents about what happens next, please keep it to yourselves over break unless someone specifically asks you to tell them. Some people don't want to know everything all at once, so no spoilers, guys."

"No spoilers? What does that mean?" asked Josie.

Max raised his hand and spoke at once. "Miss Vallejo, do you know about Batman?"

Chloe smiled. "I know a little bit about Batman. Yes. I was kind of familiar with some of the movies – but it started as a comic book, actually."

"My dad told me about Batman," continued Max. "Bad guys killed his mom and dad so now he is like a bat and he beats bad guys up - and one of the bad guys is a clown."

"He beats up a clown?" asked Tommy, gleefully.

"He beats up a clown and a penguin," explained Max through their mutual laughter. "Come over to my house and my dad can tell us all about it."

"Okay."

Alan, a quiet, bulky, nine-year-old, chimed in: "Can I come, too?"

"Yeah that's alright. Dad won't mind. He likes to talk about stuff from before The Fall."

Chloe dismissed the class. "See you in six days, everyone."

The full moon hit hard that evening, shaking up the base nature of each villager. Max's father, a bearded and relatively young adult named Britain, was ecstatic to have the opportunity to share a piece of his own childhood with his son and son's friends. All seated around a fire pit, he began his first story with a dramatic flair, as though he was reciting a well-rehearsed monologue. "Our tale begins in a time before this one, when people were social creatures and paper could be traded for goods and services – a time with electricity and technology." He then divulged a detailed account of Bruce Wayne's childhood and the murder of his parents. He spoke of Alfred as Wayne's adopted caretaker, and Ra's al Ghul as his eventual mentor, with a crescendo into his becoming Batman. From there, he slowly opened new doors to new characters, introducing Commissioner Gordon, The Penguin, Robin and, of course, The Joker. The children were enthralled, wide-eyed and open mouthed.

The fireside story session continued the next evening, with more children in attendance. The night after that brought even more, and some of their parents, as well. By the fourth gathering, the event had morphed into a nostalgic recounting of Batman synopses and motifs, shared openly between Britain and three other adults from the village. By that point, the number of children present had tapered off a bit, but those who remained were dedicated to the discussion. These were the tales of their ancestors, after all.

Chloe and the children returned to school, centered and lucid in the afterglow of a beautiful fall break. The onset of colder days had revealed itself and would soon be cause to drape the sides of the pavilion and start a fire in their wood-burning stove. This set a subdued tone in the class. The children were so quiet and behaved, Chloe could not determine if they were all actively listening to her lesson, or daydreaming. Ultimately, it did not matter either way to her – though their lunch break, too, seemed more quiet than usual.

At recess, a bright and popular seven-year-old named Stephanie, accompanied by her two girls and one boy entourage, rounded the activity area. "Hey, let's play

Star Wars!" she suggested to each grouping of classmates. "I'm Princess Leia," she would immediately affirm, securing the primary female role for herself. Nevertheless, many of the other children joined in, eager to pretend with a tangible narrative.

"I'm Luke!" called out Josie, to the dismay of several male students who would have loved to have had the role, but would not dare cross Josie in an attempt to claim it. Naturally, Han Solo was the first character chosen by a male, followed by Darth Vader, Chewbacca, and then R2D2.

Once the roles were determined, the actual role-play was as flimsy as could be expected from children enacting the second hand fiction of their parents. Mostly, the children ran around pretending to fight with light sabers or shoot lasers from an invisible TIE fighter control panel – all while making general statements like, "We've got to blow up the Death Star!" or "Let's get to the Millennium Falcon!" At one point, Stephanie as Princess Leia had taken to wielding her supposed light saber, for some reason, against Danny – a shy six year old who had meekly chosen to be a Jawa. When she took a step backward, she bumped into another body.

Max placed his hands on her shoulders the moment she turned around. "I thought a Jedi was not supposed to let her anger control her," he said.

"Don't touch me," she shouted, stepping back from his grasp. Danny ran away.

Max stepped toward her again. "You shouldn't deny your anger, you know. You should let it give you power. You obviously feel it. I see you swinging your sword at poor little Danny."

"It's not a sword. It's a light saber, you idiot."

"It's still a weapon."

"Shut up, Max," she said, "You didn't even want to play."

"I didn't want to play *Star Wars.*"

"Well that's what we are playing here and I am Princess Leia. So what are *you?*"

Max grabbed her by the front of her blouse and pulled her face close to his. "I'm Batman."

II

Gordon built the foundation of his temple with rocks from within the Badlands. Though bricks were available to him, he felt it was important to incorporate the land, itself, into his project. He believed his area to be a sacred place, inherited from his father. Before that, his grandfather owned it and his grandfather came into possession of it by way of his great-grandfather, Max, who had fled there with his parents while he was still a baby – a few years after The Fall. After five generations, there was no question of Gordon's ownership, and the history there was rich and widely known. His ancestors were buried just a brief walk from where he built his own home with his own hands. Like that modest residence, the temple, too, would be Gordon's construction alone.

At the center of the temple floor sat a tall, metal, fireproof, safe. After the foundation, Gordon next gave priority to building a tight, stone box around this safe. Once completed, this box was to raise as high as the walls, touching the ceiling, and appearing as a pillar in the center of an otherwise open space. The walls, contrary to the pillar, were to be made of evenly cut, gray bricks. These, too, however, would come from within the Badlands, hand forged by a local artist, from silt collected from along small streams; purchased at a discount because the artist shared enthusiasm for the vision of the temple.

Inside the safe, at the center of all this, were stacks of boxes filled with hundreds of *Batman* comic books and graphic novels. These boxes were piled one on the other, hoarding nearly all the space within the metal container. All of the books inside were decades old, preserved in plastic sheaths. The jewel among them was a badly tattered and yellowing *Detective Comics* #27, which was Batman's first appearance in any literature; his inception from the olden year of 1939.

These, like the land, were passed down through the generations from his great-grandfather Max. A staunch Batman devotee, Max spent most of his twenties traveling the remains of America and seeking out these comics – collecting them and building as complete of a canon as he could obtain. He became a scholar on these tales and, by the age of thirty-four, had worked with a team to complete a quintessential, strictly literary translation of the Batman story. As more copies were printed and distributed over time, their book, *The Batman Odyssey*, became the standard account that people referenced. By sheer luck of ancestry, Gordon now possessed all the raw materials, which he felt duty bound to preserve and protect.

As he laid brick one day, Shilo, his wife, approached. "I'm off to my Star studies now," she said.

"Are you taking the kids with you?" asked Gordon.

"Yes. I will."

"They can stay here if they would rather."

"No that's alright. I want them to learn and develop Star Wars principles. It's good if they come," she said.

Gordon knew where this discussion was going. They had been down this path with greater frequency as time persisted. "I understand that," he said, "but let's make certain that they don't forget their roots in Batman. There are a lot of good lessons there, too."

"Gordon, I know. You don't have to tell me every time. I know why you are building this temple. I know about your grandfather and your family and I know how close you are to Batman. I understand that – I respect that

– but Gordon, I just want to raise our children to be respectful and, most importantly, nonviolent."

The violence thing again. "You know, Batman does not condone violence," he retorted.

"Oh, right." Shilo rolled her eyes. "Your figurehead throws people off buildings, Gordon. He shoots guns and punches people in the face."

"He doesn't shoot *that* many guns. And what about Star Wars? Star *Wars*? *War*? It doesn't get any more violent than *war*, Shilo, and *your* figureheads chop people up with laser swords! Don't even talk to me about violence."

Shilo scoffed. "Whatever. Goodbye." She turned, walked back into their home and retrieved their children, Ivy and Nigma. The three mounted their bicycles and pedaled away.

Gordon worked on his temple until Shilo and the children returned a few hours later. The family ate dinner, did some reading, and turned in for the night. In the morning, Gordon woke and began his day before the others, as usual. He walked to his temple, and was disturbed to see half of the wall, completed just the prior evening, had been collapsed. The remaining half was defaced with large green letters that asked: "BATMAN? SERIOUSLY?"

He wondered how anyone could have known the purpose of his temple. His great-grandfather's picture books were of extreme value and so it was of no benefit to explain his intention to anyone at that time. Passers-by could only see that he was building a structure, neutral to any ideology or the mythology from which it was birthed. He did plan to open the temple to other Batman devotees for study and praise, but only once the entire thing was completed and the picture books safely and secretly stowed in what would be the Sacred Pillar.

Suddenly a thought occurred to him. He walked back into the house and to his wife, still asleep in their bed. "Hey. Shiloh."

She responded with a sound somewhere between a grunt and a moan.

"I'm sorry to wake you but it's important. My wall got knocked down – on my temple. I think it was someone from your Star Wars group."

Shiloh turned over and looked at Gordon through squinting eyes. "What?"

"The only person that knows what I'm building is you. Who did you tell?" demanded Gordon.

"What the hell? What are you accusing me of?"

"You did tell someone, didn't you?" He asked.

Shiloh stammered.

"It's okay," confided Gordon, "I'm not blaming you. I just need to know. Who did you tell?"

"What makes you so sure that it was someone from our group?" she asked. "Why not just random vandalism?"

"Because it was specifically motivated against Batman. They painted a message about it on my wall. They know what the temple represents."

"Still, they are civilized people. They wouldn't do something like that."

"Shiloh! You are the only person, other than me, that knew what I was building! Not to mention, that the paint was green! Your top figureheads, Luke and Yoda, I know for a fact are represented by that color!"

"Calm down," struck Shiloh, sternly. "I told one person. Okay?"

"Okay! Who? Who did you tell?"

"I only mentioned it briefly, in passing, to our director," she admitted.

"I knew it! What is her name?"

Myth

"*His* name is Steven and he wouldn't have told anyone else."

"*Steven?*" mocked Gordon, "What is he? One hundred fifty years old?"

"He is a nice guy and, more importantly, an adult." defended Shiloh. "He would not vandalize a building."

Gordon stepped away from the bed and paused in the doorway. "I'm going down there to talk to him."

Shiloh protested heavily, leaping out of bed and following Gordon out to his bike. The children stood in silence, watching their mother scream, as their father disappeared in the distance. Once futile to continue, Shiloh turned to her children. "Go inside and lock the door. Don't open it to anyone who may come. I have to leave but I'll be back." She mounted her bike and followed Gordon down the road.

When she arrived at the ovular assembly hall where she had attended so many Star studies before, she was quick to find her husband shouting, his fingers in poor Steven's face. She excused herself as she pushed by a small group of onlookers, only to place herself directly in-between the two men. "Enough!" she shouted, facing Gordon. "This is not a place for being loud or being angry!"

"It's okay," said Steven as he cupped Shiloh's shoulders.

Gordon raised his fist in the air, "Get your hands off my wife, you garbage pile."

Steven immediately complied. He was desperate to make peace. "Look, Gordon. Shiloh has told us a lot about you. You know, I have been really eager to meet you actually. I – I respect a difference in beliefs. You know? And I know you come from a Batman family, but I had no idea your building was at all idealistic in nature."

Gordon extended his finger toward Shiloh. "She told me that you *did* have an idea, Steven. She told *me* that she told *you*!"

Steven continued, exasperated. "I mean, maybe she did. I just don't specifically recall. You know how it is. Things go in one ear and come right out the other sometimes. But look, Gordon. We run a place of compassion here. We want to help people in need. Not fear them and not turn them away."

"What are you saying?" yelled Gordon. "Get to the point."

"Gordon, I'm just letting you know that we did not damage your temple, we believe in people working *together* despite their differences, and our congregation would *love* to not only help you repair your temple, but to help you complete it, as well." Steven exposed his palm to the air, "Right Hand to The Force."

Gordon was seething mad, but had no powerful reply. "I don't need your damned help." He jerked away from Shiloh. "You Star Wars people just stay off my land, okay?"

"No problem, Gordon," replied Steven. "I'm sorry for what happened to you and may The Force be with you."

"Fuck you," retorted Gordon as he walked away with his bike, middle finger in the air.

Gordon rebuilt his fallen wall and added three more. Each was, on multiple occasions, defaced again with green paint. Every morning that he woke to such vandalism was similar to the first. He would confront Steven, make a scene, and embarrass Shiloh in front of the Star studies group. With every such occurrence, however, the effectiveness of the drama was diminished in the minds of the observers. The vacuum that remained was filled with a mix of humor and pity. By the fourth verbal pummeling, Steven simply stood smiling in silence and waited for Gordon to get it all out of his system and ride away. A routine had been established.

As Steven and Shiloh could see his desperation, so could more sympathetic minds in the village. Zedmore Greene was the first to approach him about his observations. He did so on a cool, sunny day as Gordon sanded down a window frame. "Could you use some help, brother?"

Gordon turned and faced him. "I think I'm alright. Thank you."

"Well, how are you gonna get that roof on?" called Zedmore, stepping closer. "You're gonna need a few more hands. No doubt about it."

Gordon looked up at the open top and then back to Zedmore. "Yeah. I don't know. I guess I was just going to cross that bridge when I came to it. Figure it out as I went."

"I see. Well my name is Zedmore Greene. People call me Zed, and I've got great people. We could save you a lot of pain on that."

Gordon sighed. "That sounds nice, but I just don't have a lot of money to spend on this thing right now. It's pretty much a labor of love."

"Love like Batman?" asked Zed.

Gordon felt a tingle run up his spine as the volume of his tinnitus increased. He didn't need any more people empowered to work against his vision. The intrusions had to stop.

"I bike by here almost every day on my way into town. I've seen all that nasty graffiti and I know what you're doing here."

"I just want to be left alone," pleaded Gordon. "Please."

"You don't understand," continued Zed, the two men now facing one another directly, "I want to help you. I love the Batman. I want to honor the Batman, just like you. My men – they're all the same way. We're a fellowship, based around the Batman."

"A fellowship?"

"That's right. We're devoted to learning about the Batman, praising the Batman, and sharing the Batman with others. So to see you here doing the exact same thing makes me realize that there are more of us out there. We just need to come out of the dark and unite together."

Gordon thought about how Shiloh found such meaning in her Star studies. Oppositely, he had always considered his devotion to Batman to be very personal and internal - something more of his blood than his skin. Zed's assertion that this mythology could be meaningful within a community *before* his temple was finished felt revelatory. "So you would help me put a roof on there for free?"

"Well, in exchange for letting us praise and meditate here, of course," replied Zed.

"Oh. Yes. Certainly," beamed Gordon, more positive than he could remember being in several years.

"Do you mind if I take some measurements?

"Right now?"

"Yeah."

"Um. Yeah, sure."

"Great," smiled Zed. "And whenever you're ready for us, we'll get that roof on. We could set a time today, if you like."

"Well I've still got some ways to go before the roof," replied Gordon.

"We don't just do roofs either, by the way. We can lay bricks. We can clean up graffiti," laughed Zed. "I'm sure we would all be happy to assist in whatever way we could."

Gordon looked around at all the raw materials stacked about. There was plenty more to be done. The open areas had to be reinforced before installing the windows and doors. The pillar also had to be completed, and of course, the roof. "Would you like to come by tomorrow morning?" asked Gordon.

"I would love to," smiled Zed, "But I already have an all-day job scheduled out east. How about the day after?"

"I look forward to it," nodded Gordon. The men shook hands.

As stated, Zed and his group showed up early, two mornings later. Among them were nine men: Conner, Hoth, Harvey, Griedo, Grayson, Egon, Obi, Big Alfred and Threepio – as well as three women: Harley, Gozarinne and Layah (an incredibly fashionable name when she was born forty-some years prior, though spelled differently from its origin). Though apprehensive and shy at first, it did not take long for Gordon to open up to the group, as their helpfulness and dedication were quickly made apparent. There was a rhythm between them, compelling Gordon to comfortably and naturally relinquish a degree of control over the project and, instead, do what he could to assimilate. Yet, they made no major decisions without his consent, respecting his land and his idea.

Gordon quickly found a home unlike the one that he and Shiloh had attempted together. And so it was no surprise that their family routines also changed over the matter of a few weeks. Shiloh began waking before

Gordon and the children. She would depart for her Star Studies early in the morning, sometimes before the twilight. She also stopped taking the children with her, citing that they had lost interest and would soon be starting school, which would cause a schedule conflict anyway. Gordon could appreciate that she, too, was giving up some control and he was happy to have Ivy and Nigma there among his Batman brethren, witnessing the raising of his temple and learning the finer points of the mythology from people who were pleased to discuss it.

Harley and Gozarinne soon took on the daily duty of cooking breakfast and a later afternoon meal, from a selection of food that was provided communally. Everyone sat outside and ate together at a long wooden table that had been constructed by Obi. At each meal, Ivy and Nigma helped set the table, as the food was prepared. Once it was served, the group would all hold hands and engage in a brief, silent contemplation on Batman before eating. After a usually jovial, often boisterous feast, they would begin their work in good spirits.

The days pressed on, the temple grew, and the group became closer, however the vandalism did not stop. Nearly every four days, some antagonistic new mark of green paint would appear and each time, Hoth and Harvey would painstakingly scrape and scrub it off. Gordon, in a more peaceful state, stopped tromping up to the Star Studies group in order to yell at Steven every time the graffiti returned. He had taken that path one time since he had met Zed and his inability to control his anger in front of the group had left him feeling embarrassed. He still felt very strongly that the Star Wars people were to blame, but he also found himself to be made inherently wiser by Zed's suggestion that he "pick his battles."

Myth

One morning, not unexpectedly, the group arrived to immediately see illegible green words scrawled across the face of the temple. A collective sigh ran through them as they sat down to breakfast, knowing that a portion of their day would be spent cleaning up a bigoted mess. They ate their meal and walked out to the construction area in relative quietness. Hoth filled a bucket with soap and water. Gordon, Layah and Egon stacked stone in a wheelbarrow. Big Alfred entered the temple to retrieve his sandpaper and pick up where he left off.

He had only just stepped inside before calling out, "Hey you all might want to get over here and look at this!" The others dropped what they were doing and ran to crowd the door and witness what Big Alfred had seen: a gangly teenager with green hair, passed out cold between a can of spray paint and a bottle of rum, mostly empty. The boy opened his eyes suddenly and flopped up to standing position at once. Startled and terrified, with a large group of adults between he and the door, he sprung toward the window. Big Alfred plucked him from the sky, mid-leap and threw him on the ground. He pinned him there, foot against chest. "I believe this is our guy."

"Please let me go!" the boy screamed, "It was just supposed to be a joke!"

Gordon, enraged, picked up the paint can and pressed the aluminum cylinder against the boy's soft face. "A joke? You think this is funny? *Do you think this is funny?*"

"I'm sorry! I'm sorry!" screamed the boy.

"How did you know this was about Batman here?" demanded Gordon, "Who told you?"

"I heard you talking about it to my dad! I'm sorry! Please just let me go!" pleaded the boy.

"Your dad? Your *dad?*" Gordon scoured his mind. "Who *is* your dad, you little shit?" He pressed the can harder against the boy's face, bending his nose awkwardly to the side.

"Dyson Mabry!" the boy shouted. "You bought your bricks from him!"

Gordon realized he had been wrong. He had taken so much anger out on Steven, believing that Shiloh had shared his plan with the Star Studies group. Really though, it had been his own loose tongue that lead to the vandalism. He had completely forgotten that he had revealed his plan to the brick maker, who had even charged him less because of it. His anger began to subside and he removed the can from against the boy's face. "Why would you do this to us?" he asked.

The boy, too, deescalated a bit. "I don't know," he answered. "I'm sorry. My friends and me – we were raised on Batman and I guess we just like the Joker better. We really just thought it would be funny. No other reason, I promise."

"So there are more of you?" asked Big Alfred.

"Just my friends!" The boy grew excited again. "But if you let me go, I can talk to them and make sure it never happens again. I promise!"

Gordon and Big Alfred subtly nodded toward one another. "Alright. We're going to let you go," said Gordon, "but I know where you live and if this ever happens again, or I ever see you or your friends on my property…" He abruptly slammed the base of the paint can to the ground, centimeters from the boy's head. "You understand?"

"Yes!" cried the boy, "I'm sorry!" Big Alfred removed his foot, freeing the boy to stand. He breathed heavily and coughed dramatically as he stumbled out of the temple and ran away.

Gordon turned to Zed. "Well you know what this means? I owe Steven an apology." He mounted his bike and pedaled toward the Star Studies building. Such a fool he had been. He had harbored so much displaced aggression that he alienated his wife and pushed her away. It was clear to him now. Poor Steven had taken on so much of Gordon's animosity for things that did not otherwise involve him in the slightest. He even offered to assist with construction of the temple the very first time it was vandalized. If only Gordon had calmed down and taken him up on it, what different versions the men would have known of one another. The perception of conflict, between them or their respective mythologies, had been purely subjective and heavily influenced by outside emotion. Gordon was relieved to have been wrong. A changed man, he felt no shame in finally, humbly, confessionally, laying this burden down.

He entered the building with both hands in the air, palms out – a position of surrender. Still, his presence in the room was met by the handful of older women there with groans and the rolling of eyes. "I'm not here to accuse anyone of anything this time," he assured. "I promise."

"Then why *are* you here?" asked the little blind lady, seated by the window.

"I want to make amends. I promise. Is Steven here?"

Another lady spoke up. "This is a *women's* study group. The main Star Studies don't begin for another two hours. Steven will be here and you can talk to him then."

Gordon snapped his fingers. "Drat! Well I'm sorry to interrupt your studies. If you could just point me to my wife, I'll be out of your way."

More disparate sighs and whispers filled the room. "We haven't seen Shiloh all morning," continued the lady, "She only ever comes to the main study. Can you please leave us be now, Gordon?"

He could not. "Where does Steven live?" he asked.

None of the women uttered a word.

"Just tell me what street."

More silence.

Gordon was beginning to feel uneasy but was determined to leave a peaceful wake. He smirked, nodded and exited the building. Undeterred, he crossed the breezeway to a smaller building there – one he had never entered. Through the glass, he could see two young women moving about. He pulled open the door and stuck his head inside, startling both the women, and revealing a group of several children seated on the floor, awaiting a story.

"I'm sorry to bother you," he explained, "But I have a meeting with your director. Steven, right?"

"Yes?" said the woman with curly red hair.

"Well I forgot that I was supposed to meet him at his home and I came here instead, by accident. I have his address, but I left it at my house and the meeting should have already started by now. So it makes no sense for me to pedal all the way back home."

The blonde woman looked at the red head, then back to Gordon, from whom the red head's stare never left. They each smiled through furrowed brows. "I wish we could help you," spoke the blonde, "but we don't know his address."

"I know its somewhere on Rhiannon Avenue," added the red head. "I've been there a few times." The blonde gave her a stern, side-eyed glare.

Gordon thanked her and headed for Rhiannon Avenue. By the time he arrived, he had developed an intense tightness in his stomach and his immediate mission had become blurry. He walked his bike slowly up one side of the street and down the other, scanning every home. When nothing stood out, he went around to the back of the house on the corner and then walked the other way, cutting across the back yards. Finally, parked beside the garbage bin, three houses from the end of the street, he came upon the one thing he had been looking for but hoped not to find: Shiloh's bike.

Like all the homes on Rhiannon, this one had a simple, rectangular, one story design. This afforded Gordon the ability to trace the perimeter and explore every window. Most of the blinds were closed, obstructing any visual action beyond them. They could not, however, muffle the sound of the action, and so it was at the third window that he could clearly hear his wife's voice inside, mingling in laughter with another man.

Gordon stormed to the front door and knocked three times. When there was no immediate response, he next pounded three more, with the side of his fist. After no answer still, he began to kick the door, rather stomping it repeatedly with the bottom of his boot. Harder and harder he stomped until the door flung open. He marched inside and kicked open a weaker door on the right. He crashed into the room, grabbed Steven by his neck and smashed his head into the large mirror he had been using to adjust his hair. Shiloh, who had been in the process of buttoning up her blouse, turned to the wall and cowered as Gordon approached her. He grabbed the open part of her shirt and tore it off her body, popping buttons on to the floor. "If you take it off here, then you can leave it here!" he screamed as he shredded the fabric.

Steven put his arm around Gordon's neck and attempted to restrain him. Gordon, scrappy as he was, ducked and pivoted around quickly, then swept Steven's legs out from under him. Once on the ground, Gordon straddled his chest and punched him three times in the face, drawing blood from the nose. At the same time, Shiloh screamed and hit Gordon repeatedly in the back. Finally he stood and flung his elbows, shrugging Shiloh away from him. He kicked Steven once more in the side and then exited the house without a word.

Gordon was confused now. When he returned to the temple and the others there saw the blood on his shirt, they were also confused. Yet no one addressed him as he walked silently by them and into his home. Inside, he took a shower and a brief, accidental nap.

It was still only the mid-afternoon when he realized he had let himself doze off. He buttoned his shirt and made his way out to the temple, with a determined, steady focus to take his mind off its lack of clarity. Straight to the middle of the room, he stood at the foot of the pillar. He loaded the basket there with large chunks of stone and raised it almost to the ceiling with a simple pulley system Zed had built. He secured the rope by tying it to the handle of a wheelbarrow - weighted down, itself, by rock. He climbed the ladder there beside it almost to the ceiling and continued his work of stacking stones one on the other, building the pillar higher.

He installed one basket of stones, scurried down the ladder, and had just raised another when Big Alfred entered the temple. "Sir," spoke Alfred, "You have a visitor."

Gordon tied the rope again to the wheelbarrow handle. "Who?" he asked.

"Steven – and your wife."

Gordon exaggerated a false and hearty laugh as he climbed back up the ladder. "Send them on in, I guess."

"Shiloh doesn't want to see you," informed Alfred, "But Steven has requested a meeting. I can send him away if you like."

"No, no. Send *him* on in then."

Alfred exited, to be replaced moments later by Steven's wiry, well-dressed presence. Gordon threw a rock at his head before he could speak a word. He dodged it narrowly with a sloppy, hunched jut to the side, then stepped back and raised his hands. "Look, I'm kind of here to apologize, Gordon!" he shouted. "I understand why you are angry!"

Gordon bounced another large stone in his palm. "Where is my wife?" he asked.

"She's inside your house." Steven's volume lowered. "She's getting her things."

"Getting her things?"

"I came here with her, hoping you and I could speak man to man. Could you come down and talk to me?"

Gordon chucked another massive stone toward Steven, who sidestepped it, more casually this time. "Everything I have to say to you, I am saying with these rocks."

Steven stepped to the bottom of the ladder and grasped one of the rungs with both hands. "Let's not allow this to get ugly," he seemed to threaten, just barely jolting Gordon's support.

Fearing the possibility that Steven might actually take advantage of such a vulnerable position atop a ladder, Gordon swiftly descended. Holding the sides, he kicked out his feet and slid down, skipping nearly five rungs at a time – an action that more closely resembled repelling. His final drop was aimed at coming directly down on Steven's head, hopefully kicking him in the face. Here too, however, Steven dodged the attack. Gordon hit the ground hard, but landed on his feet and crouched. He lunged up and pushed Steven's chest with all his might. "Why are you even here?" he demanded.

"I want to work this out with you," answered Steven. He then pushed back against Gordon, while at the same time protesting this very violence. "I want to work it out by talking to one another – not *pushing* one another."

Gordon shoved him again; stepping back a bit, himself, as Steven used the wheelbarrow to maintain his ground. "My pushing *is* talking. Why can't you understand what I'm saying?"

Steven grabbed a rock from the barrow and held it up defensively. "Look. I will smash you in the head if you don't stop."

This statement drew intense ire from Gordon who grabbed Steven's throat with one hand, while using the other to disarm him of his rock. "Are you threatening me on my land?" he demanded. "A Star Wars person is *threatening* me?" He pushed Steven hard up against the side of the barrow, lifting the closest wheel off the ground. "Star Wars people don't *threaten*. Aren't you all supposed to *control* your emotions? Isn't that your whole *shtick*?"

Steven gasped for air, contorting his body and flailing his arms around wildly. Still, none of it was enough to break Gordon's hold. He tried to take more ground for himself, pressing his thighs harder against the side of the wheelbarrow. A cloudy blackness began to fill his vision as he struggled harder and harder. Finally, he pushed so hard against the wheelbarrow that it tipped over entirely, spilling its load on to the temple floor.

When the rocks tumbled out, there was no longer sufficient weight to counterbalance the basket of rocks at the top of the pillar. The basket dropped a bit and the wheelbarrow was lifted into the air. The uncertainty of these large moving objects was enough to startle Gordon into loosening his grasp. He pushed Steven again, to the floor this time, coughing and hyperventilating. Then he stood there, in awe of his dangling devices.

The knot in the rope was no match for the wheelbarrow, especially having only been tied around the handle, which was an elongated spindle shape and not enclosed. When the handle slipped from the loop, the wheelbarrow came crashing down and the basket of stone did the same. Steven had the foresight to roll his body out from under this mess before it occurred. High on his aggression, however, Gordon did not; and so he was struck and knocked to the ground by the falling basket of rock.

Steven crawled to Gordon's outstretched wrist and felt for a pulse. It was faint and intermittent. When he lifted himself up to his knees, he could see a pale dust intermixed with Gordon's blood and coating his open eye. Above that was a crater in his skull, hemorrhaging through small pieces of shale. Steven stood up quickly and darted to the door. "We need a doctor!" he screamed as he ran out into the yard.

Alfred naturally restrained him the moment he realized Steven was hysterical. "Why do we need a doctor?"

The rest of the group gathered around the scene as Steven tried to explain. "Gordon has been hurt but it wasn't me! I swear it was his own fault!"

A pediatrician by trade, Griedo darted into the temple to assess the scene.

Shiloh and the children emerged from the house and joined the others in the yard. "What's going on here?"

"There was an accident, Shiloh," explained Steve. "Gordon needs help right now. Please tell this guy to let me go!"

"Is daddy okay, Mommy?" asked Ivy.

"I don't know," she replied. "What happened, Steve?"

"He had me by my neck. I didn't know what was going on. The wheelbarrow fell over and the rocks fell down."

"*What happened, Steve?*" Shiloh demanded a better explanation.

Griedo appeared from within the temple with a look of shock. "Gordon is dead," he announced.

Alfred spun Steven around and pinned him to the side of the temple. "You better come clean right now," he directed as he pushed his massive thumbs into Steven's ribcage. "What did you do?"

"I didn't do anything! I promise!"

Ivy busted into tears. "Mommy! Why is daddy dead?"

Nigma took Ivy's hand. Stone faced and silent, he led his little sister away from the calamity, back inside and to the bedroom they shared. They sat across from one another on their respective beds. "If daddy is really dead, then I am the man of the house now," he explained.

Ivy wailed.

"Shhhh. Stop. Please," requested Nigma. "Listen to me. This is my house now – and yours too. Not mom's house. Do you understand?"

Ivy looked at him inquisitively through her tears.

He continued. "Daddy is dead because of Star Wars. Mommy brought Steven here and she was going to leave with him. I think that she still should. Star Wars is for her – not Batman. And this is a Batman house. That is a Batman temple out there."

"I hate Star Wars!" scathed Ivy.

"I do too. We need to destroy Star Wars."

"Let's kill them!"

"We *will* kill them but we need a good plan and we have a lot of decisions that we have to make *right now - today*. Do you trust me, Ivy?"

"Yes!" She shouted enthusiastically, no longer sobbing so distinctly.

"Then stick with me no matter what and I promise I will protect you and we will get revenge for Daddy," ensured Nigma.

Ivy stepped across the rift and hugged him. She was no less disturbed and saddened by her father's death, but had complete confidence in her brother. She also saw that Steven was ultimately a weak man – the antithesis of her father. In that moment she realized the strange power found in having nothing to lose, once everything had already been taken away. She knew that she, too, was stronger than Steven – stronger than Star Wars. She suddenly understood her mourning as a tipping point, rather than an end. The moment was as temporary as any. She found herself with no fear of what was to come, and anticipated more major changes for everyone involved.

Myth

III

The microphones and slide projector were each checked by a trained technical team of two in order to ensure there would be no disruption during the day's business. "Some lady's gonna be speakin' bout history today. Talkin' bout the old old times after The Fall," informed the first technician.

"Talkin' bout the Black Period?" asked the second. "How do you think they held these meetings way back in the Black Period?"

"I guess with no amplification they would have to speak direct to one and another instead of yellin' all on top *at* one and another."

The two technicians laughed.

About an hour later, the room slowly filled with members of the congress, with the Council for the Aversion of Religious Crises to be positioned front and center across from the speaker's podium. On either side of the podium sat a long table of the day's scheduled guests. After twenty full minutes of chatting and glad-handing, the congress, the council, and the guests took their seats.

The Master Speaker stepped to the podium and slammed his gavel three times. "Alright, everybody. We're gonna get things started here," he spoke into the microphone. "As we are all very well aware, we are having a major problem in this nation – well in this world – with religious extremism."

Representative Whollox, sitting in the back of the room, leaned over to his nearest constituent and whispered, "It's the Batmaanics. Everybody knows it. I don't know why everyone is so afraid to just say it."

His constituent snickered.

Representative Krishnan, seated in front of them, overheard the comment and turned around. "There have been far more murders committed by Starwarinai than by the Batmaanic people over the past decade," she scolded.

Whollox scoffed. "Yeah. Worldwide maybe, but not in this country. Plus, Darkside Starwarians are not the same as regular Starwarians. Regular Starwarians don't kill anyone. We're lovers."

Krishnan rolled her eyes and turned back to the front.

"Bitch," whispered Whollox and his constituents chuckled.

Krishnan raised the back of her hand to him and extended her middle finger. Everyone within the viewing radius laughed loudly.

The Master Speaker banged his gavel and scolded the back of the room. "This is serious business, people. If you don't wanna be a part of this, then don't waste the time of the people who do."

Whollox made a loud fart sound with his mouth. No one laughed.

The speaker continued. "Our first guest, Miss Onell Brookens is an archeologist with the University of Leavenwerth, and a scholar, specializing in the Black Period. We have her here today in hopes that she will be able to make us wiser to the issues we face with religious extremism, by introducing us to the roots of the problem. We're really hoping that through her testimony today, as well as the testimony of our other speakers, we can all come out of this with a better sense of where we can and can't step when we eventually write new legislation around these sensitive religious issues. And make no mistake about it. We *will* have to write that legislation whether we like it or not - whether our *donors* like it or not. Okay?"

Myth

Whollox made a motion with his hand as though he was ejaculating a large penis. He looked around, but no one was paying him any mind.

"So with no additional delay," said the Master Speaker, "I give the floor to Miss Onell Brookens."

Miss Brookens commandeered the podium to a mix of light applause and a few scattered catcalls from the back rows. She flipped her long, straight, blonde hair over the back of her shoulders and adjusted the small, black, microphone before her. "Good afternoon," she began. "My name is Onell Brookens and I'm pleased to be here with you today. The purpose of my visit is ultimately education. I aim to teach you the origins of the major, modern religions, with a particular focus on the misconceptions about them which have opened the doors to the wave of extremism and terrorism that we have been experiencing globally. It is my belief that by tracing these behemoth religious systems back to their roots, we can understand them more objectively, providing a unique insight that you can then apply to diplomacy, legislation, and of course, problem solving."

With a turn of a white dial, mounted to the side of the podium, she dimmed the lights. She next pressed a button beside this, illuminating the screen behind her with a projected image of a variety of religious symbols. "So the question I want you to focus on here is, 'where *did* all these beliefs come from?' And I will let you know right now that the simple answer is myth – storytelling." She changed the slide to a photograph of a statue of Batman, juxtaposed with another photograph of a fresco style painting of the exalted Star Wars Jedi, Yoda. "So which is right? Which is wrong? Is one more dangerous than the other? Is one more accurate? Can any of them actually save your eternal soul? And if so, then from what?"

She pressed the button again, this time changing the slide to an exaggerated, gothic style illustration of Ivy and Nigma, as adults, rising from a flaming pool of blood and each holding the skulls of their enemies high in the air. "Surely, even you all have heard of the Batmaanic crusades of the late 2100s. These two young adults pictured here were an incredibly consequential pair of leaders from that era. Perhaps you are most familiar with them as Ivy the Tempest and her brother, Nigma the Darkness – originators of the crusades and major purveyors of the Batmaanic religion as we know it today. Both of these names – The Tempest and The Darkness – we believe were taken on as a means of making greater impact on the public as they rose to power. We now know, however, that the family name they shed was a bit less remarkable. It was simply, 'Jones.'" A smattering of light laughter spread across the room and then dissipated. "Not so threatening when you know that, right?"

Once more she changed the slide. This one showed an image of Gordon, laid into an elaborate stained glass window. "We know their family name because it appears on the grave marker of this fellow, Gordon Jones - their father. He is more commonly known, of course, as Martyr Gordon, one of seven who have been ordained and celebrated as such since the church's inception. He is also considered the founder of the first Batmaanic temple. It is this guy here, whose death was so profoundly affecting on his children that they spent every moment of their waking lives after that trying to both seek vengeance for the loss of their father, while at the same time spreading the Batmaanic faith."

The next slide depicted a painting of Gordon in a physical struggle with Steven, as a crowd looks on. "The main problem with all of this is, as you hopefully know,

Gordon Jones died at the hands of a man named Steven Jacobson who was, at the time, a pioneering member of the Starwarian faith. This murder if you are Batmaanic, or accident if you are Starwarian, was the crucial event that threw these religions into a long history of violent disagreement, which still stands today, stronger than ever. There is, of course, a differing array of versions of this story, but with neither faith willing to concede one way or another, we end up with what is ultimately a black hole in place of this historically very important event – an event that quickly escalated two simple myths into the two most powerful, global religions that any of us have ever known. But can we go back further?" asked Miss Brookens as she changed the slide again, this time to a photograph of the ruins of Gordon's temple. "What happened *before* this event?

"I wanted to know and so, thanks to a very generous grant from the Council for the Aversion of Religious Crises, I was able to lead an archeological exploration at this site, located in the Badland area of The American States." She pointed toward the slide projection. "This is what is left of the very first Batmaanic temple that we are aware of, built by Gordon Jones himself. It's construction dates back to the approximate year, 2125, or 107 P.F. for those of us who go by the Post Fall calendar. Of course, we know this as the era named the Black Period, a time in which the human race had lost its ability to harness electricity. So a lot of details about the temple are unknown, but through our studies and excavations in the area, we have been working hard to fill in the gaps."

The next slide was that of an overhead view of Gordon's land. Miss Brookens powered up a green laser pointer and aimed it at each relevant site on the map as she described it. "This is the main temple here. Just across this spat of land, opposite the temple, are the remnants of the Jones family home – really just a foundation is all that is left. To the south of that, up on this hill here, is the temple's graveyard, with headstones just barely in tact after so many years. Thanks to the National Gravestone Archive, recreations of these monuments have been digitally preserved and are publicly accessible. So we know that this corner up here, kind of separated from the rest of the monuments, are the Jones family plots. Gordon is here, so are Ivy, Nigma, their children and their children's children. Curiously, their mother is absent from the area and so we do not know her name, her age, or anything about her."

She changed the slide to a digital rendering of the temple, closely resembling the original. She ran her green dot up and down the area where the pillar protruded through the top of the roof. "This stone monument, believed to have been laid by Gordon's hands himself, has since collapsed, but we thought pretty proud of ourselves to have discovered that it once rose, not just to the ceiling of the inside of the place, but also *through* it and quite high in the sky. This discovery, however, was nothing compared to what we found hidden away inside the base of the pillar."

The next several slides showed photographs taken at the excavation site. Miss Brookens continued. "Walled into this massive obelisk was a very old, metal box – a safe, in fact, which took considerable effort to get into. And inside that safe, the largest collection of ancient Batmaanic texts ever discovered – still relatively preserved by plastic coverings. These are the source stories on which the Batmaanic holy book, *The Batmaan Odyssey,* is based and thusly so is the entire religion, by and large. To add even more shock to the discovery, we also quickly realized that these stories were almost exclusively dictated in *picture book* form. We found this to be rather curious, considering that the oldest of these books appears to date back to the first half of the twentieth century – 1939 on the old Gregorian calendar, 79 B.F. in more modern terms – obviously predating the Fall that lead to the Black Period, but still having been drawn and written well after the invention of the English language and the publication of many other, wordier texts, both academic and religious."

Her next slide was another photograph; this one of a grayed man with a tiny goatee and thick rimmed glasses that magnified his kind eyes. "This is Dr. Slima Marton, a fellow of my field, with a focus on Starwarian studies. He and his team have, through their own excavations, unearthed some texts similar to these - and almost as ancient- but depicting the Starwarian mythology in various forms." She changed the slides steadily though a variety of photographs of *Star Wars* literature, including junior novels, unlicensed fan fiction, and even coloring books. These images gave way to additional *Star Wars* merchandise, such as lunchboxes and action figures. "These storage containers and dolls were not exclusive to the Starwarian studies either." The dusty old *Star Wars* merchandise was replaced by dusty old *Batman* merchandise in the images. "As you can see, we have turned up plenty of similar Batmaanic affects, ourselves. In fact, these kinds of items have been discovered in the mythology of nearly every one of our nation's primary religions today, with no exception. And what do they all have in common? As prolific as they are, they are all based on stories designed for the entertainment of children and adolescents."

The range of merchandise shown in the slides branched out into a massive display of cultural artifacts from the late twentieth century. "So with consideration to how out of hand these religions have become – how seriously they are being taken by their extremist fringes – let us not forget their roots in *children's* mythology. Yes. The Starwarinai have a very principled set of standards based on dark versus light and a person's ability to reach a certain state of enlightenment, but it also has rocket ship laser battles fought in space. Yes. The Batmaanic faith also carries ideas of dark and light, as well as a particular God figure, but his origin was that of a rich guy in a bat costume who fought a clown. Even our more passive religions originate from – well, I don't want to say *ridiculous* concepts, but for example: The Ghosbusser faith; sure, it's based on this lovely notion that we are in constant communion with the dead, but it began with the story of four guys who zapped ghosts with electricity and trapped them in little boxes. And what of the Terminatiatic religions? All of them originate with this strange tale of a robot traveling through time to kill an unborn baby. They have obviously blossomed into a web of popular faiths, full of beautiful rituals, but still – in the beginning – a little absurd, right?"

Miss Brookens hammered her point a bit further before retiring from the podium to a strong, steady applause. Even Representative Whollox understood and appreciated her presentation. Beyond that, she stayed to watch some of the other speakers, but departed during the recess.

Upon returning to her office, she listened to a message left on her phone recorder. "Hello, my name is Skynost Marcini and I am a film maker located out here in Indio on the coast of Lower California. I just finished watching your speech to congress today and I really think your expertise could be monumentally helpful to me regarding a particular project that I have in development right now. Just thought I would see if you might be available to fly out west here for a couple days and have a chat with me in person." He then left his phone number, which Miss Brookens scribbled down. She called him back, accepted his offer, and found herself on a plane to Indio at Mr. Marcini's expense just forty-eight hours later.

A robust, older, well-dressed, bald man, Mr. Marcini stood to greet Miss Brookens at their table at an upscale restaurant downtown. "Miss Brookens!" he beamed, extending his hand. "Thank you for being here!"

"Oh! Thank you for getting me here! And please, call me Onell." Their handshake lingered warmly for a moment.

"Surely! You can call me Sky. So pleased to meet you in body."

"Likewise!" The two sat.

"This is the best Dakotian restaurant in the whole city," ensured Sky. "I felt it an appropriate choice, considering the location of your most recent line of expertise."

The waiter arrived before she could respond. Drinks were ordered, including a moderately expensive bottle of wine for the table, per Sky's request. There was small talk about her flight and traveling and the weather. Food was ordered and then business began.

Sky brought it up. "So this project that I called you about. I fully intend to discuss it with you – tell you what I'm trying to do. What I am looking for is a consultant to tag along and make sure that I'm doing it the right way."

Onell had done consulting work before for museums and special projects, but nothing as exciting as cinema. Still, she felt it best to obscure her enthusiasm. "I understand," she confided.

Sky continued. "The thing is; this is a very – how should I say – *delicate* project. And while I think you are an ideal candidate for this job, I would like to hope I could confide in you not to disclose to anyone what I am trying to do here, should you not accept."

She nodded.

"Can I confide in you?" asked Sky.

"Yes," replied Onell without a second thought on the matter. "Absolutely."

"Good. So all this religious war that's going on these days; I think its just insanity, and I am pretty certain that you share these sentiments. Right?"

"Yes again."

"So my industry, cinema. I've been in the game a long time and it's had its ups and its downs. Maybe we got a little too self-aggrandizing for a while. I know that, but believe me when I say that we were *all* humbled by the tsunamis. All that destruction to the sound stages and cameras; sets and costumes; none of it found in nature. All that money lost on ornate pieces of metal, wood and plastic that sat around for years doing no good for anybody. And hey, forget about the financial loss and what all that tied up cash could have otherwise gone to. The toll on human life was awful. I lost fifty friends in one sudden gulp of the earth when the quake took down Tempest Towers – about thirty more in other places around the city." Sky's eyes grew red and swollen. He cleared his throat and continued. "So I want to be very clear that this project is not about money or fame or studio control – nothing like that. When I was forced to move out here to Indio, it was like starting over for me – a complete mess. I lost my home, my friends, family members. My pets." His eyes were clearly watering. "I gained perspective and, in time, I found purpose. This project is about doing the absolute best that

Myth

I can do in order to make the world we live in a better place. Nothing more and nothing less."

Onell laid her hands on his. "I'm so sorry."

Sky broke from Onell's touch, leaned back in his chair and dabbed his eyes with his napkin while grinning. "Sorry for you to see me like this; crying to a stranger over an event almost a decade old now. Like I said, it's a very personal project."

"No need for apology," consoled Onell. "Grief is best not contained."

"You're right. Still, I went a bit further than I had intended. Let me get down to it here. I want to bridge the gap between the Starwarinai and Batmaanics."

Onell was intrigued, but uncertain how to react to the notion.

"Cinema can be such a powerful art form," continued Sky. "Cinema has been the cathartic release needed by so many people – so many nations of people – to evolve their understanding of the world around them. We lost that somewhere before the tsunamis, but have been slowly building it back since. I want to get back to that."

"But with a religious movie?" asked Onell.

"Not a religious movie, but a movie about religion - but not a parody or satire of religion. Something that treats the source material with respect, while focusing on how these two warring factions can coexist both dogmatically and practically."

"Well dogmatically is tricky," spoke Onell. "It would be a lot easier to approach it mythologically."

Sky slouched back in his seat and then straightened up quickly. "See? This is why I need you!" He picked up his glass of wine and extended it toward Onell. She tapped her glass to his.

Onell relocated to Indio and spent the next three years working with Sky on his project. The script was rewritten and edited until it could pass Onell's inspection for accuracy, clarity, and, most importantly, reverence. Once cast and put into production, Onell remained on set to make certain that no props or staging were contradictory or discourteous to either faith. She was also the third person to view the final cut of the film, only after Sky and the editor. Lastly, she was granted final approval on the title, *Everything is One*, which she would have vetoed if given the choice to do so strictly based on how contrived she felt it was, rather than how offensive. Sky was adamant about it, though.

Controversy surrounded the film well ahead of its release, or even its official announcement, as it was impossible to keep a secret with a staff that large. Religious leaders, both Batmaanic and Starwarian, took to speaking out against the movie without ever having seen a frame of it, or even contacting Sky's studio about its content. As their disdain dripped down on to their congregations, protests began, centered on any theater that would carry the film. All of their anger and loud objection, along with the endless news programs and talk shows that covered it, only served as free advertisement for the film. The first two days' tickets sold out just under a week prior to release.

The evening before the premier, the Mancinis invited Onell over for dinner. This was nothing new to her by this point in her professional relationship with Sky, but her anxiety (as well as his) was being exacerbated by all the stress surrounding the release. Each of them had a need to talk through their worry, and so in the middle of the meal, Sky broke the ice by proposing a toast.

He stood and raised his glass. "Bottoms to the top for *Everything is One*. Come what may."

"Come what may," repeated his wife and Onell together – a customary response when toasting, born of the same psychological protection provided by knocking on wood.

"I knew the film would cut a few people up there and here, but the back burn against us has really surprised me," he continued.

"Back burn from people who have not even seen the film, I will remind us all again," interjected Onell.

Sky's wife sighed. "These are such ignorant days we live in."

"If people just watch it – if they just give it a chance – then they will see what we are trying to do here." Sky scratched his chin. "And it doesn't look like audience will be a problem. Surely, if enough people see it, word of what it is portraying will make rounds. Right?"

"We can only hope," spoke his wife.

"I mean, if our intention is good, people will pick up on that. A new understanding, right?" Sky could not contain his concern.

"Frankly, if the intention is good, it doesn't matter what other people think," coddled Onell, almost apprehensively. "How bout another toast?" She raised her glass of wine again and then continued. "Bottoms to the top for good intentions for a greater good. Come what may."

"Come what may."

The movie was pulled from theaters after only the first nationwide screening. This was due to a wave of mass shootings, sixty-seven in total. The title screen was speculated to have served as some kind of trigger or "go point" for the shooters.

Representative Whollox zipped up his pants as he read aloud the news on the ticker that ran across the bottom of his hotel television: "Over sixty theater shootings accompany opening of *Everything is One* – hundreds dead."

"That is just horrible," spoke the prostitute on his bed. "Religion just needs to lighten up. Why so serious anyway?"

Whollox snickered. "You know who does all these shootings? The Batmaanics."

"I don't know," said the prostitute, "It all feels the same to me."

"Well it's not the same. Starwarians are good people," demanded Whollox, " I go to Star Studies four times a cycle."

"If you're so good, then why am I here with you now instead of your wife?"

Whollox snickered again. (Snickering was commonplace in his expression.) "Because my wife is back in Florida," he replied simply.

The prostitute scoffed and began to dress. "So basically, whatever you say is good is good and whatever you say is bad is bad, then. Total subjectivity. Is that what you believe?" she asked.

"Amen, baby. Amen."

Earthlings

I

Technically, Elmer and Clark died in their sleep. Two days prior, they had left together to hunt deer at Hillman State Park. It had been a tradition of theirs for nearly five decades and had started with a group of sixteen men. As the years passed, though, so did their friends. Even most who simply moved away still continued to embark on the pilgrimage to western Pennsylvania each autumn, but they, too, eventually succumbed to the inevitable. Year after year, the friends were taken by heart failures, cancer, diabetes, war and a car crash. Clark saved all the obituaries.

The shape of their event fluctuated in other ways with the ages, though remained always anchored in October. In its infancy, it had begun as a weeklong excursion of strong men, guns, cannabis and alcohol. As the men grew more "civilized" and settled into marriages, parenthood and steady jobs, the duration slowly shrunk to accommodate their stiffer lifestyles. The increases in their incomes also afforded them harder drugs, cocaine being choice for many of them, particularly in middle age. This too tapered off with the passing of time and their dwindling numbers. When the hunters aged into seniority, multiple days of camping had become rough on their bodies and so they eventually reduced down to just one weekend, three men and strictly alcohol. When Oscar passed away that June, not a week after his wife, Elmer and Clark were the sole survivors. Accurately, they figured that their time would arrive as well - sooner than later now - but until it did, their retreat would continue in honor of days past.

They camped for two nights, but not on a weekend. Both retired, with not much sense of what a weekend really was anymore, they decided on a Tuesday through Thursday sojourn. By the third day, the trip had seemed a bust. The tone had been solemn and neither man had killed any of the three deer they had encountered. There before them was the naked fear that they would exit existence with a whimper, rather than a bang.

"Well isn't a whimper how the whole damn world is supposed to end?" asked Elmer. "Everything'll be alright."

Clark wasn't trying to be a downer. Hard truth or not, he was dedicated to realism. Elmer handed him the whiskey and he took two rapid pulls. He chased it with some beans they had been warming on their breakfast fire. "You're right. Maybe we'll both still be here next year. We'll kill two bucks to make up for this time; maybe more."
Neither man actually had faith in that prospect and so a silence fell over them.

Elmer took a glug from the whiskey, wiped his mouth on his flannel sleeve and stood. "You're right, buddy," he spoke, "This is bullshit. We need to get back out there and bag one before we leave." Clark laughed nervously, aware that Elmer was serious. "What do you have to do today, Clark?"

"Well, I was going to try to get some work done in the yard; rake some leaves."

Elmer extended the whisky again to Clark. "Take a gulp," he demanded, and Clark complied. "Now," he asked again, "What do you have to do today?"

Clark continued to passive aggressively protest. "I didn't bring another change of clothes," he said. "I'm not equipped to stay another night."

"Who said anything about another night?" asked Elmer. "Take another gulp."

Clark gulped. "I told Helen I would be home for dinner," he reasoned once more.

"Well then," started Elmer before swiping the bottle from Clark's hands and imbibing its contents, himself again. "I guess we better get out there and get that deer so that you won't be late." He handed the bottle again to Clark, turned and removed his firearm from the rack on his truck bed. "If worse comes to worst, you can eat leftovers can't you?"

Clark stared at Elmer, pummeled by his neighbor's confidence as usual. "Damn it, man." He took yet another pull from the whiskey and joined Elmer's standing position.

"One kill and then we head home," reminded Elmer.

Clark took his gun down from the rack. "What if night falls first?" he asked.

"Yeah I suppose it might take us longer than we think."

"Exactly."

"Well, you better grab that other bottle then." Elmer walked toward the tree line beyond their camping area. Clark sighed, retrieved a second handle of whiskey from the truck cab, and walked briskly to catch up with his friend.

The men trampled through the woods as they had done the prior day; now with less reservation regarding their alcohol intake. By three o'clock, they had finished off one bottle and continued to the next. It helped to calm

Clark's nerves and kept him moving ahead with Elmer's insistent ambition, though his wife's twisted, down turned countenance never quite left the back of his head. He knew Helen would be irate upon his return, and steeped in worry every moment until then. He simply *had* to keep drinking, if for no other reason than to numb himself to the hell that surely awaited.

The time passed with an unacknowledged quickness, faster into the future as they drowned their concern in liquor, along with the rest of the daylight. With dusk upon them, and their remaining bottle almost depleted, the men had no choice but to accept their empty handed fate, return to their campsite and then to their wives and lives. Back through the thicket they slogged, silently passing off the remnants of the whiskey until none was left. Elmer reluctantly devoured the last sip. Though he would normally never dispose of litter in such a pristine and meaningful place, in this moment he was too drunk and depressed to give a second thought. And so, just on the edge of their camp, as the gloaming dissolved into darkness, he flung the barren glass vessel hard into a thick of brush about fifteen feet out from their path.

The impact of the bottle against its resting place stirred some creature that had been hiding there, watching and waiting for the hunters to pass. The dark, furry mass darted out from its cover and ran away from them, down the same well-worn trail that they were already traveling. Without a second thought, Clark raised the barrel of his rifle, almost casually, and pulled back on the trigger. A single round was all it took to drop the fleeing shadow. The men staggered tiredly to it and, by the light of a single match, felt great elation to discover the motionless carcass of the healthy young stag, toppled in their path.

With Clark's blessing and, in fact, to Clark's relief, Elmer removed his knife from his boot and immediately began field dressing the deer. Heavily intoxicated and with only moonlight to see by, his handiwork was atypically sloppy. As he twisted the creature around all different ways to achieve the leverage needed to complete the job, blood, organs and other sinewy insides formed a thin, morbid blanket on the forest floor. He grabbed the stag from behind, just below it's front legs, and attempted to drag it backward to rest on a large rock. This was unsuccessful, however, as his feet slipped in the darkened gore, putting Elmer on his back, somewhat underneath the carcass. He laughed and made several attempts to stand but his inability to gain traction in the mess of blood and guts kept him crashing back down again. At last, he rolled off to the side of the trail; propped up on his knees, and maneuvered the large rock over to the deer. He used it first to regain his balance. Then he braced his shin against it, leaned over and awkwardly grabbed the deer's leg. He used both hands to pull it toward him and propped the animal's shoulder up against the rock. "I'm gonna leave him here to drain while I run to the truck and get my tarp," he said. "I'll be right back."

"Bring back the flashlight, too!" hollered Clark as his friend disappeared. He stood and waited, lighting match after match to reestablish his bearings in the darkness while continually glimpsing his kill. Here he crossed the threshold into no regret. His dinner may be cold and his wife may be angry, but the achievement for which these things were sacrificed was solid and permanent.

Elmer returned with a flashlight, two canned beers and a large blue tarp. Together, the men unfolded the plastic sheet, spreading it out flat beside the deer. They pushed as one to roll the stag over on to it. To celebrate this job well done, Elmer cracked both beer cans at once and handed one to Clark. They toasted and they drank. The empty aluminum cylinders were tossed on to the tarp with the carcass, and they drug the macabre collection back to Elmer's truck. There they lifted the mass into the bed and closed the tailgate.

Inside the cab, Elmer had two more cans of beer waiting. As before, he popped them open and handed one to Clark. "We damn did it!" he exclaimed as he tapped his can to Clark's. "We damn did it."

Clark smiled. "We sure did. Couldn't be better." He took a sip of his beer. "But Elmer, buddy, I really must get home." Sobriety was slipping back in.

"Alright. Alright." Elmer turned his key and put the truck in gear. "I'll have us back in an hour and a half." He pressed his foot to the gas and guided the vehicle out of the park - one hand on the wheel and the other holding his beer.

Not ten minutes into the drive, Clark passed out in the passenger seat, his beer falling out of his hand, spilling on to the floorboard. Elmer didn't mind. He, himself, was still covered in fresh blood that was smearing all over his seat and steering column. He figured he could wipe the whole thing down as soon as he returned home. As his eyes grew heavier though, his thoughts on this priority shifted more realistically to the following day.

Just inside Allegheny County, the truck crept up on an old railroad crossing. Elmer eased slowly to the edge of the tracks and looked left, then right. Then his head dropped in exhaustion. He opened his eyes and looked straight ahead again, slowly inching forward. As he moved across the rails, he nodded down once more and his foot weighed the break into a complete stop. Unknowingly, he joined Clark in drunken, tender slumber, the engine purring and the vehicle still in gear.

Time ended there for the men, though they each had at least one good half hour of sleep before the crossing lights began blinking. Left light and right light and back to left, they never saw this radiance. Nor did they hear the dinging of the bell or the distant whistle of the locomotive. And as that whistle grew louder, closer, neither man was the wiser to it. The engineer spotted the truck's lights straddling the path ahead, and the brakeman did everything he could to prevent collision, but it was of no consequence. The wheels shrieked as the train crumpled and tore the truck like paper. When the investigators arrived to assess the scene, they could not differentiate between the blood of Elmer, Clark or the deer.

Earthlings

II

"Neighbors in life, neighbors in death," smiled Vida. Helen could not share in this attempt at humor. Her husband's mangled remains were sealed in a closed casket in the east room, adjoined to the lounge where she sat. She had not seen him since the morning he left for his hunting trip, and it was apparent that no further memories would be made. Vida's circumstance mirrored this, with her own husband stowed in his own fancy receptacle in the west room. She had always been a better sport than Helen.

The elegies had already been delivered; one hour apart to assure their mutual friends would have time to recharge their grief between emotional releases. Even so, Helen was concerned that the fanfare for Clark was diminished by the funeral director's decision to schedule his service second. She could not reasonably voice this complaint, though, knowing that the choice had been made strictly by the flip of a coin. And so she sat, trembling and stuck inside her head. Vida grasped her quivering hand and suggested that they step outside to smoke a cigarette.

The women quietly emerged from the back door of the funeral home, into the alley. Vida extended her cigarette pack to Helen after removing one for herself and placing it between her lips. Helen was not a regular smoker, but indulged secretly and occasionally. For *this* occasion, she helped herself to two cigarettes and held no regard for anyone who may have been watching her breathe them away. "This is so unbearable," she finally spoke, "How are you keeping yourself together?"

Vida's smile returned inappropriately. "It's all for show," she admitted. "Mind over matter."

"Hogwash," asserted Helen as she exhaled a large cloud.

"Well you asked." Vida shrugged.

"Where is your sadness?" asked Helen. "Don't you have a soul?"

Vida's smile faded. "I feel like you're taking this out on me, Helen. Don't forget that we're in the same boat, you and I."

"The same boat? *The same boat?*" She erupted with all the venom she had been withholding since the bodies were found. "You know as well as I do that my Clark was not even half the boozer that Elmer was. But with all the pressure Elmer would put on him, he always felt obligated to keep up. And I'll bet you any money that, had Elmer not been persuading him, he would have returned by noon like they were supposed to and none of this would have even happened."

Vida inhaled the rest of her tobacco and tossed the butt to the ground. "Clark was a grown man," she said, "He was capable of his own decisions. You can't blame Elmer for everything."

"Don't even try to tell me that," scorned Helen. "It was Elmer's booze and Elmer's truck. He was the one driving the damned thing – not my Clark. All Clark did was try to be a good friend and he thought that meant going along with Elmer's demands and his stupid *stupid* ideas. For years I warned him to be more mindful of that influence. Now look where it got him."

Vida's façade was punctured. She lit another cigarette and turned her face away to obscure her watering eyes.

Nearly two full weeks passed before the women spoke again. An unseasonably warm November day drew them each to their respective back porches. Vida stood at her banister and smoked. Helen sat on her stoop and stared mostly straight ahead, relinquishing quick peripheral glances toward her neighbor. These were nonetheless apparent to Vida who turned her full body toward Helen, held her cigarettes in the air and asked simply, "You wanna smoke?"

"That sounds nice," replied Helen.

"I'll come to you." Vida descended her brief stair set and crossed the concrete walkway that separated their yards. She stepped to Helen's porch, presented her with a cigarette, and subsequently ignited it for her.

Helen kept her eyes fixated on a stand-alone tree in her yard. "You see that bird?" she asked.

Vida looked to the tree and quickly noticed a bluebird perched on a low hanging branch. Its chest bore a distinct, bright yellow mark, shaped almost like a trapezoid. "You mean that little blue one?" she asked.

"Yeah that's right," Helen replied. "I've seen that bird out here every single day since Clark died. Every day."

"Maybe it's a sign."

"It's more than a sign. It's my Clark. He comes back to watch over me."

Vida smiled. "Elmer has been visiting me, too," she said. "There's a black cat that showed up in my yard right after the funeral. I don't see him everyday, but at least every other. I know its Elmer."

"So you know what I'm talking about."

"I do."

Helen removed her glasses and wiped tears from the sides of her eyes. "I'm sorry I got so upset at the funeral. We're both grieving and my blame was just uncalled for."

"It's alright," consoled Vida. "I think that's part of the human condition. We think we have dominion over the world, but we really don't. And when that illusion of control breaks down, we just don't know what to do with ourselves."

"Too many words," said Helen, "We have too many words and when we're desperate, we just spill them everywhere. I'm sorry."

"I'm sorry, too." Vida gave Helen another cigarette. "I guess we should be glad to see our husbands reincarnated as animals. They're enlightened now."

"Enlightened?"

"Yeah. Free of that human condition. Free of all those words you're talkin' about. Free to just exist. Think about it. You've had pets, right?"

"Of course."

"You and Clark had a dog for a while, right?"

"A long time ago," confirmed Helen, "Been almost a decade now."

"I remember. That little black poodle - what was her name?"

"That was my Trixie."

"Trixie. That's right. How many words did Trixie know?"

Helen took pause to digest the question. "Only about four, I guess. She knew 'sit' and 'stay.' She knew that 'pee pee' meant I was going to let her out to use bathroom. And she knew what a 'treat' was, also."

Vida continued. "But how many of those words did she ever say back to you? Could she use any words at all?"

"I don't follow."

"I'm just adding to your point about words. Trixie only knew to bark, growl and cry, right? No emphasis or dialect, right? No sentences to put together. No verbs to conjugate. Just barking, growling and crying – but were you ever in doubt as to what she was expressing?"

Helen drew contemplatively from her cigarette. "No I guess not," she agreed.

"See we've lost that," said Vida. "Human beings have lost their ability to withhold our speech until there is an actual need to let it out. Instead we just make things more difficult on ourselves by over speaking and trying to control everything in advance."

"I see what you mean."

"We should be pleased if our loved ones return to us as cats or birds or whatever," Vida pressed. "Those are not lower forms of life. They are *higher* forms of life. Wearing clothes and drinking cocktails; buying cleaning products and breaking your back for paper money; those things are *not* evolution. Those are steps backward; away from freedom, away from God."

"Animals have it right," agreed Helen just as the bluebird sprung from its branch and took flight. "Goodbye, Clark," she called as it left her sight.

Vida continued. "You know what the largest structure built by earthlings is?"

Helen thought for a moment. "The pyramids?" she asked. "No wait. It has to be the Great Wall of China."

"Neither of those," informed Vida. "It's actually the Great Barrier Reef."

The wonder drained from Helen's face. "Honey, the Great Barrier Reef wasn't built by people."

"I didn't say it was built by people. I said it was built by earthlings."

"It was built by nature."

"It was built by coral polyps." Vida's answer was final. "Little sea creatures built the Great Barrier Reef and they keep on building it every day."

"Well I said it was nature." Helen hated to seem incorrect. "Sure sounds like nature to me."

Vida rolled her eyes. "Yes, dear, it is in the nature of the polyps to build it, therefore it *is* nature, yes. But for that matter, it is in the nature for humans to build skyscrapers, therefore the Grant Building or the Gulf Tower would be just as natural. That's beside the point, though."

"Well get on with the point then."

"I'm trying, Helen. Look, the point is that you automatically assumed that the largest structure in the world made by earthlings would have to be made by human earthlings, in particular. And I'm not faulting you because that's what I thought also when Elmer first told it to me. It seems to be a very clear indication, though, that we human beings really overvalue ourselves. You know what I'm saying?"

Helen nodded slightly.

Vida's spiel continued. "We think we're so great because we can make our worlds to be overly complex. But we are far outnumbered by other earthlings who do amazing things together with simpler lives and far less thought. Practically no words whatsoever."

"I try to live a simple life," inserted Helen.

Vida pierced her with her eyes. "No, you don't," she said direly. "You try to live a *convenient* life. So do I. Most all humans do. We lost simplicity a long time ago. We could have had fire, but we traded it for electric heaters. We have to pay money to keep that electricity going, and for our air conditioners in the summer. Well we can't make that money without a job, which also gives us a schedule we have to keep up with. So then we need clocks and calendars. We also have to get to that job somehow so we need an automobile. The automobile runs on gas, and we need money for that, too. All this just to stay warm? What was wrong with the damn fire?"

Helen understood. "And where did our lives go while chasing those things, too?" she pondered.

"If Clark is a bird, then he is free now. If Elmer is a cat..." Vida sobbed into her hand.

"Hey. Speak of the devil," said Helen, her eyes fixed on Vida's adjacent yard. "Is that the cat?"

Vida turned around and, sure enough, the black cat she associated with Elmer was slowly crossing her yard. "Oh yes! He must have heard me!" said Vida excitedly.

"Yeah, Elmer wouldn't leave you crying, would he?" asked Helen.

"Absolutely not." Vida smiled and wiped her eyes one final time. Then she knelt, extended her hand and ran her thumb and index finger together in the cat's direction. "Here Elmer Elmer Elmer!" she called. "Here Elmer Elmer Elmer!" The cat ceased his step and sat down. Vida handed another cigarette to Helen. "Here's one for later if you need it. I'm going to go put some milk on the porch for Elmer."

Earthlings

III

By proxy, the onset of cold weather brought Helen to Vida's home one night. It had been a week since the temperature abruptly dropped and two days longer than this since she had seen the bluebird she associated with Clark. The loneliness had become central to her thoughts. As much as she disliked her, Vida did have a comforting way of putting the world in perspective. She also had cigarettes. And so Helen dressed herself in her green parka and crossed the concrete to Vida's yard. She ascended her stoop and knocked on her back screen door, rattling it in it's slightly bent frame.

Vida answered, still in her pajamas. "Well good morning, Ms Helen," she said.

Helen hated being called "Ms" by someone who was only five years her junior. "Good afternoon, Vida. Do you have a minute?" she asked. "I just need someone to talk to."

"Sure," replied Vida. "I was just making tea. I'll grab two cups." The women moved into her living room and sat down opposite one another before her blazing fireplace; each in her own soft recliner beside an end table for tea. "So what's on your mind?" she asked.

At that moment, cigarettes were on Helen's mind, but she went ahead with the larger issue that brought her there. "I haven't seen my little Clark bird in over a week now."

"Oh well it's getting cold outside. He probably just migrated somewhere else for the winter. You know how birds are. I'm surprised that he stayed as long as he did, really."

"I just feel scared that he won't come back in the spring," explained Helen.

That fatalism earned her what she had been waiting on. Vida handed her a cigarette without a word, and also lit one for herself. When she was completely certain that Helen would expound no further, she went ahead and spoke. "If he doesn't come back, then that just means he was visiting you one more time in that form and then moving on. He could have come back just to say goodbye, you know?" She could see Helen's body become tense. She had to change direction, but this was a tough one. "And then next year maybe you'll see him in *another* bird that comes around," she continued, "Maybe not even a bird. Maybe a squirrel or a dog or something."

Helen sighed as she exhaled the cigarette. She needed her misery to reach further, dig deeper. "What about Elmer?" she finally asked, hoping for some reason to believe that her problem was not unique.

"Oh, he's around here somewhere," replied Vida. She then turned away from the fire and yelled out toward her hall, "Elmer! Where are you, Elmer?" A sleek, feline silhouette appeared in the doorframe. "There he is. Come on, Elmer." The cat stepped forward and was revealed clearly in the light. He rubbed against Vida's varicose legs as she scratched the top of his head.

"So Elmer lives with you now?" asked Helen.

"Yeah. Been about two weeks since he started coming inside. One day he just finished his milk then walked on in like he owned the place." There was so much more Vida could have told her: how he kept mice out of the basement for her, or how he knew to relieve himself outdoors and so did not need a litter box, or how he slept in her bed curled up in the small of her back – but she knew it would only add to her neighbor's sadness. "Another cigarette?" she offered instead.

The winter was dense, with snow and cold and silence. Helen mostly kept to herself, watching television, phoning her sister, and sleeping on the living room couch. Vida made certain to check in with her from time to time and twice helped to clean up her house. Otherwise, Vida sat by her fire; reading books, with Elmer nestled in beside her.

As the weather warmed, Vida would walk to the end of the street and back with Elmer at her heels. Through her living room window, Helen envied and so despised this. "Who does she think she is; parading her dead husband around in front of my house everyday?" She would ask this question aloud and stringently. Her resentment would grow within her until a mental breaking point gave way to a fleeting clarity. Her final solution, found repeatedly in these moments, was always for Clark to simply return. And with that, for a few precious hours at a time, she could direct her animus away from her neighbor. Blaming her bitterness instead on Clark allowed her to subconsciously meditate on their relationship. Every time, her curses turned to prayers, "Please, Clark. Please come back to me."

Though rather overdue considering the temperature outside, Clark did finally return; the same bluebird with the semi-trapezoidal orange marking on his chest. Helen noticed him through her kitchen window early one morning. He was poking around in the grass, presumably searching for food. She wanted to run into the yard and scoop him into her palms, but knew better than to scare him away. It was evident that her relationship with

Clark, at least for a time, would be strictly voyeuristic. Still, his return to her was enough to validate her prayer.

Clark had many housing options now, complete with feeders and a birdbath – all products of Helen's desperate hope. He tried each one, but never really found a preference. As the sun subsided, he retired to the same tree he inhabited the prior year. The next morning, Helen rose before daybreak, made coffee, sat and waited for the bird to emerge again. Once in her vision, she spoke to him through the glass. Her dialog continued for hours before she excused herself to the restroom.

When Helen returned to her window, Clark was involved in some engagement with another bird. This one appeared to be of the same species, but more gray than blue. Together, they pecked at one another while circling, on the ground and in flight. She wanted to shoo away the little gray nuisance, but was again wary of how Clark might react to her involvement. So she sat and watched. Her observations lead her to conclude that the gray bird was not fighting with Clark, but was a friend. She could see quite clearly that they had only been playing together. Her head tracked the movements of the two birds as, practically in tandem, they jetted from one house to another, to the feeders, to the bath and back again. At the end of the day, Clark returned to his tree and the gray bird joined him there.

Over the next two weeks, Clark and the gray bird worked tirelessly to assemble a nest in each of the three birdhouses. Though she was ebullient to see Clark taking a firm residency, Helen thought this property grab to be rather greedy. "Clark would never be so intrusive or selfish," she thought to herself. "I bet it's that little bitch putting him up to it." And so from that thought on, this was the name by which Helen would refer to the gray bird. She would call her: "Bitch."

For a time, Helen stopped making long speeches through the window. Her level of dialog stepped down to about where it was before Clark was killed – curt and routine. As the renovations moved forward, however, she ramped back up in new ways. Though she knew nothing about building a nest, herself, she took to making lay criticisms of Bitch's handiwork, as well as her effort. "You're letting her just sit there while you do all the heavy lifting," she would complain. "She's got no cooking or cleaning to do so I don't understand why she can't put forth a little more effort here. You're letting her walk all over you, Clark."

Though Clark and Bitch installed a nest in every house, they spent most of their time in the yellow one on the back of the garage. If any other birds trespassed near one of their vacant nests, Clark would take to the air and immediately run them off. All his other time seemed to be spent coddling Bitch, sometimes bringing her food or keeping her seat warm when she left the nest. This seemed pathetic to Helen, but endearingly so, as it strongly resembled Clark when he was a human, always so eager to please. It was one of his idiosyncrasies that she spent decades learning to love (and not abuse). Bitch could not have known him for even a year, though, and Helen did not like the way she was treating him.

Neither bird paid much mind when Helen marched outside, even letting her screen door slam. She, too, looked away from them as she crossed over to Vida's yard and stepped on to her porch. She rapped three times sternly.

Vida answered, again in pajamas. "Well hello, neighbor."

With no smile to reciprocate, Helen asked bluntly, "Can I come in and smoke a cigarette? Clark and I are having some issues."

Between Vida and her sister, Helen relayed her eccentric foible ad nauseam for days. Each of her listeners served her the same common sense: "You are a human. Bitch and Clark are birds. Enjoy them before they leave for the next winter." She couldn't voluntarily change her feelings, though. It was not that Clark had taken a new mate, but that the new mate took advantage of his kindness. She felt pulled two ways between the need for Clark's presence, and the sadness for his circumstance. Thinly veiled by these concerns, jealousy festered at the core of Helen's problem, which was ultimately with Bitch.

On a rare afternoon in which both birds left the yellow house unattended, Helen took advantage of their absence to survey the area. She did not expect to find anything of value in doing this, but felt a need to exercise dominion over her yard and the little wooden birdhouses she purchased with her own money. She lifted the top of each of the green and red houses. The nests there were nothing special; just twigs and some trash stuck together. In the yellow house, though – the one in which the birds spent most of their time – she found the nest was sheltering six blue ovoids. "Thirty years of marriage and Clark could never give me children," she observed out loud, "But he can give Bitch here six in just a few months? I'll be damned." This was Helen's final gasp of jealousy.

Throughout the incubation period, she reached an enlightened understanding. As she repeatedly recalled the image of the eggs in her memory, her perception of Bitch slowly evolved. She came to no longer see her as a lazy, domineering home wrecker, but as the mother of Clark's

Earthlings

children. Beyond that, she anticipated that the eggs, once hatched, would serve as surrogates for the offspring she was never afforded when Clark was a human. In Helen's mind, the dynamic had shifted. In her mind, she and Bitch had met at a level of mutual respect, woman-to-woman. It took some time, but now she realized they could all be one big happy family.

Earthlings

IV

In the mornings, Clark routinely gathered food to share with Bitch. A varying collection of neighborhood finches usually explored the yard the same time as he. There was a regular cardinal and two titmice that would also join in the daybreak sweeps. Everyone remained respectful of the area each other bird was exploring (except sometimes the finches would bicker among themselves). Though they assembled because that particular yard at that particular time of day allowed for the choicest pickings, their community also provided the feeling of safety. To be grounded and preoccupied is a very vulnerable position for a winged creature to be in. Together, through fight or flight, only one bird would be needed to signal all the others to a threat.

As he often did, Clark procured the area around the yellow birdhouse and expanded his field outward toward the tree. Helen watched him from the kitchen, with a respect she had not had for him when he was human. She, in fact, viewed him as more manly now that he was a bird. She was proud of what he had become: no speaking, strictly action. Closer to the tree he moved, with no consideration for stopping until their meal was uncovered. He was soon out of Helen's sight, near the trunk and obscured by the shadows of the branches.

A loud rustle in the tree abruptly disturbed the calm of the prodding birds. Everyone looked over to the source of the noise, wings poised to flap. From within the leaves erupted Clark, sending the other birds into flight. Helen looked up from her crossword puzzle just in time to see Elmer following him out. She rose from her seat with impulsive concern, but before she could even reach her door, Elmer sprung from the ground and plucked Clark from the sky. Helen ran outside in an attempt to prevent a massacre, but it was no use. As she approached, Elmer simply walked away with Clark in his teeth. He would sit down and chew on the bird until Helen was too close, then he would relocate again. "Please let him go!" she screamed. "Please, Elmer!" Confused as to why anyone would be anything but proud of his kill, Elmer scuttled off, carrying Clark's lifeless body to the other side of Vida's garage. He sat on the concrete slab that bordered the alley and shredded his avian breakfast.

Helen was in tears as she collected Clark's feathers from the yard – feathers he had just lost in his scuffle with Elmer. She found six in total. She laid them out on her counter, arranged in two rows of three, and screamed at them while pounding her fist. Utterly beside herself, she bounced around the kitchen, weak kneed and rolling on the balls of her feet. She screamed a few more times, punched some cabinets and pushed over a chair. Then she went to the bathroom and washed her face.

After finding her bearings enough to cease her violence, it was determined that a visit to Vida was in order. Helen put on her shoes, crossed to her back door and knocked sharply but with no rhythm. Vida answered, wearing pajamas as always anymore. Immediately she noticed Helen was trembling. "Ms Helen you look like you've seen the devil, himself," she said. "Why don't you come on in and have a cigarette? Tell me all about it?" Helen stepped into the house and the women walked into the living room. Vida dispensed a cigarette to her and sat down in her usual chair. Helen remained standing, her back to the unlit fireplace. "So what's the news?" asked Vida?

"Can I borrow your lighter?" asked Helen.

"Oh of course. Sorry about that." Vida handed over her lighter.

"Thank you." Helen turned toward the fireplace, dropped her head and lit the cigarette. She slipped the lighter into her bra, touched her brow to the mantle and wrapped both hands around the fire iron. As casually as Clark had shot the deer, Helen turned and swatted the poker at Vida. She deflected the attack, taking the hit to her wrist, but Helen persisted. Vida could not stand and defend herself at once and so it was only a matter of time before Helen would cleanly connect with one of her thrusts. After she cracked Vida's head on about the fourth or fifth whack, it was easy to keep beating her. Once Vida's defenses ceased, then so did Helen's assault. She tossed the iron to the floor, took a deep drag from the cigarette and asked, "Hey are you still alive?"

Vida, her face a mess, did not respond.

Helen picked up Vida's copy of the *Valley News Dispatch* from her end table and walked into the kitchen. She opened the oven and, crumpling one page at a time, tossed the newspaper inside. She followed this with the remnant of the cigarette, slammed the door closed and turned on the heat. She exited to find Elmer licking his paws on the porch. She tried to kick him, but he ran away as soon as he saw her.

Back at home, Helen unfurled her garden hose from the side of her house. She turned on the water and walked up and down the property line, saturating the concrete walkway and the grass on either side of it. Once she felt it had been adequately soaked as to prevent the spread of fire to her parcel, she walked inside and went to bed.

As Vida burned away, her essence ascended with the smoke. Her consciousness, free of its earthly vessel, stretched out into the dimension above. She looked down on the material world as though into a fish tank. There she saw the path that her life had taken. Restricted by the human body, this path was only visible to her one moment at a time, but in death she became aware of the shape of all those moments strung together; the design of her existence.

As her reality in the material world had grown, it wrapped like a vine around the reality of other people and things. The intermeshing was a slow chaos, expanding outward in all directions. From the fifth dimension, this looked very much like rich foliage. As each life moved across the earth, it grew as though it was a stem. Each path not taken was a leaf or a thorn on that stem. Some people's lives grew thickly enough together to resemble a tree. Fruits and flowers, filled with color and detail were born of crucial synchronic moments in a life. She realized that, when one zoom outs, all earthlings are quite like plants, or perhaps like the polyps that built the Great Barrier Reef. The separation between earthlings was purely perceptual. It is simply in the nature of humans to obsess over details, confining our own moments and inflicting that confinement on others.

Vida felt no hate for Helen and, in fact, still wanted her neighbor to be happy. And so, instead of progressing outward into further dimensions, or better exploring the one she was in, she decided to follow the path that put her back on earth - into the body of one of the baby birds. She began pecking out of her shell at the sound of activity at her old home. (Detectives and damage assessors were all over the place but, of course, she didn't know what any of that was.) She had several sisters and brothers that joined her over the next few days and, without Clark around, Bitch took over the feeding duties herself. Helen looked into the nest a handful of times. Though she aroused nervousness in most of the hatchlings, Vida felt a comfortable familiarity toward her.

After a couple weeks, Vida grew curious for what existed outside the nest. She began stretching over the edge, trying to see where she thought she might be able to one-day visit. She reached so far that she eventually toppled out. This was the first time she attempted to use her wings, feeling an instinctive notion to do so. Though she did not take flight, her landing was softened. She used her new perspective to explore on foot, wandering almost right up to the old charred lot where her home once stood. She felt a discomfort and began to cry out for Bitch.

A black cat that had been sleeping in the alley answered her calls. Elmer entered the yard and followed the sound. When he pinpointed and faced her, they were each taken back by a mutual feeling of exhilaration. Her crying ceased and he devoured her on the spot.

Earthlings

Oblivion

I

Like most people, he longed for the Next Thing. It's not that Markie felt contempt for his current occupation, but he was acutely aware that life outside of it went on without him. Five years and two months of anything was at least two months too long. He could have been working on something – some thing – that he could move to laterally, once it was built. He instead burned through his money for travel – pursuing that life outside as a tourist and a voyeur.

This desire for movement was the reason he applied for his job in the first place. It seemed something closer to freedom to be paid to drive ones car around town. Sure, there was the downside of having to wear a uniform, which seemed contrary to the whole idea of freedom. Sure also, Markie could not choose where he was to travel to, nor when. What counted was that, when in route, the only job in those moments would be to drive. There would be no boss to loom over him. There would be no coworkers to entertain. There would only be a driver, his car, and the road – a fleeting circumstance, but one that occurred many times in a workday. For the most part, his presuppositions about the job had proven truthful. This is why he was not so quick to escape the occupation sooner. The resulting five years of complacency were now enough, but he could not yet see a clear exit.

"Hey, you bum. Wake up."

Markie nodded awkwardly toward his boss, who was briskly walking from the freezer to the manager's office. "Put that in a box and come here a minute, Mark," continued his boss.

Markie pondered the chance that he was going to be reprimanded for daydreaming, though this would not seem characteristic of his boss, who was gruff and hard working, but not much of a stickler. He quickly cut the pizza that had been sitting on the table before him, shoveled it into a box, and sat the finished product on the order window. He crossed over to the office, but before he could step fully beyond the doorframe, his boss presented him with a ticket.

"Here's your run. Two deliveries, all the way out to Lake Ridge. I figure you'd appreciate that." Markie *did* appreciate it. The Lake Ridge area was on the absolute furthest reaches of their delivery jurisdiction. It was so far away from the store that addresses in the area were exempt from the company's policy of providing the customer with a free pizza if not delivered within thirty minutes. There was no longer drive that one could make in a single run there. It was an ideal route for a fluttering mind.

Markie removed his orders from the window and slid each one into a separate, insulated bag. He carried them out of the store, now with a bit more swagger, and stacked them in the back seat of his Nova. It was a 1979 model, with a tape deck that sang "Your Saving Grace" by Steve Miller Band when he started the car.

He ejected the cassette immediately. This suited him well on the way to work, but the tone of his thoughts had since changed. Now he had arrived at an inevitable long drive north, at sunset, on a clear day. Night would fall within an hour or less. He scanned his assortment of random cassettes, many without cases, and many of which, intentionally or not, came with the car when he purchased it. The answer was immediately clear. The Rolling Stones. *Their Satanic Majesties Request.*

He slid the cassette into the player and immediately "The Lantern" began to play from about a minute in. He loved this song, but figured it best to start at the start. He ejected the cassette, flipped it in his palm, and inserted it again into the player; with the local public radio affiliate filling in the small amount of time it took for him to complete this action. "2000 Man" now played just long enough for him to reach up to his console and press the rewind button. He then put his car in gear and proceeded to a right turn out of the parking lot.

Being such a long way to Lake Ridge, he figured he had better fill his gas tank before committing to the drive. Better to disrupt the moment at the beginning of a new experience, then in the middle when the feeling of the thing is at it's most powerful. Just as he pulled into the station, the cassette had reached its head and began to play. Markie ejected it, for to save it to accompany the drive. Again, public radio came through his speakers for only a moment before he killed the engine and ran up to the station's convenience area. Inside, an elderly clerk sat behind the counter, listening to country music radio.

"I'd like to get twenty on pump two please," said Markie as he removed a bill from his back pocket and presented it to the clerk.

"That be all?" asked the clerk.

"Yes. Thank you." Markie exited with just enough time to hear the music interrupted by a special news bulletin. He had no time for this now. He had pizza to deliver and a cassette to listen to.

As he pumped his gas, he noticed the clerk sitting stiffly on his stool, glancing up and parting his lips. The old man anxiously rubbed his legs and scratched his head before placing his elbows on to the counter and resting his mouth in his hands. Markie turned his attention to the numbers on the pump. The gas flow slowed as the twenty-dollar mark grew nearer. In this elongated, encapsulating moment, Markie took one more look at the clerk, who was now standing, despite there being no customers there to serve. Suddenly he smacked his palm on the counter and spun around to the window, holding his chest and appearing very exasperated. Markie quickly ran to the man's assistance, but was shooed away through the glass before ever reaching the door.

The clerk's demeanor returned to being calm and collected enough. Markie turned and walked back to his Nova. Sitting in the driver seat, facing the store, he had no way to avoid one more look upon the clerk, who was now standing just on the other side of the entrance. Having walked away with his back to the man, Markie had not witnessed the prior moments when the clerk flipped the hanging sign on that door from the side that bore the word, "OPEN" to the side that said, "CLOSED." He still had not noticed this nuance before returning to the road.

The public radio station was also broadcasting a newsbreak. Someone from NASA was going to be addressing the listeners shortly regarding the impact of something. "Blah blah blah," spoke Markie to himself before pushing the cassette back in and then…silence.

II

Tears ran down Marilynn Montgomery's cheek as the man from NASA addressed the cameras. "This is the end," was all that Ed could think to say, but refrained from doing so. Stating the obvious would only aggravate the emotion in the air.

"Why are you crying, mommy?" asked Jeffrey. Ed turned off the television immediately.

"I didn't see you there," she replied.

"I didn't mean to scare you, mommy. I didn't mean to make you cry."

"No, Jeffrey. I'm not crying because I didn't see you. I'm just saying that you snuck up on me, but it's not your fault that I'm crying. I'm not saying…" She did not know how to proceed.

Ed stood up. "Jeffery, get your brother and go to the prayer room."

Jeffery did not ask any of the questions in his head. He walked up the stairs and into his bedroom, took his brother by the hand and proceeded to pull him away from the toy cars that were occupying him.

"Stop it!" protested his brother.

"Dad said we have to go to the prayer room. Come on, James." James conceded without further inquiry.

"Start the prayer chain and I'll be there in just a few minutes," said Ed, "I want to secure the house." Marilynn turned toward the hall. "Wait." Ed grabbed her arm and she faced him. "I love you." He rubbed a tear from her cheek and kissed her mouth before releasing her.

Marilynn lit two long, red candles on either side of the massive crucifix that hung above the fireplace. She spread pillows down below it, where she, Jeffery and James knelt, joined hands, and bowed their heads.

Ed walked upstairs to the bedroom and turned on the small black and white television that sat on their dresser. He kept it on just long enough to confirm that rioting and looting were beginning in the major cities - as he figured. He plucked the television from the dresser, yanked its power cord from the outlet and lunged it into the wall behind the bed.

Lake Ridge was a mostly affluent place, but Ed felt great concern for the valley on the northern side. The area had been developed earlier in the century, built to affordably house the employees of Lake Ridge Steel and their families. This worked for a time, until the mid-nineteen-eighties, when a South Korean company purchased the mill. Only three months later, the Koreans ceased operations there so they could build a modern, state-of the-art replacement for it in Canada. This devastated the valley. Over the course of a few years, as people moved out by choice or foreclosure, the government had purchased much of the property, tearing down the blighted homes and replacing them with cheap, low-income apartment housing.

Ed had always been wary of the inhabitants of the valley, but now he could not stop his mind from turning over countless scenarios that their reactions to the news were going to lead to. His home could be prominently seen up on the ridge by anyone in the valley. He regretted his vain enthusiasm for that very detail, which largely influenced his choice to purchase the place. He now realized that such naked bravado, in a time of crisis, would only become a prime target for desperate men. He had to protect his wife and children from the horrors that were surely to come.

Ed reached high up in the closet and retrieved his pistol from under a stack of folded towels. He exited the bedroom and stepped quietly down the stairs. Hesitating outside of the prayer room, he thought about whom it made the most sense to kill first. He did not want his children to see their mother die, but it seemed unnatural for the children to die first. After contemplating the possibilities, he decided that, so long as he acted quickly, he could shoot Marilynn first and then probably follow up with the children before they could quite realize what was happening. In fact, it had to be Marilynn first because she was the only one who could possibly overpower Ed if she decided to fight against his plan.

Marilynn and the boys were deep in whispered prayer. Ed extended the gun toward the back of Marilynn's head and slowly stepped forward into the room. Carefully he rolled his heels across the carpet, as not to make a sound. Intuition, however, was enough to make Marilynn break her focus on praying and turn around. Startled, Ed lowered the gun. Marilynn broke from the children and, before they could notice why, she quickly pressed her body up against Ed's, with the gun in between them.

"Keep praying," she told the boys. "Your father and I need to have a talk." Marilynn put her arm around Ed's waist, rolling him against her own body, so as to obscure the gun from any potential glances back that the children may take. Without a word, she escorted him out of the room, down the hall, and into the kitchen.

"I'm sorry," said Ed. "It needs to happen, though, Marilynn. Hell on earth is here and our only escape is going to be to remove ourselves."

"That choice should be mine to make," she protested. "Why would you not tell me about your intentions?"

"Because I didn't want you to agonize," said Ed. "But the choice should be simple since our deaths are approaching either way. The only question is whether we want to be tortured and raped before we go."

"Tortured and raped?" Marilynn had not considered how the valley might have been reacting to the news.

"Yes," said Ed, " I turned on the television in the bedroom. The cities are falling into chaos. It's only a matter of time before it reaches us here. I hate to say it, but we are sitting ducks up on this ridge and we have nowhere else to go."

Marilynn now realized the fear. She did not want to die, but she knew there was no way around it. She thought about the electrical grid losing power as the time grew near. She imagined people from the valley, climbing up the ridge and smashing the windows on their large French doors. She envisioned toothless drug addicts sodomizing her in front of her children, and her children in front of her. The home alarm system that they pay for every year was rendered meaningless. What reason would any police officer have to answer a call now? Surely, they too, would have been wiser to go home to protect their own families in these final hours. She now understood Ed's intention. To postpone death was a senseless gamble that could jeopardize them all. In death, as in life, the family had to stick together.

Marilynn felt no other choice than to allow Ed to take their lives. Her adherence to this idea came with one single caveat, however: There must be no risk of the children knowing the truth of the situation. They were not to see their death advancing and their concluding moments were to be as joyful as could be mustered. Ed agreed to these terms and wasted no time in reworking his plan. He placed the pistol in his waistband, grabbed Marilynn's hand and walked her back to the prayer room.

"Hey boys, we're going on a trip, okay?" James and Jeffery looked at one another with confused, semi-excited exchanges, each waiting for a signal that the other had an idea of what Ed was talking about.

"Where are we going, daddy?" asked James.

"Anywhere that you want to go. Anywhere at all."

"Anywhere?"

"Anywhere," said Ed as Marilynn began to cry, "We have to go now though."

Jeffery and James stood up. "I need to put on my shoes."

Ed assured him that he did not. "We are traveling on a magic chariot through a – a wormhole in space."

"How will we breathe in space, daddy?" asked James, "We need space suits."

The questions were stirring anxiety in Ed. "It will all make sense when we get there. We're going to use dream power. So we have to go to where we dream at night."

"We have to go to sleep?" continued Jeffery.

"No. We have to – get in a trance – basically." Ed needed movement. "Come on. Let's go upstairs to your bedroom."

The family proceeded up the stairs in a slow line. Though he felt great urgency, Ed was careful not to expose his boys to it. At Ed's request, the four of them split into two pairs and stationed themselves, respectively, on the outside of each of the boys' beds. With a count of three from Ed, the family pushed toward the space between them, bringing the beds together.

"Okay. Okay. Everyone on the dream machine and prepare for departure!" said Ed, enthusiastically. "Pull the covers down first." Together, the family stripped the sheets and balled the covers up around the exterior edge of the bed set. Ed took the largest and thickest blanket, a blue one that used to fit a king sized bed that the family no longer owned, and unfurled it over the middle. It covered both beds with slack remaining. Ed lifted the corner of the blanket, "Everyone in!"

Jeffery jumped first into the black hole. James next. "I need to stay out here," whispered Ed. Marilynn wrapped her arms around his torso as tears filled her eyes. "We can't make a show of our sadness. I will be right behind you and the boys. I promise." Ed held her hand loosely as she sat down on the side of the bed. "I love you." Marilynn then crossed her legs together, lifted the corner of the blanket, and spun around into the black hole. Jeffery and James were now giddy with delight.

"Why are you not in here with us, daddy?" asked James.

"I'm here," replied Ed. "I am in the cockpit though because I have to pilot the dream machine. But I will see you as soon as we land, okay?"

"Okay, daddy."

"Now everyone form a prayer chain." Marilynn and the boys joined hands. Ed walked around the exterior, determining the positioning of each of their heads under the blanket. "Concentrate very deeply about where you want to go."

"Anywhere in the world?" asked Jeffery.

"Anywhere in the universe," replied Ed. "Any place and any time. Any dream you have had. Any thing you can think of."

"I want to see grandma," announced James.

"Grandma is in Heaven," reminded Jeffery.

"Then let's go to Heaven!" suggested James and Jeffery concurred. The boys began to chant: "Hea-ven! Hea-ven! Hea-ven!"

It was now or never for Ed and the children had to go first. He raised his pistol and made three quick and concise shots - one for the top of each pillar before him. Without another sound, each pillar collapsed.

Ed tossed the gun on to the corner of the bed. He took a deep breath and exited the room. He trembled slightly as he descended the stairs. He walked into the praying room and stood with his face just inches from the giant cross, as if in conflict with the painted, white wood. He screamed. "I'm not crazy! I did *your* will!"

The cross did not reply.

Ed stepped backwards into the longer part of the room, stumbling slightly after reaching the green ottoman that accompanied the red chair. Marilynn would accuse this set of cheapening the aesthetics of the room. Anytime she protested this tacky mismatch of furniture, Ed always quickly shut her down with a reminder that red and green represented Christmas colors. Christmas celebrated the birth of Jesus. Who could argue with that?

The truth is that Ed never cared about the aesthetic either way. For him, it was simply a matter of convenience, regarding a vice that Mailynn was never to be made aware of. He needed that ottoman to access his secret sins. Or rather he had grown accustomed to its use to that end and, like any addicted personality, simply feared the change. Whatever the circumstance, Marilynn was no longer there and Ed saw no harm in one final self indulgence before he joined her across the divide. He did not wish to die in a stressed state, after all.

Using his foot, he pushed the ottoman to the corner of the room in two moves. He stood on it and, reaching out, grasped a large, decorative light fixture with his left hand while cupping his right hand below. He pulled the piece out from the wall just slightly and a pack of cigarettes fell into his palm. He stepped off the ottoman and reflexively drug it back over to its original position beside the red chair.

He moved outside and into the garden, as usual. Marilynn was never going to know about it, but he still felt it imperative to respect the rules of their home. He wondered for a moment if she might be watching, after all. Were they still there with him as ghosts? Waiting? He pictured Marilynn holding the boys tight while fighting against ascent into the tunnel of light. He saw her looking back towards the earth, desperately anticipating his appearance. Was he, in these moments, condemning his family to purgatory? As soon as soon as Ed tasted the tobacco on his lips, it didn't matter anymore.

He inhaled slowly and deeply. He felt the polyps burning inside the bottoms of his lungs. He imagined them bleeding more with every drag. He saw the blood filling his body and pulling his skin tightly until his arms were involuntarily lifted. It seeped from his pores, slowly at first, but the process sped as he continued to inhale and exhale. It was not long before his skin was fully breached, and his body quickly torn apart. His remnants were carried away on a sea of blood, where his mind was now sailing.

The sound of a car coming up the driveway pulled Ed immediately back into his reality. He could barely see the lights through the trees, but the engine was clunky and the music was loud. He knew a fight-or-flight situation was pending and he was not going to leave his family's bodies behind for this necrophiliac from the valley to desecrate. Perhaps he would not have had to deal with this, had he just followed them across the divide instead of hesitating for one final earthly pleasure. Then again, the other option would have simply lead to four corpses by this time, with no living soul to protect them from this rapist that was coming up the drive – with his shitty car and loud rap music. Ed had to act fast. He extinguished his cigarette on the side of the bird feeder and tossed the butt into the trash can, never missing a step on his way back upstairs to retrieve his pistol.

The music in the car was not rap. It sounded this way to Ed because the concussive elements resonated loudly and clearly in his driveway, while the finer nuances were made incoherent at that distance by these same acoustics. In truth, he could not tell what type of music was playing – only that it had a beat. In truth, the song was "2000 Light Years From Home" by the Rolling Stones.

Markie turned down the music and parked the Nova in front of the garage. The glowing sign on the roof of the car illuminated a forgotten truth to Ed. Just before the Big Announcement, in that final regular moment, Marilynn had decided not to cook. Citing the lackadaisical nature of the day, she elected, instead, to order this pizza, which had been completely removed from Ed's mind once the news came across the television. Yet, here it was. Marilynn's ghost again, pulling those cosmic threads.

Markie exited the Nova and retrieved the pizzas from the back seat. Ed saw the hat and the nametag and placed his gun on the end table. He pushed through the screen door and startled Markie.

"Hey," said Ed, "I didn't think you were still coming."

"Well we try to get it to you as quickly as we can," Markie defended, "but you live pretty far away from our store-."

Ed interrupted. "Oh. I don't mind if it's late. I forgot that we even ordered the damned thing. I just mean that with everything that's going on, I figured you wouldn't still be working."

"Everything that's going on?" asked Markie.

Ed paused. "Wait. You don't know?"

"I guess I don't."

Ed was disturbed by this revelation, for he suddenly and unwittingly found himself in the position of gatekeeper to dire information. He did not know this delivery person and believed that it would be rude to presume that he would even *want* to know the news. He figured Markie could not be more than twenty-five years old. Ed wondered whether or not he, himself, would have wanted to know such terminal and inevitable news at that age. Ignorance is bliss, of course, but truth is also truth.

"Do you have kids?" he asked.

"No," replied Markie. "I don't even have a girlfriend."

"Give me a moment, please." Ed walked back into the house and into the praying room. He stood facing the large cross again, silent with his eyes open. After a quarter of a minute or so, he shook his head and exited the room. He then walked into the kitchen and retrieved a cheap, white, plastic garbage bag from below the sink. Then into his study, he pulled back the corner of the carpet to reveal a large metal safe in the floor. It was guarded by an oversized, circular, combination lock, which Ed quickly solved.

Inside the safe were neatly organized stacks of cash. Ed picked up all but two of them and stacked them in the garbage bag, which laid flat on the floor. He then pulled the sides of the bag up and slid his hand from the drawstrings down, closing the top. He carefully pulled the excess plastic tightly against the money and wrapped it around itself. He moved back into the kitchen, opened a drawer, and retrieved a rubber band, which he bundled around the package to hold it secure.

Ed walked back through the screen door. "Sorry. I had to get some money."

"No problem," said Markie, "Your total with tax is $10.26."

Ed handed Markie the packaged money. "Here buddy. Keep the change."

Markie had no idea of what had just been placed in his hand and so reacted as he did anytime a customer gave him payment and told him to keep the change. He did not look at it. He simply smiled, nodded his head, and said "Thank you."

Ed gave a simple wave and disappeared back into the house. He closed the main door this time, leaving no transparency into his home through the screen.

Markie walked back to his car, removing the rubber band. He held the top of the bag in one hand and let the bottom drop, collapsing the stacks of money inside. When he looked in, he was first relieved to see that he was paid with cash, but then jarred to realize that it was such a large amount. He pulled out one stack and thumbed through it. All the bills were hundreds and the band around the money denoted "$5000." There were at least thirty of such stacks.

Markie concluded this was a mistake born of senility or brain damage found in Ed. He killed the engine in his car, because it seemed to him that handling this might take longer than he had initially anticipated. He walked back to the door and knocked. No one responded. He knocked again and projected, "Sir!" No response. "Sir, you gave me too much money here! Sir!" Still there was no response. "Sir, I'm going to turn this money over to my manager, okay?"

On the other side, Ed had been listening. Upon hearing that his money was going to the management at the pizza shop, he quickly opened the main door, with the screen still between he and Markie. "Don't give that money to your manager. It's *your* money, okay? Not your boss. Not the company you work for. In fact, don't even go back there. You don't need to."

"I don't understand," replied Markie.

"You have money now," reminded Ed, "No strings attached."

"This is all very unnecessary."

"Go live your life while you can, kid. Right now." Ed closed the door.

III

Markie descended silently into the valley. The interaction with Ed replayed loudly in his head, competing with thoughts of future prospects. Markie did not consider for even a moment to return the music volume to an audible level. The cassette had ended and restarted again while sitting in Ed's driveway. The Stones were all there – Brian Jones included – whispering below Markie's thoughts, but dividing no further attention. Regardless of the new doors before him, he felt certain that he still owed it to his boss and the other customer to complete the delivery. If he was to leave the job, he did not want to do so with animosity at his back. His boss had always treated him well and his coworkers were mostly affable people. Out of respect, he would provide a two-week notice.

A few of the other drivers would flatly refuse to take deliveries to the valley. The tips were rarely worth the drive, but more than that, a couple of them had been robbed by gunpoint at the government housing there. Markie had not encountered anything so extreme. There were some visceral interactions at times, usually with beggars and crackheads, but nothing that ever culminated into violence. On this particular evening, however, there appeared to be a boiling surface of precisely that.

Markie instinctively rolled up his windows and locked his doors as he slowly approached a flaming dumpster that had been rolled into the middle of the street. The scene felt ominous, but there did not appear to be anyone nearby. Reasoning that this was likely a prank by some juveniles, he bore left around the dumpster, scraping his tires on the curb. Immediately on the other side were two men intensely beating a third with their fists. One of the assailants screamed at Markie as he sped up and turned down a street just beyond the one he was to deliver to. He made a second and third left, bringing him down the target street from the other side, eluding the line of sight of the men beside the dumpster.

He parked the car against the curb in front of the modest, stand-alone house on the hill. It was one of the few remnants from the steel town days; a plot of land that remained in the hands of the original family, rather than succumbing to government acquisition. A long concrete staircase up to the front door would separate him considerably from his car. He slid the money stacks under his driver seat and filled the space around them with random garbage that had accumulated on the passenger floorboard – most of it empty soda bottles and local newspaper inserts. He grabbed the customer's order and exited, locking the door behind him.

As he proceeded up the narrow, broken stairs, he heard men yelling on the adjacent street. He paused a moment to look back and nearly lost his footing. He reached for a railing that was not there and fell forward on his right hand and left elbow, keeping the pizza bag raised and in tact. He corrected his balance and scuttled quickly to the top. There he was greeted by more concrete, now flat and leading directly to the front door.

Here he knocked.

A thin voice inside asked him to please come in. This did not seem safe to Markie. He pretended not to have heard the request and knocked again.

"Hold on! I'm coming!" strained the voice. About a full minute and a half passed before an elderly, dark-skinned woman opened the door. It clunked against her walker, which she awkwardly withdrew. "I'm sorry. I am disabled, "she said, "could you please carry the pizza to my table for me?"

"Absolutely! I'm sorry!" Markie felt obliged. Once the woman cleared the door, he stepped sheepishly inside, immediately wiping his feet on the mat. "Where can I put these for you?"

"Just in the dining area over there, please." She pointed to an adjoining room, guarded by two double doors, both open. Opposite that corridor was an old, large, jukebox, pushed up against the wall. Markie was immediately in awe of the vintage machine. He crossed the living space toward the dining area, but stopped short of the door.

"Does that thing still work?" He couldn't resist.

"The jukebox?"

"Yeah. I was just curious."

"It works very well," said the lady, "It was a gift from my son. It used to be in our little bar downtown; a place called Stanton's, named after my late husband. Things were better in the valley for just a moment after Jim Crow – all the way up until about the middle of the eighties. We did so well with that place. So many memories, too."

Markie stepped halfway into the dining room and sat the pizza on the small table there. "May I ask what became of the rest of the bar?"

She continued, "Well new owners took over the building and the rent went up. The same people developed those houses up on the ridge. I think they thought they were going to try to cut out a part of the valley to make some kind of goofy tourist stop. It never really worked out for them, but we got all the pain as they bought up more and more property and put the squeeze on us to cover their costs. We hung in there as long as we could but had to throw in the towel right around the same time the mill shut down. It was like the whole valley was just falling to pieces.

"Anyway. The jukebox was leased to us and it was supposed to have gone back to them. But my son, Sherman – bless his heart – he talked them into selling it to him cheap, on account of it was so old. He used his own time to restore it and fill it with our records. He even labeled the whole thing. Set it up to play for free and gave it to Stanton and I on our thirtieth anniversary. It was such a nice gift.

"Both of them are gone now. Just me here. Stan passed away from a heart attack in 1987 and Sherman in 1992 from the same condition. I like to use this old thing as a time machine more than anything. These songs all take me back to memories. When I play them, I can sometimes feel my boys here with me. I can feel that time, like I'm there."

Markie looked around. He saw no television or radio in the sparsely adorned room. The woman knew what he wondered and answered without the formality of his voicing it. "This old box is the only sound in this house that doesn't come from outside the windows. I have no need for a television or any of that kind of thing because I don't need those signals getting in the way of my time traveling - or my knittin' or my readin', for that matter. I don't care at all to know what happens in a world without my boys anyway."

"I'm sorry for your loss," said Markie.

"Well I appreciate it," she continued, "death is just one of those things. We hate it for others, but for ourselves, you kind of warm up to it as you get closer. You kind of start to see it as a distant friend or something."

Markie had no idea how to reply.

"Say, how much do I owe you for the pizza?" The woman recovered the moment.

"Oh, nothing at all, ma'am." Markie remembered the money in his car. "It's on me."

"On you?"

"Yeah. Don't worry about the money."

"Honey, you don't have to do that for me," replied the woman.

"I insist," said Markie.

The women began to rummage through a handbag that sat on a wooden chair. "Well let me tip you something," she said.

"No no!" insisted Markie, "Please. Let it be totally free to you."

The woman pressed harder, "You drove all the way out here and you don't want no kind of money? I don't mind to pay, you know."

By some strange instinct, Markie took her hand and looked directly into her eyes. He felt calm and his voice expressed nothing less. "No. It's free. I promise."

The woman felt a rising wave inside herself. It was something akin to vertigo with butterflies. "Well would you like to play something on the jukebox?" she asked.

"That sounds good." Markie released her hand, surprised at himself for having held it for so long. He walked to the jukebox and leaned over the top. A long sleeve of seven-inch records sat under a glass dome. Beneath that, laying flat under a single pane, was a large sheet of paper, baring a list of what each record contained, written neatly by hand in thin black marker. A thicker marker and a straight edge had been used to define a grid to separate each selection.

"You don't need to put any money in," said the woman, "just make your choice when you find what you want."

There were several rare vintage recordings, which Markie was unfamiliar with, as well as some more popular songs from those same bygone eras. He chose the first thing that he recognized without question: "Shake" by Sam Cooke.

"Now if you're gonna choose this one, then you have to dance with me," pressed the lady. What reason did he have not to, anyway? His car was full of cash and the future was endless. He took her hand again and swung her arm in an arc, in rhythm with the beat of the song. She pushed her walker aside and reached out her other hand, which Markie grabbed immediately. They would break each time Sam hollered, "Shake!" Their hands flew above their heads for this singular word, only to reconnect immediately thereafter. Halfway through, Markie broke the grasp of one hand, raising the other above their heads and spinning himself around her. She was elated. When the song ended, they hugged deeply.

They said nothing, barely parted, as the mechanical arm in the jukebox reached out and flipped the record. After a few moments of silent anticipation, the b-side began to play and the song was "A Change is Gonna Come." Both of them melted as the strings swelled. Sam sung the opening lines, crooning of his birth in a tent beside a river. Lost in emotion, Markie acted upon another involuntary urge, placing his arm around the woman's waist and repositioning himself behind her. She closed her eyes and he wrapped his arms fully around her. Her dark hands lay in contrast across his pale skin. Together they swayed and they cried. Sam's smooth voice stretched across time, pouring over all the weight of the world.

At the conclusion, Markie and the woman held their position and their silence just a bit longer. When he finally released his arms, she fell to the floor, knees touching down first before slumping over on to her face. Markie knelt immediately beside her and jostled her shoulder. "Ma'am? Ma'am?" She did not respond. He pulled her over on her back and felt her wrist for a pulse. There was nothing.

He stood and walked to the kitchen where he remembered seeing a telephone mounted to the wall. He picked it up and dialed 911 but the line was busy. Thinking there must have been a mistake, he tried again, and then again. The result was the same. He was not certain what his next action should be, but he felt no sense of urgency. The woman seemed peaceful. If she was really dead, her final moments were perfectly tender. It would seem like a cruel affront to life's poetic nature for her to wake up now. Markie tried calling 911 a final time and could get no further than the busy signal once again. Out of options within the house, he stepped over the woman's remains and approached the passage he had initially come in. He paused for a moment, looking back, waving lightly and whispering, "goodbye," before exiting.

He thought about seeking help from behind some random door in the apartment complex across the street, but from his vantage point atop her concrete staircase, he could see the dumpster burning brightly a few streets over, and hear the echoes of the men who basked in its light. For his own safety, he felt it a better idea to collect his thoughts in his car before making his next move.

Markie descended the long stairs with great caution, favoring a step at a time, rather than foot over foot. Unaware that the lace on his right shoe had become untied, he stepped down on to it, accidentally pinning it under his left. When next he attempted to raise his right for the ensuing step, he was anchored there, his balance too far shifted to prevent him from toppling headlong down the steps. Again, he instinctively reached for a railing that was not there. His final motion was an attempt to throw his hands out in front of himself to soften the impact of the fall. This gesture, however, proved slightly too late and his head smashed hard into the edge of a step, voiding his mind.

The sun came up the next morning, illuminating the previous night's destruction, which was now mostly silent. Markie lay on the stairs, his blood largely coagulated in a still stream that stretched almost ten steps down when counting the furthest splattered drops. Of the few souls who moved past the scene, no one had anything to say of it. For to them, by this time, Markie was just another dead body in the street.

Butterflies

I

She was a typical, North American monarch, enjoying the sunny back roads that she had learned well over her eight long months of adulthood. She spotted a deer across the road, and went to her. She did not make it, though. The windshield of a speeding sport utility vehicle smashed the poor girl to death.

The bulky, goateed anglo-jock in the fitted, backwards ball cap turned on his wipers and scraped her guts off the glass.

"That reminds me," said his fiancée, "is everything good with the butterfly house?"

"You mean the butterfly release." He corrected. "Yeah it's all good."

"No. I mean the butterfly house, honey."

"What do you mean by butterfly *house?*" he asked.

"What do you think I mean, Jackson?" Her tone was abrasive.

"I think you mean a butterfly *release*, where we open little boxes and let 'em out, no?"

"No, Jackson. I mean a butterfly *house*. A house of butterflies."

"Baby, I'm not sure that people actually do that." He felt intimidated.

"You're not sure that people do *butterfly houses?* What does that even mean, Jackson?"

"I just –."

She interrupted, as she was prone to do. "Look around. Butterfly houses are real. They are real and we need one. That's, like, our whole theme, Jackson."

He tried to speak again. "I know, but, like -."

"No buts! Our whole reception is supposed to be *in* a butterfly house. We talked about this, Jackson."

"Baby, I just thought you were just – you know – brain storming; fantasizing."

"*Fantasizing?*" A tiny red light turned on in her brain. She poised to strike. "Why *fantasize* about something that is real that people do everyday? Why do you think daddy spent twenty grand on those two big tents, Jackson?"

"You know, I just – I just thought it was – it was where you wanted to have the reception." His thought process was failing.

"It was where I wanted to have the reception? In a tent? You think daddy paid twenty thousand dollars just so I could have a reception in an enclosed tent on a yard?"

Jackson tried to defend his blindness to her wishes. "Baby, I just -."

She interrupted again. "The answer is 'no,' Jackson. He did not pay twenty thousand dollars so we could have our reception in a tent. He paid twenty thousand dollars so we could have our reception in a *butterfly house.*"

"Okay. Okay. I'm sorry. I'll call the butterfly people tomorrow and change the order."

Jackson arrived to work thirty minutes early and attempted to call them, but of course, a butterfly company has no reason to be open at seven thirty in the morning. Their answering message stated that they opened at noon so he napped at his desk for a while and clocked in at eight o'clock. He sat in his cubicle, making calls and filing papers with some autopilot of second sight. The front of his mind, however, was strictly anxious to seek resolution for his fiancée's expectations. At noon, he broke for lunch and immediately attempted his call again. He reached their answering message once more. He sat the phone down, closed his eyes and drew a deep breath. Releasing it out slowly, he watched the clock for two minutes and then dialed again.

A connection was made and a man spoke. "Butterfly Supply, this is Roy."

Jackson trusted his southern drawl immediately. He could tell that Roy was a good ol' boy, like himself. "Hi there, Roy. This is Jackson Mills. I have an order in with ya'll for a release box and a dozen butterflies."

"Mills...Mills..." spoke Roy as he flipped through a large appointment calendar on the cluttered desk in front of him. "When's the wedding?"

"It's this Sunday."

"Oh. Yep. There you are. Your order is scheduled to be sent out for overnight delivery on Friday afternoon," reminded Roy. "You'll get 'em on Saturday."

"Well it looks like I'm needin' to change my order."

"Okay. No problem. You want to add another dozen?"

"Probably," spoke Jackson. "Do you all do butterfly houses?"

"I'm not really sure what you mean," said Roy. "We've provided a few different species to butterfly houses at a couple botanical gardens, but we don't set up any kind of thing like that ourselves."

"We have a big, square, enclosed tent already rented. We just need someone to fill it up."

Roy tapped his fat index finger against the date in his schedule book. "Well, you're current order is a dozen monarchs. How many more do you think you might need?"

"Um." Jackson knew they were working with two tents that were each thirty feet by one hundred feet. When erected side-by-side for greater space, this would make their total dimensions sixty feet by one hundred feet. That meant the area was going to total six thousand square feet. He guessed a height in the tent of about ten feet, but rounded down to eight just to keep his estimates conservative. This made his total density forty-eight thousand cubed feet. With no particular logic behind it, he arbitrarily figured he should inquire about one butterfly for every five cubed feet. "Could you do ninety-six hundred?" he asked.

"Ninety-six hundred?" repeated Roy. "By Saturday?"

"Yes, sir. I'm sorry for the short notice. It was a misunderstanding."

"I presume you mean ninety-six hundred individual butterflies, right? Not ninety-six hundred dozen?"

"That's right."

"Boy, that's still a tall order to fill and a short time to fill it in," said Roy. "We definitely couldn't do all monarchs. You'd have to settle for a mixed variety if we could do anything close to those kinds of numbers."

"Oh, that's fine," said Jackson, "Whatever you could do anywhere near that would be really appreciated. My wife – she's a bit of a hard ass and I really dropped the ball on this one. I'm just trying not to spend my honeymoon in the doghouse."

"I feel ya on that, buddy." Roy considered his own failed marriage and felt truly sympathetic "I'll tell you what. Let me get your number and I'll talk to my partner, see what we can do, and I'll call you right back. That alright?"

"That sounds good."

Roy's partner was his younger brother, Henry. They inherited their company from their deceased mother three years prior. Both men were plump and middle aged, with mustaches. Henry was grayer, though, and wore glasses. He had been standing at Roy's desk, listening to the call and fidgeting with a calculator. "Ninety-six hundred is eight hundred dozen," he figured. "That would be forty-eight thousand dollars at full price."

"We couldn't charge the guy that much," insisted Roy. We would have to give him a considerable break in the price for ordering such a large quantity."

"Well of course, but I'm just sayin' that we have a lot of room to work with on that number," said Henry. "Remember he's at our mercy, especially considering that he wants all these by Sunday."

"Yeah, but whose mercy will *we* have to deal with in order to get that many butterflies that quick, ourselves? I mean, even if we gave him every butterfly we have in stock, we wouldn't even come close to that number – even if we gave him the ones that have already been reserved for other customers."

"I understand what you're saying. We have to outsource. But that means we can also drop ship, too, though."

"That's true." Suddenly it didn't feel so heavy to Roy and the answer came to both men at once: Lala Okeke.

"Alright. You should call him," posited Roy.

"What the hell? Why me?"

"He loves you. You know that. You can get us the better deal."

Henry felt awkward. "Well he ain't my type. That boy is a little too celebratory for me."

"Oh get over it, Henry. He may give you a hard time, but he will definitely give you the better price. You know that." Roy was correct. "If you feel weird about it, then just consider it the cost of doing business."

"Gottdamnit, I new I should have moved out west after school. Gimmie the gottdamned phone." When it came down to money is when anything became black and white to Henry.

"Happy day!" spoke Lala when the call connected.

Henry rolled his eyes. "Hello, Lala? This is Henry over at Butt-." Interrupted.

"Oh Henry! How are you?" Lala stretched out nearly all of his long vowel sounds. "It has been so long, my friend. So long."

"Yeah. Well look." Henry got right down to it. "Any way you can do eight hundred dozen to the states by Saturday evening?"

Lala laughed. "That is a crazy amount, o' Henry! You tell me early and it's no problem, but this is very late, man."

"What can you do then?" asked Henry.

Lala took a deep breath. "I will try for five hundred."

"Five hundred dozen?"

"Yes. Six thousand butterflies, only for you, Henry. It is a lot you are taking. I cannot guarantee the species or age. You understand?"

"Of course. How much?"

Lala took pause to scratch out some numbers on a small notepad. His final price was fifteen thousand dollars, shipping cost and all. "Only for you, Henry."

Yet Henry still asked, "Could you go lower for me? Maybe thirteen?" The way he spoke sounded unintentionally flirtatious, which was the real reason he pretended he did not like speaking to Lala. It was not Lala's boisterous, effeminate nature that he despised, but his own inability to hide his own latent homosexuality when he engaged with that nature. Lala had really ever only loved him out of pity, in fact, the way one may love a wounded deer, dying on the side of the road.

"I am so sorry, dear Henry, but I can go no lower than fifteen. It is my floor, my friend, and there will be much work for me to do." Lala was not a person who could easily be taken advantage of, but his force field was a very polite one. "Even the post is quite a drive and the postman does not come every day. You understand."

Fifteen was more than fair and Henry felt a sense of guilt to have even tried to talk Lala down on the price. "Okay. Fifteen it is. I'll have to confirm it with our client and then get back to you on the payment and shipping address. Mind if I call you right back?"

Lala laughed. "You're going to have to, aren't you?"

"Right." Henry disconnected the call feeling far beneath Lala. He handed the phone back to Roy. "Lala can do six thousand - that's five hundred dozen - for fifteen."

"That's great," said Roy. "What should we sell 'em to this Mills guy for? Twenty?"

"Twenty-five," stabbed Henry.

Roy whistled. "That is quite a killing from one simple drop ship. If he goes for it, of course."

Roy called Jackson back. He went for it.

Butterflies

II

The facility was housed down island on the edge of the Ifaty Forest, northeast of Tsifota. Set back from the road, it appeared to be a boring, beige, blocky building surrounded by a chain link fence crested with razor wire. Beyond the sterile exterior, however, stood a compound of actually four separate buildings surrounding a large, glass atrium in the middle. The back of the property consisted of nearly a dozen acres of undeveloped fields, heartily coated by milkweed and wildflower.

The property was paid for in full by a joint effort between the governments of Burundi and the United States. It was granted to Lala as diplomatic reparation of sorts. His sister had been a political activist turned cabinet member for Melchior Ndadaye, the first democratically elected leader of Burundi. She was also among those murdered with him; by officials within their nation's own military ranks; which opened the door to a decade of genocide and civil war.

Lala took custody of his niece, Mahera. This was natural, as he had already assisted with her upbringing through most of the previous year, after her father (a Tutsi) was shot in the street for loving her mother (a Hutu). With assistance from his sister's political ties, they were able to flee to America as refugees. It was there where Lala learned both English and capitalism. Only a handful of months after arriving, he was working steady cash jobs and able to afford a modest but decent apartment in Bethesda, Maryland for he and Mahera. They remained in the United States until the war in Burundi was just beginning to wrap up. By that time, he had made several connections within the American government and media. They not only kept up with him as a political refugee, but also genuinely appreciated him for his straight-shooting communication and hard-working nature. And so when Burundi finally extended to him a compensation for the loss of his sister, America was convinced to match this funding with very little persuasion. In some large part, the outpour of money came down to the fact that Lala had never applied for a green card and, though he should have otherwise faced deportation much earlier, none of his constituents in the US government wanted to send him away in such harsh fashion.

A large cash amount was initially offered, with the stipulation that Lala resettle back in Burundi and assist the new government with peacekeeping efforts. This was another positive attribute in the eyes of the Americans that lobbied for him. He would not just leave the United States with dignity, but would also be quelling aggression on the African continent – a place that President George W. Bush staunchly wished to assist as some personal atonement for the quagmire that his administration had been making of the Middle East. And so Lala's deal was casually earmarked deep inside the text of a larger bill written to fight the AIDS epidemic there.

Lala collected five hundred thousand dollars and moved he and Mahera back to Burundi. His stint with the government was to last five years. Once completed, he was to receive another five hundred thousand, and retire. However, after only two years into the term, his position was no longer needed and so his relationship to the deal had become gray. After another relatively simple, honest, discussion between the three parties, it was agreed that, instead of a prorated payout for his time, he would take the property in Madagascar. It was, after all, a former scientific facility that had not been occupied or funded since the late

1980s, something that the Americans were happy to remove from their asset ledger.

The atrium was the only structure on the property that was constructed after the relocation. Lala and Mahera would eat breakfast every morning there, among a variety of fluttering butterflies, a fishpond and natural light. On this morning, over fresh fruit and chocolate pudding, Mahera was informed that her lessons for the day would be cancelled, and instead she would engage in some hands-on training. "I have a very large order to fill," informed Lala, "Six thousand of our little friends!"

"Six thousand!" repeated Mahera.

"I know – and by Saturday, also! Crazy order, but not impossible, and a good bit of money, too. But I will need your help, my dear Mahera."

"Anything, Uncle Lala."

"It is a job that I know you love already."

"Catching?"

"Yes! It is all catching! So when we are done with our meal, I will need you to sweep all that you can today. There is no limit to how many we need. There is no limit to the type."

"I can't wait!" she squealed.

And so the two completed their breakfast and went about their respective duties for the day. Mahera began a slow walk out into the fields, armed with a pistol (for aggressive wild animals she may encounter), headphones (accompanied by American pop music), a net, and a large, ventilated, plastic receptacle – this with a spring-loaded trap door on the top. As she traversed the landscape, she collected loitering butterflies with nearly every yard. At times, she would acquire three or four with a single swoop of her net. A variety of sizes and colors, all were ushered through the small trap door and into their plastic cell. She kept this up for hours.

Lala, in the meantime, took inventory of his massive collection, organized by species into large, decorated, glass tanks. He attempted to figure how many he could spare from each type while minimizing the gap in reproduction that would be caused in doing so. He settled at three thousand for the moment, separating them out and mixing the species into two, large, central tanks – these plastic. This cut his inventory down by slightly more than one third.

Once his selection of three thousand was secured, he walked out into the field to assist with further catching. Eventually, he and Mahera found each other there, worked within one another's orbit for a couple more hours, and then carried their keep back into Lala's laboratory. To count each butterfly as it was added to the larger mix was no simple or perfect task, but Lala had managed to top out just short of around three hundred of them. Mahera had accumulated well over a staggering eighteen hundred, replacing her container with an empty one, half way through the day.

As they transferred and tallied, a particular butterfly caught Lala's eye. It was bestowed with rich, almost navy, blue wings, each adorned by small, orange polka dots. "Do you know what this one is called?" he asked as he lightly tapped the glass.

"Yes. That is the Rune…something," replied Mahera. She stopped thinking and cleared her mind. It came to her quickly. "It is called the Rune Emperor."

"Yes, it is," affirmed Lala. "It *is* called the Rune Emperor. Very good, my dear!" He continued. "This is a very special butterfly, you see. Her species is undergoing an evolutionary mutation at this very moment. You see, some of them are born with blood that is toxic to their predators. These orange spots on their wings are a darker shade than the ones who do not have the poison blood. The toxic ones carry more of a *burnt* orange. If a bird or rodent eats these types, then that animal will become very sick. So the birds and rodents, they learn. They know to stay away from the darker color of orange. But now the lighter colored Emperors – the ones with blood that does no harm – they are dying more rapidly. They have no defense. In only a few more generations, only the darker Rune Emperors will remain and they will be so much stronger than their ancestors."

Mahera smiled. "They are a very beautiful species. The colors compliment each other well."

"To me, their evolution is evidence of God." Lala returned the smile and then to the business at hand. "We still need nine hundred more specimens for the order. Tomorrow after breakfast we will work together to collect them. How about that?"

Mahera nodded in agreement.

"With luck, we can get the rest collected in the morning, quick enough to get to the post before the sun goes down."

Butterflies

III

Slightly more than six thousand butterflies arrived just hours before the ceremony, packed together in a set of four breathable, plastic bins. They had been stowed away with some tables and chairs on the back of Jackson's truck since only a few hours after their delivery early Saturday evening. Now they sat awkwardly stacked in front of the wedding party's table, awaiting their proper designation.

Jackson was supposed to have been assembling his tuxedo and preparing himself mentally for the giant leap he was about to take. Yet there he stood, half dressed and pressured to handle business. "I don't have time to deal with this right now," he conveyed to his brother, Reagan. "Do you think you all can get these butterflies in the tent for the reception?"

"Absolutely," affirmed Reagan without a second thought. "Don't even worry about it."

Luke, a lower groomsman, was a bit more cautious of the duty. "How do we do this, though? Just dump 'em out on the dancefloor?"

"Your guess is as good as mine," said Jackson. "I imagine they'll fly out when you open the lids. Right? I guess just let them go where they want to go, so long as they are in the tent. I mean…right?"

Reagan could feel his brother's stress. "Go relax as best you can. Do what you have to do, and Luke and I will take care of the butterflies," he ensured. "We'll have them all in the tent and ready to go before the ceremony. Don't worry about that."

"Thank you so much, brother." Jackson gave them each a quick hug and then sprinted back to the staging area.

Reagan and Luke carried the bins on to the dance floor. "Should we just open them all up here?" asked Luke.

"Probably not. Why don't you take two bins over to the other side? That way we can get an even density."

Luke carried his to the far end of the tent and sat them on an empty table there. Without fanfare or a countdown, the men dropped the plastic latches and lifted their respective lids. Both men jerked back a bit, as though expecting the butterflies to come flocking out at once and swarm their faces like bats. This was not the case. In fact, only a tiny smattering of the little creatures actually emerged on their own.

"How do we get them all out of the box?" Luke hollered.

Reagan stared intently into the colorful cube. After a brief contemplation, he lifted it into the air with both hands, and spun it in his palms so that the open side faced down. Luke did the same and they stood across from one another, shaking their bins and tapping the bottoms. The result of both actions was, indeed, a deported conglomeration of the arthropods. Some remained suspended in the air, curious, startled, or perhaps looking for a fight to avenge their displacement. Others navigated themselves to the first perch that they could find, saving their energy and observing their new surroundings. Several others, still, simply dropped out like leaves and lay dead or dying on the floor. The anti-climatic nature of the release led each man to shrug at the other before repeating his dump for the remaining bins.

"Looks like we have a couple piles of casualties here." Reagan mentioned the obvious.

"Should we sweep 'em into the trash?" asked Luke.

"I'm not sure. This is Emmie's deal and I wouldn't want to be on her bad side if we do the wrong thing."

"Right."

"Lemme see if I can figure it out."

Reagan exited the tent and walked across the yard into the large stone building where the nuptials were to be traded. He stepped to the bride's dressing room and tapped lightly. Sandra, one of the bridesmaids, cracked the door just enough to expose her face. There was a bit of back-and-forth between them, with occasional pauses so that she could consult with Emmie – the bride – on the matter at hand. Her final instructions were not to sweep the dead butterflies into the garbage, but to spread them out across the floor as though they were decorative rose petals, intentionally placed for the guests to walk upon. Not one butterfly was to be wasted. Not at that price.

Reagan grabbed two brooms from the custodial closet and darted back across the lawn to the tent. He gave one to Luke and the men began spreading the grounded butterflies out across the plastic, foldout floor. Per the request of the bride, they strived for even coverage across the area. Hence, they were the first to actually step *on* the butterflies as they worked.

Second to crush the butterflies underfoot were the caterers. The two robust women were, in fact, quite apprehensive about entering the tent. Reagan assured them that the butterflies on the ground were all dead. Their hands were full so they ultimately did not wish to question him. They did, however, rely on him to scrape an abundant lot of the butterflies off one of the tables so they could sit their food dishes there. Surely they noticed a few living ones still falling to the floor with this action, but by that time were somewhat accustomed to walking on the tiny bodies and so continued to carry in the rest of the food. Each time a new load was brought in to the tent, Luke and Reagan had to push butterflies off of the table space for it. They remained there longer than intended for this purpose only. Once the caterers had situated all of their covered dishes and assortments of drink, their hands were free to fend off butterflies, themselves, and the groomsmen ran back to the staging area.

The wedding ceremony, itself, was ironically devoid of all butterfly iconography. Apparently, Emmie had wanted the butterfly reception to be a surprise and a climax to the evening. Trading the vows, as far as she was concerned, was not much different than signing the marriage license at the courthouse. The minister, to her, may as well have been a county clerk. The real meat of the event, as with any wedding she could fathom, was going to be the reception.

As the guests trickled out across the yard, the caterers removed the covers from their dishes. It did not take long for butterflies to begin settling on the food. The women tried to shoo them away, but they were an abundant, stubborn and confused lot who would only flutter up from one meal to drift down upon another. The caterers had no choice but to end their futile attempts and agree between themselves that the butterflies were not their responsibility.

Sharon Shipley, a co-worker of Emmie's, was among the first people to enter the tent. She stopped in the doorway, her husband and son behind her. "Oh my. Are the butterflies on the floor real?" she asked, hoping they were not.

"You know, I am not really sure," lied one of the caterers. "But it's okay to walk on them. You're supposed to."

Sharon stepped lightly into the room, doing her best to tip toe around the little bodies. Her husband and son tromped through with much less regard, but equal surprise. Each other guest that entered was also visibly taken aback by the carnage, and each handled it in his or her own way, evolving their steps along that spectrum between great care and total indifference.

Several guests had to clear their seats of butterflies before sitting. There were an unfortunate few who did not think to look first at their chairs and whose trousers and skirts collected new color as they ground wings, blood and tiny limbs into their ass cheeks. Some swept their tabletops before sitting, and others refrained from disturbing the creatures so that they could be more closely observed. Still, all stood and applauded the arrival of the wedding party. A good deal more butterflies were smashed unknowingly when seats were taken again. One man, Jackson's mustachioed uncle, even pounded one into the tablecloth with his fist, amid the ovation.

As the line formed for food, everyone remained rather casual about dining around the butterflies. Though some politely refused to eat, most scooped out their portions from around them, usually startling them into flight. None of the guests had ever thought to view a butterfly as a filthy animal, and so very few of them minded much for their food to be touched by one. For them to see a butterfly hoist it's body up and down was not considered startling or grotesque. They uniformly presumed that flapping of such colorful wings could only be majestic and beautiful. This species blindness, however, meant that the guests were unaware that some butterflies had laid their eggs in the salads. Others actually copulated there, and in other dishes as well. These were, however, the minority of the butterflies that had taken up ground on the food. The

majority, though, had at least urinated and defecated there
– a few vomited and died there as well. The guests kept
eating.

The best man made a speech that everyone laughed
at, though "comical" would be too strong a description.
Most of it was sentimental pap that bordered on insult.
The high point came in the parts that he did not write
while stoned and drunk the night before. The high point
came as he joked improvisationally about the copious
amount of butterflies around them and, in particular, on
the floor. "You know what they say," he quipped. "If you
want to make an omelet, you've gotta break some eggs!"
The sound of laughter encouraged him to go forward with
his next "zinger," starting with a cringe worthy and
stereotypical comedic catch phrase: "But seriously,
though…" He proceeded, "The ones on the ground that
are still moving – they're sick! Terminally sick! So when
you squash them, just know that you're doing them a favor
by putting them out of their misery!" More laughter. "No
offense to you, Uncle Bob!" he shouted, perhaps trying to
make a genuine apology for the joke. Seated in his
wheelchair in the back of the room, breathing heavily
through a plastic mask that was hooked to an oxygen tank,
Uncle Bob never heard a word of it anyway. Everyone else
laughed heartily.

The wine flowed and the evening moved on a little
more smoothly after that. Emmie had her romantic bride's
dance among an assortment of butterflies, sweeping them
up in the train of her dress, just as she had planned. She
then danced with her father, and Jackson with his mother.
She threw the bouquet over her shoulder and it was caught
by her little sister's bitch friend, whose name she didn't
even know. They skipped the garter toss because it

offended their Christian values. They danced to Michael Jackson and Color Me Badd, "The Macarena," and then they cut the cake.

By most whispered accounts, the cake was a tacky, horrid thing; four tiers, with navy blue icing, trimmed and decorated in burnt orange. Atop the grotesque mass were the tiny bride and groom figurines, each wearing little football helmets that brandished their college letters, *A* and *U*. Though Emmie came up with the design herself, she thought of it as her single wedding concession to Jackson, though still ultimately symbolic of their relationship. For it was there at their mutual alma mater, dressed in those school colors, that they found each other. They met at a Tigers home game and followed their team all the way to a bowl victory against the Cavaliers that season. It was concreted into Emmie's memory banks as a time she considered to be magic and, though she knew the cake would raise mixed opinions, it did not bother her. Any other criticism surely would have set her on edge, but the cake was the one aspect of the event that she considered to be for she and Jackson alone - everyone else aside. It was the one visual element that roused authentic nostalgia and sadness in her and so she was excited to destroy and devour it.

The bride and groom cleared some butterflies off the large bottom tier and, together, dropped the knife on to the open space. They made a second cut and then extracted the piece. He served a bite to her. She served a bite to him and smashed it into his face. Everyone laughed as though surprised. More butterflies were removed and the caterers took over the cutting.

There was one butterfly that was overlooked, however. The Rune Emperor sat spread across the soft icing surface, sucking up sugar and, otherwise, minding his own business. He saw the other butterflies face ejection from the cake by the predator caterers. Yet finding himself in such a rare moment that his colors blended so well with his surroundings, he knew he was best to stay calmly in place until the threat had passed.

By some strange fate of this stillness, the caterer cut around and not through him. He remained right there, on a little cake triangle atop a paper plate, continuing to feast as he was passed from human hand to human hand. At last he and his vehicle were lowered back down to a new table top, placed directly in front of Sharon Shipley's son.

Both overwhelmed and bored as any six year old would be at his mother's officemate's wedding, the child paid no mind to details of dessert as he plunged his fork into the cake. The motion was quick so that the Rune Emperor first endured the brunt of the stabbing. His wings were pierced and his body bent and pinned down into the mass. With an exaggerated upward motion, the child lifted the full content of the fork up into the air, and then down into his mouth. The sweetness of the cake completely obscured the bland taste of the Emperor, who was mangled in the little boy's teeth and damned to the pits of his stomach.

Some guests exited directly after the cake. A few others took to the dance floor with the bride and groom. Most people just lingered and conversed. Such casual arrest prompted the DJ to encourage more dancers with a charismatic, amplified plea spoken over the beginning of "The Electric Slide." It worked, and the floor filled to near capacity.

Not everyone knew every step of "The Electric Slide," and so there was a bit of drunken collision at times, but nothing terminal. Sharon Shipley's son knew the dance very well for his age and was quite emphatic about his own presentation. He knew the adults were watching him and fully grasped the moment to shine. It was easy to garner attention from adults by being a *cute* child, but a *charming* child earned their actual respect. So he used the opportunity to do what the adults were doing, and made certain that he was doing it better. He kept dancing into the next song and, as he had planned, an adult complimented him.

Emmie, the bride herself, leaned down to him. "I really like your moves," she said. "Who taught you how to dance like that?"

"Television" was the correct answer, but this was a grown woman he was speaking to, and so he replied, "I just practice a lot."

Emmie threw her head back in a hearty, fake laugh. (She didn't actually even hear what he said.) "Do you want to dance with me?" she asked, extending her hand.

The little boy smiled. "Okay." Both he and Emmie had already been dancing, even as they spoke. The difference now was that he was holding her hands as they moved.

She lifted him from the floor and spun three circles with him. He began to feel a bit queasy, though not from the motion. He felt queasy because the blood of the Rune Emperor was mixing with his own. He felt very warm and removed his sports coat and tie as he danced, tossing them against the wall. The nausea came in greater and greater waves, but Emmie looked so beautiful that he could not bring himself to stop the interaction. His stomach sloshed the Emperor's broken body back and forth – back and forth with stomach acid and soggy cake. Yet he kept dancing, agitating himself; becoming warmer and sicker. His plan was to maintain his composure to the end of the song, kiss the bride once on the cheek, then walk casually to the men's room and take care of business.

Unfortunately, business came first and suddenly. The boy, at once, defecated in his pants and spewed blue vomit across the front of the bride's dress. His chance for a kiss was ruined.

"What the fuck?" she first asked, immediately apologizing and then following up with, "Are you okay, sweetie?"

He opened his mouth to say "no" but discharged once again instead. He tried to veer it away from her dress this time, but still sprayed the train when she turned away. She wailed incomprehensibly and fled the dance floor to the far side of the nearest table.

Sharon and her husband ran to their son's aid. The boy continued to vomit and defecate. His parents could not engage him in any way, as the fluids flowed with very little hiatus – regurgitated food to bile to blood. Sharon looked at her husband. "What do we do? What are we supposed to do?"

"Get him out of here!" screamed Emmie through black mascara tears. "Get him the *fuck* out of here!"

IV

The bride and groom each took two weeks of leave from work. The first week and two days were spent on their honeymoon in Orlando, Florida. They used the remaining time to recuperate and enjoy domesticating together in the home they had already shared for the past two years. It was one such blissful, quiet evening that they sat at the kitchen table together, preparing thank you cards for the wedding guests. They each signed every one, but Jackson alone addressed them. Emmie took her attention, instead, to their freezer, from which she removed a bloated, plastic shopping bag.

Inside the bag was a mass grave - a variety of stiff, butterfly corpses. It was all that she could drunkenly gather for herself at the end of the reception. Her plan then, just as it was at the kitchen table, was to preserve as many as she could in photo albums, entombed between laminate paper and thick card stock. It was on her agenda. She had already purchased the albums, even - but it would have to wait. At the moment, they were working on the cards for the wedding guests. The reason for bringing the butterfly bag to the table was strictly for the sake of personalizing one particular card for one particular pair of constituents.

This card was different from the others. It was larger, with nothing but a print of painted flowers on the front. The colors were in earth tones, which was an intentional choice on Emmie's part. She wanted to embellish the card with a butterfly, but did not want to sacrifice one with wings especially bright or bold. She dumped a small pile of the lifeless bodies on to the table and sifted through them. Some of them were in bad shape, but had really magnificent colors – something she would have to make decisions about later. For now she needed something in gray or brown, preferably in between - to match the card, of course. "And gray and brown are kind of more boy colors anyway, right?" she asked.

"Oh, I don't know," started Jackson.

"I mean, loud colors don't really go with boys," she interrupted. "Camouflage is more for boys. Like army guys, right?"

"Sure."

Finally Emmie came across a butterfly that she found to be dull enough to exclude from her personal collection. It was a dusty color and possibly just a large moth. She spread its body out in the upper right hand corner of the card and stapled it there, one in each wing, and one around its thorax.

Inside the card was blank. Emmie had intended to pour her heart out there, but could not help but keep her words concise. "We are so sorry for your loss," she wrote and then read aloud to Jackson. "Forgive us for missing the funeral while we were on our honeymoon. It had been booked many months in advance. Please let us know if there is anything we can do to help in this time of grief. God bless you."

"It's simple. Sounds good," affirmed Jackson.

"Then I drew some Xs and Os and signed both our names," explained Emmie.

"I could have written my own name, baby. I signed all these other cards."

"Too late now," she smiled after licking the red envelope and sealing the card inside. She then slid it across the table to Jackson so he could address it to its intended recipients: Sharon Shipley and her husband.

Relevance

I

"Something is off," said Mike, "I think it's my cadence."

Jimmy smiled and raised his brow, as if to appear surprised. "It sounds great to me, Mike. Really great." Inside he was cringing, not from the recording, but from Mike's newly adopted perfectionism. He could remember a time when Mike's complexities were all internal. Everything outside was simple. Bang it out in a few sessions and cut a record of the best tracks. Simple.

Every take was magic then, just because it was Mike. That charisma, coupled with Jimmy's experience in the industry, paved their way to make a hell of an impression. Mike would never be a Frank or a Dean, of course, but those guys were untouchable anyway, with huge international networks and limitless funding. There on the California coast, though, he had his own nice piece of the action.

He and most of the studio guys he worked with were based out of Salinas, a town that sat in something of a cultural vacuum before they brought it to life. They pooled their money and purchased an old local bar, tore out a wall and built a stage. It only took one live performance to shake things up. After that, the place remained packed to capacity on any night there was music. The demand grew beyond what Mike and the boys could feasibly handle by themselves and, naturally, new acts began to rise. That abundance of entertainment soon outgrew the venue and so spawned more bars with more live music. Mike never saw this as competition, or even imitation, but homage in every sense.

A budding nightlife brought new investors to Salinas, but Jimmy had come strictly for Mike. Many of the musicians that made rounds through the bar would travel to Los Angeles for studio work. Through their network, which often extended to a space that Jimmy managed, stories of Mike Lobetti were frequently traded, if not exaggerated. He had become something of a mythic figure, without realizing it.

Jimmy drove up and watched him perform twice before he ever approached him. After the third show, he was a true believer. He bought him a drink and invited him down to the studio. Noting that Jimmy's suit was much more expensive than his own, Mike took him up on it and they scheduled a week together - after that, another week, and another. Mike and his band recorded hours of material and Jimmy worked to release record after record. They were playing shows in Los Angeles regularly, out to Las Vegas and stretching down into Mexico. Of course, he was still popular in Salinas and everywhere up the coast until San Francisco. He never did perform there or anywhere North of there until Oregon. Jimmy cited "shaky connections" as the reason it could never happen. Mike knew Jimmy never actually tried anyway, which to him, was all the more reason not to press the question further.

Mike continued to tour regularly, but the mid-'60s had become something of a slow punch to his gut. Everything seemed to have gotten sluggish. Had the record sales not dwindled, it would have been impossible to meet an immediate demand anyway with so many of the new "rock and rollers" backing up the major record presses. Attendance at performances had slowed as well and his audience was increasingly out of touch. If ever a young, modern person did wander into one of Mike's performances, they were usually distracting and difficult to understand, for their use of intoxicants would often stretch far beyond alcohol. He could still acquire good work performing at weddings and other events for the web of wealthy people he had come to know, but he found it much more preferential for the audience to be there because of him, and not someone else's gala he happened to be namelessly attached to.

"Something is off." Maybe it wasn't Mike's cadence. Maybe it was the whole line of events that shaped his career. Maybe he should have taken on a less expendable occupation. For now, he had no choice but to continue documenting new songs, despite his decreasing record sales. He had come too far down this path to know any other way now.

Jimmy looked at Dobie, who was laid back on the couch. "It's really great. It sounds great, right?"

"Yeah. Better than ever," replied Dobie.

"Well tell him," quipped Jimmy. "I already know. Mike needs to get it through *his* head."

"Yeah. It's really sounding great, Mike." Dobie questioned the believability of his own vocal cadence as soon as the words passed his lips. He immediately fell back on The Kid. "It's great. Right, Kid?"

The Kid shrugged. "I'm just here to push the buttons and move the sliders," he reminded.

Jimmy eyed him angrily. "Let's take five, okay guys?"

Mike removed his headphones and exited the isolation booth.

Dobie stood up and reached out. "Let me refresh your drink, Mike. You drinkin' one third like usual, right?"

"Make it a half this time, said Mike, surrendering his empty glass.

Dobie walked to the mini-bar in the adjoining room. A thick tension remained amid the cacophonous, trying silence. Mike sat on the arm of the couch, wringing his hands, cracking his knuckles really, and staring glassy eyed at the booth he had just evacuated.

"Hey Kid," said Jimmy, " Why don't you put on some music or something, yeah?"

"Yeah sure," said The Kid, pulling a crate of records out from under the control room desk. He thumbed through the large platters, removing one that was housed in a predominantly red, but very busy sleeve. He sat the record on the turntable and the arm on the outer edge. Static crackle began to emanate from the studio monitors. No one but The Kid really noticed the ambient theater sounds that began the record, but the guitar introduction cut through the air very prominently. It had a bendy, somewhat sexual tone, which seemed jarringly alien to Mike.

"What is this?" he asked, "Negro music?"

The vocals began with the singer dating their content as twenty years prior to that day.

"It's the Beatles, man," answered The Kid.

Dobie returned and handed a new drink to Mike, who immediately drew a large gulp.

"Was this recorded live?" asked Mike, "In front of an audience? People are laughing. And there are horns?"

"Yeah. No." started the kid. "I mean they recorded all this stuff but it's dubbed in. There are all sorts of crazy things going on."

"It's really weird stuff," said Dobie.

"It's weird but it's genius," said The Kid. "No one has ever made a record like this before. It's a totally original idea."

The song segued into the next. "What the hell happened there? What is this now?" Mike took another gulp of his drink.

"Yeah, pretty neat, huh?" beamed the kid. "A lot of the songs are connected together like that. And that fellow singing – that guy's the drummer."

"The drummer?" whispered Mike to himself. He had never willfully exposed himself to The Beatles, but could not help but know the same basic information about them that seemed to penetrate most everyone's brains. He knew a few of their popular songs and was secretly fond of "I Want to Hold Your Hand" when it came out – until he heard it too many times and began to despise it. He knew they were from England, but never cared enough to retain specifically where. He knew their names and the instruments they played. He knew Ringo was not only the drummer, but also the delta male of the group – hired on once the band had already found success. Nothing more than a studio grunt, really, so why was he *singing* on the second song? Or was this still the first? Mike felt lost. He gulped his drink again.

A new song began with what sounded like a harpsichord, followed by some ridiculous lyrics about some magical land made of food – or something. "What is this garbage?" asked Mike.

The Kid did not know how to reply.

"Easy, Mike." Jimmy touched his shoulder.

Mike spun around with his hands up. "Who would listen to this, Jimmy? Who could possibly connect with this mess?"

"Well it's really popular right now, Mike. The kids really like it."

"How long has been out?" asked Mike. Jimmy turned to The Kid for an answer.

"Not even a week," he said. "But I mean, everyone's getting it. I swear I hear it played by someone every day. I've heard it twice this week at the soda shop I go to in Venice. They were playing it at that party in the hills last night. I heard it at the service station last time I filled up my tank. Also, my old lady's been playing it over and over at our place, and I can't say I mind at all. It's a real piece of work."

"Okay, enough, Kid," interjected Jimmy.

Mike finished his drink in one final gulp just as that pretentious candyass, Paul McCartney, began to sing to him that it was "getting better all the time." Mike knew better. Mike knew that the future was a steady decline once you got over that hump that you worked so hard to conquer. He knew progress was illusion and the end game was always failure – if not of one's career, then one's body for sure. He didn't need shortsighted life advice from a child. He smashed his glass against the wall.

Jimmy touched his shoulder again, "Easy, Mike. Easy." He turned to The Kid. "Turn it off."

The Kid complied, trembling slightly.

II

"I know what you're feeling," said Jimmy. "I've been in the business a long time. I know."

Dobie leaned forward from the back seat. "Mike, you know you've got people looking out for you. No matter what happens, you'll be taken care of. You don't even need to worry."

"I appreciate that, Dobie, but nobody's going to give me money if I don't work. I've got my own family to support," retorted Mike.

Jimmy steered the black sedan left around a sharp bend, easing the break. "It ebbs and it flows, Mike," he said, "and it always has."

"Well the tide has been out for a little too long," said Mike, "There used to be a lot of guys doing this. Not anymore. I'm becoming a relic."

"But that makes you one of a kind, then. If no one else is doing it, then that makes you *the guy*. Scarcity drives the market. It's good to be rare." Jimmy was doing his best.

Dobie spoke up again, "Look, Mike, if it's about the money, again, you don't need to worry. We can find work for you. There'll be more weddings. Plenty of private events."

Jimmy interjected. "And you still have a decent draw in most of the clubs up the coast. Better than decent in Vegas."

"Decent but dwindling. That's what I see," said Mike. "And it's not *just* about the money, anyway."

"What else is it about?" asked Jimmy. "Relevance? Notoriety? Is that it?"

Mike looked out the window and thought about how much he hated John Lennon's glasses.

Jimmy turned right into the parking lot of a small motel, nestled in the hills. The words, "Oasis Valley Inn" reflected in large neon letters on the windshield. He pulled up to the bottom of a stair set and Mike opened his door. Before he could exit, Dobie grabbed his shoulder. "We're gonna send a girl up. You can blow off some steam. Sound good?"

Mike nodded. "Sure."

"How much time you need?" asked Dobie.

"I don't know. Three hours."

"Okay you got it, Mike. Hang in there, buddy. Everything will work out swell."

"Thanks, Dobie." Mike exited the car.

"Well hey," Jimmy stopped him again. "I'll call you tomorrow. Maybe you'll feel up to giving it another shot."

Mike nodded, gave a small wave, picked up his briefcase, turned and walked up the stairs. He fumbled in his jacket pocket for the key as Jimmy drove away. He entered the room, tossed his briefcase and jacket on the bed and loosened his tie. He next unbuttoned the top four buttons on his shirt and pulled it up over his head, necktie and all. This, too, was given to the bed.

After pacing a bit, he stepped into the bathroom and faced the mirror. "What are you? Square now?" He lit a cigarette. "You creep. You fell behind. You said you would never fall behind and you fell behind." He gazed at himself angrily and pulled long and hard off the cigarette. "You had every opportunity to make things work; every opportunity to leave a legacy. But you fumbled. You fumbled and you fell behind!" Mike slammed the side of his fist into the mirror.

Blood splattered shards of glass tumbled to the basin. He tipped the filter of his cigarette with the red ooze seeping from just below where his pinkie met the rest of his hand. He placed it between his lips and picked one of the shards up from the sink. He held it out from his face and stared at himself again as he squeezed his palm tighter and tighter around the edges of the glass. More blood trickled swiftly down his forearm and to the bottom of his elbow before dripping into the sink. He fought the urge to faint before tossing his cigarette in the toilet bowl and wrapping his hand tightly in a bath towel. Back in the main room, he collapsed on to the bed.

Mike woke suddenly to a rapping at the door. He had momentarily forgotten where he was, before rising in a daze. He looked at the door, then to his bloody hand and back to the door. He knew immediately that it had to be the girl. He could not discern whether he regretted passing out more, or allowing Dobie to send her in the first place. Either way, Dobie may have made the arrangement, but he was not the one paying her to be there. For this reason, Mike was obligated to open the door.

The girl had large red curls of hair, and a form fitting sheath dress of the same color, hidden only slightly by a short blue jacket. Her eye shadow was also blue, sitting behind long, black lashes. Her heels and clutch purse were black, too. Her ensemble was off putting to Mike. To him, red, black and blue just seemed like a silent protest against America. He was certain this girl was a communist.

She waved her driver onward and spoke first. "So you're Mr. Mike?"

"Just Mike is fine."

"Well Mike, are you going to invite a girl in or what?"

"Yeah. Sorry. Come on in." He stepped aside and she entered the room.

"I go by Vera," she said, presenting the back of her hand.

Mike lifted his bloody towel wrap slightly and shrugged. Vera recoiled her hand. "What happened?"

"I had an accident."

"Do you need to go to the hospital?"

"No. I'm fine. It's worse than it looks.

"I'm going to take you at your word, mister," she said, "but you'd let me know truthfully if you really needed to go, right?"

"Yes. Yes. Look. Just help yourself to the mini-bar – anything you like. You'll just have to pour it yourself, though, on account of my hand."

"No problem, mister." She mixed her drink very strong. "Would you like me to make a drink for you?"

"Um. Sure. Yeah. Scotch on the rocks, please." Mike sat down on the bed.

"You got it." Vera completed the order and placed the glass in Mike's free hand. He took a sip and sat it on the nightstand. "Cigarette?" She extended her pack to him. He nodded, removed one and placed it in his mouth. She did the same and Mike lit them both. "So D'Angelo says you're a hot shot musician."

"D'Angelo?" asked Mike.

"Yeah. D'Angelo Litelli."

"Oh, that guy." D'Angelo was hired muscle and a frequent doorman at weddings and other private events. "I don't really know him that well," said Mike, "I just kind of know *of* him more than anything. Worked with him a few times."

"Well he knows you, but that's beside the point. Are you a musician or not?"

"Yeah. Yes. Yes I am," he conceded.

"I love music," she said, "You know what's really good?" Mike did not answer because he already knew what she was preparing to say: "The new Beatles record. Have you heard it?"

Mike felt his blood crystallize as he nervously gnashed his teeth together. Through the haze of a kind of vertigo, he replied, "No. I don't really care about the Beatles so much."

"Oh, but the new one," she said, "Have you heard *that*?"

"I did actually. Yes, I did."

"And you don't even like it a little bit?"

"It's just not my bag."

"But it's not anyone's bag," she continued, "It's completely unique. No one has ever done anything like that before."

Mike was getting hot. "Look. I told you it's not my bag. Okay? To me, it just seems like they stuck a bunch of sounds together. A collage. And that's art – not music. There's a difference."

Vera was not certain there was a difference. She decided to excuse herself for a moment. "I'm going to powder my nose. I'll be right back." She stepped into the bathroom and noticed the shattered mirror right away. "Wow, Mister. Was this part of your accident?"

"Yes."

After several minutes, Vera began to sing to herself, loud enough to be heard through the door. It was "Lucy in the Sky with Diamonds." Shortly thereafter, she emerged, holding a triangular shard of glass. She walked over to Mike and tossed it on the bed next to him. "You know I could clean all that up for you for two dollars if you wanted."

"I'm sure the maid will do it for free."

"Okay just offering, mister."

Mike was getting impatient. He wanted her to quit talking so he could ejaculate in her mouth and send her on her way. "You about ready to get down to business?" he asked.

"Well aren't you romantic?"

"I'm down a hand. You wanna help me with my trousers?"

"Gee whiz, mister." Vera knelt down in front of him. She unfastened his belt, and then put both knees on the carpet. "You're a pretty tough fellow. You hate the Beatles and you don't even kiss a girl." She unbuttoned his pants and drug down the zipper. "You can't be a victim of negative thinking, though." She stretched down his briefs and removed his semi-flaccid penis. "Because no matter how you feel about the Beatles, they sure are right about one thing." She firmly and rhythmically tugged the shaft. "It really is getting better and better all the time." She looked up at Mike as her speed increased. "Better...and better..." She kept fixed on his eyes as she lowered her head closer to where her hand was still working hard for minimal results. "Better...and better...."

In Mike's head, it was not his fault that his penis would not harden to capacity. It was the fact she kept talking about the Beatles. He didn't need this. "Better and better?" When was she going to obliterate those words with his dick? He fantasized about punching her in the side of the head and he felt himself grow harder. Yet there she was, still using her hands and repeating, "Better and better..." His fantasy deepened and he envisioned himself grabbing her by her curls and smashing her head into the wall. He got harder still. When he next heard, "better and better," he opened his eyes. He glanced over at the mirror shard sitting next to him on the bed. Without a second corrective impulse, he swiped it up and jammed it into Vera's neck.

She recoiled immediately as blood sprayed across Mike's pants. She flung herself back against the wall, desperately digging her heels into the carpet and applying pressure to the gushing wound. With every cough, blood filled her mouth and escaped from beneath her palm against her neck. Mike casually returned his penis to his briefs, zipped up his pants, lit a cigarette and watched her die.

Relevance

III

Mike always had something of a destructive personality. He had plenty of physical altercations in the past, but not more than a drunken fistfight here and there. In those situations, the other guy was equally engaged in the behavior, fighting just as hard. This girl, doubled over against the motel wall, however, was docile and innocent, albeit rough around the edges. This was not like a fistfight. He figured that what occurred was more on par with abuse. He had hit his wife several times, but she always took it. Of course, he never hit her with a sharp object - he could simply not justify his action in any way. Out of pure animosity, with the sweeping of a hand, Mike became a murderer.

He was in over his head more than he had ever been before. The police were one concern, though lesser so than deciding how to square this mistake with the person who paid for the motel – the person who paid for the girl. This was not the kind of guy that he could dial on the phone. Mike could only send information up the chain and then deal with the consequences. He had to act quickly in framing that information to his benefit, as best he could. It had been no real accident, though. There was nothing to frame except his own angry outburst.

He considered fleeing the situation altogether. He considered renting a car, picking up his wife and children in Salinas, and leaving California. This plan, however, would put his family in danger when Don Vigneto's men came looking for him. He felt that if he were to flee the situation, he would have to do it alone and cut all ties with everyone he knew, including his family. Still, this did not guarantee their safety. He had to face the music, but cautiously. He called Jimmy.

A woman answered. "Hello?"

"Hello. I'm trying to reach the Donovan residence."

"This is the Donovan residence. May I ask who's calling?"

"Um. Yes, ma'am. This is Mike Lobetti trying to reach Jimmy."

The woman's voice relaxed. "Oh Mike! This is Madeline. How are you?"

"Never better. Never better…"

There was an awkward silence, broken by Madeline. "Well that's great to hear, Mike. I'll get Jimmy."

"Thank you."

Jimmy took the line. "Mike?"

"Sorry to call you at home, Jimmy, but there's been an accident."

"An accident?" repeated Jimmy.

"An accident?" repeated Madeline.

"Jimmy, we need to talk about this in private. Can you switch lines?"

"No. Not exactly."

"You have one phone there?"

"Yes. Yes. What can I do for you?"

"The girl is dead, Jimmy." There was a silence as the men felt a mutual uncertainty of how to proceed. Inevitably, it was Mike who vomited out the next statement. "I'm the one who killed her."

"Mike, I'm eating with my family right now."

"I'm sorry, Jimmy. I don't know what to do."

"Okay. Okay. I'll try to make some arrangements. I need some time to think it through, but I'll call you back as soon as I do. Just stay there."

"Are you going to tell Dobie?"

"I think I probably have to."

"Well, if there's any way around it, that would be keen."

"I'll call you back, Mike." Jimmy disconnected the call. He turned to Madeline. "Mike left a pair of shoes at the studio. He's leaving tomorrow and he may need me to let him back in over there to retrieve them."

"Oh, it's getting so late," pleaded Madeline, "can't you just have them shipped back to him?"

"They're really expensive shoes and you know how particular he is. He doesn't want the risk of them possibly getting lost or damaged. He made that clear."

Mike smoked one cigarette after another. He could not bear to see Vera's body and so covered it with one of the bed comforters. He paced and drank, changed his pants and cursed the whole scenario. He knew that if Jimmy told Dobie, it would quickly reach Don Vigneto. He wondered what he could have done differently. Drug the body out to the dumpster? Called an ambulance for her? No other outcome seemed likely to keep him away from the one he ended up in. At this point he could only tough out the ride to come, no matter the next destination.

Of course, he did have the option of suicide. He removed his pistol from his briefcase, sat on the bed and placed the barrel in his mouth. All he had to do was pull the trigger, rendering irrelevant his current entanglement. Though, his family would eventually find out he killed himself in a motel room with a prostitute. Was this the legacy that he wanted? At least death by the hand of another would be circumstantially ambiguous. Plus he still had a *chance* not to die. Maybe he would simply be beaten. He could take that lesson, all things considered.

The phone rang. Mike removed his gun from his mouth and picked up the receiver, "Jimmy?"

"Hello, Mike."

"What's the score, Jimmy?"

"I've got some bad news."

Mike felt a lump in his throat as the muscles in his neck tensed. "What kind of bad news?"

"Don Vigneto would like to speak to you directly."

"No. What are they going to do to me, Jimmy?"

"I don't know. Maybe it will be a slap on the wrist."

"Maybe it will be a sleep at the bottom of the Pacific."

"Well what are your options, Mike? If you wanna run, then you better leave now. But where could you possibly go?"

Mike sighed. "I've thought about every possibility. I know if I don't face this now, then it will be ten times worse when I do."

"Facing it right now would be the respectable thing to do."

"I know."

"His men will be there to pick you up within the hour. Good luck, Mike."

Mike continued to smoke, drink and pace. He picked up his gun and sat it down again. He punched the bed at one point and kept constantly revisiting the window. He watched as two black sedans finally pulled into the parking spaces just feet from his door and six men exited, three from each car. He was slightly relieved to see that one of them was Dobie, though this relief was short lived once he saw D'Angelo Litelli within the crew. Still, all their guns were holstered, so even if they were going to kill him, they would likely have at least a small amount of dialog first. Mike worried that it may be the only space in time that he would have to work with. He opened the door before they knocked, and greeted them with a large, fake smile. "Come on in, fellas."

Dobie sighed as the men entered the room. "I need your piece, Mike." Mike nodded and handed over his pistol, which Dobie immediately passed to one of the other men. "Where's the girl?"

"Under the blankets over there."

Dobie peeked beneath the shroud and let it fall again. "Damn it, Mike. What the hell?"

"I wish I could tell ya, Dobe."

"You know who has to clean this up, Mike?" asked Dobie, "I have to clean this up."

"Look, I'm really sorry."

"Old Dobie has to erase everyone else's mistakes. Everyone relies so heavily on old Dobie."

"Again, I'm sorry. I don't mind to help you, Dobe. I don't mind to take care of this all myself, really."

"Well why didn't you?" pierced Dobie.

Mike knew he should not have called Jimmy.

"You have other places to go, anyway," spoke one of the men. "Come on."

Mike exited with a man on either side of him and D'Angelo Litelli leading the way to the car. One of the men opened the back door and thumbed toward the seat. Mike sat as D'Angelo entered from the other side. The man who thumbed then took his seat, pushing Mike to the middle. The third man took the driver seat and started the car.

The drive held a particularly awkward tension with D'Angelo on Mike's side. He wondered how well he and Vera had known each other. Did he even know that Vera was the girl who had been killed? Was he, in fact, sent because of his connection? *And what was that connection?*

Mike could not bring himself to ask. He felt it in his best interests to remain silent. The rest of the car did the same.

With not a word between them, they arrived about forty-five minutes later at a gated compound, somewhere in the Upper Laurel Canyon area. After a brief communication with an intercom there, the wrought-iron gate slid aside and the car entered. The grounds beyond were immaculate. Mike had been there several times, serving as entertainment for various functions, but it all seemed unfamiliar and disturbing amid the tension he was feeling. At last they pulled up in front of Don Vigneto's quarters, a massive fountain blasting across from the door.

The men walked Mike up one of the large staircases in the foyer. At the top was a long hall, lined with closed doors. They walked the full length of this hall, to one such door that stood alone at the end. One of the men gave a single knock, which garnered a muffled voice from the other side. The man then opened the door just enough to step inside, and then disappeared behind it. His absence was brief, however, as he emerged within less than a minute. He looked at Mike. "Don Vigneto is ready for you." Mike sought some desperate refuge in the faces of the other men, but none of them would make eye contact. He drew a deep breath and stepped sheepishly beyond the door.

A long, blue, rug lead to the large oak desk at which Don Vigento sat. "Come on in, Mike," he said and Mike stepped slowly closer. "Don't be afraid. Have a seat." Mike felt wooden as he reached the desk and lowered himself to the chair that faced it. Don Vigneto casually picked up a stack of papers and smacked their lower edges a few times on the desktop to line them up. He then dumped them into a drawer that was obscured from Mike's vantage point. "So I hear you are having a rough time lately, Mike. Is this correct?" he asked.

"I've been better, sir."

"We sent a girl to your room so you could blow off steam."

"Yes, sir."

"So did you blow off that steam with her then?"

Mike stammered for a moment and then cleared his throat.

"Did you get all that aggression out of you, Mike?"

"Yes, sir. I suppose I did."

"Well that was why we sent her up. She was there to ease your tension, but I'll tell you at the start, Mike, that I blame myself in a way for not being more specific as to how. It's largely my fault for believing that you had the good sense to make it with the girl, rather than what happened. A man in an emotional state acts erratically. No surprise there. I should have known." He laid both hands flat on the desk. "All that being said, I still have a family that I need to take care of here."

Mike spoke slightly out of turn. "I understand, sir. I have a family of my own."

"I know, Mike. You have a beautiful family. I've met them many times, as you know. Your children play with my grandchildren, which you also know. So tell me, how many daughters do I have, Mike?"

"Three, sir."

"That's correct. And how many of their weddings have you been to?"

"All three."

"That's also correct. And at all three, as well as at the weddings of my sons, who performed the music?"

"I did."

"Correct again. You have even been to our family reunions, have you not?"

"I have."

"Birthday parties. Funerals. Holidays. You're always there, Mike. You're always welcome, whether you are performing music for us of just gracing us with your presence. So in a way, one could say that your little family – you, your wife and your children – is kind of folded into my larger family. Would you agree with that?"

"Yes, sir. The Vigneto family has treated me as one of their own."

"And what does the Vigneto family ask of you, Mike?"

"Nothing, really, sir. You're much more generous to me that I could ever return. There's no doubt about that."

"Actually, Mike, we ask you to perform music. We ask you to bring the joy of sound to our ears in an aesthetically pleasing way."

"Well that is always my pleasure, sir."

"Some members of this family have to beat people up – even kill men. Some members of this family, like poor Dobie, have the job of cleaning up dead whores. I think you're aware of *that*."

Mike looked down.

"But at the end of the day, we all just do our jobs and our collective family thrives as a result. For some people, that job is racketeering; laundering money; smuggling guns – but one job that this family does not do is arbitrarily killing whores. All that does is create more work for the rest of us. Do you understand me?"

"Yes, sir."

"Good. So obviously, you are having a lot of emotional unrest right now. I've spoken with Jimmy and, of course, Dobie and it seems to me that your inner turmoil is an extension of your work." Mike could not argue with the observation. "So it seems clear to me that to fix the problem, we need to make adjustments to that area of your life. We all like you, Mike. I hope I have made it very clear that you are considered family, but your job, I'm afraid, has got to be terminated. You had your time, and I hope it was the best it could be while it lasted, but Mike Lobetti is no longer a musician in California."

"I understand," spoke Mike.

"Now you have two options, Mike," the don continued. "Your first option is to move your family out of California and go be a musician or whatever you would like to do in some other state. There would be no bad blood between you and the Vigneto family, but you would receive no funding or favors from us either. The second option would be to stay in Salinas, take care of your wife and children, and make your bread working at Joe Sapinelli's insurance firm."

"Insurance?"

"Yes. We have had a symbiotic and very lucrative relationship with Joe's company for over four decades now, starting with his father before him. The Sapinellis are good, honest people. They have an office right there in Salinas, not far from your home. If you choose this option, Joe himself has already agreed to work with you until you're adequately trained and have a good feel for the job. Now I hate to say this, Mike, but I need to know right now what you want to do."

Mike's primary impulse was the first option. He felt the immediate urge to shed the entirety of his life in California – to run away from the fire he had started. However, he felt an undeniable sense of duty to his children, above all, and also his wife. He could not simply force them out of their lives and into oblivion, away from that steady income and well kept home with a sizable mortgage. He also did not feel it proper to abandon them without explanation. The inevitability of the second choice came into sharp focus. "I'll take the job with Sapinelli."

Don Vigneto smiled. "See, Mike, it's getting better all the time."

IV

Mike came to spend his days holed away in a small satellite office in Salinas, alongside a loud weasel that went by Benji. Benji was younger than Mike by at least a decade, and had been with Sapinellis's firm for over six years. Mike, a handful of months beyond his second anniversary there, had come to feel confident in the work, though never quite at home in what he saw predominantly as Benji's domain. Still, Benji was a useful colleague who relished in bending the rules for financial gain. When a client would grow too old or confused to keep up with the monthly payments, their policies were not simply cancelled, but secretly repurchased at a reduced rate by Mike or Benji, himself. When that client then passed away, it was one of the men who collected the payout, with the family of the deceased none the wiser about it. Ultimately, these tactics generated a much larger income for both men, than did their normal commissions.

Mike only ever encountered Joe Sapinelli during his first week there. It was Benji who taught him the ins and outs. He did not know if the underhanded practices were standard to the industry, the company or simply of Benji's design. He also never again found himself in the presence of Don Vigneto, anyone in the immediate Vigneto family, or any of his men, including Dobie. Mike received his checks each week, knowing exactly why each dollar was owed to him. Even if the money was passing from Vigneto through Sapinelli, to himself, the overall aesthetics and logistics of the operation were as straight as any nine-to-five job.

If not for the extra funding garnered from buying out elderly and disabled clients, Mike would have cursed himself for choosing the option to stay in California. After all, he surely would have been able to muster a straight job on his own. On the other hand, the immediacy of being placed within Sapinelli's firm came with the benefit of sparing him all sorts of trouble. Staying in Salinas meant he did not have to relocate his family, or explain to them why they were relocating, for that matter. He also appreciated the opportunity to move laterally into a new career field, without the stress of unemployment and seeking new means. Still, none of it could compare to the rush of the entertainment industry – now just a hazy recollection of a past life to him.

The events that lead him to this point also caused a deep division in his relationship with Jimmy. They spoke a few times on the phone once the dust settled, but without any further professional connection between them, their distance increased immediately. Their communication ended completely once Mike learned that Jimmy had taken on a new, shaggy haired, singer-songwriter, hippie type as his next star client – another poseur, desperate to race the future with an imitation that could never come out ahead. Mike felt a perverse joy when that budding talent overdosed on heroin and died before ever completing a full-length record.

This new chapter of Mike's life was not completely void of music, though he ever only encountered it in a spectator capacity, no longer as participant. He was, at times, able to serve as a conduit at least, choosing every other record that the men would listen to on the modern, state-of-the-art, high fidelity stereo system that Benji purchased for the office (and subsequently refunded himself for, out of the company account). Their age difference opened a disparity among their tastes, though Benji was ever the more open to Mike's selections than the other way around. Mike, of course, stuck to the standards that he knew so well - album covers and record titles with no pretension. He would forever admire the soothing, darker sounds of Frank, Dean and Sammy, Bobby Darin, Sonny King, and even a few tunes by Louis Prima, who he felt had otherwise become a bit too pop-oriented for his tastes. Benji was naturally a fan of The Beatles and The Rolling Stones, much like every other American his age, but also had a strong endearment for the black artists that paved the way for them. He found himself enthralled by the gruff, impulsive, presences of Chuck Berry and Little Richard, and sought out music such as theirs, which was presented in more raw form than The Beatles and George Martin's fancy studio tricks. He had found this abrasive expression that he loved so much in an upcoming English band that went by the name Pink Floyd. When Benji played their breakout album, *Piper at the Gates of Dawn*, Mike refused to acknowledge what he was hearing to be actual music.

The nexus of the men's musical tastes could be found in jazz. They would have days at the office where they would tromp through hours of everything from Count Basie and Duke Ellington to Miles Davis, Charles Mingus and even some of the more contemporary artists, as well. It was all so meditative to Mike, and Benji appreciated the improvisation, ever meandering between cool and brash.

The jazz selections were particularly prominent two weeks before Christmas of 1969. Things had been relaxed within the office, which was to be expected around the holidays. The men had time to really listen to the music on a level more present than background fodder, and so Benji attempted to branch out a bit that Friday. He purchased two new records on his lunch break and played one of them, *Instant Groove* by King Curtis, later that afternoon.

Each of them found it to be too regimented for their individual notions of jazz, though Benji could appreciate the collection of songs as a unique hybrid of rock, funk, and rhythm and blues. Mike could not stomach the driving pace of the record, and so took his next turn, almost spitefully, with *Frankie Laine's Greatest Hits*. He endured the first side of the record, silently embarrassed by how outdated it sounded, but too stubborn to revoke his decision. Rather than turn the platter over and play the second side, he said nothing and let silence overtake the room. Not quite an hour passed with little more than the sound of pencil to paper and the occasional opening or closing of a desk drawer.

At last, Benji spoke, "Do you mind if I check out this other record I bought?"

"Be my guest," said Mike.

From across the room, he caught only a quick glimpse of the record's predominantly blue and gray cover art as Benji removed it from its sleeve. He replaced the Frankie Laine record with the new one and lowered the needle to the outer edge. The first song began with an ominous, sliding bass guitar and a stuttering drum arrangement that seemed to oscillate out into space. Right away, Mike felt gravity in this sound. The singer was familiar to him, but he could not quite pinpoint the voice. The words were abstract in nature, but felt menacing to him. It was dark and murky, with a depth that he had never been able to reach himself, despite all of his best efforts in minor keys. "What is this?" he finally had to ask.

"The new Beatles record," replied Benji.

Mike felt a wave of queasiness. They were supposed to be a superficial pop act. This new direction felt like an encroachment on the noir-tinged legacy of their elders – the lineage on which Mike had once worked to build his entire life upon. Such darkness, he felt, was to be reserved for the art of men, and yet here were these four boys, using their opening cut to flaunt their departure from the unobtainable hippie dream world they were previously paid to lie about. "What?" he asked, "These guys can't stay on their side of the fence?"

"What do you mean?" asked Benji.

Mike could never fully explain the way he felt. "It just seems a lot darker than I remember the Beatles as being."

"Oh definitely. My girlfriend has this record so I've already heard it a few times. It's totally insane. There's this one song about a guy who kills people by hitting them in the head with a hammer."

"You don't say."

"It makes sense on account of this probably being the last Beatles record and all."

Mike perked up. "Their last record?"

"Yeah," continued Benji. "I have some friends in New York City that run in the same social circles as Yoko Ono and they say that John apparently quit the band a couple months ago."

Mike felt a fleeting moment of joy. It would have sustained longer, had the music not been so dreadfully powerful to him. He was so relieved to hear of the demise of The Beatles, but he knew this final release was going to be permanent and monolithic. All he could do was witness it.

Four songs in, Benji said goodbye and left for the day, which allowed for a kind of release for Mike. Alone in the office, without the distraction of his coworker, he could focus more intensely on the record, and criticize it flippantly to himself. He never thought he would be glad to hear their corny drummer singing another corny song, but the levity of "Octopus's Garden" provided a subtle release from the suffocation that Mike was feeling. "Yeah stick to this, you sons of bitches," he spoke aloud to their music. This only lasted, however, until the next song, which veered immediately into shadier, more enveloping realms. Mike took "I Want You (She's So Heavy)" into his ears with his full, undivided attention. The rate of his heartbeat increased as the song built upon itself with dire tones and sonic atmosphere before reaching its abrupt termination and the conclusion of side one.

Mike sat in silent pain for several minutes. He considered cutting his losses, locking up and going home, but his desperate, competitive nature ultimately forbade this. He had to know that their new record was somehow flawed. He needed to be able to pinpoint some tangibly uninspired train wreck somewhere in this collection - something to prove that these clods were actually untalented phonies who just got lucky. He stood from his desk, walked to the phonograph, flipped the record, dropped the needle and began side two.

"Here comes the sun?" he repeated back to the first song on the second side. This sudden switch to optimism angered him. "More unrealistic gloss on garbage," he spoke, and yet remained unsatisfied when the loftier, more cloaked and esoteric modes returned with the very next cut. Beyond that, he was unable to pick through the deluge of smaller, interconnected songs. Each section was vastly arranged, yet brief, with no pause between them, so that Mike felt a kind of schizophrenia by the time he reached "She Came in Through the Bathroom Window." This deranged feeling subsided by the middle of "Golden Slumbers," to be replaced again by rage during "Carry That Weight" as Mike felt he was being personally lectured by the Beatles – all at once.

Mike lifted his briefcase from the floor and popped it open on his desk. He removed his pistol from inside and pointed it toward the stereo just as "You Never Give Me Your Money" was reprised. He whispered vocal gun blasts as he pretended to shoot holes into the speakers. This pantomime continued well into the middle of "The End" before he laid the gun on the desk and placed his head in his hands. He saw an array of changing colors in his mind, mostly shades of red and blue, as the cacophony of sound flushed through his brain.

Paul's condescending voice skipped across a succinct and simple piano line. He sang the first line, and the second. Mike clenched the grip on his pistol once more and braced himself for the next lyric.

When the final line of the song was revealed, Mike's mistakes through life became immediately apparent to him. At once, he was bombarded by a wave of equal parts clarity and regret. He placed the gun in his mouth and pulled the trigger, spouting his blood and brain upon the face of the large clock that hung on the wall behind him. His body jerked back from the impact and then snapped forward again, plopping his head and shoulders down on his desk. Blood seeped rapidly out across the surface as Paul sang one short and final song, comically embodying romantic feelings toward Queen Elizabeth II.

Relevance

Together

I

The old man crossed the room with a large, pulsating, burlap sack hung over his shoulder. "Last call for Chi's," he said.

"Last call for cheese?" asked Alec.

"Last call for Chihuahuas, silly," explained Heather. Her own Chihuahua, Koko, had given birth to puppies not a day earlier. All of them were pure bred with a father from a neighboring farm, and so probably could have been sold for profit, but this was of no consequence to the old man. In his mind, things were to be done the way in which they had always been done. Under those terms, when a dog gave birth to a litter of puppies (or a cat to kittens, for that matter), protocol was to keep what one wants, give away what one can, put the rest in a bag and throw them in the lake. This is what the old man was taught to do at a very young age by his own father, and so it was, to him, not an act of cruelty, but the economic elimination of mouths that were not otherwise included for feeding in the farm's budget.

"You know. He could probably make a good little chunk of money if he sold those puppies, instead," spoke Alec.

"Yeah. I've told him that before, but he's old fashioned," replied Heather. "He works here on the farm, doing all the same stuff he did when he was a kid. He thinks it's too much extra work to stop his daily routine to fidget with strangers who want to come look at something that he was just going to throw away and be done with. I don't think he would even know where to start. I couldn't imagine him placing a newspaper ad, let alone scheduling visitors. He's so stuck in his ways that it's just too much of a hassle for him."

Alec had never considered getting a dog. The extent of his pet ownership had only ever gone as far as a goldfish that he acquired at age eight after throwing hoops around bottlenecks at the Tennessee Valley Fair. He never touched the fish. He could not pet it, or teach it tricks or even make himself believe that it was aware of him at all. It lived for four days and then floated upside down in its bowl for three more before his mother found out and disposed of it. After that, the notion of owning a pet seemed like a mundane and unrewarding prospect and so it was pushed completely out of his head for an entire decade – until this moment.

Alec's fish died naturally, stupidly, in its glass bowl. It was not tortured or shocked into death, but simply floated around in a comfortable environment until it's body stopped working. He knew this would not be the case for the puppies, and could not bare the thought of their helpless yelps and kicks as they struggled in darkness against the water that would inevitably fill their lungs. He knew he did not need a dog, but now more than ever it seemed appropriate to obtain one – to save *at least* one. "I'll take a Chihuahua," he blurted.

"Really?" asked Heather, "Well we better go stop daddy before he gets to the lake." The two teens exited the old log home and ran after the old man, who had only covered about thirty meters of distance by that time. "Daddy! Daddy!" called Heather.
The old man turned around. "Alec wants to take one of the Chi's!"

He lowered the bag gently to the grass floor and opened the top. "You want me to show them to you or you wanna just reach in there and grab one?"

Alec chose to select one randomly and blindly. He felt that seeing them all, while knowing he was only going to rescue just one, could not possibly sit well on his conscious going forward. He reached into the bag with both hands and clasped them around the first warm, furry, little body that they encountered within. The result of his retrieval was a confused, white, apple headed Chihuahua, subtly trembling in his palms. He held the dog up to his eye level, noticing instantly that they recognized one another as living, breathing creatures – unlike the goldfish, which had never made eye contact once.

Alec and Heather graduated high school one week later and never saw each other again. They had only been on two previous outings together before he visited her home, met her father, and saved a Chihuahua from systematic destruction. Those things were enough to convince him to back away from her slowly, casually, and gently. She called him a few times, but he was sure to always be kept busy with "the college process" until she decidedly washed her hands of him. It was not that he saw himself as better than her family, but simply more modern, and so more easily disturbed by less civilized ways of being – such as drowning puppies.

Because they never really got to know each other in the first place, their attempt at exploring courtship was ended with a relatively clean break. Aside from brief spurts here and there, no real emotion was lost or gained between them. The same could be said for physical objects as well, if not for the puppy, which was no loss to Heather, yet still a gain to Alec. For this reason, he felt that their brief encounter existed in the universe *solely* to pair him with this new, more palatable companion, who he named Specky, because of the dog's small size.

Alec's parents, with whom he lived, fell in love with Specky immediately, just as he had. With their assistance, the helpless little creature grew slightly larger and slightly more independent. At twelve weeks, he was as bouncy and curious, as he was eager to please. "Here." His father handed Alec a fold of several twenty-dollar bills. "Get that dog his shots and some food." Alec obliged.

The veterinarian vaccinated Specky against rabies, parvo, distemper, and various other canine maladies. She moved her hands all around his body, pushing down gently as she went. While applying pressure to one particular area on his belly, he squeaked in response. She softly ran her finger over the spot in question. "I think he has a hernia," she said. "We'll take an x-ray to be sure, but if that's what it is, then you'll want to get that fixed as soon as possible."

Alec's stomach turned in on itself. He was uncertain what such a process would demand from Specky and so felt his first fears for the dog's mortality. He had no choice but to act as the veterinarian instructed, and so an x-ray confirmed the diagnosis and an appointment was set, one week out, for surgical repair of the soft protrusion.

That evening, and for many evenings more, Specky slept in the bed, under the covers, pressed against the small of Alec's back. Alec would wake in early morning hours, his mind immediately in search of confirmation that he did not roll over in his sleep, crushing the dog. He could not find mental relief simply from verification that Specky was still there, but also needed to be assured that he was still actually breathing, as well. He would achieve this by placing his palm on the dog's chest, which not only rose and fell with each breath, but also housed the heartbeat.

On the day of the surgery, Alec's anxiety burned hotly below his otherwise calm exterior. He handed Specky over to the veterinarian's assistant, who confirmed his phone number and told him she would call when the surgery was complete. She ensured Alec that everything would be wrapped up in about five hours, smiled, turned, and disappeared with his puppy. He imagined Specky strapped down on a stainless steel table, his pupils dilated from fear, regardless of the bright lights overhead. He visualized those eyes growing heavy behind a gas mask, fitted for a dog's snout. Upon forming the image of the surgical scalpel that would make the incision, he decided to veer away from this line of thinking, exit the building, and get in his car.

He started to drive home, but concluded that he did not want to see his parents. This was a strange and vulnerable moment for him, as it was the first time in his life that he would experience such prolific concern for another living being that he was responsible for. He needed to explore this depth alone, before his parents or anyone else could infringe upon it with their own questions and opinions. This obsessive mix of love and duty could only be processed meditatively, if it could be processed at all. Alec turned into a small strip mall and drove to the alley behind the buildings. He put his car in park, turned off the engine, and reclined the seat. He closed his eyes and thought about the anesthetic drugs that would see his dog to slumber. He wondered if Specky's young age would make him more resilient against the risks of the anesthesia, or more susceptible to them. Soon, in a blur of emotion and critical thought, Alec fell asleep, himself.

When he woke, surprised that he let himself drift off in the first place, he quickly noticed that nearly three hours had passed since Specky's appointment time. He returned his seat to an upright position, started his car, and headed home to wait for the call. There, another hour and a half passed by, as his parents tried to distract his obvious worry by asking him questions about his starting college in the fall. All of this in vain, however, as Specky's safety remained firmly affixed at the forefront of his concerns.

Finally, the phone rang. As though involuntarily, Alec sprung from his seat and lifted the receiver. "Hello?"

"Mr. Tulley?" requested the voice on the other end.

"Yes?"

"This is Melanie at Dr. Prizedale's office. Just calling to let you know that Specky is all done and ready for pick up."

Alec lifted inside. "Everything go okay?" he asked.

"Everything went great. He did really well."

Later that evening, with all the business of the veterinarian's office behind them, and a bandage wrapped around Specky's midsection, the boy and his dog lay facing one another on the bed. "I was really worried about you today," spoke Alec. "I've never felt anything like that before, but it left me no doubt that I love you more than anyone – anyone and everyone. I'm responsible for you and I am going to take very good care of you. It's just you and me, Specky – until the day we die."

Alec rolled over on his back, startled by what his own words had just revealed to himself. The entire day, he had been concerned for his dog's life as though if only the one hurdle of surgery could be passed, an enriching, mutual future awaited them both. Here however, reunited safely with his friend, he realized that despite his best preventative measures, the biological differences between a human and a canine practically guaranteed they would eventually exit this world separately. Furthermore, though

Chihuahuas typically live much longer than most other dogs, it was a near certainty that Specky would be the first of the two to perish. This notion was unbearable to Alec. Separation for a simple medical procedure was difficult enough. How would he ever be able to handle such seemingly permanent separation as in death? He placed his forehead to the dog's. A tear ran down his cheek, seized in motion by a lash of Specky's tongue. "I can't lose you." He spoke, "I just can't."

Alec eventually sat up and regained his composure. He went into the bathroom, blew his nose, and checked out his swollen eyes in the mirror. When he returned to his bed, he sat down and began to speak to Specky, not as a pet, but as a colleague. "Look. I'm getting ready to start college. I'm going to study physics and I'm going to study engineering. I'm going to school in state and you and I are going to live here with mom and dad while I do. That way I can save a bunch of money while gaining a bunch of advanced technological knowledge. Then, I swear to you, Specky – some how, some way – I will put all of my resources and all of my experience together and we will solve this problem. Some how. Some way."

He used three fingers to massage Specky's head around his ears. Specky rolled over on his side in submission, his big, black eyes glaring sideways toward his master.

"I promise you," continued Alec, "Even if it takes an apocalypse, it's just you and me, Specky – until the day *we* die."

Together

II

Keeping his promise to Specky, Alec went to college locally - studying at the University of Tennessee in Knoxville, while continuing to reside at his parents' home in Oak Ridge. Aside from the money it saved, the commute back and forth was worth the peace and stability he could maintain by avoiding life in the dormitories. Splitting his dedications strictly between his schooling and his dog, he was able to earn his bachelors degree in four years and a master's degree within two years after that – performing at the top of his class regularly. By the time he started working on his doctorate, he had already taken employment in the engineering department at Oak Ridge National Laboratory. The job was acquired with relative ease, due first to his outstanding academic record, and second to one particularly effective reference.

Alec's father had worked in the processing department at ORNL for over thirty years. He would oversee the intake and export of materials through the facility, inspecting and then designating all industrial sized deliveries that appeared at the loading dock. Though this job was more menial than technical, he was well loved and respected by his peers, and considered a staple within the workplace. So then, much of the course of his life was shared with many coworkers who also served as friends and confidants. When Alec was born, it was his father's immediate supervisor who puffed a celebratory cigar outside of the hospital, before his mother-in-law ever laid eyes on the new baby. Growing up, Alec found himself present with his family at company Christmas parties and spring picnics year after year. Essentially becoming a well-adjusted, educated adult before the eyes of his father's employer and workmates, it was natural, if not inevitable, that he too would come to build a career at the same compound.

Alec proved himself a capable and innovative team player and, with the eventual achievement of his doctorate, went to work assembling and dismantling various nuclear technologies. His thesis was a contextual analysis of technology's effect on modern warfare, sharing academic ground with the rapidly expanding field of computer science. The knowledge and experience gained from his research quickly opened the door to a unique promotion at the facility, overseeing his own division that would research and experiment with wireless, internet-based, detonation techniques. He worked vigilantly with his team and was a true believer in what they were attempting to perfect in their laboratory.

His salary was nearly four times what his father was paid and so he was sure to stay close and generous with his family. He lived simply, himself, in a small apartment with Specky, who had by this time nearly aged to eleven. His monthly bills were about one thousand dollars. Everything that remained was split between keeping his parents comfortable and a savings account that he started, strictly for the purpose of furthering his secret exploration into how he could equalize his dog's lifespan with his own. The fund in that account had grown to a sizable level by the time he noticed his father's declining health; the wake up call that would spring him into action.

The Internet was growing away from being a novelty, moving towards practical standardization in nearly every American home. Naturally, Alec had become highly experienced in its use, with a specialty for accessing its darker corners. Through this knowledge, he worked aggressively to establish three particular contacts overseas, though successfully so with only two. After several weeks of trading emails with these men and building rapport through mutual desires, Alec purchased a May flight to Solwezi, Zambia. He requested fifteen consecutive days off work, which gave him a twenty-three day window once the weekends were factored in. This was granted with ease, as he had never used his vacation leave in all of his years there. (This is not, however, to say that he was an inexperienced traveler, as he had racked up thousands of frequent flyer miles from attending a variety of conferences and test detonations across the globe – all technically part of the job.) When the day arrived, he slid his passport into his back pocket, said a long goodbye to his parents, a longer goodbye to Specky, boarded his plane and took to the air.

After two layovers, he eventually touched down at the Solwezi airport at around ten o'clock in the morning. He was greeted by his first contact, a fat, white man in a Hawaiian shirt and straw hat. He spoke with a South African accent as he took Alec's hand, "*Aweh, boet.* Dr. Reece Moodley. Good to finally meet you, Alec."

"Hello, Dr. Moodley. Likewise. Thank you for meeting me here."

"It is my pleasure. It would be difficult for you to navigate Africa alone for your first time. I have my own private plane so we can get to the property quick and easy. Would you like to eat something first?"

"Oh. No thank you," said Alec, "I've had two in-flight meals over the course of the past few hours."

"Okay. No problem. *Mugwaai?*" Dr. Moodley extended a pack of cigarettes to Alec.

"No, thank you. I don't smoke."

Dr. Moodley lit a cigarette for himself and led Alec to a small, nondescript hangar on the east side of the runway. There, they boarded a small blue and white, private plane and left the ground once more. A few hours later, they touched down at a tiny airport in Cazombo, Angola, traded the aircraft for an older, black sedan, and drove south to a gated property on the outskirts of Parque Nacional de Cameria. Dr. Moodley exited the car and used a key among many others in his collection to remove the padlock there and swing wide the orange, metal obstruction. The men drove on to the area, mostly flat, with sparse trees and a variety of scrub and brush. Dr. Moodley stopped at a seemingly arbitrary location, turned off the engine, and stepped out of the car again. Alec followed suite.

"As you see, all around you. Open space. Open space." Dr. Moodley took a deep breath as though relishing the oxygen around them. "This is the middle. All that way we drove goes the same distance to the other end. You see?"

"I do see," confirmed Alec. "What about the neighbors? What are they like?"

"I do not know. I have never met any neighbors here. There are no buildings on any of the adjacent properties. I don't know who owns them."

"If I built something out here, would it be safe? Alec asked. "Is there crime in this area? Vandals? Thieves?"

"I don't hear of these things," consoled Moodley, "but the fence goes around all five acres."

"I don't know that fence would be able to keep out anyone."

"Well, let's look at the rest of the land." The two men returned to the car and continued their drive to the other end of the property. They reached the chain link fence on the opposite side and Moodley contemplated it through the windshield. "See, the fence is not so bad. You could always upgrade it with some razor wire."

Alec, too, was in contemplation. "So you want seventy-five thousand? How would payments work?"

"Well we would draw up a contract and, by its terms, you would be held to a monthly amount of three thousand dollars deposited to my bank account, with an interest rate of six percent, fixed. My name would stay on the deed as an owner until you have paid all that is owed. After that, I would be taken off and you would own the land free and clear."

"What if I paid you fifty thousand in full? Could I get it for that?"

"If you pay all at once, I could take the price down to sixty-five."

"How about sixty?" countered Alec.

"I'm sorry but sixty-five is my floor."

"Alright. Well, I can't do sixty-five in full." Alec was lying. "Even sixty would require me to secure some additional funding. Maybe I need to check out some other places."

Dr. Moodley broke. "Alright. Alright. Sixty in full. I can do sixty in full, but I cannot go any lower."

"Alright, great. Like I said, I'm going to have to secure a little bit of extra funding so give me about three weeks and I'll contact you with a definitive yes or no. Does that work for you?"

"Yes. Yes that will be fine, but if I get a higher offer in the meantime, you may lose the deal."

"Well if that happens, then I guess it's just not meant to be for me."

Alec stayed the night at a small inn in Cazombo. The next morning, Dr. Moodley picked him up and flew him back to Solwezi. At the airport, he deliberated his next jaunt. His second contact was in Syria, but it was the third contact - the unsuccessful one - that needed to be established first. This contact would have to be secured in a nation much further east of Syria, so it did not make logistical sense when considering a flight plan. However, Alec would have to work from scratch on the ground there to establish the connection he sought, which seemed like something of a long shot, if not a complete impossibility. If he could not achieve his goal, then he would have no reason to fly to Syria and would have to rework his plan. Suddenly, he realized that, however inconvenient, the most sensible choice was evident. He approached the counter and purchased a one-way flight to Beijing. He stayed the night there before traveling by train to his ultimate destination: Pyongyang, the capital of the Democratic People's Republic of Korea.

He exited the train car in Pyongyang and observed the area around him. A security gate and guard covered every apparent exit. He chose one at random and stepped through. The gate opened without a problem, but his arm was quickly seized by one of the officers, who gently spun him around. *"Geulub eun eodie?"* he asked.

This was over Alex's head. He had no idea what the officer was asking him. He responded with his full intention: "Kim Jong-un, *budi*. Supreme leader. *Budi*, Kim Jon-un."

"No, no, no." spoke the guard before lifting his radio to his mouth and speaking in Korean, his other arm still clenching Alec.

"Budi. Budi," Alec pleaded. This meant, "please" and was one item in the limited Korean vocabulary that

Alec had learned. He spoke another: "*Bogi*," or "Look." He began to drop his backpack from his shoulders.

The officer abruptly slung him into the wall and snatched his bag. Alec raised his hands. A second officer arrived and began speaking with the first. Alec could not understand what was being said. The two dismantled Alec's bag one piece at a time, tossing his underwear and toiletries on to the floor, followed by socks, pants and t-shirts. "No," spoke Alec. "*Budi. Bogi.*" He repeated while pointing determinedly at the front of the bag. The officers stopped and looked at him. He kept pointing at the bag with one hand, and motioning back in forth with his other hand, thumb and index finger together, intending to pantomime the act of unzipping the pouch on the front.

The motion that Alec was attempting to convey was finally realized by the second officer, who opened the front of the bag slowly and removed a large, sturdy, folded paper there. "*Ne! Ne!*" exclaimed Alec. "*Chingu*," he said, touching his chest, referring to himself as their "friend." The officer unfolded the stiff square, revealing a mathematically detailed and correct blueprint for a rocket ship. "*Chingu*," said Alec. "Kim Jong-un. Supreme leader. *Chingu*." The first officer charged toward Alec, and pinned him against the wall once more. He did not resist as the second officer placed his wrists in handcuffs.

They marched him through an inconspicuous, unmarked door in the back recesses of the terminal. Inside were a handful of young officers, lounging, smoking pot, and playing a card game. They immediately straightened their postures when they realized a captive was in their presence. His arresting officers sat Alec on a long bench and exited the room. "*Annyeong*," spoke one of the men who had been playing the game. Alec smiled and nodded.

Another young man extended his joint to Alec. "Oh. I can't. Thanks, though," he said as he peeked his cuffed arms out from behind his kidneys. The men all laughed, loudly and together. Alec was not sure if the offer for the joint had been an accident or an intentional joke at his expense. He laughed with them, either way.

Hours passed as officers came and went. The card playing remained constant, though the participants changed. Alec could not quite discern what the game was, though he had nothing better to do with his time than to try. At last, an effeminate Korean man in a broad, black suit entered the room and approached Alec, a plain manila folder prominently pinched in his left hand. He stood above him and bowed slightly while cocking his head. "Mr. Tulley?" he inquired, as if he would have any reason to doubt it.

"Yes." Alec stood, finding himself in an uncomfortable proximity to the man, who relinquished no ground. He slowly slid his calf along the edge of the bench until a slightly more breathable distance was reached.

"I am Mr. Pak. I speak English. Please, why are you here?"

"I need to speak to the Supreme Leader," said Alec. "I come in peace from America where I work on rockets. I want to work on a rocket with Kim Jong-un together so that we can share that peace between our nations and show how strong North Korea is at the same time."

"Yes. I have the design from your bag," reminded Mr. Pak. We have been very curious about it. Why do you want to do this?"

"Do you even need to ask?" scolded Alec. He passionately floundered for the right words. "I don't have any kids, but I do have a dog – and I want a better world for him. Plain and simple. You guys are isolated out here and I know that America just doesn't want to show you the respect you deserve. I get it. I'm from America. I know how we treat you."

Mr. Pak interrupted, raising his folder into the air. "We have a file on you, Mr. Tulley."

"Yeah? What's in the file? That blueprint and a copy of my passport?"

"Yes," replied Mr. Pak. "That is true."

"Okay. You are wasting *my* time at this point then." Alec could feel blood rushing to his face. "I need to speak to Kim Jong-un. You tell him that I am a *chingu*. You let him know that I am here from America as a diplomat who is trying to build a bridge between our nations and that this is no way to treat a friend. No way to treat a *chingu*. You got all that, Mr. Pak?"

"Yes. Yes." Mr. Pak stepped backwards.

"You show him that damned rocket that is in my damned file, Mr. Pak. If he doesn't want to meet with me, then that is his loss and I'll take what I have to Iran or one of those guys - someone who would appreciate it and treat me as a guest instead of putting me in cuffs. I mean it. Either get me in front of the Supreme Leader or get me back on the train to Beijing. Please show me the respect that I am trying to show you here."

"Okay. Okay. I will return." Mr. Pak quickly scampered out of the room.

Alec's aggression had left a vacuum of silence among the officers. "Get on with your lives, guys. Don't mind me. I'm a little hot right now." Slowly, the tension lifted and the dialogue resumed. Several more hours passed as Alec took a nap, sitting up, his back to the wall.

Three large men in military uniforms awakened him. "*Uliwa hamkke*," said one of them as the other two lifted him from the bench, one on each arm. The speaking soldier removed a black cloth from his back pocket and tied it snugly around Alec's eyes. "*Gaja.*" The men carried him through a series of doors and hallways, his feet never touching the ground. They arrived at a cavernous area, soaked in reverberation. There they sat Alec in the back seat of a car, squeezed in on either side of him, and departed their current location. After a brief drive, he was unloaded and the suspension routine continued. He was carried through more doors, more halls, and an elevator for sure. Finally, they lowered him back to the floor, where he stood for nearly ten minutes as the room filled with the sound of foot traffic and camera flashes. When the activity subsided, his blindfold was removed. Across the room, on a large, wooden chair, sat the Supreme Leader, Kim Jong-un, and between them stood a skilled translator, Mr. Pak.

"Hello, Mr. Tulley," spoke Mr. Pak, "The Supreme Leader wishes to know more about your rocket. I am grateful to say that he has asked me to translate between you."

"That is excellent. Thank you," spoke Alec. He then smiled toward Kim Jong-un and nodded his head. "*Gomabseubnida!*" he called to him.

Jong-un rose from his seat and approached Alec. He looked him up and down as he drew nearer. With a gravely serious, contemplative stare, he fixated on his eyes. Alec felt like his mind was being pierced. The intensity of the gaze pushed harder and harder against his frontal lobe, but he did not dare look away. Then, suddenly, the gravity broke as Jong-un smiled and patted his shoulder. "*Annyeong.*"

"*Annyeong.*"

"*Sugab-eul jegeo,*" spoke Jong-un to the military men, one who promptly removed the cuffs from Alec's wrists.

"Thank you. Um…*gomabseubnida,*" replied Alec.

"The Supreme Leader wishes to discuss your rocket while sharing his fine tobacco with you," spoke Mr. Pak.

Alec had never smoked, but did not want to insult his host. "*Ye. Joh-eun*," he said.

Jong-un directed he and Mr. Pak into an adjoining room and motioned for them to sit at a large, white table there. Before joining them, he removed two hand-rolled cigarettes from a small wooden box on a shelf. He presented one cigarette to Alec and then extended a small butane lighter toward his face. He sparked the flint and Alec leaned in toward the flame. Jong-un then lit his own and took a slow, long drag. Being a novice smoker, Alec erupted into a nearly immediate coughing fit. It was through that chaotic euphoria that he made a surprising discovery: This tobacco was marijuana.

Jong-un spread the rocket blueprint out on the tabletop. Through Mr. Pak, Alec stated his education and credentials. As he then explained the basic mechanics of the rocket design, the marijuana hit him hard. This was only his second time ever being under that particular influence, the first being a camping trip in college. He decided back then to swear off it because of how paranoid it made him. Here in North Korea, however, sitting at a table with Kim Jong-un, he felt strangely comfortable. He got lost in his own explanation of the rocket, resituated himself in his chair and chuckled. "I'm really high," he said. When Mr. Pak translated this, Jong-un and Alec laughed together.

In his original idea, at this point, Alec would have started using aggressive language to step closer to revealing his ultimate agenda. He had not planned to threaten anyone, but simply to emotionally engage Jong-un in a dialogue about how disrespectful America had been to North Korea. He had figured this would encourage Jong-un to be more open to the idea of showing power with something like a rocket. He had wanted to rile Jong-un's anti-American sentiment and then align himself with it. The marijuana, however, ensured that none of this dialogue would ever occur.

As though restrained from any other way to express it, Alec instead painted a picture of unity for Jong-un. He explained that the rocket was not one of war, but one of technology and a new age of brotherhood among all living creatures. "If you are interested in being involved, it could really open some doors between our nations," he rambled. "You have America working together with North Korea on this – rainbow rocket – right? And we can take a video of the launch and send it to the news and show them that, no matter what they say, or what the president says, our two nations are working together in solidarity. But here's the best part: We can build that rocket and launch it from Africa – completely neutral ground and that means three continents coming together for this symbolic purpose." Mr. Pak did his best to translate. Alec continued. "I have some great land lined up in Angola. We have my designs and my engineering know-how. We have your leadership and workforce. It wouldn't take but just a little bit of funding to get the project going."

Jong-un nodded in understanding. "*Biyong-eun mueos-inga?*" he asked.

Mr. Pak translated, "What is the cost?"

Alec had not fully considered that yet. "Well, it wouldn't be anything as expensive as a full fledged space mission. A few million in the end, maybe. Possibly not even that much. I figured that would be something we would work out as we went. Ultimately, though, it would all be construction costs. I already have the land. I would need your help in producing or sourcing some of the materials we would need for the rocket, and then a few of your scientists and laborers to assemble it. And they would have to do that there in Angola. They would have to be flown there on private aircraft, obviously and was hoping you could assist with that also."

He could see that Jong-un was feeling a bit anxious, considering the logistics. "Look," he continued, "You don't need to worry about all that. Getting it together and getting it done is up to me. I just need you to provide what I ask for in order to do it, and if you want to draw a line in regards to the highest amount of money you want to spend, that is totally fine and we will honor that. I have other sources that can also hopefully contribute. What I'm trying to say is that you don't even have to visit the launch site. Though, you probably will want to once it's finished so that you have something to pass along to the world press, right?"

"*Ye*," spoke Jong-un.

"And that is what we need you to be: a figurehead. Your birthday is January eighth, isn't it?"

Jong-un looked at Mr. Pak, then back to Alec. "*Wae?*" he asked.

"Why do you wish to know?" translated Mr. Pak.

"Because that's why I wanted to bring this whole plan to you, Supreme Leader. I know that birthday – January eighth. You share that birthday with David Bowie and Elvis Presley. Do you know those guys?"

Jong-un grinned massively and quipped, "Oh, Major Tom." in steady English.

"Yes! Exactly!"

"Elvis all shook up," he next exclaimed, cocking his upper lip for a moment before collapsing into laughter.

Alec also laughed. "That's what I'm saying. You're cool like those guys. Cool Capricorns. Cornballs. Aliens. That's what you Capricorns are."

"*Naega yujoe ibnida! Geugeon jinsil-iya!*" laughed Jong-un.

"He affirms what you say," spoke Mr. Pak

"Great! That's great!" said Alec. "Then let's work together and you be the starman for this thing, Jong-un! We're building a rocket! You *are* the starman!"

"I am starman!" shouted Jong-un. "*Ye! Ye!*"

After a bit more romanticizing, Jong-un pledged his assistance in building the rocket and provided Alec with his personal email address and phone number. He showed Alec around his compound, his classic cars and personal movie theater that screened *Star Wars* in high definition. He lit another joint and passed this one between them as he played his wife's electronic pop music through his computer speakers. He spoke of his daughter, and America, and how he desired to better his nation and break free of the militaristic stigma left by his father.

"The Supreme Leader says that he is a lover and not a fighter," explained Mr. Pak.

The men ate a terrible dinner that evening and Alec stayed overnight in a guest bedroom on the compound. He was awakened early the next morning by a soldier rapping on the door, and was subsequently ushered to breakfast with Jong-un and Mr. Pak. A variety of fruits made this meal much more tolerable than the last. Upon its completion, and a giant, parting, bear hug from the Supreme Leader, Alec was given back his belongings and taken to the train station. A soldier and Mr. Pak accompanied him the entire way, purchasing his ticket for him and seeing him on to a train bound for Beijing.

Standing in the Beijing airport, Alec felt relief that his plan had carried through, but also anxiety in regards to the final leg of his journey. The residual marijuana in his bloodstream was of no help, clouding his brain and slowing his decision-making. He wanted to go home, but he had already progressed his plan further and in much less time than he had anticipated. His land was lined up. The rocket was in place. A satellite was all that remained. He used his mobile phone to access an email from his final contact. He took note of where he would need to go, and replied to the message, letting it be known that he would arrive in Syria within the next two days. He then approached a kiosk and sighed as he purchased a nearly twenty-hour flight to Aleppo.

He disembarked from the plane and used a payphone to call his contact there. An hour later, two bearded men in skullcaps and sunglasses arrived to retrieve him. Not unfriendly, though not very talkative either and clearly armed, they led him to an armored Humvee. They drove northwest to a remote area cradled by the Nahr 'Ifrin River, a bit south of Afrin. Paved roads gave way to gravel, which gave way to dirt. They proceeded between large, gray boulders and tall wooden towers with snipers perched atop, nodding to them as they passed. The gate at which they arrived was also made of wood and stood very high. It slowly swung open a few minutes after one of the men said something into a radio. They entered and another man closed it behind them. They turned quickly right into what appeared to be a parking lot, joining several dozen other vehicles there. The three men exited the car and walked a short distance to a small office, roofed and set back from the large, open area that comprised most of the compound. One of the men knocked on the frame of the open door there. "*Ladayna hdha alrrajul*," he stated.

The man at the desk inside swiveled his chair around, away from his computer screen. Like the transporters, he also wore a beard and skullcap - but no sunglasses. With only a slight delay, his eyes and mouth widened as he stood and extended his hand. "Hello, Alec. Pleased to meet you in person."

Alec completed the handshake. "Pleased to meet you as well, Sayid. I've been looking forward to it." The men sat down across the desk from one another. The transporters exited, closing the door behind them.

"We have much to discuss," said Sayid. "I respect the need to be ambiguous when communicating through unsecured email. You say that we can be of use to one another. So now, face to face, I imagine that you are as eager to tell me as I am curious to know."

"Absolutely."

"But before we get too deeply entrenched in details, please allow me to move us beyond one major hurdle first."

"Sure."

"Given your credentials and nation of origin, what can be said for your motives?"

"My motives? You haven't even heard my plan yet. Don't you think that my motives might become self evident as we talk?"

"American entrapment is not something invented by your Hollywood, Alec," reminded Sayid. "Let me ask you this. Are you here to join our organization? Do you wish to work within our structure or do you expect us to work within yours?"

Alec sat back in his seat, overwhelmed. He took a deep breath. "Look, Sayid. I am here as an individual – not a representative of any nation or any body outside of my own. I am not looking to *be* a representative of anyone, either. So no. I am not here to join your organization and I am not here to carry the flag for another. I am here because I need a good project manager and a reliable crew."

"Okay. I understand this, Alec. But why choose us?"

"Two reasons. First, I need an international team and you guys are rooted everywhere. But also, similar motivations."

"Like what? Do you follow Islam?" asked Sayid.

"I don't follow any religion. My mind isn't made up on that."

"Then why should we work with you?"

"Because I watch the news, Sayid. I see your fight and I see the problems with America. I live in America so I know them intimately."

"And what problems are those?"

Alec snorted. "Where do I even begin? Greed? War? You don't know?"

"Your nation is removed from Allah."

"Yes. Allah, God, the Universe - whatever. Morality isn't even a word in America anymore. We share this sentiment."

"That may be true, Alec, but how can a godless man have a pure intention?"

Alec threw his palms up. "Woah," he said, "I never said I didn't believe in God. I just said I wasn't sure about religion. There's a big difference there."

"You have come very far to push your agenda."

Alec sighed and dropped his head on to his thumbs. After a pause, he looked at Sayid again. "Suffice it to say that the enemy of my enemy is my friend."

Together

III

Alec returned to Tennessee and deposited sixty thousand dollars into an escrow account. It was released to Dr. Moodley upon delivery of the key and deed to the land. As an extra courtesy, Moodley also filed the required legal documents with each respective local and regional authority, providing paper receipts for proof of the transactions. Impressed by the gesture, Alec inquired about further business together. After a rather concise discussion, it was agreed; Alec would wire an additional five thousand dollars to Moodley's account and, in return, Moodley would hire a team of men to begin laying asphalt on the property. This is to say, rather, that he would hire a man to hire a team. He had a go-to contractor in Huambo who would ultimately come to negotiate the price and specifications directly with Alec. Moodley's job was to put the men in touch, and then to stop by the property every few days to make sure the work was getting done.

Of course, none of the work could begin in the first place without some funding up front. Three hundred sixty thousand dollars was actually a bargain for an asphalt runway over thirty-five hundred feet long, but considering how shrewd Alec had been in their prior negotiation, Moodley had his doubts about the legitimacy of the plan. In truth, Alec had bargained down the cost of the job by nearly fifty thousand dollars. A rounder, even number, he figured, would be palatable when introduced to Jong-un – and he was correct. After two months of warm pep calls officiated by Mr. Pak, North Korea was all in for the full amount – or half of what they were led to believe was an eight hundred thousand dollar project. What of this amount was not paid immediately to the contractor for materials was withheld until completion and inspection of the job. Within a few short weeks, Alec visited the finished site, landing there directly in Moodley's airplane. He paid the remainder of the money to the contractor, who in turn provided him with a bill of sale. Everyone was pleased with the outcome, though Moodley wished he had sold the land at a higher cost in the first place. Still, he dared not to burn his bridge to a man who could raise over three hundred thousand dollars in two months.

Alec told Jong-un that he had approached the American government about the project and that they wanted no part due to North Korea's questionable record of human rights abuses. "But they did offer to sell us a rocket for one billion dollars," he stated. Jong-un knew this was an astronomical price for an unmanned launch and took the stated proposal as evidence of typical American gouging, if not entrapment. He suggested instead that North Korea provide the rocket from the materials they had already acquired for previous test launches of their own. Indeed, Alec had intentionally funneled Jong-un toward this idea. He then lauded it as if it were Jong-un's own, before feigning apprehension about it. When their discussion concluded, it was agreed that the vessel was to be constructed not just entirely out of the North Korean stock, but also by North Korean engineers who were already familiar with the mechanics of such things. Alec's stipulations were that he would provide a satellite for the rocket to launch, as well as general laborers to perform the less technical, more physically demanding tasks; something he ultimately planned to leave to Sayid.

North Korea sent their resources across the Indian Ocean through a questionable, but ultimately reliable Chinese shipping company. Sayid's network of assistance was spread all over the planet and highly dedicated. With his clout in their movement, he only needed to give the word and he could activate men nearly anywhere, for nearly any reason. True and frightening power, to be sure, but Alec was strangely relieved to learn that these services could be rendered in Tennessee as they could in Angola. He was going to need them, after all.

The death of Alec's father had been anticipated for quite some time. His health had been declining through obvious coughs and chest pains, but he never resigned himself to a hospital, or even a leave from work. "I can sit around in an infirmary, I can sit around at home or I can sit around here," he would tell his supervisor, "so I may as well go with the option that pays me." Though he fully expected to eventually die on the job, it actually came quite peacefully, asleep in his favorite chair on a Sunday afternoon.

The funeral was a Tuesday and Alec remained absent. "When someone is gone, they are gone," he told his mother. "I have my final memories of Dad and I don't need anymore. I don't want to see him in a box." She understood.

Instead, with permission from his superiors (all of which who *did* attend the funeral), Alec aimed to spend that time alone, working what would have been his father's shift at the processing dock. "We understand that you need to grieve in a way that makes sense to you, and we want to do everything we can to cater to those needs," said the head of processing. "Your father was beloved by every person he met - every person here for sure. He was family to us, and you are, too, Alec. So if you want to honor him through his work here, I see no problem with that at all. But so you know, we won't have anything scheduled in or out. The processing department is practically closed that day – that was *our* way to honor your father. A day of silence and stillness. So be aware that you're just going to be basically sitting at his desk the whole time doing nothing."

"Well that's all *he* did anyway," replied Alec and the men chuckled. "It sounds good and somber and I look forward to sitting in his chair and remembering all the times we had."

"Not a problem, Alec. Just go down there at some point today and get a basic run-down from Terry. Just so you have an idea of the formalities, in case some rare circumstance occurs that you might actually have to check something in or out. Not counting on it, though."

The day of the funeral, Alec was predominantly alone at his father's post, but for the security guard that monitored the station's cameras in a small room off an adjoining hallway. One hour into his shift, Alec walked down to the security room, tapped twice on the door, and then let himself in. The guard was standing, a muscle car magazine in his hand. Alec spoke immediately and sheepishly. "Hey there."

"Hello."

"My name is Alec. You're the only other person on the floor today so I thought I would say hello."

"I go by Robert." The men shook hands. "Pleased to meet you."

"You're relatively new here, aren't you?" asked Alec.

"Yeah. Been here about a month and a half now."

"Still a baby, then," proclaimed Alec. "I guess that's why they have you working here by yourself today," he steered the conversation.

"Oh yeah. Everyone went to that one guy's funeral. I didn't know him, so I don't mind."

"Well I knew him quite well. He was my father."

"Oh, I'm sorry," retorted Robert, going over his best recollection of what he had just said, hoping he had not been offensive in any way. "So why are you here today, if you don't mind my asking?"

And with that, Alec laid down a gut wrenching account of what his father had meant to him, and what the job had meant to his father. "I miss him so much," he whispered before turning to the wall and pounding his fist there. He placed his head to the sheetrock and sobbed into the bend of his elbow.

Per Alec's intent, Robert felt awkward. "I'm really sorry, man. Is there anything I can get for you?"

Alec was barely comprehendible through his muffled crying. "Would you mind to get me a bottle of water?"

"Sure. Sure," replied Robert. "I was wanting to go to the vending machines anyway and I think you need a moment for yourself, too."

"I really appreciate it." Alec fished for coins in his pocket.

"Don't worry about the money, buddy. I got it." Robert slid out of the security room and headed for the elevator to the second floor.

With no hesitation, Alec ceased his apparent grief and positioned himself over Robert's desk, his upper torso squeezed in between the security monitors. He unplugged the video feed from cameras one, two, three and seven. Then, using video splitters that he had stowed in the inside pocket of his jacket, he fed secondary images from cameras twelve, ten, nine and five back into the monitors he had disconnected. The result was a wall of thirty-six monitors, displaying images from thirty-two cameras, with four sets of two scenes that would each be identical – something that an inexperienced employee would likely never notice on a day with so little traffic. Alec then sat down at the desk and waited.

Robert returned with a bottle of water, three chocolate candy bars and two packs of crackers.   Alec took the water, and declined the offer of anything else. "I'm really sorry I got so emotional on you," he said before taking a sip.

"Don't worry about it," comforted Robert, "It's good to be honest about your grief. Let all it all out, brother."

"Thank you for understanding." Alec returned to the processing desk. Robert returned to his magazine.

When Robert took his lunch break, Alec stood out on the loading dock and watched him drive away. Once out of sight, no time was wasted as Alec reentered the building and sprinted down the hall; his cell phone to his ear just long enough to instruct Sayid's men to arrive immediately. He entered a door to his left, the holding room, guarded only by camera seven on the inside and camera three outside, both now defunct. There, he retrieved a sturdy, metal box from beneath a covered steel table that inconspicuously inhabited a corner of the room.

This box was adorned with, among other things, yellow and black, diagonally slanted stripes, and a plated warning against engaging in direct contact with the contents inside. It was locked, but Alec had been stowing his own copy of the key ever since he brought the box, and two others like it, down to the holding room about three weeks prior. The order that he fulfilled in doing so only demanded two such boxes, each containing a supply of six discs of highly enriched uranium-235. On the inventory management form (the form he had to complete in order to get the uranium in to the holding room), he made certain to scribble a quantity that appeared as some hybrid between the number two (with a loop at the "bottom" and a long tail) and the number three (with a loop in the "middle" and a short base). In doing this, the absence of three such containment units would appear correct on the departing end, while the intended receiver would sign off on their requested two cases, as normal. The carefully scribbled number could have been read either way. Only Alec would know that the third unit – the one that he intentionally let fall through the cracks – would be nonchalantly stowed away behind its fabric veil until a convenient moment to retrieve it.

Sayid's men arrived at the loading dock within minutes. Alec had never met them before and, in fact, they had never personally met Sayid. Both of them were polite, young, white men with southern drawls - named Lance and Marty, respectively. They had come to adopt and cherish a radicalized version of the Islamic faith through an initial interest in September 11th conspiracy videos, which eventually lead them to propaganda pieces distributed by Sayid's own organization. Though they openly referred to themselves as a "sleeper cell," it was clear that, in reality, there simply just wasn't an abundance of terror work to be found in the southeastern United States. The conservative legislatures there tended to push many of the same extremist agendas already: smaller government and lower debt, reduced rights for homosexuals and women, controls on media and morality, rule by religion, etc. With so little conflict in this regard, Lance and Marty were enthused to have any work whatsoever to perform for their cause - this despite receiving very little monetary gain for their efforts.

"You boys came straight off the main road and directly to this dock, right?" asked Alec.

"Yes, sir," replied Lance.

"Make sure you leave the same way."

"Yes, sir."

Alec wanted to be certain that their truck would only ever be in view of the disconnected camera number one. With cameras two and three also no longer picking up the hallway and processing area, Alec simply walked the case of uranium to the dock and slid it beneath a blue tarp in the bed of the truck. He did the same for a few additional components that could go missing without raising alarm, casings and pre-erected suspension units and such. He instructed his helpers to deliver the materials to his home address, to park in the back yard so that their vehicle could not be seen from the street, and then wait for him to get off work.

They made their arrival at Alec's home before Robert even returned from break. Alec considered using the remaining time window to reconnect the cameras now that his mission there was complete. He decided against this once realizing that doing so would leave a time stamp on the recorded video loop, which would be uncomfortably approximate to the moment of his actual theft. Of course, the video would be recorded over just forty-eight hours later, and no one would even view it unless there was a pressing and specific reason found to do so in that time, but Alec wasn't taking any chances. Instead he waited for the end of the workday and Robert's exodus, precisely at five o'clock. He then retrieved his video splitters, reconnected the cameras to their proper channels, exited the building and drove home.

The next several months were accompanied by a wellspring of daily productivity. As the launch vehicle was erected in Angola, Alec worked on his satellite in the privacy of his back yard. Lance and Marty were present to assist on weekends and every other evening. Their skill sets, fostered by their auto mechanic fathers and solidified in their high school vocational classes, were invaluable to the project. Though Alec initially believed their only purposes were going to be lifting and carrying heavy objects, he soon came to all but rely on their abilities to weld and repair small engines. Furthermore, they were quick learners, seasoned tinkerers, and upbeat company, seeing each setback as but a challenge, and each challenge as inevitably solved. They were young men that whistled while they worked, and sang country rock ballads; who loved Allah with all of their hearts, and offered no place for the devil to reside. Though Alec was more expensively and diligently educated than they were, he came to feel slightly inadequate in the presence of their vast mechanical knowledge, natural wit and positive, simple dispositions. Conversely, these very things invigorated him in the way that a father could feel pride in his son's accomplishments, even if greater than his own. The summer was pleasant and memorable for them all.

Less than a week after the special satellite was completed, the three men carefully moved it's parts on to the back of a flatbed trailer, attached to the hitch of a passenger van that was provided through Sayid's network. Also strapped to the trailer was a storage pod, filled with a two-week's supply of nonperishable dry goods, and a dense, metal trunk containing a multitude of automatic firearms. "Is it very safe for us to be transporting all these guns, guys?" asked Alec, alarmed when Lance lifted the top.

"Is it very safe for us to go on this trip at all?" laughed Marty.

"I mean, we'll be going through some pretty rough areas in Africa, sure; but I'm more concerned with getting pulled over by police on the way to North Carolina."

Lance perked up. "Hey mine are all registered."

"Yeah we ain't worried about that," smiled Marty, "We were more concerned with crossing through international waters. Ain't no law out there."

"But let's be real, brother." Lance picked up the dialog again. "You're worried about these here guns, but we're gonna be hauling a damned nuclear bomb with us."

"We'll be hauling a satellite," corrected Alec.

"Yeah okay. A satellite with a uranium center."

"I get your point," said Alec, "but it *is* a satellite and do you think some local yokel police officer is going to be able to tell the difference anyway? And you know what? Even if he *can* tell the difference – even if we get pulled over by some cop with a doctorate in nuclear technologies – I could show all the credentials I would need in order to be in possession of something like this."

"Well you can do the talkin' on that one and we'll do the talkin' on our guns," said Lance. "How's that?"

Alec looked to Marty. "Are yours registered, too?"

"Yes, sir," Marty replied.

"Well alright, then." Again the boys left Alec essentially wordless against their simple, adorable, competency.

They drove through the night, straight out across interstate forty to a stretch of beach just south of Nags Head, North Carolina. They arrived before daybreak, to a massive, self-propelling barge that awaited them at the end of a long, quiet pier. The captain, a burley, bearded, Pakistani man called Mujo, made no haste in unfolding a wide ramp out over the sea between them. They drove on to the boat and were directed into a small, sheet metal box, obscuring their vehicle and it's tow.

Mujo introduced himself to the men and then made them sign a waiver, establishing each man as responsible for his own potential death. "I have made voyages like this over one thousand times by now and I will do everything I can to keep us safe, but the further we get out in that water, the more things will be able to go wrong for us. After a certain point, it's every man for himself. I just want to be real about that. Don't misunderstand. My boat well is equipped for the sea. My hull is strong and my freeboard is long. It's the desperate men out there that cause concern. Men who take to the sea with no plan and nothing to lose." He then showed them where his own collection of firearms was located.

Sure enough, the sea was not without peril. Twice on their journey, each time in the North Atlantic Ocean with no land in sight, they encountered speedboats overfilled with tan men, racing up on them from behind. The first came at sunset and were quickly turned around as Mujo, Lance and Marty fired their guns toward them. The second came in the night, about twenty-eight hours later. This time, Alec felt confident enough to join the defense with one of Marty's smaller handguns. Somewhere amidst all the loud explosions, the sound of the approaching boat's engine switched down to a low hum, which grew softer as the barge continued on.

After four days at sea, they reached Cape Verde and stayed the evening after a decent meal and a few drinks. One more day of sailing got them as far as Mujo would go: Dakar, Senegal. There, they disembarked the barge and drove the van eastbound across the south of Mali. They clipped the top of Ghana, strafing south across Nigeria and Cameroon. A group of armed men in sunglasses blocked the road in the Congo, allowing passage in return for a toll of two guns and a case of canned beans. (This was not unreasonable to Alec, though Lance and Marty were frustrated that they lost some guns.) At last, they crossed into Angola and reached the rocket site. Their drive took about six days total, with time factored for dining and camping.

There was confusion when Alec's satellite was unloaded. A group of the North Korean engineers had been working on a satellite of their own and its construction was nearly complete. Alec aggressively insisted to them that he was to provide the satellite, per his agreement with Jong-un. The engineers apologized profusely and immediately abandoned their workstation.

Alec took the opportunity to peruse their work, which he found to be rather well crafted. He realized how much simpler it might have been had he just let North Korea in on the full extent of his plan. It would have taken so much less effort to transport the uranium to the site and let the scientists build the rest of the system there. On the other hand, they would certainly come to know that the satellite held a destructive potential and if that information made it to Jong-un, he surely would want a piece of the action or he would pull his funding altogether.

It almost came down to this anyway when Mr. Pak called Alec the next day. He expressed that Jong-un was very concerned about the misunderstanding with the satellites.

"Our deal, from the beginning, was that I would provide the satellite," reminded Alec. "You all should not have even started building one in the first place."

The dialog continued as Mr. Pak did his best to give a measured voice to Jong-un's frustrations. Alec, however, could hear Jong-un speaking in the background and his tone was recognizably heated.

"Tell Jong-un that he should be glad that this is the only part of the plan that I am being controlling over," scolded Alec. "I have provided my property for you all to practically have free reign over this whole thing," he elaborated, though never mind that Alec alone drafted the blueprints they were using. "So why is he trying to deny me the one part of this whole thing that means so much to me?"

"The Supreme Leader would like to know what you mean when you say 'means so much' to you," replied Mr. Pak.

"I told him very clearly that I wanted to build the satellite myself because it had been a dream of mine since I was a small child. Was he not listening?" asked Alec. "Did you not convey this part to him, Mr. Pak?" In truth, this was never stated at all. Nor did Alec ever even carry such aspirations until he bonded with Specky.

"The Supreme Leader states that we have put very much money into this project. He wishes to know how he can trust that you will share access to the satellite's functions with our nation."

"He does not trust me now?" Alec scoffed. "You ask him this from me. Does he remember when I told him that his birthday being on January eighth made him a David Bowie or an Elvis Presley? Does he remember that?"

Mr. Pak covered the voice receiver on his phone as he relayed the question to Jong-un. "Yes. He remembers," he finally replied.

"Well let him know that I was thinking about how Korea is almost twelve hours ahead of my time in America. So his birthday is actually January ninth in the west - which means he is probably not a Bowie after all. You tell him that I'm beginning to think that he is actually more of a Richard Nixon."

IV

Alec's satellite had won the position atop the rocket, mostly with leverage held from his ownership of the land. After this was settled, he returned to America and did not speak to Jong-un (as interpreted by Mr. Pak or otherwise) again until a few days prior to the rocket's launch. This brief phone interaction was strictly for the purpose of synching the logistics of their mutual presences around the event.

"The Supreme Leader would like to know which American news outlets will be reporting the launch," declared Mr. Pak.

"That's not how it works," said Alec. "Don't worry about that part anyway. I'll bring a video camera and we'll make our own footage. Then I'll *give* it to the media. Jong-un, of all people, should know that we need to control our own content. *We* release the image of *our* choosing. Plus, I don't think it's a very wise idea to give away our location before the launch."

Jong-un could not argue with any of this.

Alec picked up his aforementioned camera at a pawnshop the day before he flew out. It was an older model of a popular brand, which recorded to eight-millimeter magnetic tape. The outdated machine cost him only twenty-five dollars and he purchased a cheap, plastic tripod for eight more. There was a Hi8 cassette already inside the tape bay.

For the flight, he tucked these items away in his medium sized bag, along with his toiletries and a few changes of clothing. This went into the overhead compartment. Specky also came along on this trip, sitting quietly and comfortably in a soft carrier that hung from an

oversized strap around Alec's neck. In Solwezi, they
transferred to Dr. Moodley's little blue plane and landed at
the launch site nearly forty-eight hours prior to the arrival
of Kim Jong-un.

Alec's early timing was deliberate so that he could
conduct his own thorough inspection of things. Indeed,
his satellite sat securely at the head of the launch vehicle,
but that was the least of his worries. He needed to know
that the Korean engineers knew what they were doing and
that the launch would go off as planned. He found that,
like their own rejected satellite, the launch vehicle, too,
appeared to be very precisely built - and to his own
specifications, at that. He called for a test of all thrusters
on the ship, both primary and secondary. Everything was
functional and clean.

The control room was quite less sleek and mighty
than the ship. It was built of sheet metal, not unlike their
box on the barge. The observation window was open, with
a long awning to keep the weather out. The floor was dirt
and grass. At night it was lit with furniture lamps. Still,
Alec tested each knob, wire, power generator, button and
headset. He found no apparent flaws. In fact, he was quite
impressed, and so felt warmth for the Koreans that had
been absent for some time.

When Jong-un finally arrived, Alec experienced
something like the anticipation of an old friend, despite
their recent rift. The slow lowering of the steps on his
jetliner added a kind of suspense to the moment, quickly
increased by the appearance of six armed men in military
fatigues. The soldiers marched down to the asphalt,
stepped aside into two groups of three, and placed their
saluting hands to their heads. One of them shouted some
sort of unintelligible introduction as Jong-un and his wife,
Sol-ju, appeared next in the door of the plane. Dressed

very stylishly, they smiled and held hands, as a woman and two men in identical black suits stepped out from behind them and dashed quickly down the steps. The men were carrying large, digital video cameras, and the woman a boom microphone at the end of a long pole, which she extended immediately upon touching the ground. They turned their respective instruments up toward Jong-un and Sol-ju, who then descended gracefully, receiving the flurried media fanfare that had been prepared for them. Only the engineers applauded their presence. Others rolled their eyes. Alec felt some ways moved by the presentation, and might have clapped for them had he not been so taken back by the presence of the film crew. Sniveling Mr. Pak came oozing out last, never being caught in a single frame of footage.

Alec also wanted no part of being on their film, but avoiding their lenses was impossible. One camera turned its eye to him while the other remained on Jong-un. Having no escape otherwise, he greeted Jong-un with a firm handshake that rolled into a one-armed hug. He was unable to get a good read on Jong-un's disposition.

The North Koreans then disappeared as quickly as they arrived. They had rented out the entire inn, forcing the engineers and assistants to give up their rooms and instead camp on Alec's property. Jong-un and Sol-ju claimed the entire north side of the motel, keeping one room for them selves and leaving the others unoccupied. Five of the soldiers paced back and forth along the row of doors, in synch and equidistant from one another so that one was never more than three feet from The Supreme Leader's room. Mr. Pak and the camera crew were relegated to the south side of the motel, where Alec, Dr. Moodley and the lead engineer kept the rooms they had already been renting. There were no guards for the south side.

Alec, Specky in his arms, cornered Dr. Moodley in his room. "I need you to get those cameras. I'll give you five thousand dollars to do it."

"What? To steal them?" retorted Moodley, startled by the proposition.

"To steal them or destroy them. I don't care. But I can't have them filming their own footage of this thing."

"Well what would you suggest I do to get to the cameras?"

Alec didn't hesitate. "Just kick the door in and take them."

"That's criminal!" declared Moodley.

"That's why I'm offering five thousand dollars to you."

"I don't know, man. I'm not much on breaking and entering."

"Alright. I guess I'll go talk to those guys that shoot dice behind the bar," threatened Alec. "I can probably get one of those guys for just a couple hundred."

Moodley perked up. "I didn't say I wouldn't do it."

"Alright then. Let me get them out of the building." Alec sat Specky on the bed and requested, "Sit with him for a moment, please." Moodley sat beside the dog, lest Specky would have certainly followed at Alec's heels as he exited the room. Alec knocked on his neighbors' doors all in a single pass. He stepped back out from the building and watched them each emerge from their respective rooms. The sound tech had a room separate from the others, this on account that she was the only female among them, but for Sol-ju. She was divided from the others by a vacant rental that was to be used by the guards in two-hour shifts of two men each between the hours of six o'clock in the morning and noon. Beside this room was a room shared by the two cameramen. Alec could see their equipment sitting on the floor, neatly stowed in the corner of the dresser and the wall. Beside their room was Mr. Pak.

Alec bowed slightly. "*Annyeong!* Would you all like to have a few drinks at the bar next door?" he asked, turning his head from side to side, scanning the lot of them. To blank stares, he formed the fingers and thumb of his right hand into a cylindrical shape and placed them to his bottom lip, attempting to mime the act of sipping a drink.

"I can translate," spoke Mr. Pak.

"Then why aren't you?" asked Alec.

"I'm sorry. Your presence was confusing." Mr. Pak turned to the others and spoke to them in Korean. They all began to nod and smile. "Okay. We will meet you there in one hour."

"I'll see you there then." Alec returned to Dr. Moodley's room and explained the plan to him; told him where the cameras were and when the quartet was to leave the room. Their actual exodus, though, occurred thirty minutes ahead of schedule.

"So if they left already, then why don't you just go break into the room yourself right now?" asked Moodley.

"I'd be afraid of it being a set up," explained Alec. "I'm going to just take the full hour and go over there like I don't know anything. Being with them is my alibi, after all. Plus I'm paying you five thousand dollars."

"Alright. I get the point."

Alec dropped Specky back off in his room and, as discussed and on time, he walked over to the tavern and went inside. Of course, the film crew sat together at a table, their black jackets draped over the backs of their chairs, with an open seat between them and Mr. Pak. The sixth soldier, the only one not assigned to Jong-un's own security detail, sat at the bar alone. Alec smiled and nodded to him as he passed by in route to the others, but the soldier did not react. Instead, he removed a short-range, two-way radio from the front of his fatigues. He pressed the square, red button on the side and spoke something into the receiver. Moments later, more Korean words were returned through the speaker, loud enough to be heard from anywhere in the room.

"Take it outside, man," demanded the bartender. The soldier ignored him, but returned the device to his pocket.

Alec took the empty seat at the table with the others. Everyone sat huddled too closely together, stiffly and slowly sipping mead. "So will Jong-un be joining us?" he asked.

"Jong-un intends to rest before the launch tomorrow," replied Pak.

"More of a smoker than a drinker, ay?" joked Alec.

"Yes. Mostly so," was Mr. Pak's answer.

"Is he still upset with me?"

"Just slightly. He is pleased to be here for the occasion, and the satellite is no matter to him any longer. He does feel, however, that Korea has put far greater resources into this project than the Americans."

"But he understands that I am just one guy, right?" retorted Alec. "I don't have a blessing from American's political leaders at all. I'm hoping they will be more open to such things once this is all over with."

"Yes, well, eight-hundred thousand dollars seemed very expensive for the runway," Mr. Pak pointed out.

"You only paid half," defended Alec. "And did you consider the exchange rate?"

"We also provided most of the components for the launch vehicle."

"But that was your choice."

"Perhaps you have taken advantage of the Supreme Leader's enthusiasm and kindness."

"Well I'm sorry you feel that way," scoffed Alec.

Meanwhile, away from their dismal discussion, Moodley was smoking a cigarette and casually assessing the outside of the cameramen's room. He looked to either side of himself and charged the door, throwing the entirety of his body weight against it. It did not open. He looked around once more and then proceeded to kick it, just left of the handle, again and again, repeatedly with no success. His next thought was to enter through the large window, though that would be much more of a show to anyone who would have caught on to him. He had his tools in his airplane and figured he may be able to merely pop the glass out, dispose of the cameras, and then replace the pane. Upon observation, he discovered that this was impossible, for the glass was installed from inside the room. Breaking it would be the only way to enter through it. A crawl space was his next consideration. If he could get under the room, then – well – he didn't really know. "Okay. Not for me," he whispered to himself.

By this time, Alec, Mr. Pak and the film crew were all out of their seats and playing darts. This was Alec's suggestion, a way to lighten the tension in the air, and it seemed to be working. Everyone grew a bit inebriated and shared a positive, competitive experience. More importantly to Alec, however, was that it removed the film crew from their jackets, still over the backs of their chairs at the table across the room, and just out of view from anyone focusing on a dart game. His only obstacle was the soldier at the bar. He could see everything from his vantage point. Aside from that setback, Alec even knew precisely which pocket of which jacket contained the key, as he had seen the corresponding cameraman remove it with the other contents of his pockets when fishing for his cash stipend.

Then, a miracle of coincidence: Alec obscured his internal labor about how to retrieve the key but quietly cursed the soldier's very existence. In that moment, as though he had received these profane prayers himself, the soldier stood and departed for the restroom. "I have to use the bathroom," spoke Alec immediately to the group. "Skip my turns and I'll make them up when I get back."

When he rounded the corner from the small hall that housed the dartboards, he bumped face-to-face into Dr. Moodley. "What are you doing here?" he whispered sternly to him.

"I just can't do it," wept Moodley. "I want to but I don't know how. I'm sorry."

"Did you try breaking the window?" demanded Alec.

"I mean, I thought about it…"

"I don't have time for this," spoke Alec, grabbing Moodley's shoulder and swinging him around the corner to where the others were still involved in the game. "Hey look, everyone!" he beamed. "Dr. Moodley is joining us. Just let him take my turns while I'm in the bathroom, please." Mr. Pak translated and the film crew bowed a little. "Don't lose this game for me," spoke Alec to Moodley. "I have a five thousand dollar bet on it."

Alec then sprinted across the room, keeping his eyes on the bathroom hallway for fear that he would see the soldier. He placed his hand in the black jacket pocket and fished within the paper there until his fingers felt the key. He placed it in his own pocket and then walked briskly toward the restroom. Down the hall and into the men's room door, the soldier stood inside at the sink, washing his hands. Alec nodded to him again and, again, was ignored. The soldier did watch him through the mirror, though, as he entered a stall, sat down on the toilet, and waited.

Through a sliver of space, the crack in the stall door, Alec watched the colors of the soldier disappear, replaced by the washed out teal, drenched in fluorescent. Heavy boot steps clopped out of the room and down the hall. Alec counted to one hundred-twenty, slowly, and then exited the restroom. In the hall, he did not turn left to go back into the bar, but right, past the women's room and out an inconspicuous back exit. He passed by the men shooting dice and smoking marijuana – the men who may have performed the task that Moodley was not up to completing; too late now. He carried on, out past the lake and into the tiny wooded area. There, he stayed inside the tree line and moved lightly, determined to remain out of consideration from Jong-un's guards. At last, he popped out on the south side of the inn and scuttled up to the cameramen's room. He inserted the key and turned the knob. The door opened and he entered, stepping directly to the camera equipment. He lifted it all from the floor: two cameras, each stowed in its own weighty black box, and a satchel style bag of wires. He turned back out of the room and the heavy door slammed behind him. He left the key in the lock, and ran back into the woods, balancing the cameras on either arm. He leaned slightly left into the weight, as the satchel ultimately tipped him to the right. Further out into the woods he stepped, so as to ensure he could tromp around a bit more loudly without stirring the guards. Finally he arrived at the lake and, without a second thought, tossed all of the equipment into the water.

Exasperated, Alec stretched out his fingers and arms, attempting to exercise the burn they were feeling. He walked casually back into the rear of the bar and into the bathroom. He washed his face and hands, dried well, and then returned to the group, still playing darts. "So did Dr. Moodley keep up my winning streak?" asked Alec.

Mr. Pak translated and the film crew laughed, "No! no!"

"Well I guess he owes me five-thousand dollars then. Wasn't that the bet?" Alec laughed at Moodley's discomfort. "Seriously, though, I wanted to finish the game, but I'm afraid this mead was making my stomach ache something terrible. I had to run to the bathroom to, well, fight the sickness."

"Do you feel better now?" asked Mr. Pak.

"Yes I do, but no more drinking for me. It's not something I usually do anyway, but I wanted to celebrate tonight."

About an hour later, the soldier declared that the time had come for the group to retire for the evening. Everyone trudged back to the inn together, with a sense of drunken ease. Each person presented their key to the lock on their respective doors, but for the cameramen. They paused momentarily, each man checking his pockets profusely. Then one of them noticed the key already protruding from the lock. Relieved, their first instinct was to laugh at the notion that they were so careless as to leave it there in the door without realizing it. They tried to keep this lightness when Mr. Pak got involved also, but he did not find the apparent error to be so funny. When the soldier spoke into his radio, all lightness was immediately vanquished.

Alec pretended not to notice or understand what was going on. "Well goodnight, everyone," he said, "See you tomorrow for the big launch."

Specky kept nestled in Alec's armpit through the night, popping up on occasions when the commotion outside got especially loud. Alec, himself, slept soundly, and when he woke, he started the day as though he had known nothing of the previous evening's events. He showered, brushed his teeth, leashed up Specky and headed down to the launch site, all smiles.

Mr. Pak stopped him outside of the control room. "Mr. Tulley, I'm afraid we have a problem."

"What's that?"

"The camera crew will not be joining us for the launch," he explained. "They are very sick. Perhaps there was a problem with the mead yesterday. I know it made you sick, too."

Alec was not certain why Mr. Pak was lying to him. Was it a trick? Was it even a lie at all? "Oh. That's too bad," he proceeded, "Well, what can I do to help?"

"You stated earlier that you had brought a camera of your own, yes?" asked Mr. Pak.

"Yes. That's correct."

"Perhaps you should retrieve it."

"Sure thing." Alec felt nervous for the first time on this endeavor. He and Specky walked to his rented jeep and he stood in the door, fastening the twenty-five-dollar camera to the top of the eight-dollar tripod. When he returned to the control booth, instead of entering and presenting his cheap rig to the Koreans, he positioned it outside the window, facing the launch pad.

Jong-un exited the booth and approached him but did not acknowledge him, instead focusing all of his attention on the quality of Alec's camera. When at last he turned to Alec, he spoke in English: "What is this?"

"It's my camera. It's really popular in America – this brand."

Jong-un was visibly angry and withheld none of his immediate suspicion against Alec. Mr. Pak translated Jong-un's strange accusation, that Alec had some hand in the "sickness" of the crew. "You poisoned them," he asserted.

"Look. I didn't poison anyone," Alec defended. "They were there drinking before I even arrived. You should talk to the bar if you feel they were poisoned." Not being the actual event for which Alec was guilty, he found it easy to deny his involvement and, obviously, there was no evidence for Jong-un to determine otherwise.

"Well they are very sick," explained Mr. Pak. "We are afraid they may die."

Alec changed the topic. "Let's get some footage together, right?"

Mr. Pak interpreted Alec's suggestion to Jong-un and, without a word, the Supreme Leader walked a few yards out and turned to the camera. Alec moved the tripod a bit to center Jong-un in the frame, and then joined him in his spot. He placed his arm diagonally across Jong-un's upper back and smiled as the little red camera light blinked in the distance. "Come on. Get into it!" he implored. Still, Jong-un's face remained stoic, if not seething. Alec raised his thumb out from his face and punched the air. "Come on, Jong-un. This is a happy moment! A great accomplishment! Let's do thumbs up!" Reluctantly, Jong-un raised his thumb for about four seconds. He could not bring himself to smile.

After a few more of those awkward moments, Alec turned and softly tapped Jong-un's arm with the side of his fist. "So we gonna launch this puppy now or not?" Jong-un immediately began walking to the control room. Alec closed in on his head start and walked by his side. "We should feel happy for what we are about to do, Jong-un. Do you not want to go through with this? I mean if the mood isn't right, then we can reschedule."

Jong-un did not completely understand everything Alec was saying, but he knew what lip service sounded like in any language. He stopped walking, turned and looked Alec deep into his eyes. "Lots of money," he reminded. "We pay lots of money."

"And money well spent. You'll see," encouraged Alec.

Again, Jong-un did not understand every word, but he knew what an American sounded like when he was trying to make a sell or lessen a blow. It *was* lots of money, though. Jong-un was well aware that there was no way to walk it back now.

The men sat down at the control table, Mr. Pak, Dr. Moodley, and the lead engineer beside them. Five of the soldiers stood behind the men. Specky was also present, curled up in Alec's lap. "Would you like to do the honors?" he asked Jong-un as he motioned toward the power dial.

"Camera," scorned Jong-un.

"Right. Right." Alec sat Specky down on a towel beside his seat and dashed to the other side of the booth to retrieve the camera. It was still recording, so he pressed the stop button. Then he pressed rewind, and as he pretended to attempt to set up the perfect shot, the tape returned to its head. After much apparent deliberation, he positioned the tripod up against the outside of the window, the far side away from Jong-un, aiming down the row of men. He checked the viewfinder and zoomed in to be certain that both he and Moodley were cut out of the frame. Then he began recording.

Alec powered up the console and took his seat with Specky again in his lap. Everyone wore headsets through which they could speak to one another, even though they were all sitting side by side. Jong-un barked launch orders in Korean and Mr. Pak barked them back in English. Alec knew what he was doing and mostly ignored the commands as he readied the thrusters and prepared for launch.

The camera filmed only Jong-un, Mr. Pak and the lead engineer as the arm released for lift-off. Now Jong-un was finally involved in the play of the thing. As a plume of smoke and flame ballooned against the ground, he smirked just enough to look as though he was in total control and acting with great intent and meaning. Mr. Pak and the lead engineer clapped. Moodley clapped, too. Being certain to stay low to the ground and hence out of the camera's view, Alec sat Specky down again and slipped up behind the shot. He swung the eye away from the men, aiming it at the launch itself.

The vehicle took flight with relative grace and surprising ease. Alec held the camera on its position until it was no longer visible in the sky. Everyone stood in quiet awe, even beyond this point.

V

As planned, the rocket cleared the earth's atmosphere and jettisoned its payload fairing. The satellite was launched into orbit, balanced appropriately against the pull of the earth, and the rocket descended back down through the atmosphere. It landed somewhere in the South Atlantic Ocean and is probably still there today.

The Hi8 footage ended up in Jong-un's possession. Alec first attempted to exit with only a promise that he would send the footage to major media outlets, but this was not satisfactory to Jong-un. A North Korean soldier pressed his chest to Alec's and demanded the tape. Of course, Alec presumed something of this sort would occur, which is why he was sure to keep his presence removed from the film; and so he complied, presenting the soldier with the entire camera.

Alec returned to Oak Ridge and was not home forty-eight hours before seeing his rocket launch on cable news. Only this was not the footage that he had procured with his twenty-five dollar camera. It was, rather, a shot taken from much further away, and captured on higher quality, digital film. The launch, though primary to the sequence, was but background action. In the foreground was the cameraman himself, one of Sayid's men who had been guarding the gate, arms extended and pointing his camera's lens back toward himself. "Haters gonna hate," he spoke, lips pursed as the rocket lifted off in the distance behind him. "But I don't see *you* guarding no rocket ships at *your* job." He squinted his eyes and raised his chin.

The newscaster framed the launch as an act of terrorism, disregarding the fact that no one was hurt in the process and no property was destroyed. In the troubled minds of Americans, a headscarf and tan skin was enough for this designation. Alec watched with bemusement, underlain by a tinge of discomfort, as more and more news agencies expanded their coverage of the video. Droves of supposed experts and former government agents lined the walls of the television studios, each waiting his turn to cash in with his shortsighted theories and gloomy projections.

Alec received a phone call from a foreign number. He did not answer. This was followed by thirty-six more attempts, though Alec turned his phone off after four. Finally, the caller left a message. It was Mr. Pak, breaking from his typically calm demeanor, and speaking sternly and erratically through the mouthpiece. He rambled for nearly three full minutes about how angry Jong-un had become, accusing Alec of betrayal and theft. Alec never called back and changed his phone number a few days later.

Sayid also called, but Alec did not answer for him either. The message he left was profusely apologetic. He ensured Alec that the guard who filmed the video (and subsequently posted it to a social networking site) had been "fatally reprimanded." He made clear his desire to be forgiven for his employee selection and managerial oversight.

Alec genuinely respected Sayid, but chose not to return his call. He had said all that was necessary between them weeks prior when he gave him an access code for the satellite. He told him that he also had a code of his own, of course, and that both codes would be necessary to make use of the program he had built in order to control the craft. Therefore, neither of them would be able to position or detonate it without the consent and action of the other. This, however, was not true. Only Alec had a working code, and only his code was needed to access the system. The code given to Sayid was simply a random string of numbers and letters that Alec assembled together on the spot. It was useless in any context.

Within only a few days, the American government traced the origin of the guard's camera footage back to Syria. This led their investigative agencies to believe that the entire operation had been based there, as well. Two months later, Sayid was killed by a drone strike on his compound.

Specky hobbled away from Alec, to the other side of the couch, and slowly lowered himself down into an awkward position. Everything had become awkward about him that morning. He was slower than usual, and more rigid. His posture was becoming stiff, as though he was in pain to move. Furthermore, he had thrown up twice in the hour since the two friends had been awake, drank an intense amount of water, then vomited it up as well, just minutes later.

Alec stood and leaned over Specky, lightly scratching the top of his head. "My poor friend," he whispered as a tear rolled down his cheek. "I guess this is it then. Well hang in there for a moment, please." He walked back to his bedroom and into his large, walk-in closet. From high atop a shelf, he pulled down an old shoebox, filled with small trinkets from his past. From among these unique stones, ticket stubs and other odds and ends, he fished out a small, black thumb drive. He walked back to the living room, picked his laptop computer up from his coffee table, sat down next to Specky and lifted the screen.

He typed his password ("Specky", naturally) to gain entrance to his desktop, and then inserted the thumb drive into his USB port. Once the contents of the drive were shown, he opened a file called "GOODBYE.EXE." This executed a program, which requested another password to enter. This one was much more deeply encrypted; so much so that Alec had to copy it from a text file, misleadingly named, "VACATION.DOC, and saved in a series of seemingly trivial folders buried deep in a "TEMP" directory. Once inside the program, a unique data set appeared on the screen. In the field beside the word, "X-axis," he typed the coordinate of 35.980840 and beside the "Y-axis" field, he entered a latitude of -84.097306.

When Alec pressed the "Enter" key, a series of prompts dominated the screen, one after another. "MOBILIZE THRUSTERS? Y / N" asked the first, and he pressed the Y key. "THRUSTERS MOBILIZING," stated the next, and then blinked for about thirty seconds. The next prompt displayed the coordinates he had previously entered. "ARE THESE COORDINATES CORRECT? Y / N" asked the next prompt and he again pressed the Y key. The next was the blinking, informational type, stating, "GLOBAL POSITION LOCKING." Once complete, another question, "INITIATE LAUNCH SEQUENCE? Y / N," to which he pressed Y once more. "LAUNCH SEQUENCE INITIATING," was naturally the next, blinking prompt, followed at last with a simple, "PRESS ENTER TO LAUNCH."

Somewhere out in space, the satellite's thrusters were activated, and a simple push of a single button would send it on its journey back to earth. Locked into the given coordinates, it would gain speed as it traveled. It would only take a few hours after that to crash into Alec's Oak Ridge home. The uranium core would undergo a violent fission, destroying practically everything in a two-mile radius and releasing poison radiation into the east Tennessee air.

Alec squeezed Specky against his leg. "Here we go, boy." He pressed the enter key and closed his laptop. He placed the computer back on his coffee table, then lifted Specky up so that he could spin himself around and spread his legs out on the couch. He lowered Specky to his chest and kissed his, old, dry nose. "I love you." He closed his eyes and the two friends drifted into slumber together – forever.

Together

Faith

I

The green and brown brush was thick, but not debilitating. As Maki approached the edge of the ravine, she felt only exhilaration. She sprung over the edge, lifting higher and higher into the open sky. When at last she descended, it was a slow drift, softly down to the other side. One of her American friends, Deb, was waiting there for her, except she did not quite look like herself. All the same, the two girls continued to run and leap, each time springing high and sinking slowly over long distances like balloons with slow leaks. The jungle soon turned to concrete and the girls were floating and laughing in an empty parking lot, enclosed by a chain link fence. This is where things began to make sense to Maki.

"Wait," she asked, "Are we in a dream?"

"No!" shrieked Deb. "You're not supposed to say it!" Her voice echoed away with the imagery – sucked into darkness.

Maki opened her eyes, but the darkness continued. The new moon could not pierce her heavy curtains and all electronic devices were turned off. Her alarm was a classic wind up, inherited from her grandfather. Without seeing any of these things, she maintained a sense that her sleep was still ongoing, and that she was but in between dreams.

Stagnation was no way to travel and so she pushed through the darkness to her door, in the place she felt it naturally would be. Beyond it, she stepped into a hallway not unlike the one she saw outside her bedroom daily. She glided down the stairs and out the back door, all of it familiar from her waking dream, and perhaps no different from an apparent sleeping one. To Maki, in that headspace, it may as well have been either. She had been dreaming before, so why not now?

Barefoot, she stepped off the concrete slab and ran across her yard. Faster and faster into the clearing behind her parent's home, she focused on the soft moisture of the grass beneath her. She felt a kind of wind rise inside her chest and she leapt into the air. Unsurprised, she lifted about ten feet up before descending slowly, over a large patch of space, just as she had in the jungle and the parking lot.

She turned around and ran the other way, aiming to repeat the action, but at once came to the realization that she was awake. The environment had become repeated space and she was no longer moving forward with abandon. This did not keep her from leaping a few more times, but she failed to achieve such height as before. She walked the rest of the way back to her house, where her parents were waiting up with the living room light on. They met her at the back door and her mother handed her a cloth to wipe her feet. "I am sorry. I was sleep walking," she explained, not entirely certain if this were accurate.

"This is a first for you," said her father.

"I know. I will return to bed." She hugged her parents and did just that. There she laid in the darkness, her mind racing and keeping her awake. And how long had she *been* awake? There had been no darkness between the time she leapt high in the pasture, and the time she turned around. What if she had just kept running forward? How does one lose the properties of a dream both when one realizes it *is* a dream, and also when one realizes it is *not*? Eventually she fell asleep again.

Maki sat around a table with three other students in her afternoon art class. They were weaving yarn in and out of a loom they had made of thread and cardboard. It took her a moment to bring up her experience from the night before. She was among friends, but sometimes they would be critical simply to criticize, which she thought uncomfortable. Nevertheless, she felt great urgency to speak of it and so made mention at the first break in their regular flow of dialogue. "I had a very strange experience last night," she said meekly. No one spoke, so she continued. "I think I brought a dream into real life." Now she had their eyes upon her.

"What do you mean by that?" asked Crispin, sharply.

"Well." She proceeded with caution. "I was having a dream where I was running really fast and jumping high off the ground and floating down a long distance. And Deb Powers was there."

"American Deb Powers?" asked Crispin.

"Of course," scolded Gabija. "She is the only Deb Powers in school and you know it. Stop being a bloody prat!"

"She did not look like Deb in the dream," continued Maki. But we were running and jumping very high and then I realized it *was* a dream. As soon as I did, it ended, but when I woke, I still felt as though the dream continued. So I went outside and kept running and I was able to jump very high just like in the dream."

"So you were sleep walking," shrugged Crispin.

"No. That's just it. I actually *did* make the jump. It was real. And when I realized it was *not* a dream is when I lost the power to jump like that. It was very strange. I woke my parents up, too."

"It sounds like sleep walking to me."

"Belt up, Crispin!" demanded Gabija. Crispin had always been a naysayer – even back as far as first grade when they met. She rarely took what he had to say seriously and she would not begin now. She believed in what she had experienced and she believed she could replicate it again.

"I believe you, Maki." spoke Khalil softly. Maki loved Khalil.

That night in dreams, she found herself atop a grassy hill with a large and long slope, scattered with other people. Beams of lights lined up to display a full coverage color spectrum across the sky. A fleet of rocket ships lifted in the distance and passed overhead, weaving in and out of the rainbow of lights. She never caught on that this was a dream, but when she woke from it, she held the moment as if she always knew.

Through the darkness of the room, and down her stairs, out the back door and into the yard, she never let her mind slip away from exactly where it was when she woke. Naturally, she ran out into the pasture and she waited as she went. She waited for the wind in her chest, and when she felt it, she leapt and took flight. After her slow descent, she hit the ground running and continued on until the right moment to leap again. This one was also successful. She repeated the action one more time even, just beyond the third property line that she crossed.

Before she could leap again, she came upon a neighbor's fence, ceasing her forward progress. She tried pivoting right and running alongside it, but by that time it was too late. Having to choose which direction to go ultimately grounded her outside of the dream state, back into that which she was accustomed to perceiving as reality.

She walked back to her house, elated by her accomplishment.

Her parents were awake, waiting on her as before. "Sleep walking again," she smiled.

Faith

II

She lay silent in bed, mind racing as the night
before. Once she was certain that her parents had returned
to their room, she snuck over to her computer and turned
it on. With soft pecking, one key at a time, Maki scoured
the Internet for some sort of experience that resembled her
own. She dug through sleep studies and new age websites.
She read about REM sleep, astral projection and collective
consciousness; tried to understand chakras for a few
minutes. Still, nothing she could find was quite relevant to
her own discovery. She eventually settled on a message
board dedicated to dreaming. Here she registered a
username, MakiYume1995, and posted this question:

> Hello. I am new here, so please forgive
> me for being so forward with strangers,
> but I am in need of some help.
> Recently, I have experienced something
> where when I wake up, I feel as though I
> am still dreaming. I am able to do things
> much like I can do when I dream. Then
> when I realize I am awake, I can no
> longer do those things. Is there anyone
> here who has had this happen to them?
>
> Thank you.
>
> <3 Maki

When she woke the next morning, she found only
one reply to her question. It was from a user called

BaDaZZ6969 who made his post not ten minutes after she did. BaDaZZ6969 asked only a single question:

> what do u mean by much like u can do
> when u dream? no one knows what u r
> talking about noob

Maki felt embarrassed by her apparent lack of clarity. The school bus would be coming soon, but she felt a strong desire to better explain her situation on the message board. She ran into the bathroom and brushed her teeth and long black hair haphazardly. Quickly back into her bedroom, she stowed the hairbrush in her backpack so she could put more effort into her appearance once at school. For now, she attempted to better explain what she had typed the night before:

> I am sorry I was not clear. When I say
> "much like I can do when I dream," I
> mean that I can run and jump very high.
> Maybe ten feet! Then I come down very
> slowly like I am floating. I am actually
> awake when this happens, but can still
> do these things like if I was dreaming.
> Have you heard of something like this
> before?
>
> Thank you.
>
> <3 Maki

She posted her explanation to the forum, turned off her computer and ran to the bus stop. She only shared her prior night's experience with Gabija, privately at recess.

She was not certain that Gabija actually believed her, but appreciated her enthusiasm and listening ear either way. She slogged through her afternoon classes, anxious to return to her computer. And so she did immediately that, once the students were dismissed and the bus returned her home.

Back to the message board, she found the thread she had started and scrolled down. The reply from BaDaZZ6969 was rather a disappointment:

> yah its called sleepwalking bitch.

Maki was startled when she read the word, "bitch." No one had ever called her that before. Having only ever heard it used flippantly between drag queens and American entertainers, this context seemed mean spirited by comparison. She could not restrain herself from replying again:

> No it was definitely not sleepwalking. I
> don't mind that you disagree or do not
> understand, but there is no need to call
> me names. You don't even know me.

Though typically not of her nature, Maki seethed and paced. BaDaZZ6969 was not even this person's real name, rendering elusive the pinnacle of her frustration. She slapped her window frame and reread the offending words over and over again in her head until she could not help but to go back to her computer.

BaDaZZ6969 had already replied:

> i know u enough to know u r a bitch. i
> know u r a bitch because only a bitch

would lie about something like that. but
maybe i m wrong. maybe u r not a bitch
but a dumbass. dumbass people r not
always liars but r just 2 stupid 2 know
the difference between reality and
dreams like u.

Maki was utterly devastated by these words – an
insult to her outstretched hand. She screamed at her
computer, turned it off, and bolted out of her room.
Down the steps and through the back door she sprinted,
out across the pasture. She ran harder and harder and tried
to leap at times, though she did not feel the wind in her
chest before attempting, nor did she clear very much
ground. She crossed the property lines and arrived at the
fence again. She slammed her fist into the wood and then
slapped it with both hands. She wailed as she pulled up
patches of grass and threw them at the fence.

A mustachioed man in a cowboy hat emerged to
her left. "Why in the hell are you hitting my fence?" he
demanded.

"I'm sorry! It was an accident!" yelled Maki as she
fled back toward home.

The cowboy shook his head and inspected his
fence for damage.

Once she felt safely distanced, Maki slowed to a
walk. She tried to process her anger. She knew that she
would never knowingly encounter BaDaZZ6969 in the real
world, and it would behoove her to thicken her skin in
regards to his words. This was difficult for her, however,
because she was blindsided by his hatred. She sought
fellowship and understanding, expecting kindness in a
forum that was dedicated to the very thing for which she
desired clarity. But *hatred alone* was returned instead? She

knew that somehow she had to let it go and chalk it up to human behavior. She knew that she would be better served by feeling excited to explore the dream world again, rather than endlessly interpreting the words of a person who didn't even believe in such a place. It was too late, though. His venom had already poisoned her blood.

When she went to sleep that night, she dreamed of Crispin. He extended a large weasel type animal out toward her and she refused to touch it. He told her he was disappointed and withdrew the animal. She apologized but he said nothing in return and walked away. Through the remainder of the dream, she sought him among towering, gray buildings along empty cobblestone streets. When she woke, her mind was already a mess. She only went as far as the bathroom, and then back to bed.

The next morning, she deleted the message board from her browser history as soon as she woke up. She went to school and spoke very little to her friends. Gabija asked her if she had any more dreams, but she told her no. When school let out, she returned home with slightly more hope than she woke up with. Her routine became of some new comfort, knowing that BaDaZZ6969 did not exist there in her regular universe. After dinner, homework, and some boring adult television with her parents, she was back in bed and feeling much more relaxed than the prior evening.

Her dream that night seemed piecemealed together. There was something about riding backwards in a boat with the mother of a friend she had not seen since elementary school. It did not cause her to feel any particular emotional release, but the bouncing of the boat felt akin to heavy breathing exercises at the starting line of a footrace. And when she woke, she was off! Out of her bedroom, down the steps, out the backdoor and across the yard.

She knew she had to maintain the feeling that the dream was ongoing. As she ran, though, she was not entirely sure *what* she was feeling. She pressed on, contemplating breath control, rather than the grass on her feet. She crossed one property line and was still waiting on the wind to rise within her. Maybe she felt it, or maybe she had been anticipating it for too long, but eventually she leapt. The height of her jump was no different than it would be for any other girl in her class. Attempting to ignore it as a fluke, she kept running, pushing harder and harder. She crossed the second property line and pushed off the ground again, this time stumbling a bit and never really gaining air. Exasperated, her running slowed. She crossed the third property line and then reached the fence with tears pouring out of her eyes. She laid her head against the wood and cried loudly. A light turned on somewhere on the other side. She turned and walked back home, unable to recapture the feeling she believed she had mastered just two nights prior.

III

The monitors almost formed a small pyramid, with two on the bottom and a much larger one looming above those. The computer mouse that shuffled control between the screens was wireless and greasy in some places, crusty in others. Of course, this could be said for most of the entire room, really, but the greatest concentration of substances was certainly found around the computer desk.

The giant creature that sat at this desk was bestowed with the name Donnie at birth. His mother died when he was seven and he never knew his father. He always told people he was not affected by this, but his behavior clearly showed otherwise. He became argumentative over small things and insisted constantly on his own correctness. He took great interest in guns and swords at a very young age and kept to himself in school. He was an early user of the Internet, for to obtain weaponry that he was too young to purchase in a store; and the more he explored those dark corners, the more reclusive he became. His grandmother, genuinely sad for him, provided her basement, spending money, and endless home cooked meals at no cost. With time, her kindness helped to form Donnie into the adult he would become: an obese blob with a heavy beard and thick glasses, semi-bound to a wheelchair, his legs atrophied from poor circulation and diabetes.

A passing storm put his Internet service out for about two hours. He spent the entire time masturbating to offline pornography while his grandmother cooked their dinner upstairs. He zipped up his pants when she knocked on the door.

"Come on down!" he yelled.

"Shew. It stinks down here something awful, Donnie," she observed as she descended the stairs with a tray of food.

"It's *your* house, mamaw."

"Oh, don't you give me that," she scolded. "This is *your* area. When is the last time you took a bath?"

"I took a sponge bath just the other day," he lied. It had been longer.

His grandmother folded two metal rectangles out from underneath the tray and maneuvered them in between the junk and outright garbage that covered the top of a short, elongated set of dresser drawers that sat perpendicular to the computer desk. (The drawers, too, were full of junk and garbage, mostly.) "So have you thought about maybe getting out of the house sometime?" She asked this question frequently in one amalgamation or another.

His answer was also always a bit canned. "What? You wanna wheel me down a sidewalk or something?" he asked facetiously, though such a prospect would have been completely rational. "Out in some grass? It just doesn't make sense, mamaw. You know that."

"I know. I know. But you know how I am, Donnie. I just hate to see you wasting away down here."

"Mamaw, I'm not wasting away, okay? I'm stimulating my mind and that's the only part that matters. Eventually we'll all be one with machines anyway and our minds may be the only thing we have left. Jeeze."

"Okay, well I just thought I'd ask," she said with a sigh. "You know your ol mamaw loves you."

Suddenly, the Internet service was restored. "Hey I gotta take a pee, mamaw, so you better go back on upstairs. Thanks for the food."

"You're welcome, Donnie." Back up the steps she went and she shut the door at the top.

Donnie did not have to urinate too terribly, but he wanted his grandmother to leave so that he could resituate himself on the Internet, now that service had been restored. Still, he believed very strongly that one should never lie to one's grandmother and so slid open a drawer and removed a plastic, hospital grade, thirty-four ounce urinal with a lid and a handle. He relieved himself into it, underneath the desk, and then placed it back in the drawer for later use.

He took two bites of his dinner and then opened up an array of high-resolution video games and Internet websites across his monitors. Frustrated that he had to log back in to a message board, he cursed as he typed his password and user handle: BaDaZZ6969. As he ate, he typed, posting comment after comment in thread after thread. Half reading the words of others, and degrading them with badly abbreviated insults; this is where Donnie felt powerful and comfortable. There and in his video game universes, those in which he would manipulate avatars of himself as elves, warriors, spacemen and such.

A user who went by MakiYumi1995 had been newly posting in a forum on dreams that he would sometimes visit. He despised her cutesy naiveté and the youth that was reflected by the number in her handle. Furthermore, she believed in forces outside the material world, which was always a target topic for Donnie to defecate on. He checked her thread for a reply, but his words were the last that had been posted. He left that screen open, refreshing it periodically as he moved about his other two monitors.

As the evening persisted, well after his grandmother had told him goodnight, Donnie began to fall asleep himself. He exited his video games, as those required more critical thinking than his brain would allow at that time. A social media website remained open on the top monitor, pornography displayed on the left, and to his right was the dream message board. MakiYumi1995 had still not replied and so he obsessively refreshed the screen as he fell into slumber.

Before he was able to commence dreaming, Donnie awoke with a sharp pain in the center of his chest. The intensity was greater than anything he had every experienced before, aside from kidney stones, but those were different. He attempted to yell for his grandmother, but could not bring himself to make a sound. He squeezed his face tightly into its center and pressed his fists hard against his sternum.

In a blink, the pain was suddenly cancelled. Donnie repositioned himself in his chair and retuned his attention to his monitors and the websites they displayed. He saw a reply from MakiYumi1995. It said something about how intelligent he was, and how large his penis had to have been. He typed a corroborating reply. As he shifted his gaze from screen to screen, he saw several more replies, some from people he had not seen in years. He responded warmly to some, exaggerating how wonderful his life had become. To most, though, he simply condescended to their every word. He also saw replies from beautiful women; women who wanted to show him their breasts through their webcams. He criticized their bodies as he masturbated to them.

A woman more refined placed her hand on Donnie's shoulder from behind. "Hey baby," she said.

"What do you want?" he asked, without looking back at her.

"Don't you recognize me, Donnie? Look at me."

"I don't want to play games," he insisted. "If you can't just tell me who you are, then I guess I don't need to know."

"I am you mother," she spoke with such softness.

"My mom's dead," he fired back.

"Donnie, don't you see? *You* are dead."

Donnie scoffed. "Whatever. If I'm dead then why am I still sitting here on my computer? I don't think I'm talking to ghosts on the Internet. It's not a ouija board."

"You're talking to yourself, Donnie," she informed. "Your computer is just an extension of yourself. You're recreating it here in the afterlife."

He snorted. "Okay whatever. You can leave me alone now. I'm not interested in religion. Only idiots believe in God."

"But Donnie, this *is* God. Will you just look at me?" she pleaded.

"I told you to leave me alone," he demanded again. It was the last time he would ever feel her presence.

Donnie went on reading and typing, gaming and masturbating. Many of his discussions wrapped around endlessly and stated virtually nothing. Not only did sentence structure fall away, but words, themselves, began to lose meaning. Donnie felt that plobloy could sometimes vrestlyn but there was always some other asshole who rather believed that frapmul actually hindersnot. Words piled on words. Meaning slipped away.

Donnie's grandmother came to his side. "Hello, young man." Her voice sliced cleanly through all the semantic build up.

"Hey grandma."

"What are you doing on your computer?" she asked.

"Just setting some dumbass people straight like I always have to do."

"Well why don't you move away from all that?"

"My chair only wheels back about two feet before it hits the bed," he replied. "You know that."

"But you don't need the chair anymore, Donnie. Look around you. We're in Heaven!"

Another scoff. "Heaven is fiction, grandma."

"Well Heaven is just what I call it, darling. It's whatever you make it to be, though. Do you remember the night you died when you told me that our minds would be the only things left one day?"

"No," he replied curtly.

"Well you were right, Donnie! Our minds are all it ever has been!" She was ecstatic.

Donnie rolled his eyes. "I don't remember saying that, but whatever. I have to pee." It was the last time he would ever feel her presence.

On and on he typed. Endlessly he masturbated. His "online discussions," being fed through himself on an endless loop, became absolute gibberish. The same could have been said for the "beautiful women" who lost form as he ran out of memories of females from when he was alive. They slowly became awkward, rolling clumps, just like his words, and eventually himself. As his essence broke apart into pieces and drifted out into the ether, he never even realized it enough to fight against it. And so the identity named BaDaZZ6969 – the identity named Donnie - succumbed to eternal conclusion.

Active Bear Area

I

William Bradley needed solitude. His ex-wife, Savannah, had just given birth to a child that he had no idea existed. He had not seen her since the divorce in September, just seven months prior. They had not engaged in intercourse in at least a year. William Bradley needed to get away.

He found everything out on a Friday. That evening he removed all the trash from the trunk of his car and checked the oil level. Inside his studio apartment, he picked up a blue duffle bag from the base of his closet and stuffed it with clothing, a toothbrush, toothpaste, some deodorant and a roll of toilet paper. He tossed it, with a pillow, up against his door. He pulled his tent and sleeping bag out from under his bed and slid them up against the other items. He paced for a moment, and then opened one drawer after another in his kitchen until a flashlight was discovered, removed and tested. He placed it, along with a small bag of marijuana and some rolling papers, into his pillowcase. Finally, a book by Michel Houellebecq, "The Elementary Particles." He did his best to sleep before departing just prior to daybreak, all of this inventory in tow.

He decided with little internal debate to go to the desert. Death Valley felt appropriate. He needed *some* kind of death - some transformation, either of circumstance or self. Aside from the name, he also considered the high heat there, which he felt could serve as a fiery baptism to accompany his conversion.

He took his time on the drive down, smoking joints and never missing an opportunity or excuse to pull over and take in the things that he may have otherwise passed by through the window of his car. Most of the time simply driving was occupied by thoughts of Savannah. He knew that the more he could focus on the present moment, the more foreign she would become to him. And so he relied on rest areas, overlooks and roadside anomalies to drive her further and further away – as best he could, anyway.

At dusk, he reached Lone Pine, just outside of Death Valley. A crumpled piece of paper sat on his lap, handwritten by a coworker, displaying directions to a campground there. It had no street address but was located in something called the Whitney Portal. The further out into the desert he drove, the more uncertain he grew as the sun slowly extinguished itself. A sign on the road bore the words, "CAUTION: ACTIVE BEAR AREA." He shuddered.

Tension eased at once upon seeing a sign for Whitney Portal Road, and then vanished almost completely when he arrived suddenly at the pay station for the campground. He kept his headlights shining there, as the sun was now completely gone. The registration form, printed on a small envelope, demanded a camping permit number, which William did not have. As he pondered the ramifications of this, a college aged girl appeared from the shadows and shared in his headlights. "Do you know how this works?" she asked.

William was startled at first, but then felt a quick kinship with the girl, for she was as confused as he. "I was trying to figure it out, myself," he said, "Do we need a camping permit to stay here?"

The girl shrugged. "I don't know but *we* don't have one."

"Me either," he replied.

She consoled. "Well, the worst that can happen is that someone asks you to leave."

"I think the worst that can happen is probably a bear attack." William laughed nervously at his own statement. "Did you see those signs coming in?"

The girl smiled but William could tell it was forced. "Well, we are already parked in a space and we saw they have bear lockers here."

William did not know what a bear locker was. He smiled falsely, himself, and stated, "That's good." Without another word between them, he completed the registration form (leaving the permit number blank), placed twelve dollars in the envelope, and slid it through the pay slot. He then returned to his car and pulled on to the grounds, leaving the girl in the dark.

The place was relatively empty. He drove to the back, passing two quiet RV's before pulling into a site. Illuminating the area again with his headlights, he quickly pitched his tent and tossed his sleeping bag, pillow and flashlight inside. Also present were a picnic table, a fire pit with a grill attachment, and a large metal cabinet, which he realized was the bear locker. After turning off his headlights, and after his eyes adjusted, these things were still visible under the light of the moon and stars. He could also hear water flowing somewhere nearby. He wanted to brush his teeth.

Toothbrush and toothpaste in hand, William trudged back up the hill, across the grounds, to the bathroom beside the pay station. When he opened the door, he found an incredibly modest design, with no sink and not even a mirror. There was only a high, plastic cylinder, with an open top that led to an assortment of underground waste. He placed his dental supplies in his pocket and approached this toilet to urinate. When the door swung closed behind him, however, the small window there did not provide enough light to instill confidence in the aim of his penis and its pending liquid flow. He zipped up his pants and elected to try again *behind* the bathroom, this time successfully.

As he stood there, self in hand, he looked at the moon and thought about starting a fire. He had not the foresight to have purchased or collected wood for this purpose, but recalled seeing plenty of small pieces strewn about on his walk up to the bathroom. Shaking the last drips of urine out of his head, he concluded that a small fire would be better than no fire. He headed back to his camp, collecting each ornate piece of wood that he saw until both fists were full, with branches protruding all through his fingers. The take was a total of six pieces, an average of one foot in length each. He dropped them inside the fire pit. It occurred to him that these pieces may have been intentionally and decoratively placed within the campground, but in his mind, it was now too late.

He picked one of them up and held it in his left hand, out from himself. With his lighter in the right, he married it to flame. The wood burned momentarily, but the fire, itself, quickly retreated to a smolder. He tossed the segment back with the others in the pit and walked to the passenger side of his car. He opened the door and pushed aside some of the trash - mostly plastic bottles - that blanketed his floorboard. Reaching under the seat, he captured his target: an old, collapsed cereal box.

It had been there since he and Savannah drove up to Vancouver two years ago, in what would later reveal itself to have been the beginning of the end. She ate the sugary cereal dry with her fingers, entirely by herself before discarding the empty box to the floor and gradually, accidentally kicking it under the seat until it was out of sight and presumably out of mind; William never forgot it was there. Tonight, this final evidence of her would be gone forever, and its destiny revealed. Tonight, he would rid himself of the stowaway juju that was hexing him from just a foot away every time he drove his car. Tonight, he would have his fire. "I should get high first," thought William.

He was not finished smoking a joint before he began stuffing the wood pieces, along with tufts of toilet paper, into the box. The awkward package bulged and tore in places, with branches hanging out both sides, but ultimately it was of solid construction. He placed it in the fire pit and used his lighter to set it aflame with relative ease. It burned brightly for a time, emanating a distinct and musky smell. Once the box and tissue had quickly burned away, though, only a pile of glowing, hot sticks remained. The fire was a failure, but at least Savannah's final curse was reduced to ash. All in all, he felt good about it.

He took a heavy drag from his joint (which had outlived the fire), and exhaled the smoke against the stars. To his left, he believed himself to be gazing upon a large mountain with lit homes all up its slope. It was not until his eyes focused on all the other space above him that he realized these were not homes on an earth formation, but actually the constellation of Scorpio against a sky of varying opacities. From this new focus, he could see a stronger definition in the heavens, penetrating deeper and deeper into the stars. A few stragglers darted across the sky, sporadically, though most seemed gathered in clusters, and others confined by clouds. It was vast, if not endless. William soon felt a strong sensation that it was the stars that were actually watching him. Feeling a bit paranoid by these esoteric imaginings, he broke from their majesty and returned to the fire pit. He laid the end of his joint atop the glowing embers.

It had been a long and eventful day for William and now he was ready to lie on his sleeping bag and read Michel Houellebecq by lantern before turning in for the night. This desire was postponed, however, by the continued glow of the wood. He could not simply trust that it would take care of itself. This was California during a drought, after all. Leaving fire unattended, no matter how low the heat, was not a safe action. William decided to read at the table to give the burning more time to subside. He retrieved his lantern and book from the tent and planted himself on the metal bench. Spreading open the pages, he picked up where he left off.

William could not really pin Houellebecq down by his writing. Where was it going? What was he saying, exactly? William really liked the guy's style – overtly sexual and often incredibly dismal, but tender and forlorn in so many ways. Houellebecq seemed delighted to expose the new age movement as fraudulent, and also carried a defined lack of empathy for the human condition. This brash perspective seemed to be coming from the right, but was this the writer or the character? Was it even the intention? The subtext felt agreeable to William, which caused him to wonder about his own place on the sociopolitical spectrum. He had always thought himself to be rather liberal, but what if this was a misinterpretation all along? He felt that he was largely in agreement with Houellebecq's observations – whatever those were. *Hey, is that fire extinguished yet?*

William collapsed the book and stepped over to the pit. The wood was still glowing, with no finality in sight. He needed to extinguish it somehow and get to sleep. He considered the inside of his vehicle. He had no central water source there, as he elected to purchase bottled drinks at each stop along the way of his southbound journey. He still had all of those bottles lying on his floorboard, which could have theoretically transported water to the fire, except there were no sinks from which to fill them up. He then remembered that he had not yet finished his current drink, a soda, which was still sitting half full on his console. He opened the door to his car, pulled the warm can out of the holder and sat it on the roof. After smacking on his dome light, he lowered himself to the floorboard and rummaged through the bottles there. He gathered the few that still contained final sips of water and sports drinks. Arms full with five bottles of this type, and the can of soda in his hand, he closed the door with his hip and turned back to the fire pit.

He lined the bottles up haphazardly beside the pit and removed each lid. He felt it was necessary to have them all ready to go so that the flow was constant and abundant enough to overtake the heat. He poured the soda from the can first, since it was holding the most liquid. It had no problem blackening the branches, though there was still some glow outside the drenched area. William quickly picked up the remaining bottles, one in each hand, and ejected their small pools into the remaining smolder. Though it was close, the last bit was ceased with the final bottle, a cherry flavored sports drink.

He felt a very sudden and euphoric relief within himself. He had been hung up on Savannah, a silly ex-lover, this whole time, but why? Here a real world problem presented itself and he persevered using random trash and his wits. Compared to that self-gratifying moment at hand, Savannah had become insignificant. Well, not so insignificant that William could not keep himself from noting her insignificance, but it felt like a large step to him, either way. He could sleep contently tonight.

He gathered the bottles and their lids and tossed them back on to the floorboard of his car, his book on the seat. "My car can serve the same purpose as the bear locker, right?" he thought to himself. "Yes. Of course." He shut the door, grabbed his lantern from the table, and entered his tent.

William had been asleep less than an hour before he woke with a horrifying realization: He dowsed a fire with soda in an active bear area. Even if the small pours of water had somehow rinsed it away, he still ended with a syrupy sweet sports drink. This was no different from leaving food out, and though this mistake demanded immediate remedy, he remained paralyzed in fear for at least five minutes. Utterly still and silent, he listened for the Ursidaen intruder that his terror could not prevent him from expecting. Once he was able to convince himself that the camp was empty, he slowly unzipped the tent flap.

He poked only his head out first, trying to focus through the dark. Again, he waited for a sense of security in the moment before moving to his next action, illuminating his lantern. With the camp visible and no visitors in sight, he moved to the fire pit to assess the situation. Lowering his light to the bottom, he could not see or smell the sugary drinks. Could a bear, though?

He picked up a palm full of sand and dropped it on to the burned area. He repeated this action several more times, intermittently checking the area with the lantern. He wondered how far under the ground a bear could smell. A simple dusting did not seem to be an adequate solution. William could not take a chance on something of this sort. He graduated to clenching handfuls of the sand, two at a time, and throwing them into the pit. Sense of security achieved, he smacked the dust off his palms and crawled back into his tent.

He fell asleep with relative ease, but it only lasted around a half hour before he awoke to a shuffling outside. An intense terror pinned him to the ground again. This time, there was definitely something there. It sounded perhaps too small to be a bear, but even a coyote would not have been a welcome visitor. William had no plan to find out. He thought he heard a sniffing nose and a scratching of the ground, certainly movement. Within a few long minutes, the sounds all faded to the outside of the camp and then silence. William considered exiting the tent and spending the rest of the night in his vehicle. He waited to regain his sense of security so that he could make his next move, but fell asleep before it arrived.

Active Bear Area

II

William still felt stoned when he woke to the daylight, relieved to be alive. He stepped out of the tent and stretched amid the cloud-capped mountains that surrounded him. He felt it was this view that would define his memory of the journey. His bear fearing shenanigans, proven to have been of no determinable consequence, would be another amusing story from the road, if he could tell it the right way. This was his life. This was his moment. Then he remembered that he had forgotten to think about Savannah. His morale ticked down slightly, but only due to frustration for allowing himself to insert her back into his psyche. He pissed in a nearby stream, rolled three joints, packed up his camping gear, and set his course for Death Valley.

He drove an hour to Panamint Springs and stopped there to fill his gas tank. Fuel was over five dollars per gallon. This was a privilege of location, considering that most people entering there have no concept of where the next service station exists. Running out of gas in Death Valley was the specific fear that allowed for such audacious prices and, hence kept the money flowing. The drinks and snacks were also slightly more costly than what he was accustomed to, despite no greater variety than in any store of that type in his hometown. He settled on a bottle of water and a strip of local beef jerky. The girl behind the counter spoke in a heavy accent. She was not American, but perhaps something European - maybe a Russian.

William drove northeast on 190, toward Stovepipe Wells. The road and the sky were both wide open. He turned the radio on to static. After pressing the automatic scan button on his stereo, the channels cycled endlessly, never settling on a frequency. This, in turn, lead to the insertion of a compact disc: Neil Young's *Harvest* – an apt fit to the tone being emitted by the rocks all around. William settled into his seat and lit up a joint. Mountains passed by. The music carried the moment.

He came upon an uninhabited overlook with a small restroom, which he entered, again with his toothbrush and toothpaste, in hopes of finding a sink inside. This time, he was in luck. The joint burned out as he first urinated down into a circular, raised hole, not unlike the toilet at the campground. He put his penis away and removed the burnt roach from his mouth, next debating where he should leave it. A coffee cup, with a small opening in the lid, sat on the top of refuse in the garbage can. If he dropped the remains through the hole, it would be concealed by the cup, though its final resting place would be ultimately synthetic, and within a machine-made convention; a Styrofoam coffin. Suddenly it did not feel like a correct tomb for this mystical herb, which had brought him such meditative mental balance. It deserved better. He instead chose the organic option, dropping the remains of the joint into the toilet.

As he brushed his teeth, unease began to rise as he second-guessed the toilet grave, as well. He remembered when he was five and his beta fish, Fishy Jo, had died. Fishy Jo's fate was also the toilet, by the hands of William's mother. Then too, it seemed like the simpler, more fitting action, only until the deed was complete. Immediate regret followed and five year old William walked into his bedroom and cried alone with his thoughts. He was not so sad that Fishy Jo was dead, but that he had done a disservice to the body and final memories of him. Fishy Jo, he realized, should have been dropped into a river or a lake. Even a large puddle would have been more respectful than a porcelain chute into human fecal matter. Twenty-five years later, eight hundred miles from home, it still made him weep.

He exited the bathroom, taken back to find a man waiting on the other side of the door. The moment he saw the man's weathered face, partially hidden behind mirrored sunglasses, William looked away and mumbled, "Excuse me," as if he had caused some inconvenience. He did not walk to the overlook, but directly back to his car. "There will be plenty more," he thought. His chief concern was that the man had smelled marijuana smoke, and secondly that the man had noticed he was crying.

He continued down the road, the rocky desert sprawling out before him. A black car with tinted windows came quickly up behind him, but slowed to allow for distance between them. William grew concerned by their refusal to pass, even when the road allowed for it. A bit paranoid, he wondered if the car was holding the man from the bathroom. His mirrored glasses had made him look like a cop. Was this about the marijuana?

William pulled into another overlook. The black car followed. He felt conflicted as to how he should handle it - pull over and act natural or keep driving out the other side and on down the road. He decided that immediately exiting would appear suspicious, but had already driven past all the parking spaces. He nervously tapped his breaks as the black car pulled in between the designated lines. Impulsively, William steered toward a third option – a dirt road that continued up a large hill that rose up beyond the overlook.

It was not but thirty yards or so before the ground leveled out and he stopped the car. He stepped out, walked a few feet, put his hands on his hips and looked out at the mountains on the other side of a gap. The man and woman from the black car were pressed up against a metal rail, imbibing the designated scene down below him. Theirs was the greater of the two views, as they were able to see much further down into the valley. William realized this from where he stood and so wondered if they knew it to be true as well. He felt stupid.

He held his awkward stance as if he was looking at something *really* interesting. He planned to do so until they returned to their car and drove away. Then suddenly, and from out of no determinable point, a military fighter jet screamed through the valley. It turned up on its side as it navigated space that was precisely eye level with where William had found himself standing – truly the best vantage point for this rare occurrence. Then, as quickly as it had arrived, it was gone, rising back up into the sky. William walked back to his car casually but immediately, as if he has just seen exactly what he had come there for.

He sat inside and watched the man and woman take pictures of one another before finally returning to their own car and driving away. He felt a sense of lightness and inner peace now, as thought he had witnessed a divine moment there with the jet. When he placed the car in reverse to turn it around, he knew it was the wrong decision, and so stopped. The path to glory, he felt, was not backwards. He picked up his beef jerky and bottle of water from the passenger seat and exited the car once more. Further up the hill, on foot he continued, heading forward now, to whatever waited among those ancient boulders.

William stepped with only the ground in mind. He knew this was what he had come there to do – to be present. Savannah was not there anymore. She was finally, completely, outside his head. Here instead, he knew rock and the casual tearing of his muscles with every step. Here too was sky and life, both plant and animal. Here at last was the infinite. Here was pure truth and ultimate meditation. Here was oblivion by the meter. Here was actual, undeniable bliss.

William spotted a coyote, watching him from behind some brush. Yesterday, this would have made him turn around. Today, under the bright sun, he felt bold enough to coax the animal closer, using sounds like those one might use to vie for the attention of a cat. Realizing she had been recognized, the coyote scrambled a few feet away before returning her gaze to William. He climbed upon some large rocks and patted the surface, attempting again to call the coyote closer. She ducked her head cautiously and stepped forward. "Hello there!" spoke William, "What's your name?"

The coyote did not reply.

William climbed higher still, from one rock to another until he was approximately fifteen feet off the ground. He began to howl loudly, causing the coyote to retreat slightly. This made him laugh. He removed the cap from his bottle of water and held it into the air, "To you!" he proclaimed, "My coyote friend!" He then tipped his head backward and opened his mouth. From as far as his arm could reach, he poured the water down into his throat from above. This pour was, however, miscalculated as the liquid accidentally dumped almost directly into his windpipe. With a single shallow cough, he lost his footing on the rock and spun off the top. On the way down, his head clipped the side of a smaller, neighboring formation, knocking him out immediately. When he hit the ground on his back, the water pushed deeper into his lungs. As he lay unconscious, his breathing began to slow. The water he had aspirated depleted his oxygen intake within a few minutes. Alone in the heat, William had asphyxiated to death – drowned in

the desert. The coyote approached him with relative
confidence now.

III

The coyote licked William's hand and sniffed his crotch before scampering back into the desert. It was a skunk that next appeared, some hours later, near sundown. He, too, sniffed around the body curiously, as it lay only a dozen or so meters from his den. He noticed a strong and gamy smell emanating from Williams's hip pocket. The skunk dug frantically against his jeans, attempting to route out the source – the beef jerky. His claws, though very well suited for dirt, were no match for denim. After a couple of hours, he gave up his fight and continued into the night to search for an easier meal.

A kit fox had been watching the skunk's efforts from behind a nearby brush pile. He wanted a piece of the action, but knew better than to disturb a skunk. He could smell the scent of the last skunk he bothered; still deeply embedded in the fur on his hindquarter - and it had been many moons since that encounter. He waited patiently for the skunk to give up and move on before approaching the body, himself. Immediately he went to the beef jerky. Like the skunk, he scratched at the target area, paw over paw. Like the skunk, he had no luck at penetrating the pocket. He smelled it intensely for a bit, and then paced around the body, stealing quick sniffs here and there. None of it was as pleasing to his olfactory sense as was that pocket of jerky. Since he could not reach it, he acted upon the next best idea that he had and instead urinated on it. After kicking some dirt with his hind legs, he, too, moved out into the night, in search of simpler food options. Kangaroo mice were much less trouble for him to acquire.

Several more hours passed and the sky had become a lighter shade of blue, obscuring most of the stars. A glossy snake, tired from hunting lizards all night, slithered into William's pants leg. She was indifferent to the body, and simply looking for a place that would be shaded against the pending sun. The softness of the fabric on one side, the flesh on the other, and her ability to stretch fully out were of particular comfort to her. She fell quickly into slumber.

The sun was fully visible when the skunk returned home. Though he was exhausted from the previous night's adventures, he decided to revisit the body before settling down to sleep. As before, and undeterred by the urine splatter of the kit fox, he dug rapidly at William's pocket, still unable to reach the jerky. The glossy snake was awakened by the scratching and so slithered ahead, emerging from the opposite pants leg than the one she had initially entered. She slid her long body atop William's hip, opposite the jerky, and watched the skunk in sheer curiosity. It was not until he paused his scratching that he noticed her and, acting hastily but with great prejudice toward snakes, whether venomous or not, sprayed his scent in her direction, misting William's crotch. Startled by this sudden aggression, she immediately defecated and urinated at once, all over his jeans. The skunk fled to his den and the snake to as far out in the desert as she could carry herself.

The second day of intense sun eventually lead to sparse blistering on William's skin. As he slowly cooked in the heat, three vultures circled overhead, beckoned by the smell. They maintained their formation for nearly a half hour before one of them dove down to inspect the baking corpse. He landed on William's chest, first facing his legs. When he encountered the mix of skunk spray and snake waste, he winced and pivoted around. He stared at William's solemn, red face for a few minutes before making a quick peck at his eye. The others watched from above as he pecked again, this time penetrating the eyelid with his beak and nicking the sclera inside. A series of similar, rapid attempts loosened the eyeball within the socket, little by little, until it was completely free from William's countenance. The vulture raised it toward the sky, gripped within his beak, sinewy streamers dangling. The eye promptly lost its position, dropping to William's chest. The vulture made a few awkward dips to retrieve it once more, snagging William's shirt in the process. Getting a firmer grip around the tissue on the back, he raised it again to the sky and opened his beak, dropping it into his throat. Carcass confirmed, the other two vultures swooped down to join in the feast.

The first to touch down did so near the top of William's head. She attempted to peck at his other eye, much to the consternation of the first vulture, which responded to her intrusion with a guttural hiss. She hopped to her right, closer to the neck, and proceeded to peck his throat as the first vulture began work on the remaining eye. The third vulture, crowded out by the others, had the unfortunate circumstance of landing on William's pungent smelling pelvis, covered in dried snake dung. He flew back up immediately and landed several feet away, rethinking his approach. He stepped cautiously toward the left hand, which was outstretched and open. He pecked a few times at the upright palm before tearing out the skin between the index finger and thumb in one decisive move. After rolling it down his throat, he continued to sear the skin from that point, down toward the wrist, in large chunks.

The massive birds had made incremental progress over the course of a half hour. The first had moved from William's chest to above his head, where she was plucking chunks of dura mater out through his eye socket. This allowed more maneuverable space for the second, which had, by this time, completely exposed the thyroid cartilage in the neck. The third vulture had torn William's forearm skin down to the where the elbow bent, pulling out the veins and devouring them. A fourth and fifth vulture circled above them now, assessing the scene. It was, however, the sudden appearance of the coyote and her mate, which caused all of the birds to abandon the corpse at once.

She had watched this creature fall off a rock and die barely even one moon ago. She had seen plenty of creatures like him in Death Valley and many times they had attempted to coerce her or her kin toward them, usually with an offer of food. She could never once recall a completion of even one of these attempts at bonding. If the creature were too bold in its approach, then the coyote would stand down, but if the coyote were the bold one, then the creature would retreat. Here, though, was a creature with no essence anymore. If it had seemed harmless to her in life, then it must be completely powerless in death. She returned to the body for the sake of sheer scientific curiosity.

Her mate walked immediately to William's pocket of beef jerky. He smelled the urine of the kit fox and casually marked over it with his own. The two coyotes spent nearly twenty minutes sniffing around the body and urinating in a few other choice spots around the legs. Each of them licked the bloody wounds, the female on the hand and the male on the throat. This, however, was short lived, as they soon grew bored and began to, instead, wrestle and chase one other away from the gruesome area.

Aside from the flies that laid eggs in William's eye sockets, his body laid relatively undisturbed until a few hours after sunset. It was a mother bobcat that found it next. After a soft and cautious approach, she closely smelled his outstretched, shredded hand. She then moved to the area south of his arm and sprawled her legs across it, pinning it to the ground. She bowed her head and chewed on an exposed tendon. She remained in this kind of rhythm for a time until her focus was broken by a badger rolling around in a near by brush. Seeing no threat, she licked the meat a few more times, and then her lips, and she stood again. She next smelled the lower part of William's body but like all animals before her, was repulsed by the mix of waste that covered his pants. She slinked up to his throat and smelled the thyroid cartilage, which had been severely mutilated by the vulture. Here, she put her full mouth over the throat and gnawed there until the remains of the cartilage, as well as the larynx it had obscured, were free from the corpse. With the organ in her jowls, she dashed back to her rocky den where it would come to serve as the first meal of meat ever consumed by her litter of twelve hungry kittens.

The final visitor that night was the badger that had been rolling in the brush. As soon as the bobcat departed, he waddled confidently up to the body. Undeterred by the snake waste, skunk spray, and urine, both canine and vulpine, his direct focus was on the beef jerky in William's pocket. Unlike his furry predecessors, the badger was able to tear through the denim with relative ease. He then simply extracted the processed meat and hobbled away.

The vultures returned early the next morning for breakfast. By midday, nearly three-dozen of them were gorging on his flesh. Even his shit covered lower half did not survive the gradual onslaught. When they wrapped up, William was a skeleton in tattered rags.

A park ranger had seen William's car up on the hill two days prior and thought nothing of it as he left work. He arrived home to a delicious meal, intricately prepared by his wife, and took the next day off to play golf. The rookie ranger covered for him, got high in the middle of the shift, and never spent a moment of thought on the car. Upon the senior ranger's return the next evening, he noticed it still parked there, almost forty-eight hours after he had first seen it. He pulled his truck up beside it and followed the obvious path to the corpse.

William's bones were shipped back to his family and subsequently interred in a Catholic cemetery. He may not have appreciated his final remains being sealed in a stainless steel, carefully crafted, fancy trash casket. His soul, however, could rest easy in knowing that his flesh and blood, at least for a time, would be raining down over the desert – in vulture feces.

Alone

I

Inside the house and outside the house, they called for her. "Cleo! Cleo!" Everyone moved about rapidly, checking and rechecking every room. She was not present in any of her regular spots and no one had seen her all morning.

"I think I found her!" yelled Jon Jon, his face pressed against the small space beneath the couch. His siblings, cousin and mother came running into the room.

Victor retrieved a flashlight from a kitchen drawer and ran to the couch. "Move," he demanded of Jon Jon, and took his little brother's spot there. He shined the light into the opening and clearly saw her black fur. "It is her!" he yelled. He called for her. All the children did, attempting to coax her out from under the couch.

Their mother knew why Cleo was not responding. She became reluctant to solve the situation, but she knew the ensuing series of events were going to be inevitable. The kids had to learn some time, after all, and so she ushered the children back and lifted the couch forward from against the wall, letting it fall over on to its front. "Everyone pet Cleo goodbye one more time," she told the children. "It looks like she has passed on."

The children all broke into tears and their mother retrieved a towel from the linen closet. Once all the goodbyes were said, she wrapped the cat up and laid her just inside the garage door, up against the wall.

When her husband returned home from work, she greeted him at the door and stepped outside before he could enter. She whispered. "Go easy on the children, Clarence. Cleo died today."

"Well that was a long time coming," he replied.

"I know, but the kids are taking it hard. It's the first time any of them have ever experienced death."

"I imagine Jon Jon is taking it the hardest."

"He is."

"And the other three?" he asked.

"Coping but sad. Victor wants nothing to do with it – wouldn't even pet her goodbye. We've all been crying though." The husband drew his wife close and kissed her on the top of her head.

Dinner was more quiet than usual. The children's father offered his condolences as soon as he saw them. The memories, burial arrangements and high emotions were mostly talked out before the food made it to the table. Still, there was one question that kept eating away at Jon Jon. "Why was Cleo hiding away from us when she died? Why did she not want to be with us?"

"Honey, that's just what cats do when they die," consoled his mother. "They go off on their own because they don't want to make us feel sad for them. She was thinking of us."

"Well I don't know about that," popped the father.

Their mother looked at him with pure animosity. Her eyes said, "Shut up before you give our children psychological damage." It was too late, though. His voice had reached his children's ears. There was no letting it pass.

Victor spoke up. "Why don't you know about that, dad?"

He fumbled for an answer. "I mean – I'm just saying – I'm not a veterinarian. Your mom probably knows better than I do."

"But what *do* you know?" asked Victor.

His mother then looked at him with the same foreboding gaze that she had given his father, except her head cocked silently toward Jon Jon.

Victor understood immediately. "Oh, I get it," he said, "Cleo was protecting us from feeling sad. She thought that if she could just disappear, then we would go on thinking that she was somewhere out there alive forever. Right?"

Their father received another scathing glance from his wife. He shrugged as slightly as he smiled.

Later that night, after a small burial and service for Cleo, Victor visited his father in his work shed. He was cutting a piece of wood for one reason or another, listening to a baseball game. He handed a pair of safety goggles to his son, turned the radio down slightly, and kept cutting strange angles as they spoke. "What's on your mind, son?"

"I want to know what you meant at dinner," said Victor, pointedly. " – the thing you didn't want Jon Jon to hear about Cleo."

His father could not quite remember the exact context. "Oh I'm just feeling a little blue over her and I didn't want for it to start bothering Jon Jon is all."

"I know, but you said you didn't know about Cleo going off by herself so that we would not be sad. So what do you know then?"

His father stopped cutting and placed his goggles on his forehead. "I don't want to upset you either."

"I just want to know," replied Victor. "I'm the oldest, except for Charles, but he's your nephew. I'm you're son."

His father chuckled a bit at his son's headstrong demeanor. "Well look. Don't tell your brother, your sister *or* Charles, but what I was going to say is that the reason cats go off by themselves is for their own protection. They know they are vulnerable since they are sick so instinct tells them to hide so they don't get eaten. That's all."

Victor sunk a bit. "Oh."

His father immediately felt it was a mistake to have stated this. "But hey all cats are different, you know? Just like people. Maybe they all have different reasons for going off alone. But you know, dogs – they go off alone too. And if I'm not mistaken, *they* are the ones that go off so that you don't feel sad. Yeah they're different from cats."

Victor found it obvious that his father was backpedaling desperately to keep from upsetting his son. He did not feel it was necessary and only replied curtly to his father because he was processing what he had just been told. He was by no means upset or offended. In fact, he achieved a clarity he did not have before. He realized that, cat or dog, for their own instinctual protection or the protection of their master's feelings, there was no downside to going off and dying alone.

II

Ora Lee Williamson passed peacefully in her sleep in November of 1961. The matriarch of the Williamson family, she was beloved by them, and survived by her two daughters, as well as four grandchildren: Victor, Jon Jon, Sylvia and Charles. Hers would be the first funeral for a human being that any of the children had been to, less than one week after Victor's birthday that year.

At the viewing, a parade of family and friends lined up along the east wall of the church. They slowly shuffled along beside the casket, whispering their final goodbyes as the organ player and Miss Violet Jane dueted with some uplifting hymns. The Williamson grandchildren were accompanied to the casket by their father, once the line had tapered off. As with Cleo, Jon Jon had more difficulty with the situation than the other children. He held himself together well for most of the evening, but the moment he saw Granny Williamson's outstretched corpse, his emotional control fell to pieces. He jumped back from the coffin, as though startled, and became quickly engulfed in a mass of tears and snot, accompanied by blubbering shrieks. His father walked Jon Jon back to the lounge where his mother was mourning with other relatives. Victor, Sylvia and Charles remained, looking down on the pale individual that used to be their grandmother.

"You were mean, granny," spoke Sylvia contentiously to the body.

"Be respectful," demanded Charles.

"Whatever," Sylvia scoffed. "At least her hair looks good for a change."

She was right. Granny Williamson's hair did look very well styled and full. This stirred unrest in Victor. He had seen Granny wash her wig many times, using a half inflated balloon in a cooking pot as a makeshift stand to dry it on. The wig on this body was not Granny's wig. This one was newer. It was thicker, with a more modern design. Her makeup was also not an accurate representation of the grandmother he knew. Victor did not know enough about lipsticks, foundation, eye shadow and such to pinpoint quite what it was, but her face was not of its standard adornment. In life, Granny applied her own makeup with her own hands, forming the day-to-day avatar that she reflected to the world. Here though, it was apparent that someone else had taken the liberty of remaking her face while laid out in that vulnerable position. Victor realized that this was no longer his grandmother, but rather a mannequin on display – decorated by the mortuary company that was paid to do so. His grandmother was long gone by that point.

Not one year later, Victor celebrated his sixteenth birthday on the back porch. It was a casual affair, per his request. His mother maintained a steady supply of soda and jambalaya as he and a handful of friends listened to popular music on the radio. They discussed sports and girls, mostly.

Due to its location in a floodplain, the home was raised on stilts. An old oak tree growing in the yard arced its limbs toward it, almost touching the edge of the porch. For years prior, the children had made an activity of climbing the tree, shuffling out on the longest branch and leaping down about five feet to the wooden deck. This summer, however, was the first one in which not one of them performed the motion, or even climbed the tree. Feeling alienated among his brother's older friends, Jon Jon decided it was time to give it a go.

Climbing in the autumn, a first for Jon Jon, was much different than in the summer. The leaves had mostly been shed and the branches were clearly displayed. Stepping sideways, he had no green foliage to chunk into his palms. Instead he slid each barren branch slowly through his hands, removing his grip from one and connecting it to another in careful succession. Without the illusion of density that would have otherwise been provided by the leaves, he grew nervous at the site of the ground below him. Still he continued through the skeletal limbs, steadily, with a firm, sweaty clutch, more anxious than he had ever been to reach the safety of the deck. With only another three or so feet to go before a position squarely above the porch, he elected to make a hasty leap to his goal. He might have cleared the space there, but for the force of his bounce, which cracked the branch, separating it from the rest of the tree. Jon Jon toppled with the limb, falling just short of the deck.

Victor and his friends all stood at once, rushing to lean over the banister. Below them, Jon Jon laid motionless, his head against the concrete block used to secure one of the stilts. Victor first called his brother's name, and then his mother's when there was no response. She emerged through the French doors, unknowing of what had occurred. "Jon Jon fell!" exclaimed Victor. "The branch broke!"

Their mother rushed back into the house to appear again, down below. She blasted out of the downstairs door, over to Jon Jon, gathering his limp body up into her arms. She shook him violently and screamed his name as blood trickled from his ears, his eyes half open, glassy and still.

Jon Jon's wake was a quiet and subdued affair, unnaturally opposite from his capricious, emotional existence. Victor sat against the wall outside the viewing room, immersed as best he could be in a paperback copy of *Stranger in a Strange Land*.

His father sat down beside him, his voice quivering slightly as he spoke. "We have to leave here in an hour," he informed.

"Okay. I'm ready." Victor never looked up from the book.

There was a pause before his father spoke again. "It's your last chance to say goodbye to your brother."

"I already said goodbye."

His father sighed deeply. "Your mother would really appreciate it if you saw him one last time."

"I'm fine," said Victor. "I already saw him one last time."

His father nodded, sniffled, stood and walked away. Victor turned two pages and read a third of the way down before his mother took the place that his father had relinquished, sitting sideways on the soft, polyester velvet couch. "You need to say goodbye to Jon Jon," she demanded.

He remained in his book. "I already did."

"When?" she asked.

"The night he died."

She was flustered by his answer. "Victor Williamson, put that book down now." He complied and she continued her plea. "Your brother will be in the ground *tomorrow*. We have to leave here in no time at all. You will pay your respects this moment, young man."

"I'm paying my respects *every* moment, mama."

"Victor, this is not a choice," she continued. "He is your brother."

Alone

"And that is how I will remember him: as my brother."

She was uncertain how to reply to his curtness. "You get in there right now and you say goodbye." A tear slid down her cheek.

"No."

"Why not?"

"Just let it be, mom."

Her countenance grew wetter and the wrinkles in the corners of her eyes more defined. "How can you say to let it be?" she asked. Her volume increased and her voice began to break. "This is your last chance. That is your brother laying in there."

"You already said that." Victor was also losing his cool, overwhelmed by frustration rather than sadness. "But Jon Jon is *gone*, mama. That ain't him in there."

"What do you mean that ain't him?"

"*It ain't him*," he pushed back. "He left on my birthday."

"Victor Matthew Williamson, you go in there and pay your respects to your brother *right now*." Vertigo began to set it.

"No," he demanded.

"Why not? *He is your brother.*" Her tears were now prominent.

"I know my brother," he scorned. "That is *not* my brother."

"How can you say that?" His mother's tone and tears were now clearly recognized by the other attendees in the room.

"My brother is gone. He's just gone."

"Do you know what you are doing to me?" she cried. "You are breaking my heart."

"I'm sorry mama. It's my choice."

"Damn you," she said softly, before wailing again, *"Damn you!"* She curled her fist up into a ball and raised it as though she were about to strike him.

Her brother, Victor's Uncle Marvin, appeared at her back and laid his hands on her shoulders. "Easy. Easy," he said. "Victor, why you doing this to your mama?" he asked.

"Why is she doing this to *me?*" Victor replied.

Her words were replaced by loud, incoherent howls. She stood and wrapped her arms around her brother. Victor removed himself immediately, exiting the funeral home and relocating to beneath a single halogen bulb illuminating the back door of the building. He sat down cross-legged; his back against the brick, and opened his book once more.

Victor's mother never fully forgave him for his reluctance to view Jon Jon's body. Their relationship remained strained over the next passing year. When his birthday came back around again, neither of them acknowledged it, shadowed instead by the anniversary of Jon Jon's death. He didn't mind. He walked to school that Friday like he would have on any other day. In the morning, before class began, the other students sang "Happy Birthday" to him at the behest of his homeroom teacher. This made him feel awkward, with no idea of how to hold his face through the excruciating attention he was being paid. He was relieved to finally begin their lesson; relieved to feel the normalcy return.

At lunch, he sat in the cafeteria with the same friends he had sat with for the past three years. "So what are you gonna do for your birthday?" asked Martin Lasternick.

Victor shrugged. "I might walk down to the park maybe, if you guys wanna play some ball."

"It's your birthday," reminded Martin, "so whatever you wanna do, I'll be there."

Robert Mayall piped in, "But we play ball at the park all the time. Don't you wanna do something special?"

"We can get ice cream at Jimmy's, I guess," added Victor.

"Jimmy's is closed for the winter," reminded Martin.

"Oh yeah. That's right. I don't know then."

After lunch, the students returned to their classroom, but the teacher was not present there. The quiet whispers that typically accompanied that time of day slowly crescendoed into a boisterous sea of teenage dialogues.

At last, their teacher appeared, her skin unusually pale and her mouth turned down. "Class, come to order," she said. The room fell silent and she continued. "I'm afraid that I have some very troublesome news." Her eyes teared up. "President Kennedy has been shot – in Dallas."

A small, collective gasp swept the room. That was it for Victor. In that moment, he knew what would come next for him on his birthday. He would not go to the park, or Jimmy's. He would not play ball or eat ice cream. He would never see his friends again, in fact. After an early dismissal from school, he would walk in the opposite direction from his home. He would keep his pace as long as he could, extending his thumb to passing cars and taking any ride that would allow him to travel as far west as possible.

Alone

III

Victor hitchhiked to the middle of Texas where he hopped a train across the desert. The charity of strangers kept him fed for a week as he slept on beaches and benches in southern California before realizing he needed some kind of steadier income to continue on. And so out of sheer necessity, coupled with a refusal to return home, he entered into a recruiting station in San Diego and, lying about his age, enlisted in the United States Army.

"It's a fantastic time to sign up," his recruiter ensured him.

"I know we are doing a lot of things in Vietnam," nudged Victor, half expecting to know immediately if he might be deployed there.

"Oh that old thing?" asked the recruiter with a smile. "Don't worry about that. We figure that should all be over by Christmas. We're actually in the process of bringing one thousand of our boys home right now. No, I wouldn't worry about that at all."

Keeping focused and to himself, Victor excelled over the course of two months in basic training. He went on to Advanced Individual training at the Defense Information School at Fort Benjamin Harrison, just outside of Indianapolis. He immersed himself in six months of courses there, dedicated primarily to photojournalism and print media. In September of 1964, he was placed in a unit and shipped out to South Vietnam. He had heard of many American casualties in the region by the end of the year, but never saw much action himself until the following February in Qui Nhơn where he photographed an exploded hotel. Twenty-three Americans were killed in the blast, but the experience only made Victor more interested in his work.

He completed that tour in 1966 and entered directly into another straight after. Two more years in Vietnam afforded him a slew of interesting subjects to photograph, Buddhist protestors and the surreal devastation at Bến Tre being his personal favorites. The second tour led to a third - this one supposing to be four years in length.

Victor had grown comfortable in the army, and was well respected by his commanding officers, as well as most of his peers. This affability, coupled with his skills as a photojournalist, afforded him a quiet leeway that was well earned, but not commonly granted to the other soldiers. Though some grew envious of his freedoms in the field, most of his compatriots shrugged it off and, in fact, were positively drawn to him for his apparent independence. When present, he never quite gave enough of himself to wear out his welcome.

Not quite halfway through that third tour, Victor found a natural friend in a Philippine soldier named Dakila. They met on a joint reconnaissance mission into Cambodian territory. Neither of them was certain exactly what they were doing there, each only obeying orders. Victor followed Dakila around with his camera, photographing him as he made jokes and exaggerated his heroism through a series of fruitless, one-man raids on abandoned buildings; teeming with slapstick. It was this mutual lightness that drew the men together and, as the war grew sloppier and more discombobulated, they found themselves often in close quarters. Their inside jokes and giggling irreverence with one another kept their respective units dumbfounded, though at an odd and fragile ease when in their presence. Their peers subconsciously believed that the men's relaxed relationship was born of special knowledge that they, themselves, simply were not privy to. They trusted this joyfulness as a measure of danger's distance, though in reality, Victor and Dakila were simply indifferent to the prospect of peril. Either way, the effect on their fellow soldiers was positively construed and their commanding officers considered their interactions to be a boon for morale. And so they were ultimately left to their shared humor, if not encouraged.

When the tour concluded, Victor signed up for yet another, but he would not return to Vietnam. Given his acquired familiarity with the Filipino language and his apparent proclivity for their people, he was given a unique assignment to the Philippine province of Davao del Sur where he was to assist in Ferdinand Marcos's call for martial law. It was here in which he witnessed a share of mass violence that had tended to largely forego his presence in Vietnam. Brutal homicides became near weekly commonplace in the streets and he knew that, politically, he was serving the side of the oppressors. Still, a job was a job, and when considering the long view, he was nothing more than just another random male, walking around with a firearm. He kept his head low and stayed as uninvolved as he could, the majority of his workday spent seated safely at a desk in the American base.

Dakila, having been discharged from the Philippine Army, joined the protest movement and lived with his family in the neighboring Davao Oriental province. Victor would visit him there on his days off, and became well acquainted with his sisters and parents. Though they found Victor's employer to be a dark and merciless force, they saw none of those attributes in him personally, and so were pleased to extend their hospitality as though he were one of their own. Above all, they were thankful for the friendship he provided to their son, as Dakila had also grown up as something of a loner, himself. They would become engrossed in the two men's stories of Vietnam, as they all sat around a large table on the patio, eating home cooked meals of adobo and utan.

On a rare extended break from duty, Victor used his vacation to fly north to Cavite with Dakila and his eldest sister, Malaya. Cavite was Dakila and Malaya's hometown, and much of their family still resided there. They rented a car and drove to the rural homestead they would occupy for a week; put up by their aunt and five cousins. A cassette copy of Leonard Cohen's *New Skin for the Old Ceremony* set the tone of their drive. It was as new to Victor as any of his surroundings, but "Field Commander Cohen" welled rare, deep and affecting emotion inside of himself. The car remained silent but for its engine and the song, and for those few, sacred minutes, it was almost too much for him to bear. His internal workings had become only slightly more normalized as they reached the gate to the property, "Who By Fire" guiding them in.

As they made their way down the long dirt road to their aunt's home, they passed several small huts, constructed along the sparse tree line. "Are these guest houses?" asked Victor.

Dakila and Malaya looked at one another and traded smiles. "Kind of," spoke Dakila. "They belong to our ancestors."

From her position in the passenger seat, Malaya turned to Victor in the back. "Our *dead* ancestors," she added.

Dakila chuckled. "We don't want to sleep in those. I promise."

Victor accepted this without question. "Okay," he agreed simply.

"Our ancestors died in those little rooms," explained Malaya anyway. "And they are resting forever in those trees."

"Are you speaking poetically?" inquired Victor.

"No, sir. It is our custom on this land – a custom for several families in Cavite."

"I don't understand," said Victor. "How are they up in the trees?"

"Not *up* in the trees," corrected Dakila. "*Inside* the trees."

Malaya continued the explanation before Victor could ask another question. "When one of our ancestors was close to death, they would choose a tree they felt a connection to. The rest of the family would build one of those huts beside it and that is where they would live their final days. And when they passed away, we would hollow the tree and stand them inside."

Victor was intrigued. "So there are people actually entombed in these trees?"

"They are probably skeletons by now," laughed Dakila.

"It's not as common as it used to be," answered Malaya, "but yes."

In early autumn, Victor spent one lunch break strolling along San Pedro Street by the cathedral. As he admired the architecture he had seen so many times before, a group of protesters approached from further down the street. Nearly fifty strong, they wore colorful costumes and held banners proclaiming such sentiments as "*Laban ng Masa*" and "*Marcos Walang Bayani.*" They stopped their march at the capital, raised their signs and their fists and chanted something in Filipino that Victor could not quite understand. He stepped off the curb, apprehensive about quelling their demonstration, though he knew it would be for their own safety.

One of the protesters, wearing a gaudy, bright yellow chicken costume, turned around and caught a glimpse of Victor timidly advancing. He immediately broke from the group to meet the American soldier in the street. As soon as Victor noticed this change in direction, he placed his hand on his gun and prepared for conflict. The protester froze mid-step, grabbed his mask by its beak and lifted it to reveal his sweaty face. It was Dakila. Relieved, Victor continued the path to greet his friend.

Each man took only a few steps more before a flurry of skyward gunshots erupted from somewhere closer to the capital building. The demonstrators parted as two men in police uniforms walked boldly through the crowd, waving their clubs manically and smashing them into the faces of any dissident within their proximity. One of the officers continued around the perimeter of the group, bludgeoning them randomly. The other came for Dakila, who turned and raised his arms, taking the strike to his wrist.

"It's okay!" Victor called. "This man is with me."

The officer lowered his club and stared deeply, angrily into Victor's eyes. "America has no power here," he proclaimed. He then removed his pistol again from his holster and placed it against Dakila's temple.

Victor begged the officer to lower his weapon, but this was of no consequence. Without breaking his gaze, he pulled the trigger and Dakila collapsed, his yellow feathers stained crimson.

Alone

IV

Dakila's wake lasted for three days and Victor stayed with his family through this period, per Malaya's request. Many loved ones visited in that time, laying hands on the body and leaving small gifts around the casket. Victor tried to stay engaged if not useful, assisting with the preparation of food, sharing stories from the war and playing cards with Dakila's uncles. He never approached the body, of course, and if anyone noticed his reluctance, they did not mention it to him.

Unlike his ancestors in Cavite, Dakila was given a solemn burial in the grounds of a Catholic cemetery in Davao Oriental. Before being lowered into the ground, his casket was again opened and a rosary strung around his hands. His friends and family crowded together for one final viewing, again touching the corpse and whispering prayers into Dakila's functionless ears. Victor stood to appear involved, but remained outside the group. Malaya threw her arms around him and wetted his shoulder with tears and makeup.

Traumatized by his friend's death, Victor was put on indefinite leave and underwent several weeks of therapy with an army psychiatrist. This led to an honorable discharge from his service, though he remained for a time in the Philippines. He took out a one-year lease on a small apartment, a short drive from Dakila's family home. In this time, he grew increasingly close to Malaya and they were soon married in the San Pedro Cathedral, just yards from where her brother was murdered. When his lease was nearly expired and he was posed with the prospect of renewal, it was Malaya who expressed a desire to leave her country of birth and all the sadness that engulfed her there. She wanted to see Victor's home, though he could not quite recall where that was. They decided to relocate back to the United States where they purchased a few acres of land outside Santa Barbara and built a house.

After obtaining the required certifications, Victor began employment with the park service, as a ranger for the Los Padres National Forest. In this time, Malaya worked as a manicurist, performing jobs for cash until her American citizenship became official. With a new social security number, she migrated into the paralegal field and times were very good for them. With two incomes on top of the money Victor had saved from the military, they paid their home off quickly - but not without Malaya twice taking leave to give birth to two children in a three year period. Their eldest was a girl who they named Sarah, and the second child was a boy. They named him Dakila, naturally.

As the family aged, Victor's roots remained a mystery to his wife and children. Many times they asked about his parents and siblings. He freely shared the stories he knew, of cousin Charles being adopted in to their home, of Sylvia's gruff ability to dominate her brothers and, of course, of Jon Jon's death. Beyond these things, however, he had no family stories to divulge past his seventeenth birthday. His wife would liked to have met her in-laws, and their children remained forever curious about their grandparents, but as far as Victor was concerned, that chapter was forever closed. To him, the expiration of time and place were as finite as the life of his brother, never to be known in any other context.

Victor found great peace in his job with the park service and remained happily employed there well into his mid-sixties. Even then, retirement was not preferable to him, but his mind had seemed to be declining beyond what was acceptable for him to adequately perform the work. Species names of trees that he encountered daily for decades were beginning to slip away. This was also true for water and land formations and the names of his coworkers as well. When he began to find himself repeatedly lost on the same roads that he traveled daily for years, he knew the time had come to relinquish his position.

At home, too, his ability to communicate had become fleeting. His children had children of their own, but he eventually struggled to keep their correct names in tact. He tried to share stories with them; stories he believed he could withdraw easily from his memory banks. When actually spoken, however, only a mosaic of garbled concepts emerged. A dead president, tree people, a burning hotel and bloody feathers – why could he not put these things together in a way that made sense to others? Eventually, the rooms in his home, as well as the people in them, became foreign to him. Sylvia may have tracked him down and reunited with him in their old age, but unable to differentiate between her, his wife and his daughter, he could never be certain.

As the world around him collapsed, he was well taken care of by familiar strangers. This slight acquaintanceship, too, dissolved until one morning he found himself laid out across a bed in a sterile white room, draped in an awkward gown. A variety of machines clicked and hummed softly around him. Thin, plastic tubes draped the rails of his bed, attached at one end to the machines, and the other to his body. Fixated in place by surgical tape, they carried strange fluids into his nose and the back of his hand. Other fluids were carried out of his body, into grotesque transparent sacks that he wore like a belt.

For a time, friendly but impersonal orderlies came and left, stopping to place small electronic devices temporarily in his mouth or around his arm and index finger. Sometimes they would dispose of the fluid that had collected in his belt bags. On one such day, amid this flurry of intrusion, a gallery of vaguely recognizable faces displayed themselves around his bed. He felt a tinge of nostalgia and could almost remember his connection to these people. One, an elderly female, remained longer than the others. She whispered a song to him; some military hymn about a field commander wounded in duty, and she wept as she repeatedly referred to him as "my love" at the end. She said nothing beyond that, only kissing his forehead and exiting the room. Minutes, or possibly hours later, an orderly turned out the light.

Deeper into the darkness, Victor sunk. In some meditative waking dream state, his life returned to him in large chunks. His remembered his parents and Jon Jon, Sylvia and Charles. The elementary school came back to him; and the ice cream shop and the park – even Martin Lasternick. He saw some of the men from his unit and his commanding officer. There also was Dakila and his family; and Malaya – sweet, beautiful Malaya, still young and vibrant. Their home was lucid to him, filled with their children and grandchildren. Yes, these had been his visitors, he was certain. He could see them as though they were still beside his bed. And then he could see them as though they were beside his casket, then kneeling at his grave, mourning his buried vessel.

Victor rejected this possibility and sat up quickly in his bed. He could not allow this cloud of death to hang over his loved ones after his ascension. He refused to leave his empty body behind for his family to deal with. It could not linger as a relic of his life. When he was gone, he needed to be gone absolutely.

He was weak, but his intuition had become suddenly pointed, and with no second thought, he ripped the tubes from his nose and hand. He rolled his body over his bed rail and buckled to the floor. Grasping some unseen piece of furniture, he pulled himself up atop his bare, wobbly legs. He stepped backwards and then forward to calibrate his bearings, then pushed through the darkness to the exit. As though moved by some unseen, intelligent force, his hand descended directly over the handle. He pushed down and pulled back, opening the door just enough to see the dim corridor outside. To the left, some distance away was the nurses' station where the night crew was immersed in their own conversation, none the wiser to his pending escape. And to the right, just yards away, were the elevators. With a newfound grace, he slid through the passage and pressed a button on the wall. Immediately one of the steel slabs slid open and he stepped inside. He pressed another button on the panel there, the lowest on the left, seemingly at random. The box dropped down several floors and released him into a quiet parking garage.

There was no definitive direction to be taken from that point. Victor merely ran to an opening in the concrete and, once his bare feet pressed down on the sidewalk outside the structure, he followed it with little haste. He sprinted only one block before ducking on to a side street to catch his breath. From there, he moved determinedly, at his own pace, in the direction that felt correct to him. The sky was dark and the presence of other people was infrequent. The sparse people he did pass paid him no mind, too enveloped in their own concerns to attempt dealing with what appeared to be a lunatic roaming the streets at that hour. And so he pushed on until he reached the Mission Canyon area where he found abundant cover beneath the trees. He continued just off the road, cutting across private properties and eventually finding himself mingling with route 192, eastbound. At last he came upon the Los Padres foothills and, though he was fatigued, and his feet badly abused, his faint recognition of the area kept him in motion as he ascended in the direction of Cold Spring Trail.

As the sun broke the sky, Victor stumbled off the path and slogged through thick foliage that bloodied his legs. His belt of fluid bags was long gone, inadvertently torn away from him and abandoned randomly along his journey. He crumpled his body into the brush and pulled himself further off the trail into uninhabited space, scratching up his arms to match his lower extremities. Small animals scattered as he pressed on beyond them until he could touch the beacon that had subconsciously called him there. Far enough out from where any future hiker may think to explore, obscured by thorny growth and lying on its side, was the remnant of a tree that once stood on that spot. The hollowed timber stretched nearly twelve feet in length and Victor knew with great certainty that it was there for he alone. Exhausted, but content, he crawled inside, closed his eyes, and exited the earth within minutes; his disappearance forever riddled with mystery.

Alone

Diamond Dogs

I

All the doors were wide open. Summer was giving way to autumn and a group of friends were enjoying rare, true leisure together. A light breeze repeatedly lifted and dropped some napkins on the coffee table as the new Sparklehorse record drifted sweetly from the stereo, mixing with the marijuana smoke. There were three on one couch: Bran, his girlfriend Sadie, and Joshua. A second couch positioned perpendicular to this, seated Jacob, Parker and Melanie. Beth sat alone in the recliner, her legs pulled up into her oversized shirt.

It was Beth's family home, rented from her grandmother. She kept a somewhat rotating cast of roommates, but for the time being, Bran and Sadie shared a room there. The other four were present in some capacity or another at varying intervals, sleeping on a couch or sipping beer on the deck or something. They never contributed to the rent, but freely shared their collective array of skills, which ranged from cooking, to car repair, to musical interpretation.

They were all in a rare spot, a few years out of college, but not yet exposed to the desperate ruin of adulthood. Food service was still okay to them as they chased artistic dreams. Still unblemished by the world, their awe within it was tenable. They were still young enough to experience this moment: smoking dope with friends and listening to Sparklehorse with the doors open, void of politics and duty; void of worry or loss.

"Ghost in the Sky" was about halfway through when a new being entered through the front door. She was a dog, some kind of mutt, with boxer and pit bull evident somewhere in her lineage. She entered the living room and, without so much a glance toward anyone else, shuffled directly to Bran. Up on her hind legs, she balanced against his knee and stared into his eyes, her tongue dangling.

"Hey dog!" Bran chimed in a silly, higher register.

She hopped, pushing herself into his leg.

"Hey dog!" he repeated.

She hopped again – then again. Undeterred she dropped to all fours and sprung up once more at his other side, this time successfully, on to the couch between he and Sadie. Much closer now, she licked his face and rested her head against his shoulder.

No one knew where she had come from and she had no tags that could have indicated such information. This was all the better for Bran, who felt a magic in their connection and did not wish to see her given up to another master. He felt in her, and in the room, a strong sense of family – something essential to a Capricorn like himself.

Bound by the duty of the golden rule, Bran embarked upon a quest to find the dog's owner, however half-heartedly. He hung up some "found dog" signs around the neighborhood and hoped no one would answer them. He and Sadie had taken to calling her by the name Zeta, which she began responding to very quickly. At one minute after midnight, on the thirtieth day of no inquiry, Bran went outside and removed his postings.

"She's ours now," he assured. "It's where she should be anyway."

Sadie agreed.

"And I think we should change her name."

"Change her name?" Sadie disagreed – strongly.

"Hear me out," continued Bran, "It should still sound the same, but we should spell it Xeta, with an X rather than a Z. It can be like a rite of passage into our family."

Sadie had no issues with this amendment. Bran was taking on the bulk of responsibility for the dog himself, anyway. "Okay then. Xeta – with an X."

Within the year, Bran and Sadie moved out of Beth's house and into a rental in the residential outskirts of downtown. Twice a day, Bran and Xeta would circle a few blocks, sometimes passing by the Lutheran Church and entering the unaffiliated garden cemetery across the street.

Xeta would grow excited to be among the graves there, breathing in each monument and relishing the smell of death. With their limited olfactory perception, humans tend to perceive this smell as primarily sour, if they smell anything at all. To a canine, however, there also emanates a sweet side. And though humans ultimately determine death to be something of a *concept*, to a dog it is recognized as a physical entity in and of itself. For by smell a dog knows its master, as it knows any other creature on earth, too by smell it knows its god.

Once Xeta was comfortable with the new location, after a few months of walks, she was able to accompany Bran without her leash. There were exceptions, such as during block parties or holidays that involved fireworks, but the restraint was precautionary then. Even at those times, she kept steadily at Bran's side. Only in the cemetery did she ever break her step, and within its walls this was a constant; charging immediately to the back recesses of the place, where the smells were less trampled by human steps. It was her custom there to go ahead of Bran and wait for him to catch up.

Diamond Dogs

II

The 'oughts carried an odor very similar to that of death, but with the sweet attributes on the surface, and the sour hidden below. It was a soft, round decade, as it's written numeral forms implied. Solid, bold colors washed through the fashion of the time, with clothing that was both stylish and comfortable. The vivid fabrics were accompanied by equally textural sounds as music, too, had become clean and bright - positive even, if one's ear was in the right place. Technology was allowing people to remove blemishes from their art, and to share it with the world through a growing Internet. America stayed high on the Clinton prosperity of the nineties, enjoying an oblivious slide into the gutter of the 2008 financial crisis.

Barack Obama took over the American presidency just in time to clean up after the party and deal with the collective sticker shock. A Leo by birth, there was no better leader for the new age. Yet, his benevolence and pragmatism were shrewdly limited by a congress of men who still desperately clung to the old. Through the rise of social media, this division came to be prominent between private citizens as well. Everyone felt duped or hurt in some way and so defenses became high and frequent. On frail legs, the world entered the twenty-tens with its head down, as though it were an abused animal.

Art and music had always been dicey ways to make money. Tech industry executives found ways, though - on the backs of the creators. This left the artists themselves shortchanged on royalties, as the cost of living kept rising. As usual, creativity stood little chance against process. It was in some ways fortunate then that Bran's thirty-sixth birthday would fall on a Saturday, for his wonderfully imaginative friends all had the weekend off from the dismal office jobs they had resigned themselves to.

An anemic but involved sampling of those friends met he and Sadie at a small, unmarked speakeasy on the ground floor of a stylish downtown hotel. The drinks were pricey but well crafted, and the atmosphere was quaint. Beth, Parker and Melanie were all in attendance, as well as Parker's girlfriend and Melanie's husband. Beth had remained single and took over the mortgage on her grandmother's house. Joshua sent his regards, though was busy with a wife and three children in Atlanta. Jacob moved to Arizona and lost touch with everyone. Bran and Sadie were married. Mark Linkous from Sparklehorse died a few streets over from the one they lived on.

Another death had occurred in the neighborhood the evening before Bran's birthday. Beth brought it up: "Did you all make it out for the lights last night?"

"The lights?" asked Bran.

"Yeah - on Eleanor at Third. Right down the street from you."

"I saw it," spoke Sadie. "What was it?"

"A suicide. Alan Placido."

Parker spoke up. "Wait. That's what that was? Alan Placido? Really?"

"I don't know who that is," said Bran.

"I used to work with him at Chez Lib back in the day," Parker explained. "That's shocking to me. He was a really super nice guy."

"He really was," agreed Beth. "I hadn't seen him in a couple years, but it was always a pleasure when I did. You know it would have been his birthday in just about another week. I think his was the sixteenth."

Beth's wording seemed alien to Sadie. "It's so weird how we switch to past tense the moment someone

III

On the morning of January tenth, in the wretched year of 2016 the world woke up to learn that the legendary musician and artist, David Bowie, had also passed away. To some, this was every bit as startling and sudden as the deaths of Xeta and Alan Placido. To Bran, Xeta's departure was naturally the most difficult of the three to handle. There was no question to anyone, however, that death had commenced the year with a heavy pound of its gavel.

As aforementioned, Bowie's final album, *Blackstar*, was released on his birthday that year, January eighth. Its poetry was misinterpreted for a brief time until his sudden passing, not forty-eight hours later, made it all so direly clear. The theme of the record crystallized around Bowie's own awaiting death; its close proximity obscured from the entire world but for a small inner circle. Suddenly, there it was, glaring shrewdly at generations of shocked people.

And yet, there was also the sweet side of his death – the side more familiar to canines. Undeniably, his sudden disappearance held mystical qualities, but mythical as well. The way his departure was made, be it intentionally by the artist or by some force of synchronic events within the universe, was masterful in it's ability to tie his entire life together into an apposite, organic, package. That *strange magnetic depth* was not there to satisfy demographic testing garnered through focus groups. It was there because nothing else would have made sense.

Intentionally, Bowie came to the world at large as an alien from another plane of existence, introducing himself with a song about an astronaut drifting through space eternally. He called himself Ziggy, and a parade of other aliases would follow. Perhaps it had been fiction, though perhaps not, once his full story arc could be determined and analyzed. Simply put, his final album was called *Blackstar* and was released on his birthday, which occurred one day before the moon itself was entirely blacked out by the shadow of the earth while in the constellation of Capricorn. Then, one day after that, just as the moon saw the slightest of illumination, David Bowie exited with that shadow. And so it seems that, be it premonition or coincidence, he was taken by the darkened satellite that he had conceived, and at precisely the most appropriate time.

The world may never know if David Bowie had constructed his own tunnel out, or if this passage opened up for him from the other side. It was apparent, though, that on the ninth of January, between Bowie's birthday and death day, the portal was at its widest. To unsuspecting human beings, paying most of their attention to handheld glowing screens, the new Bowie record was merely released the day before a new moon – if even those things were apparent to them. The open tunnel that would carry home the alien artist simply passed overhead, mostly undetected. Those who did perceive an inkling of this sacred formation were quick to turn away, for this passage was death, itself, and the avoidance of sour smells had grown inherent in most people.

The presence of the passage was not lost on dogs, of course. Like most all other dogs in the neighborhood, and most all other dogs on the earth, Xeta smelled the sweet underbelly of death. It hung crisply in the air, more strongly than she had ever experienced on her jaunts through the cemetery. It was so present to her, there on her master's birthday, that she became aware that she could step right through it, herself. She was, at first, reluctant because Bran was not with her. She felt it at once unnatural for him to not be accompanying her through that particular scent. Yet there she was, in their home as she was so many times before. Xeta did not believe that her master would allow such a smell into their home if not to interact with it. She was uncertain though and so changed her respiratory pattern and took the tunnel in through her nose a different way, with short, shallow, repetitive sniffs. She found finer olfactory nuances in doing this, but one in particular stood out above the others.

Through the sweet and the sour of death, beyond the home she slept in every night, she smelled the Capricorn essence. This was Bowie's essence, as well as the essence of that time of season. It was the essence of the moon that night, and it's particles flooded through the passage. This being also the essence of her master, her confidence to pass through only increased. She felt more comfortable to go that way; determined even, but still she had not seen Bran, and wanted to make certain he was near. She lay down on the floor and stared into the blackstar, anxious but obedient.

Somewhere outside the tunnel, a familiar white door opened. It was the same white door she went through daily to go on her walks. Within its frame, Bran appeared. He spoke her name, and she turned to look at him with great relief. With him there, she knew their walk could commence as usual. And so she went ahead and waited for him to catch up.

Diamond Dogs

Legacies

I

A new desktop computer sat on the long counter at work. Nolan stared at the screen and clicked the mouse, diverting his attention only momentarily to greet Daniel when he walked in the door. "So we have the Internet now," he stated coldly, eyes fixated on the glowing box.

"Oh wow. How come?" asked Daniel.

"They would like us to each list three records per day on some weird auction website. Doug left instructions."

I wonder how long that will last."

Nolan concurred. "Yeah. He always talks about how the Internet is killing business, but I never took him for an if-you-can't-beat-em-then-join-em kinda guy."

"Nope."

"But as long as we have it, I'd like to learn about it. I've been looking at different websites and there's some weird stuff out there, but I'd like to learn about email and how that works."

"Oh email is easy," said Daniel. "I can kind of show you how it works. You have to set an account up somewhere, but they're usually free."

"Cool. Yeah I found this one website all about Colin Blunstone, from The Zombies. I guess some fan of his made it, but they had some really psychedelic old pictures, you know? And, like, a complete list of all the records he has ever released. Stuff I had never seen before. I was, like, 'Wow, this is really cool.'"

"Geeze. This really is new to you, isn't it?" asked Daniel.

"Well it's new to the store, and I don't have it at home."

"I guess I've actually been on the web longer than most people," Daniel realized. "I was trading bootleg Beck cassettes with people I met on BBS dial ups back in eighth grade."

"BBS?" asked Nolan.

"Pre-Internet, basically." Daniel suddenly felt the need to make his knowledge relatable. "So did you see the Spectre Subworlds website?" He took over the keyboard and typed in the web address. "Check it out." A website with a gray background appeared, it's pixels made to look like stone. The text was in burgundy, typed out across rectangular, black boxes. Within the options listed along the top of the screen was one to "search by state." Daniel implored Nolan to click it and he did as requested. A list of all fifty of the American states took over the screen, laid out in two columns of twenty-five each, in alphabetical order. Nolan clicked "North Carolina." The screen next displayed a long list of supposedly haunted locations and the ghost stories attached to them, organized by town. Just four entries from the top was theirs, Asheville, with more related haunted stories than any other listed, most of them centered around the Biltmore Estate. The two men read them all and were familiar with most of the locations.

They skimmed the rest of the list and Nolan scrolled until they reached a submission form at the bottom of the page. When he realized what it was, he pulled the keyboard squarely in front of his body and began to type. "I'm going to submit a haunted place."

"Where?"

"You'll see." Nolan typed and typed. When his story was complete, he stood from his stool and offered it to Daniel. "What do you think?"

Here is what he typed:

> Hi. I would like to submit a ghost story about a haunted place in Asheville, North Carolina. It is about the area that is now the parking lot across from the Fine Arts Theater on Biltmore Avenue. Back during the 1800s, this area was dirt instead of asphalt and people in town would park their horses here. When the civil war ended, everyone was downtown celebrating. A man named Daniel Patton was late to the party, but found a place to post up his horse in the lot. A few blocks over, some men were drinking and shouting and shooting their guns in the air. No sooner had Daniel gotten off his horse, before one of those stray bullets accidentally struck him in the head. He fell to the ground bleeding. His horse began to lick his blood and quickly acquired a taste for it. Then, as he died, his horse ate his face off and his body was not found until the next morning. They say that if you stand in just the right parking space on a full moon, you can hear the ghost of Daniel Patton, moaning in the night. Thank you.

"Why am I the ghost?" asked Daniel.

"Why not?" Nolan grinned broadly. "I'm going to send it. Do you care?"

"No I guess not," surrendered Daniel. "It's kind of funny, I guess."

With that, Nolan clicked the tiny gray "submit" button underneath the white typing area. "Your submission has been received!" read the website text. "Please check back in a few weeks to see if it is posted! Thanks!"

Daniel rolled his eyes and snorted a bit. He removed a sheet of paper from the brown copy shop bag he had brought in with him. He picked up the tape dispenser and walked to the front of the counter, taking in the whole of it from a few feet away. Three of the advertisements posted there were for events that had already passed. He ripped them each down with slightly unnecessary force, then plucked off each paper corner that held its space under tape. In the most central new void, Daniel hung his own paper.

"You got a show coming up?" inquired Nolan, though he already knew.

"Yeah. In a couple weeks at Vi-Bo."

"That's that new place?"

"Yeah."

"Like a coffee shop or something?"

"Yeah."

"Do they have a stage or something?"

"They're just clearing out some tables," explained Daniel. "Gonna play on the floor."

"Oh okay cool. So is this one with your band?"

Daniel's spirit dropped a notch. "No. It's just another solo thing. I don't really know what's up with the band these days. Just trying to do my own thing until they come around, I guess."

"Solo. Cool." It was easy for Nolan to view it indifferently. He had his own band, with its own issues, but ultimately took all music in stride. It seemed that *all things* were casual to him, in fact. "So last time you had a keyboard running through a pedal board or something, and a guitar maybe?"

"Yeah this is nothing like that. This is just me and my acoustic guitar. Some songs I wrote."

"Cool. Cool. Well I will probably be there, then."

September arrived. Daniel attended classes at the University of North Carolina on most weekdays. He would work at the record store on evenings and weekends. His free time was divided between developing his music and going to parties. He had written several new songs and was sure to find a few hours each night (or technically the very early morning) to practice and refine them. Smoking marijuana was the only constant across his occupied days.

Every other week, his uncle would pull his truck into Daniel's driveway and mow the lawn while he was in class. His living quarters were a family home, set on slightly less than an acre of land, which he rented from his father. Uncle Jake was in some kind of financial debt to Daniel's parents and so the yard maintenance, it was agreed, would allow him to work that debt down. He used a riding mower, but not a very good one. It got the job done, but was susceptible to becoming sometimes stuck by divots in the terrain. This week, Uncle Jake had finished up just shortly before Daniel arrived home and the two crossed paths in the driveway. Each spoke from the window of his vehicle.

"How's it going, Uncle Jake?"
"Oh, it's going, buddy. It's going."
"Well thanks for mowing."

"Ain't no problem," ensured Jake, "But hey, you got some holes in your yard. I don't know what kinda animal makes em but my mower don't handle em well."

"Sorry about that. I don't know where they might come from."

"Well if just you're ever out there and ya see one, please just kick some dirt back in it for me – if you think to."

Inside Daniel felt that this was not really his problem, but he was not a fan of conflict. "I'll keep that in mind."

"Alright partner. Thanks. You have a good'n." Jake pulled out of the driveway.

Daniel parked his car and ascended the steps to his front porch. Sitting upright on a plastic chair, just to the right of the front door, was a small object that was foreign to him; a wood cut statue of a person's head. It was long and boxy, not unlike those giants found on Easter Island, but with a less prominent brow and an obvious smile. It had been intricately carved out of a dense section of white oak, with a flat top and much detail to the eyes and teeth. Daniel felt a kind of déjà vu when he picked it up, and the feeling followed him into his house.

His roommates were passing a bong of marijuana smoke, preparing to go to their respective workplaces. Alec sat down, altering their handing pattern from a line to a triangle. "Does this belong to either of you?" has asked, holding up the statue.

"Not me," spoke one roommate.

The other squinted and furrowed his brow. "What is it?"

"I have no idea. It was just sitting on the porch," he tossed it to the squinting roommate who observed it from every angle once in his hands.

"It gives me a weird feeling. I don't know about this thing." He tossed it back.

"I just wonder where it came from," said Daniel. "You guys were here all day and didn't see anyone come by?"

"Just the lawnmower man."

"I mean, it's in a really prominent place by the door. I definitely didn't see it when I got home from work last night, but I can't say I even looked on my way out this morning." Daniel's gears were spinning. "So if it wasn't left here today, it could have been left in the night."

His roommates both shrugged.

The show was four days away. Daniel's plan for the evening was to arrange the songs into some sort of order, and then record a rehearsal of the complete performance.

After a quick urination, he walked back to his room and retrieved his guitar and songbook. He had been working on his set there, but tonight he would move his sessions downstairs to the music room. He placed the wooden statue on the detuned, old piano and leaned the guitar against the wall. He retrieved microphones and cables from their respective bins and affixed them together atop a couple of stands. One was set low to pick up the guitar and the other set high to receive Daniel's voice. The wires ran to the inputs of an old VS-2480, controlled by a mouse and keyboard from the late nineties. Once his configuration was in place and ready to go, the guitar also tuned, he slipped back upstairs again. There he obtained a beer from the refrigerator and another pull of smoke from the bong. He saw his roommates off to work and returned to the music room. He placed his beer on the piano, about a foot away from the statue, and pressed the record button on the 2480. Lifting by the fret board with his right hand, he passed the guitar to his left and draped the strap down over his head to rest on his shoulder. He formed a simple E chord, cleared his throat, and began to strum.

Daniel was not a particularly proficient guitarist. He learned new chords as he wrote songs, experimenting with different sound changes, but he knew nothing of theory and had no technical ability. His vocal range was also lacking. Chunky and brash in execution, the essence of his songs were still carefully crafted. The chord changes, though not often standard, were yet emotive and the lyrics prolific. Stubbornly, he clung to absolute control of his songs, never considering the success he may have garnered from writing for other people, instead.

He pushed through his rehearsal, song-by-song, recording every moment with no stops. He was aiming to document the session in a version as close to what it was to be when performed at Vi-Bo. He would not correct mistakes or start songs over. He would not even open his songbook until the set was complete. The songs were rough and abrasive, political and fiery, sometimes sad, with a potential for softness that he could simply never fall into. Though he wished to move forward through the set with no interruption, he did have one momentary stumble near the end of the fifth song. It was an older one he had written, but somehow he had become lost in the moment, slowing it down and spilling unnecessary chords on his way to the end. It was a kind of vertigo that tore at his thought process, and when he finished, he paused, almost deciding to sit the guitar down for a moment before moving on. He didn't though, instead electing to ignore the temptation and push on to the conclusion he had planned.

The final song of the set was also an older one, written two years prior about the end of a romantic relationship. Being of the theme of departure, he always felt it a practical song to close with. The lyrics to the chorus were these:

> So you know
> You can go
> Anytime you want to leave
> I hope you know
> I love you so
> But you don't have to wait for me

In time, Daniel had come to find these lyrics a bit contrived. When he wrote them, he was moving through an incredible emotional wave and he really *felt* what was coming out of him. About eight months later, he wondered why he didn't ever revise it to be more poetic and less simplistic; maybe get rid of that crambo mess on the C lines. He never ultimately cared enough to actually rework it, but did continue to perform it live, obviously. The relationship it was based on had become a decent memory, and the girl remained a casual friend and ally. Both of them felt they were better this way. All that emotion had been settled. There was nothing left in it for Daniel, except one more showpiece for his arsenal.

Something was different this time, though. This time Daniel *did* feel it. He felt it in a way he could not explain. He was not pining for the relationship it was based on, but an image of the girl did flash quickly in his mind. Beyond the blackness behind her flat, quantum appearance, he sensed something just out of reach and so much more powerful than himself. It was also a *part* of himself. The collective consciousness was floating out there, divinely, tenderly, touching him. He was not only aware of it but also engaged with it, as his hands knew every position needed to form around the guitar and his voice sang in perfect harmony with the universe. For just a few minutes, about half the duration of the song, he was one with God. He removed his guitar, leaned it against the wall, took a seat and wept heavily for the next ten minutes.

Daniel attempted no second take. He saved his work, however rough, and burned it on to a compact disc. The disc was placed in his computer's drive and the session was extracted, broken into separate tracks, and digitally archived. Over the next few days, he rehearsed some more, without recording. He then performed his set at Vi-Bo, to a small, sitting audience and no reviews. This same cycle of events spun for a long time - a decade or more - though some details were ever changing. Sometimes there *was* a second take. Sometimes there were more musicians - different projects. The technology he used also changed, and so the quality. The audience sizes varied and the venues that held them changed *a lot*. With them, so did his life beneath that version of himself.

Money was a necessity to keep funding his musical projects, as most of them operated at a loss. With age, he found himself in need to fund more things: his own food and shelter, comfort and bills. The record store closed as Internet piracy became mainstream. Daniel began delivering pizza. It was decent income and flexible hours. His music gained exposure on the growing Internet, but it was short lived, diminished by a flooded market. Still he trudged on, recording and performing as the value of music sunk with each new technology.

His knowledge of maps from years of delivery earned him a perfectly scored written exam for the United States Census Bureau. After a very successful assignment as an enumerator, he found himself assisting with the digitization of their maps into hand held devices. Once that year's census ended, Daniel had little problem moving from a temporary federal job into working permanently for the state. Things were okay for a time at North Carolina's Child Services division. He earned enough to live alone finally, and his coworkers were mostly aligned with him politically. Even removing meth babies from shanty houses was not enough to interrupt the jovial candor between he and his workmates. Then Pat McCrory became governor and those workmates, as well as candor itself, were swept away by partisan efficiency. The new regime tried to push Daniel out with the others, but the money was too good and so he chose fight over flight. The toxic atmosphere depleted his energy and his involvement in music tapered down to just a few hours per month. He wanted to be inspired and focused, but found it difficult not to pass out drunk in front of his computer most nights.

One Saturday evening, Daniel had been out at a bar, drinking heavily and smoking pot out back with the kitchen manager. A sloppy mess, he probably should not have driven himself home, but arrived nonetheless unscathed. He plopped down in front of his computer, illuminated its screen, and packed another pipe of marijuana from his desk drawer. Browsing his archives, he pondered the course of his life. He lit his pipe and wondered how the music he produced in his twenties may seem to him now in his thirties. Randomly, he chose the September rehearsal for the Vi-Bo show, queuing the tracks in his computer's media player and pressing play. He remembered that session but his recollection of the set list was hazy as he moved to the couch and continued to smoke.

He listened intently to the recording. At times he cringed at his own naïveté, but could not deny there was a passion back then which had become lost somewhere along the way to his present moment. His musicianship had notably improved since that time, to be sure. Half asleep by song three, the fifth song stirred him back awake again when he heard his flubbing in the second half. And when the song was over, as the tone of the guitar had trailed almost completely out, he thought he heard the sound of another man's voice cut through the quietness. He listened again, just to the fade, with the volume higher. Yes, it was clearly another man whose southern drawl was caught to tape – richer in speech than Daniel's voice, and seemingly set out further from the microphone.

After a few more listens, the disembodied words were quite clear: "Keep on playin'," they seemed to encourage. The context, these words spoken at the end of a music performance, made Daniel realize at once that this person, whoever he was, was sharing in the moment on the recording. The feeling of vertigo struck him again, before he could even attempt to rationalize it. Yet when he did, he hit a wall in every direction. Not only was the voice unrecognizable to him, but also he remembered recording that session and remembered being there alone. Such was the case for all of his solo acoustic sessions, as he was embarrassed to rehearse so minimally in front of others - certainly strangers. Finally, there was no other point in the rest of the thirty-six minute session during which any other human voice could be heard, but for Daniel's. He concluded he had accidentally recorded a ghost.

Fascinated by the discovery, he opened the track in his sound editing software and isolated the voice out from the rest of the recording. He amplified the overall sound, filtered out the background hiss, adjusted the bass and treble slightly and saved it among his music files in a folder named "EVP." He listened to it again and again, wondering who this visitor was, and if he was still present in the house. His initial shock had cooled to a warm hum as he yearned to *know* this apparently friendly ghost that seemed to appreciate his music.

Daniel took to the Internet, in search of information about the land he lived on. He wondered if he could find a history of the place, before it was his great grandfather's farm. His quick search of the words "property history" alongside his address only turned up services requesting money for such information. He figured his parents would be much better to speak to about it, anyway. His home was at one time theirs, for it was they who parceled the land and built it.

He tried a new search, half assertively typing the words "ghost" and "Asheville." This provided many more results, of course. He clicked on one that felt most scientific to him. It was called "The Ghost Aggregator," and it served as a streamlined database of ghost stories, pooled together from across the Internet, and searchable by location. As he clicked through the Asheville items, he came to one that jarred him with nostalgic shock. He found the story about himself, his face eaten by a horse in a parking lot, posted to the Spectre Subworlds website by Nolan over a decade prior. Furthermore, The Ghost Aggregator was sourcing it from four different websites: Spectre Subworlds, of course, but also three others that mirrored the content under different site names.

Daniel listened to the ghost recording a few more times. He felt a strange solidarity with the speaker now.

Legacies

II

The slaves were declared free in the winter. Lewis wanted to leave, but he had no plan and nothing to protect himself from the cold. Colonel Calhoun's plantation was the only home he had ever really known and things had changed so much there that, by the time emancipation came around, the slaves mostly had the run of the place anyway. Colonel Calhoun had lived a decade and a half beyond the suicide of his wife and his children's subsequent abandonment. He was a sick and shriveled little man well before 1863. His accountant was the only visitor he ever had and even he usually only dealt with Isaac, the senior of the slaves. Calhoun had no closer friend to designate as an authorized representative for his estate, and so Isaac was the one who worked to reform the context of the farm from that of a plantation to that of a commune. The only thing that made any distinction between the two, ultimately, was whether or not Calhoun was still breathing. Everyone was polite to the Colonel, but would surely rejoice his demise.

As far as ownership went, Lewis had no stake in any of it. The estate was going to legally belong to Isaac and his wife, eventually their children. It practically already did. Lewis, though, was a free agent. He was brought there at eight months of age, with two unrelated adults, all purchased by Calhoun at the port of Charleston and personally transported to his land in Greensboro. Lewis had been there ever since, not quite three decades, but still much less time than Isaac. Though he was well liked and relatively comfortable where he was, he knew that these winds of change were to be embraced. And so as Colonel Calhoun lost his grasp on the business within his own plantation, Lewis stayed through the remainder of the winter, working for Isaac.

It was near the end of March, as the weather began to warm, that Lewis made his departure. He was sent off with a blanket, some clothing and a supply of food, all packed with care by the women of the house. He headed out west, with an aim to resettle in Tennessee. This had been at the suggestion of Isaac, who was told by the accountant that Union held Knoxville had become very friendly in integrating newly freed slaves. As he traveled toward the Great Smoky Mountains, he moved at a casual pace and kept to more rarely trampled paths.

Outside of Salem, he came upon a stout branch of white oak that had broken cleanly from its tree. He picked it up and observed it as though it were alien to him. He used his knife to shorten it down to a stumpy section that fit his grasp. Each time he sat to break from his travels, he would whittle the piece further, into a new, distinct shape. By the time he had reached the mountain town of Asheville, it had been well formed into a dumb, grinning head, with particular detail to the eyes and teeth.

Lewis took a seat on a log, facing a clearing just off the road. Three deer grazed there, undeterred by his presence. As he watched them, he continued to whittle the oak totem, rounding the head so that he could carve out some ears.

Unaware, he sat with his back to the sight of another man's rifle. "I could get him in one shot," ensured that man to his friend.

The friend took a pull of whiskey. "You can't just shoot 'em no more," he explained. "Lincoln gave 'em rights." He passed the flask.

"Well the war ain't over yet," said the first man before imbibing. He then shot Lewis from afar, hitting him square in the back of his head. Lewis fell forward and collapsed on the ground. The deer scattered and the wood sculpture flung from his hand. The shooter and his friend walked casually down to the main road and continued their eastbound journey.

Lewis was a young soul, and so death was a new sensation. He saw his body stretched out beneath him, still connected to his present form by sinewy astral threads. It didn't make sense to him. He sat again on the log and continued to carve his totem, but no matter where he cut, he could no longer alter its form. He noticed that it, too, was connected to its own identical counterpart in the grass. When he followed its thread from his hand to the ground, he found he could only possess the one he was already holding. The other could be rattled slightly, but never lifted from its position in the physical world.

He found himself on the edge of life, rather than directly submerged. No longer bound by time, the speed of his experience was relative to the movement of matter around him. This is to say, more obvious changes in his scene would slow time down, while incremental changes sped time up, and so the astral connection that ran to his body was quickly atrophying. It dissipated completely when a random man, possibly the man who killed him, grabbed his ankles and drug him into some thick brush further off the path. Though he would have preferred a proper cremation, he was at least relieved that he no longer had to look at himself lying there on his face.

After that, the material change around him was mostly slow and structural. The path he was on when he fell out of life had become overgrown and ignored. Animals slowly picked apart his body, carrying it away in pieces too small to notice. Foliage and weather worked to cover both his bones and the wooden statue. The clearing became parceled and sold and homes were erected in the distance. He saw the evolution of the road from dirt to asphalt. What once was dominated by walking people progressed into the transport of strange, four wheeled pods; against which walking people would never have stood a chance in physical battle. Possibly horses neither, for that matter. Lewis watched it all from the log and held firm to his totem, its own astral thread still very much in tact.

A new home was built much closer than the others, the back door about one hundred feet from Lewis's log. A family lived there: a mother, a father, a son and a daughter. Due to a series of interpersonal matters that Lewis was never privy to, this basic core of people came and went in varying intervals. Only the parents and the son lived there initially. The daughter was born during that arrangement. The mother and children exited, with the kids still visiting for sporadic, brief spurts. Other women came and went through this period, exotic women who Lewis was pleased to see. Then the mother returned with the children and they all lived together again. Just the mother and son exited after that, and then the father departed as well. Once only the daughter remained, a random flow of her strange, modern acquaintances became normal. Lewis took great interest in watching the bizarre parade, but then suddenly it all stopped and the house sat empty. The leaves changed a few times and then a new parade began. This one was a bit more meditative and subdued, as they were the friends of the son and his two roommates. There was also, of course, a lawnmower man who regularly came in closer proximity to the old log than anyone else in the house. Lewis never approached any of them the entire time, and wouldn't know how to interact with them if he did.

A stray dog had been coming around the yard, after learning that this was a house where food waste was thrown back to the earth, rather than the garbage can. On a Thursday, there was nothing there for him, but this did not stop him from sniffing around the area. He pissed here and there, ate some grass, and then, just as he was ready to move to the next lawn, became suddenly transfixed by a particular spot on the ground. He breathed it in deeply and obsessively, to the point of shaking. He took a step back and gazed up and down, as though a column or king had been placed on his spot. He submitted to it, laying down his head and front legs, hindquarters still poised to spring and run at a moment's notice. This was temporary, though, and soon he relaxed, wagged his tail, and flopped over on his back. Stomach to the morning sun, he wiggled and writhed on top of his spot. The call of a crow startled him into resuming a standing position. He smelled the spot some more and then began to dig. He kept this up for nearly three quarters of an hour, eating ants and throwing inconstant dirt mist behind him. At last he uncovered a small piece of wood; not a root, but with an end that had been sanded flat. He smelled it. He clenched his teeth around it and tried to pull it out, unsuccessfully. Slowly, he dug out a bit more dirt around it, but then stepped back, whimpering. Then he turned and walked away, moving on to the next yard, but stopping to glance back every few meters.

Later that afternoon, Uncle Jake showed up to mow. He drove his machine around the yard, beer in hand, in as neat a back and forth as he could maintain. Inevitably, he reached the hole that the dog had dug, but had the foresight to stop before plowing over it. He dismounted his mower and used the side of his foot to push some loose dirt toward the gap. Just as it crested the side and dropped down, he noticed the flat, wooden object poking out of the ground. He sat his beer on his mower and used his hands to dig out some more dirt. Once loosened from the ground, he lifted it from its grave, revealing the artifact to be, of course, Lewis's statue. Uncle Jake was a superstitious man and found the piece to be a bit too macabre to keep for himself, but too unique to simply disregard. He switched off the engine to his mower, walked to the front of the house, proceeded up the steps and sat the statue on the seat of a plastic chair there on the porch. He then completed his job and went home, briefly catching his nephew in the driveway as he left.

Lewis looked down at the totem in his hand. Its astral thread was no longer buried, but now stretched out all the way around the front of the house. In that moment, he realized he could move away from the log, and so followed the path of the thread. Suspended in the air, it swung wide around Daniel's roommate's car, and up the small embankment to the wooden porch. There the statue sat, upright on a strange white chair. Lewis reached for it, but again could barely move it, let alone physically attain it.

Daniel, fresh out of class, stepped on to the porch and saw the statue for the first time. Lewis attempted to speak to him but was not heard. Daniel picked up the statue and brought it into the house. Lewis followed him inside, where the smell of marijuana triggered deep memories from some of the days on Calhoun's plantation. Accurately, he presumed Daniel and his roommates to be of similar age as he was when he died. He found himself amused by the enigma they believed his statue to be. It was the most comfortable he had felt since his death.

He followed Daniel through some of the rooms. When Daniel urinated, Lewis respectfully remained in the company of the roommates. One of them actually noted his presence, stating that she felt like there was someone else there with them. The other roommate told her she was just paranoid from the weed. She denied this and then they left for work. Lewis went downstairs to the music room with Daniel and would have been elated to pick up one of the instruments there, if only that had been possible. The lights on the VS-2480 filled him with anticipation until, finally, Daniel strapped on his guitar and began his performance.

Aesthetically, a guy and a guitar was nothing new to Lewis and so he may of well had been back in the 1860's with regard to what he was listening to. He never considered this, though, because he had no concept whatsoever of modern music. Bass drops, turntable scratches, even electric guitars, were conceptually foreign to him. So though he might have heard something slicker and more modern at any other time in that room, he would only ever bare witness to Daniel, chunking away on his acoustic. And since he did not know, he did not mind. He was pleased to hear any music at all after one hundred and forty some years, and so when Daniel flubbed the fifth song and almost quit, Lewis spoke out almost involuntarily: "Keep on playin'."

Daniel did keep playing, all the way through the rest of the set. When he reached the final song, he sang words that resonated very deeply within Lewis. They were these:

So you know
You can go
Anytime you want to leave
I hope you know
I love you so
But you don't have to wait for me

Lewis heard these simple sentiments and felt shaken. So clearly they stated something that he blankly had not considered since he died. He had no further business in the material world. He could have let go and moved on long ago. It was clear to him now, and he released his totem. It's astral thread wound back into the statue, forever forbidding any further access to Lewis. It didn't matter anyway, though, as a distant light grew to consume him. His senses fell away, one at a time. It seemed that the last to go was going to be sound, but that one ran eternal.

III

Daniel got old, married and fat, in that order. He never had children, but he did have a pension and a retirement fund, as well as a good bit of coin put up in a savings account. His wife had very similar assets and so old age was decent for them both. He never completely stopped with music, but it simmered to a slow hobby. Travel had become prioritized higher among his uses of leisure time. Still, his life's work amounted to several hundred gigabytes of information, most of it music, split across two external hard drives.

He, himself, died on his own property, just feet away from Lewis's log. He had thrown wildflower seed along the perimeter two weeks prior and walked over to check for sprouting. As he knelt there, essentially where Lewis's body lay for so long, his heart malfunctioned suddenly and he collapsed in the same place. He lay there for hours before his wife returned home from a hairdressing appointment and found him lifeless.

She continued to live in the house, but never removed Daniel's personal affects. She instead convened with her attorney and worked out a plan to sell it all off after her own death, and donate the money to a foundation that rescued abused animals. That day came in not two years time when she tripped over one of her cats and fell down the stairs. She was found about ten days later after failing to show up at her weekly card game and remaining unreachable by phone. Per their agreement, the lawyer handled the estate sale, taking a standard cut for his self. He did not drag the couple's belongings out into the yard, but rather just hung signs and allowed visitors to browse the inside of the house, themselves. It all had to go, after all.

A young man, barely in his twenties and sporting greasy, shaggy hair and dark sunglasses, walked downstairs. The lawyer, suspicious of the man, followed him. The mistrust dissipated when he heard the man speak: "Woah, dude!" His mouth open, he scanned the room from side to side. String instruments and drums were everywhere. "So this guy was a musician?" he asked.

"That's right," spoke the lawyer, "And all these instruments are for sale."

"I'm a musician too," spoke the man.

"Oh well maybe there's something here you can use then. What do you play?"

"What do I *play*?" asked the man.

"Yeah, what instrument?"

The man appeared to be stumped. "Well, I use my computer and a couple decks."

"Decks?" asked the lawyer.

"Yeah that I can affect the sound through. I can take a *wheeeeeeee* and push my slider to make it wobble like *weeweeweeweeweewuuwuuwuuwuuwuuwoewoewoewoewoewoe* and then drop a beat in time with the oscillation of the sound. Then I can trigger mad samples from some crazy old jazz or something and turn my knobs and make it so dirty and rough."

The lawyer had no idea what he was talking about. "So you're more of a producer then?" he asked, and then spoke again before the man could answer. "You should check out that little control room over there. He's got some recording equipment. Some microphones and that kind of thing."

"Ept, dude. Sick ept. Let me at it." He stepped into the cramped room and attempted to smile through his diminishing enthusiasm. "Oh, so he had a lot of vintage stuff. That's always pretty cool. Yeah." With the lawyer looming behind him, he felt pressured to make a purchase of some kind. He noticed Daniel's external hard drives, perched like bookends around his outdated eight-channel interface. Recognizing them as the only things in the room he could tangibly make use of, he asked the lawyer for a price.

"Fifty dollars and you can have them both."

"Official!" said the man, unplugging them from the wall. "I can always use more memory for my tracks."

The lawyer smiled and they walked back upstairs.

When the transaction was complete, the man placed both drives under one arm and shook the lawyer's hand. "Thank you so much, dude," he spoke with a false sincerity. "Hey, by the way," he retrieved a small rectangle from his breast pocket. "Here is my card." He handed it to the lawyer.

"Cheeky D?" asked the lawyer.

"That's just my stage name," said the man, "You can call me Petran. But if you ever need a DJ for a wedding or a bat mitzvah or something, I can tailor a set to whatever you need – dance, pop, rock, rap, soul, oldies, any era, whatever. I mean, don't read me wrong, I'm a club DJ first and foremost, but I will take any job where I can make peeps happy by playing music. And really, I just like you, dude." He shook the lawyer's hand again.

"Well I will keep that in mind, Petran." The lawyer removed a small, flat, silver case from the inside of his suit jacket and popped it open. He extracted his own business card from within and extended it to Petran. "And if *you* ever need a lawyer, my name is Laken Groshman. I'm an attorney."

The men smiled warmly toward one another's separate life.

Malik had a stressful, busy night at work and so was agitated to come home to thumping bass at two o'clock in the morning. "Can you please turn it down?" he asked.

Petran complied. "I'm sorry," he apologized, "I have been working on this track all night."

"I don't mean to stop your flow." Malik kissed him. "It's just that work was rough and I need just a little bit of veggie time."

"I can put on the headphones," offered Petran.

"That's not necessary. I don't mind to hear it. I just can't take it booming at high volume right now. That's all."

"Well if you don't mind, then check it out." Petran played the track he had been building, starting at the beginning. It sounded indicative of his typical work: modern, droney keyboards wrapped around a glitch beat, with a tone reminiscent of the 2030's and dubstep drops dating back to the 'oughts. In the space before one such drop, as the keys whistled out into white noise, Petran pointed at the speakers, for to tell Malik to pay close attention to this part. And there, hanging in the atmosphere, was the sample of Lewis, clearly requesting, "Keep on playin'." His ghostly voice preceded a cacophony of grimy, stuttering drum samples, and dissonant, spooky synthesizer tones. This mode gave way quite suddenly to a simple, bouncy beat, alone but for muted bass taps. And here again, Petran motioned toward the speakers as the recording of Lewis returned. This time his voice repeated the line, "Keep on playin'," multiple times, establishing a pattern and then altering it with a multitude of filters and effects. Before the next drop, the words slowed and stretched as though everything was coming to an elastic stop. By the end of the song, the sample of Lewis was saturated in reverberation, overlain on top of itself, with one of them climbing higher and higher in pitch. The result was a full and ethereal conclusion, reminiscent of an insectoid alien chorus.

"I like it," said Malik, though disingenuously (he didn't care). "It has a kind of haunting feel to it."

"A haunting feel!" repeated Petran. "I am so glad you used that word! The part that I was trying to point out to you – that sample –."

"Keep on playing?"

"Yes! 'Keep on playing' – that is a sample of a ghost! I have a legitimate ghost in my song!"

"How do you have a legitimate ghost in your song?"

"I mean I presume it's legitimate. See, I went over to Dawdry's place to pick up some more psilly for the weekend and, like, two streets over they were having an estate sale. So I check it out and there are just mountains of instruments and old recording stuff. The dead guy was, like, a grind-all type musician. So I ended up buying two of the dead guy's hard drives. Three terras each and fifty bucks for both – so the price was bang. I figured, 'why not?' I'll use 'em sometime eventually, right?"

"Right."

"So I got them home and hooked them up just to see what was on them and the guy just had thousands and thousands of sound files. Most of it, I guess, was his own music. Nothing really spoke to me that I listened to, but there was this one folder titled EVP. Inside was just one file." Petran navigated to the file as he spoke.

"Keep on playin'," of course. Daniel's original waveform of Lewis's voice had been unearthed like the wooden statue.

"I don't undie, dude. How is that a ghost?" asked Malik.

"What don't you understand?" followed Petran. "It's a recording of a ghost."

"But how do you know?"

"Because it's the only file in a folder titled 'EVP.'"

"I don't know what that means," admitted Malik.

"EVP is a ghost hunting term. It stands for *electronic voice phenomena*. It's the thing where you record a ghost talking. You know?"

"Okay. Okay yeah. I didn't know what that was called. So you think that is one of those?"

"It has to be. And it's so apprope that what the ghost is saying is music related because that's what gave me the idea to put the sample in the song." Petran's demeanor grew quickly serious. "Mark my words, Malik. When peeps find out there is a wet new track with a *ghost* on the vocals, it will spark and catch fire. Peeps in the club will be *begging* for it."

Petran was correct, though he worked hard to make it so. He toured nationally as Cheeky D and promoted the track to every outlet that would speak to him. Ultimately, just as he had predicted, the novelty of using "ghost vocals" was a real door opener. Within a year and a half, he found himself on the morning entertainment news, saturating more and more people with his sound – old people, new mothers and small children, among others. Cheeky D had become famous. And as he moved up in station, he left Malik behind - exchanging him for Laken Groshman.

IV

Cheeky D's second national tour, the one funded by an energy drink company, wrapped up with a homecoming show at the old Orange Peel building on Halloween night. Fetishists and pop culture references flooded the streets, moving in and out of buildings, consuming drugs and making love. One such group of friends stood beside their cars in the parking lot on Biltmore, across from the Historic Fine Arts Theater, sipping beer and smoking pot as preparation for the show.

"I was lookin' at this thing," spoke the leather bound twink. "You know the Daniel Patton story about this lot, right?"

"Yah, dude, of course," replied the tall man in a sequined dress and long, blonde wig.

"Well there was this study online where they used the lay of these old buildings around here, and the trajectory of the bullet that hit him or something to figure out exactly which parking space he was killed in."

"The trajectory of the bullet? Who would know that?"

"I don't know. Probably death records or something."

"So which space was he killed in?" asked the crossdresser.

"I think it was 22D. Somewhere over there." He motioned toward one of the corners further out from Biltmore Avenue.

"Who is Daniel Patton?" asked Soliday from beneath her wide brim hat. (She was not dressed as a witch but as an aristocratic woman with bacon taped to her face,

Legacies 325

a popular advertising image that year.) She was from Maine, and was only visiting Asheville for a week.

"Daniel Patton is the ghost that haunts this parking lot," answered the twink, Soliday's cousin. "He was this dude from, like, the seventeen hundreds."

"The eighteen hundreds," corrected the crossdresser. "Almost the nineteen hundreds."

"Whatever," continued the twink. "It was horse times. Back when people had to abuse animals to get around. Anyway, this dude got shot and killed right in this lot. It was a stray bullet and no one saw it happen, so he just laid there dying. And as he died, his horse for real ate his face off."

Soliday found this too ridiculous to be believable, let alone scary. "Why would his horse eat his face off?" she asked.

"When animals get a taste for blood, there's no turning back."

She rolled her eyes.

A man in a priest's robe and collar spoke up. "You wanna *see* that ghost?" he asked.

The twink knew immediately what he meant. "Oh! What'chu got? What'chu got?" he kept asking as he pressed his body into the priest.

The priest pushed him back. "I got tabs of concentrated psilly crushed with deemst and kay. I mean, if we're gonna see a show, we might as well see a *show*."

"Yes please!" The twink was equally enthusiastic. "And one for my cousin?"

"It's Halloween. Take two!" The priest dropped four tiny ovals into the twink's hand.

He turned to his cousin. "Open up, darling!"

"What is it?" she asked.

"Just go with it," he requested, but she still wanted to know what she was about to put into her body. And so the twink explained the mix of drugs. Once convinced that each of the three primary ingredients was of natural origin and completely safe, Soliday opened her mouth and accepted the strange wafers.

She could feel the first rises of the drug as the group traversed the sidewalk a few blocks to the show. The feeling was foreign to her, if not slightly uncomfortable, but she was determined to hold on to her wits. As they approached the club, it appeared fake to her in a way – plastic and airbrushed. And she just knew the doorman was on to her, but maybe he was on weird drugs, too. Didn't he want to also have fun on Halloween? Was he mad at her for being there and making him work? Was he going to tell on her? Was she being latently racist? Her wits! She was determined to hold on to her wits!

She kept on marching, keeping close to her cousin and his friends. They walked in a line through the open spaces between bodies, finally filling in somewhere closer to the right of the stage, but as near the middle of the room as the path of no resistance would allow. Cheeky D was already performing, a silhouette behind a giant table of computers, basked in colorful, strobing lights and lasers. To Soliday, the music sounded difficult and slightly off, like the road moving beneath a bent bicycle wheel. She thought they had come to dance, but the repeating sample disrupted the rhythm, removing the perception of a flow within the music. She was a student of the classical violin though, herself; so who was she to comment on such contemporary works? She reminded herself to breathe again.

As those sounds led to others, the tension was slowly eroded away in waves. Soliday found herself not quite dancing, but rather loosely slogging her mass from side to side. Certain higher, more sparsely utilized tones caused her to see sparkles in her periphery. The lowest tones buzzed her body as though an invisible force were hugging her. Slowly, naturally, her eyes closed. Everything became meditative and underwater.

Her cousin pulled her back to the surface to say, "This is the song I was telling you about," when Cheeky D started the beat pattern that would prelude and eventually cradle Lewis's voice. "Spirits" had become the title of the song.

Soliday closed her eyes again and took in another deep breath. As she released the air from her lungs, she felt a sensation she would later describe as "falling sideways down a hole." Both sound and vision were distant, cavernous. To her, the sample of Lewis's voice became almost indistinguishable from the beat. She saw the stage and the lights and then up up and up to the ceiling she looked. She fixated momentarily on the large, spinning fan, then gazed higher and higher until she was falling again, backwards and down. There was no soft cushion of breath this time, but rather a solid jolt to her body and then complete blackness.

Through the silent sea, an unseen hand pulled Soliday up from the floor. A kind, dark face came into her focus – it was Lewis. He smiled toward her as she looked around. The entire club was empty now, though a constant, distant beat remained. "Did I overdose?" she asked.

"Overdose?" asked Lewis. "I don't think so. You're epileptic. You didn't know that?"

"No. I didn't," she replied. "Am I dead?"

"Nah. No one's really dead. I think you're just startled. In shock maybe."

"Oh."

Lewis felt a tinge of anxiety emanating from Soliday. "Hey, you wanna dance?" he asked.

"Okay."

The two wrapped their arms around one another and stepped a slow circle around. "My name is Lewis," he said.

"I'm Soliday."

"I know," he smiled. "You hear that annoying fella talkin' over the music? Keep on playin?" Soliday started to make out the song, but could not remember the title. She also failed to remember Cheeky D's involvement with the song, or that authorship or possessions were even real concepts. But she recognized those words. "Keep on playin'." Lewis continued: "That's my voice sayin' that. That's why I'm here, so you know."

"Why you're here?"

"Yeah. Here in this building with you now. I'm here because that song with my voice opened up a path for me to this place so I came to check it out. Saw you strugglin' and thought I'd try to help you relax until you went back."

"Went back?" Soliday had many questions.

"Back to where *you* came from: the material world. Like I said, you ain't dead. You're gonna go back. Anyway, the whole reason I'm telling you is just so you don't think I'm some creepy guardian angel always lookin' over you or nothin'. I ain't stalkin'. We're just in the same place at that same time. That's all."

"I'm really confused."

"Sorry. I'm not trying to confuse you. Don't worry about it, though. It'll make more sense when you get back."

In an unanticipated millisecond, the music returned to full presence, a new song now, and Soliday opened her eyes. She saw the priest, his hand atop her head. He removed it as soon as he saw she was conscious. Her cousin shouted her name and pushed the priest aside. He extended a plastic cup of water to her.

"Where are we?" she asked.

"We're in the lounge," answered her cousin. "You took a hard fall."

"Darlin', you were fishing out," spoke the crossdresser. "We were terrified that you got some bad chemicals."

Soliday sat back in the large, soft chair that she just realized to be supporting her. "I met Lewis," she said. Her cousin, the crossdresser and the priest all returned blank, uncertain stares. "The guy in the song," she attempted to explain.

"Cheeky D?" asked her cousin.

"No. The ghost. The 'keep on playin'' guy on the song. His name is Lewis. I met him and we danced. He told me I have epilepsy."

Soliday's cousin and his friends took her claims very lightly for a time. She returned to Maine and obtained a referral for a neurologist. After some testing, she was indeed diagnosed as epileptic. The professional recognition of this malady within her sent new validity of her story back to Asheville, and with it, a new curiosity to be explored.

Experiments started small, casually even. Soliday's cousin and the apothecary priest had many times discussed the notion of attempting to replicate her experience with a mix of the same chemical cocktail, the same song, and some kind of meditation or light effect. When this discussion drunkenly spilled out to a room of people at a party, they found themselves with volunteers on hand for such an occurrence. And so for a small fee, the priest administered his specialty mix of psilocybin mushrooms, DMT and ketamine to ten willing participants, the twink and himself. The group then walked all together, away from the dusty house, across the large back yard to the edge of the woods.

Cousin twink unfolded his microspeax to amplify the music from his handheld. He played a variety of soft electronic music for around thirty minutes, as the group grew more comfortable with the drugs and with each other. When he and the priest both felt it appropriate, they wrangled the attention of the group and the twink gave these instructions: "When the song, 'Spirits,' begins, close your eyes and focus on the sample with your mind, but let the beat pulsate your body in the background. Fall into a breathing pattern with the rhythm and mentally pick apart the qualities of the voice that states, 'Keep on playin.'" Focus on that voice until the speaker appears in your head. Remember this person. Hold them there and try to send thoughts to them."

"Should we all join hands?" suggested the priest.

"Nah," said the twink. "That will just add an unnecessary use of our sense of touch. I think we need as much sensory deprivation as we can get, except for sound." He started the song, and turned the loop setting on. The group stood in deep meditation, sinking into the drugs and slowly, but certainly, bringing each of their lungs into concert with the bass drum, and subsequently their hearts. As instructed, they focused sharply on the sample of Lewis's words, and when it was all over, not one of them denied seeing him. Still, to be more scientific about it, the twink took each other person aside, one at a time, to hear their descriptions. The priest kept the others in a close huddle so as to be assured that none of them compared stories. All participants described Lewis basically the same, though none claimed to have spoken with him. Seven of the ten also described Lewis as having stepped into the circle between them, appearing somewhat offended, turning to walk away, and disappearing. This is also what the twink and the priest saw, and the other three, though unable to verify any kind of offense in his countenance, would still substantiate that he disappeared abruptly from the middle of their circle.

Talk of the experiment and its eerie results lead to other groups attempting to reproduce it. Their positive outcomes lead to others, and others yet. Though not always successful, people attempted their own variations on the method. Holistic substitutes for the drugs did not work. If one was not open to that specific mix of hallucinogens, he or she was not going to conjure any spirits. The sensory deprivation was also imperative, and the twink was correct in noting that hand holding would distract from the process. Also, the song, or rather at least the recording of a spirit's voice set to a constant rhythm, was a necessary element, or else no connection could be made. One evening, a group attempted to conjure Daniel Patton in the parking lot on Biltmore, right in space 22D. Though his soul never actually parted from his body at that spot, he still could have likely shown, except they had no recording of his voice. (Unfortunately, all Daniel's songs would conclude their digital existence in a police evidence room after the raid and arrest of Petran and Laken Groshman for heroin trafficking.)

Once the formula was solidly established, music producers mined the Internet for EVP recordings to sample in their songs. Ghost voices soon became a hot commodity and the kids stopped coming to the shows to take drugs and dance. Now they were coming to take drugs and commune with the dead. As these experiences opened them to new ideas of death and the afterlife, the dancehalls morphed into holy chapels. Gone were the lights and laser shows. Gone even was the stage, replaced by three hundred-sixty degree surround sound and no central visual reference point. No one cared who was playing the songs anymore. What mattered to the devout were the entities behind the voices that the producers were exploiting. In fact, putting ones name on such a thing became regarded as such an act of arrogance, that anonymous production became commonplace.

Lewis, on the other hand, came to be considered something of a saint inside the new faith, though he could not have cared less about such a thing. He felt awkward about the idea of fleshy earthlings hoisting him on to a spiritual pedestal. Yet, how could he simply abandon the poor creatures, knowing that they still consciously existed in only four perceivable dimensions? How could he disregard the one practice that helped the most to calm their bodily fears? And so he eventually spoke with those who conjured him, kindly and casually, in an attempt to be seen as an equal, rather than the godhead that he was becoming to them. He explained that, just because he was the *first* spirit to be contacted through their method, it did not mean that he was any more important or powerful than any other spirit. After a few more years, most people agreed.

A new wave began when a schoolteacher claimed she had been taking dance lessons from Gilda Radner by conjuring her through samples clipped from old episodes of *Saturday Night Live*. Her story grew within the zeitgeist for two reasons. First, it was evidence that the practices had outgrown the dancehall chapels and moved into the mainstream. Second, and more importantly, it was the first time anyone had considered using a recording made of the deceased from *before* they died. The devout were quick to attempt this, themselves, of course, and the results were exactly as they had hoped – exactly as the schoolteacher had stated. The voice of the living could be used to contact the speaker later in death. Suddenly, sparse EVP recordings were no longer necessary, and the world found itself surrounded by a near infinite number of connections to the afterlife – at least as far back as the old-time radio era. Consequently, as Lewis's small sainthood evaporated, David Bowie and Prince Rogers Nelson were promoted to gods.

The new religion eventually outpaced all other major faiths in the Americas, Europe and Australia. It also grew very large in Asia, though not large enough to overtake Buddhism (or Hinduism in India, naturally). It was banned in the Middle East. By near unanimous agreement, the god statuses of Prince and Bowie were globally upheld. Problems arose with the formation of councils, who designed their agendas to determine who *else* was to be considered worthy of such sacred elevation. Whereas the androgynous alien musicians were natural choices, adopted lovingly and easily by the masses, the councils began to feed a nasty idea that artistic merit alone should also garner consideration.

The original councils were in unanimous agreement that The Beatles and the Rolling Stones deserved the transcendence before any other candidates were discussed. Freddie Mercury, Dolly Parton and Jimmy Hendrix were next promoted to gods. Miles Davis was also elevated, though he seemed to pay little mind to the idea. Madonna and Bob Marley came after that, their names being in close alphabetical succession when announced as nominees at one particularly late and drunken vote. Lou Reed and Iggie Pop were added next, for the council felt it overdue as the natural compliment to Bowie. Johnny Cash made the cut at the same time as Tupac Shakur and Leonard Cohen. Beck, Snoop Dogg and Willie Nelson were inducted together. Frank Zappa, Radiohead and the Beastie Boys entered the godship somewhere in there also. Surprisingly, Elvis Presley went for quite a while without so much as a single consideration. When he did finally acquire his god status (almost by default), it was alongside Stevie Wonder, Stevie Nicks, Ray Charles and Garth Brooks. Outkast, everyone in Pink Floyd and N.W.A., Bob Dylan and Doc Watson all became noted gods. Beyonce and Jay-Z ascended. So did Wesley Wyrick, Brian Wilson and Jerry Garcia. Eminem made the cut, which raised contention in David Byrne supporters that felt overlooked. With some determined lobbying, they went ahead and deemed David Byrne a god also, right after the Wu-Tang Clan (but not before Miley Cyrus). Yes, Wayne Coyne, too. There were countless others. A Japanese council advocated strongly for the inclusion of Mana from Malice Mizer, citing the progress she made for the transgender community. Once she was accepted, the Americans were quick to answer back with RuPaul.

RuPaul, being a recording artist who was more famously regarded as a screen star, raised a major issue among the councils: should their gods continue to be limited to musical subjects? On the conservative side, the popular thought was that since music was the bridge to the spirit's domain, only musicians should be eligible for god status. The liberal members, however, felt that the previous decree of artistic merit should be expanded to all mediums, be them actors, painters, or even journalists or sportscasters. After several years of debate on the issue, the liberal minds persevered, and more gods were determined. Fred Rogers, Martin Luther King Jr., Bill Murray and Bob Ross were all added, one of who staunchly declined the position. By that point, however, the councils had no further regard for whether or not their selections accepted the designation. Their desire for celebrity overrode their ability to deliberate. Soon, Barack Obama was considered a god (Michelle a goddess), then Joan Rivers, Rachel Maddow, Kurt Vonnegut and the Monty Python guys. John Stewart and Stephen Colbert both earned quick godship. Gene Wilder became a god. Chris Farley became a god. Tina Fey and Amy Poehler, Dave Chappelle and Louis C.K. – lots of comedians became gods. Larry David made the cut early and so did Richard Pryor. LeBron James became a god. Harrison Ford became a god, Carrie Fisher a goddess. Robin Williams, Muhammad Ali, Nina Simone and Dan Castellaneta all became gods. Basically, everyone became a god until the whole idea of anyone *not* being a god became ridiculous.

Once the decades long fervor had subsided, and the religious components became obsolete, the scientists stepped in to pick up the pieces. They practiced the sacramental conjuring in clinical settings, streamlining the process. The ideal conditions were then quantified, packaged and sold. The proper mix of hallucinogenic drugs became available for over the counter purchase at any drug store. Audio technicians had abundant work recording people's loved ones and fixing them to a beat pattern. The cries of newborn babies were recorded straight out of the womb. Pets were recorded for post-death visitation, and old people on the way out. Grief therapy became succinct and simple. The so-called gods became too many to matter, and communication with the dead became a practical concept.

Eventually, the entire idea of grief was stripped away from the human psyche, at least as it applied to the loss of other earthlings. It became a lesser feeling, reserved for the loss or destruction of material objects. For the soul ran eternal, but carbon based shapes were bound for ruin. This welled up a new kind of sentimentality in humans, causing them to horde artifacts while taking their ancestors for granted. In a distant past, this might have been considered callous or greedy, but in a more modern world, it was the natural standard. In a modern world, material objects were cherished, for they were alien to the soul. They reached across time, connecting people to their memories. Without worldly totems, the notion of separate identities would inevitably become abstract beyond recovery. They were all we really ever had.

Legacies

Thanatalia

I

Alvin slipped deeper into his coma, eliciting a sensation beyond the sleep. The silence and nothingness were now replaced with a feeling of being dragged through a thick liquid, or perhaps the weight of a gravitational pull through dark matter. In any case, this viscous space soon gave way to a distant star, which was fast approaching, and seeming to grow in size. When Alvin reached this star, it revealed itself to be a tunnel, and he became encapsulated by its white light. Beyond the light, Alvin found himself in a green field, which he seemed to recognize, but could not specifically pinpoint from memory. His mother stepped immediately into his vision and greeted him with a deep, warm embrace.

"I've came back for you, Alvin," she spoke, "but you are not supposed to be here yet." Quickly then, he was flung back into the light, back through the tunnel, back through the sludge space, and toward another star. It neared more quickly than the prior. He felt no soft surrender this time, but rather a coming crash.

A spasm came over Alvin's entire body, jouncing him nearly a foot above his bed. He opened his eyes at the peak of the rise and called for his mother as soon as he touched back down. She returned his name with obvious surprise and came immediately to his bedside. "Alvin!" she repeated as she stroked his hair.

His father turned on a small fluorescent lamp beside the bed, revealing a modest hospital room. "Hey buddy." He touched Alvin's shoulder. "I'm gonna go get someone." He exited the room.

"Oh, Alvin," his mother repeated as she hugged him tightly.

His father quickly returned with a nurse. His mother stepped aside to let her work. "Hey pal," she said, "can you tell me your name?"

"Alvin."

"I'm sorry," interjected his mother, "I just said his name to him three times."

"Uh oh," said the nurse lightly as she removed an oxygen tube from his face. "Can you breathe okay, Alvin?"

"Yeah, I can breathe okay."

The nurse wrapped a cuff around his arm. "Can you tell me how old you are?"

"I'm six."

"Very good!" She placed her stethoscope on the bend in his arm and listened as she squeezed a black ball, pumping air into the cuff. "Your blood pressure is good, too," she finally said before deflating it and removing it from his arm. "Do you feel okay?" She placed her palm on his forehead.

"I think so but I don't know where I am." Alvin looked at the bundle of tubes that was taped to the back of his hand.

"You're in the hospital, honey," she said. "You were in an accident but I think you're going to be okay." She turned to the parents. "He seems to be just fine, but we will come back and check on him every two hours. He doesn't need the oxygen anymore and once that saline bag is empty, we won't have to worry about getting another. Dr. Plank will make his rounds tomorrow morning and, as long as he doesn't see any reason to keep him longer, we should probably be able to discharge him tomorrow afternoon."

"Wonderful!" spoke Alvin's mother.

The nurse turned back to the patient. "Can I get you anything, Alvin? Some water? Ice chips?"

"Water would be good."

"No problem. I will be right back." The nurse exited the room.

Alvin's mother moved to the side of the bed and his father sat on the arm of the chair beside it. "Do you remember anything?" she asked.

"I remember a tunnel of light," he said. "I think I went to Heaven."

His parents exchanged serious, silent, proud glances.

"It was like I was in space," he continued, " and then I went in the tunnel. And then the tunnel went to Heaven and everything was really nice there. But then you told me that I wasn't supposed to be there."

"Who told you that you weren't supposed to be there?" asked his mother.

"You did." he said. "You told me that you came back for me."

"Came back for you?" His mother did not know what to say.

"Yeah," spoke Alvin, simply. Words escaped him, as well. "You're alive, right mommy?"

"Yes, Alvin. Yes we are all alive. Everyone is alive."

"Why were you in Heaven then?"

She opened her mouth but produced only a stammer. Her husband shrugged and shook his head when she looked to him. "God is mysterious," she finally uttered. "Would you like to watch some television?"

"Maybe it wasn't Heaven then," concluded Alvin.

The nurse knocked twice before entering. She presented the patient with a Styrofoam cup of ice water.

The next morning found Dr. Plank in Alvin's room, slightly contradicting the nurse's prognosis. He wanted to keep Alvin admitted twenty-four more hours for monitoring. The family would stay for one more night.

Over the course of that period, Alvin learned the cause of his hospitalization. He had fallen down some steps and hit his head on concrete. He was on life support for five days and had lost his pulse at one point. The net result was a concussion and some blood clotting in his brain – and of course the coma. When the sun rose again, he was unhooked from the machines, prescribed some blood thinners and discharged.

His mother and father took him to eat at Shecky's, his favorite restaurant. "Did I die?" he finally inquired, over dessert.

"Well your pulse stopped," answered his father.

"Is that my heartbeat?" asked Alvin.

Alvin's father was not an educated man and looked to his wife, who offered no answer of her own. "Yeah I guess it is," he settled.

"So then I did die?" asked Alvin again.

"Maybe you did. You said you saw a tunnel of light, right?"

"Yeah but why was mommy there?"

His mother repeated what she had told him the first time, "God is mysterious, Alvin."

"But why were you in Heaven if you weren't dead? How could you be there and be here too?" Alvin looked down at his plate. "Can I say something that might make you mad?"

His parents looked at one another. "Go ahead buddy," said his father.

"Well," he started, "I think maybe that was a dream."

His parents relaxed. "Well it could have been a dream, buddy. We'll never know I guess," said his father.

"But really it could be whatever you choose it to be, Alvin," his mother interjected, "A truth like that is yours alone."

Alvin shook his head. "I guess…I mean…that God is probably…"

"Probably what?" his mother was anxious.

"God is probably like Santa Clause," said Alvin. Two years prior, at the age of four, he reached his own conclusion that Santa Clause was fictional. He simply deduced it from his parents' slippery wording around the holidays. It also did not make sense to him that his parents and grandparents would receive gifts from one another, while his own presents came from some old fat guy that he never even met. He had difficulty relaying his suspicions to his family, fearing their disapproval. Yet, once they knew he was in on the joke, his being so was of no major consequence. Though now finding himself just as nervous in a similar situation, he felt he had a good shot at the same outcome when questioning the God story.

"What do you mean by 'probably like Santa Clause'?" asked his mother cautiously.

"I mean grown ups probably made up God, too."

Thanatalia

II

Ohio State University seemed an unlikely choice to Alvin's parents. They were unaware that he selected this school largely because of its distance away from them. Columbus, Ohio was about a three-hour drive from everything he knew in Kentucky. It was far enough to start a new life with confidence, but not so far that his familiar lifelines were unreachable in times of need. He could test new ways of being there, defining himself consciously. Back home, he had withheld more of himself as he aged, not wanting to upset his parents or cause them to second guess their child rearing abilities. In Columbus, though, his honest feelings could be laid bare, and his new life would be comprised strictly of people who did not turn away from his convictions. He had waited for this kind of freedom for many years, and so it was ironic that his roommate turned out to be a devout Christian, not unlike his parents.

Ignacio Jaramillo went by the name "Iggie." He came from New Mexico where his grandmother raised him. Casually, she had impressed Catholicism on him for his entire life. In spite of that religious signal belying the surface, or perhaps because of it, Iggie had an inherent respect for the beauty and ritual of the faith. He found it easy to be emotionally moved by these things and so a quaint comfort kept him not only dedicated, but also enthusiastic. A true believer, he sought miracles always and so found them everywhere. To him, things were simple: Jesus died so that we could live. As with most young men his age, living included recreational drugs. If not for these those, he and Alvin may not had become such close friends, despite their differing vantage points on God.

Iggie and Alvin's religious discussions would only get heated when they drank alcohol, each being insistent and annoying. Cocaine brought out similar attitudes with an end result of complete communication breakdown. Neither of them ever snorted another line in the other's presence after the first time. Marijuana, which accompanied the majority of such dialog, generally left the topic idling with a mixed bag of dissent, understanding, common cause, misgivings and misperceptions. Discussions over a joint never tied up well and were always eventually traded for lighter fare. Psilocybe mushrooms were a particularly favored indulgence of the boys, and they always felt a sense of agreement after having eaten them. On the mushrooms, neither could possibly deny that all things were, indeed, one. The atheist and the Christian were both correct, for everything and nothing were the same. When eating LSD, neither friend could bring himself to ever bring up the topic. There was always a mutual feeling that to do so would be breaking an unspoken taboo.

In early fall of their sophomore year, Iggie received a care package from his older brother, Abelardo, in New Mexico. It included toiletry items and a bag of individually wrapped, chewy, fruit flavored candies. A phone call from home revealed another surprise stowed away at the bottom of that bag. Iggie dumped the contents out on the coffee table and sifted through them until he reached a piece of candy most unlike the others. It was not in a colorful wrapper, but a small, transparent, zip bag. Inside that was a dark, sticky substance that almost resembled wet coffee grounds. In fact, this was dimethyltryptamine, painstakingly extracted from ayahuasca vine and purified. Abelardo was proud of this achievement, which he had taken on completely alone and with no background in chemistry. He enthusiastically explained to Iggie the protocol for ingesting the drug, also known as DMT, and suggested to him a book on the topic. The next day, Iggie purchased that book, and also a new pipe.

Iggie respected drugs as spiritual facilitators primary to party favors, though sometimes these aspects would overlap. The DMT, it seemed, would be best experienced squarely in the former. He never so much as opened the sticky little bag before completing the book, cover to cover. It took about a week and even then, he only smelled the drug once. He placed the book, the pipe and the bag in his nightstand drawer, believing that the right time would have to reveal itself. He also needed a shaman, if he could find one.

It was snowing outside the evening before the boys would be departing to their respective family homes for the winter break. Iggie would fly out in the morning and Alvin would head south by automobile. Until then, their apartment felt warm and comfortable, with a Brian Eno record playing low. The lamps were dim with Christmas lights outside their window blinking in occasional succession with another display across the street. Finally these simple things could be contemplated now that all the year's tests had been completed and nothing was left in the hands of the students. This was a rare moment where, truly, neither person in the room had a single care. Involuntary meditation.

"Would you like to smoke DMT?" asked Iggie.

"You have DMT?" Alvin was aware of the book Iggie had read, but presumed that actually getting ones hands on the drug would have been an impossible task. He did not realize that Iggie only read the book because he already had the drug in his possession.

"Would you like to try it?"

"Of course, I would!"

"I haven't tried it yet, myself," said Iggie, "but I think I have a good idea of how to make it effective. You know?"

"I *don't* know. I have no idea, but I am willing to do it however you think it needs to be done."

Iggie turned the music off and the two boys migrated to his room. He closed the curtain so that no outside light was piercing the window. "Sit on the bed," he said as he removed the glass pipe and sticky bag from the drawer. He pinched a small glob of the substance from out of the bag and held the pipe upright, dropping the drug into the opening, down its shaft and into the ball on the end. He turned and extended it to Alvin, along with a lighter.

"Woah. A crack pipe?"

"It's just what you smoke it out of. You're not smoking crack."

"I don't know. It just feels like it might be kind of weird," said Alvin. "Why don't you go first anyway? You want me to make sure it isn't poison for you? Is that what it is?"

Iggie laughed. "No man. My brother made this stuff. I just want to play the shaman role first so that I can get an idea of how you need to play it for me."

"The shaman role? What? The crack shaman?"

"Alright, alright." Iggie placed the pipe and lighter back into the drawer. "We can try again after the holidays maybe."

"No no no. Let's do it. Let's do it. I'm sorry," pleaded Alvin. "I said I would do it your way and I need to stick with that. Sorry, man."

Iggie retrieved the pipe and lighter once more and handed them to Alvin.

His concerns persisted. "So if I'm supposed to burn the bulb on the end, then how am I supposed to hold it?"

"By the stem." At that moment, Iggie realized that a third party administration of the drug was probably a good idea. He didn't need hot glass falling out of Alvin's hand, or being thrown across the room for that matter. "Actually, give it back to me. Let me hold it for you."

"I can do it," protested Alvin.

"*My* way," said Iggie.

"Your way." Alvin handed him the pipe and lighter back.

"Okay. Get square on the bed and sit up." Alvin obeyed as Iggie turned the light off, leaving the room pitch black. He sat on the side of the bed, facing Alvin, and flicked the lighter. "I'm right here. Breathe the air out of your lungs." Alvin exhaled. Holding the pipe by its stem, Iggie placed its tip in Alvin's mouth and held the flame against the ball where the substance was sitting. "Inhale slowly and deeply."

Alvin's lungs filled with the smoke as Iggie manipulated the airflow with his thumb and the carburetor. When he could take no more, he backed away from the pipe and exhaled a large cloud into the darkness. Reality fell away almost immediately, leaving him with a feeling that was strangely familiar. There was the thick sludgy feeling of the space around him, and in the distance, a single star. He knew he had to move to the source of light, but felt stuck there on the threshold. He began to whimper.

Hearing this distress, Iggie realized another opportunity to act as the shaman. He needed to assist his friend across the divide. "Just breathe," he said, and this single disembodied statement was precisely what Alvin needed.

Alvin was shot toward the distant star, or rather his essence stretched to it. When he broke through the tunnel of light, he felt the familiar warmth of his childhood and so expected to be released to another green pasture where his mother would send him back. This did not happen. Instead, Alvin found himself standing on a white, cobblestone street, looking at a blue, 1960's model car of some kind, parked in front of a wrought iron fence. This image was brief, and among many more that moved too quickly to engage with. He was also momentarily caught in another scene where he was sitting at a small plastic table, made for children, with an older woman that he did not recognize, but felt warmth toward. Beyond that, he abruptly found himself naked, hanging in space with large, green, circular machines all around him, watching him. He felt no fear of them and, at once, they departed.

The darkness gave way to form as he descended upon a pulsating, red and purple landscape that resembled a beating heart. The rhythm of the mass was in time with a kind of music unlike anything Alvin had ever heard before. It was at once, symphonic, but otherworldly, with a deep and steady beat. He continued his descent into an open ventricle. All up the walls of the cavity was some featureless breed of ghost, all standing on balconies and moving in syncopation with everything else. He softly touched down at the bottom, looking up to realize there were thousands of these *piller people* above him. There on the ground with him, however, was what appeared to be another flesh and blood human – a tuxedoed conductor with a piano, standing on his bench and waving his baton.

His hair whipped in all directions as he flailed around with tight eyes and a large smile. The music began to build, as if new sounds and tones were being added at once. It came to a peak and Alvin felt a tear on his cheek. It was almost too much for him to bear. The maestro then lowered his baton and opened his eyes. Alvin was immediately shot back up the tube, through the top and back into darkness where he found himself rapidly approaching another star. He crashed into himself with a jolt and opened his eyes to more darkness. "Iggie?" he called out.

"Right here, buddy," comforted Iggie as he lit a candle. "Take your time."

Alvin sat up. "I guess there is something over there," he said.

Iggie seized the moment. "Something like God?"

Alvin almost said "no," but stopped short of its utterance. Given what he had just witnessed and its curious similarity to his actual death as a child, he was now posed with new questions on the nature of his relationship to the universe. "Maybe *something* like a God," he replied.

"Are you still an atheist?"

Alvin drew a deep breath and felt the afterglow of the experience around him. "I don't know. I guess you can upgrade me to agnostic."

"I'll take it!" exclaimed Iggie. "Okay, my turn now." He added another, smaller dab of the substance to the pipe, just for good measure. "Trade me seats." Alvin slid off the bed and Iggie took his place. "I need you to take the pipe from me when I exhale, walk over and blow out that candle. Are you cool to do that?"

"Sure. No problem."

"I need you to sit down in the corner and stay totally silent, then – until I am back. One exception is that if you hear me crying or whimpering or any sounds like I am not having a good time, I need you to remind me to breathe."

Alvin remembered this from his own trip. "Yes. No problem. I get it."

"Alright. I exhale, then you take the pipe, blow out the candle, and sit down."

"Got it."

Iggie held the flame to the bottom of the pipe and breathed in slow and steady until his lungs were full. He held it in, extended the pipe and lighter from himself, and exhaled. Alvin took the pipe. He blew out the candle. He sat down.

Iggie did not need any reminders to breathe. He crossed the threshold with no resistance. His body stretched out to a distant star and he entered its tunnel of light. The first memory flash that lasted was a fire in the desert, not unlike many he had seen at gatherings in his youth. There were other people there, all men without shirts, but he did not recognize them. Back through more memories, he held for a moment in one where a baby was suckling his breast. He knew this breast was his own, and that it felt natural, forgetting his boyish Earthen body, altogether. Traveling further back made him forget that matriarchal body as well. Though somatic notions were removed, he found that the feeling of nakedness was not. Like Alvin before him, he came to be suspended in space, surrounded by the voyeuristic, green, circular machines. Iggie felt an eagerness to interact with them, causing them to leave abruptly, as before.

Down he fell over the pulsating landscape. There was the otherworldly music and the many open ventricles, one of which he descended into. Inside were the pillar people, those faceless dancing ghosts that lined the walls. When he reached the bottom, though, there was another man - not the tuxedoed conductor. This man's skin was dark and his clothing was tattered. Iggie could see the sound waves, emanating from the crown of the man's head. It was obvious that, though he had no piano or baton, this bearded man was indeed conducting the music. Iggie knew exactly who this man was and so knelt down in the glory of his king, Jesus Christ of Nazareth. As the music hit a long, emotional rise, Iggie was completely in tears. When the peak of sound subsided, Jesus turned and reached out to him. Before he could begin to reciprocate, he was expelled from the scene and sent back to his Earthen reality. After the usual spasm, he sat up immediately. "I'm back."

Thanatalia

III

Alvin and Iggie went their separate ways after school, but continued to keep in touch, first by phone, then email, then social media. Both men ended up well traveled. Iggie took an academic path, earning him an eventual doctorate in cultural anthropology, as well as a few awards for his writings on the topic. He married a pretty Italian woman and together they had two daughters. Alvin pursued no further education beyond his bachelor's degree in sociology, with a minor in philosophy, of course. Instead, he built a small real estate empire, purchasing homes and renting them out for more than the cost of the monthly mortgage payment. He had enough of a cash flow to pay the bills at his primary home, while traveling frequently to indulge new prospects. He thought he had been in love a few times, but nothing ever panned out for him. He had no interest in having children, anyway, and so focused on money.

Though the men had reunited several times over the years, more than a full decade had passed before their next encounter in London. Iggie was there to present an academic lecture at the University College. Seeing an online advertisement for the event, Alvin flew there and attended secretly. At that point in his existence, his income flowed steadily and plentifully and so he felt it an apt time to vacation in Europe and surprise an old friend.

At the presentation's conclusion, awestruck young students and fellow scholars alike swarmed Iggie. Alvin waited patiently for each of them to pay their complement, ask their questions and exit. He sat on the side in the first row of seats, head in his phone, until Iggie was finally free.

As Alvin slowly stood, Iggie picked up his briefcase and dashed toward the door, never looking his way.

"Excuse me, doctor," spoke Alvin in a false British accent. Iggie froze. "It sure is rude of you to pretend that you didn't see me over here."

Iggie turned and extended his hand. "I'm sorry. Ignacio Jaramillo."

"Pleased to meet you," said Alvin as he shook his hand. He dropped the accent. "Do you know *my* name?"

Iggie finally focused on the face. "Wait. *Alvin?*" he asked after a momentary disbelief.

"You got it."

Iggie embraced him in a giant bear hug. "I am utterly shocked to see you. What are you *doing* here?"

"Nothing in particular. Just thought I would fly to London and check out what you have going on."

"This is such an awesome, awesome surprise," said Iggie. "So what are you doing right now? Do you have time for a drink or what?"

"I have all the time," replied Alvin.

They walked to a popular restaurant just off the campus and sat across from one another beside a large front window. Each man was in his mid-forties now, rounder and more weathered than previously remembered by the other. There was distinct warmth between them as they reviewed older, more absurd memories they shared; and eventually, of course, religion. Alvin brought it up at the first natural, but prolonged pause in their exchange: "So studying Anthropology and knowing what you now know on that intellectual level, is Jesus still your guy?"

"Until the day I die."

"But that's it? Then you're moving on to Krishna or something?"

They shared a laugh at the notion. "But really though," said Iggie, "who can say?"

Alvin nodded. "Yeah. Who can say?"

A man stepped up to the window beside them, cupped his eyes to the glass and looked inside - beyond them, as if they were not there. To this man, Abdullah Maloof, they may as well not have been, for he was only pretending to seek anything on the other side of the glass. He was, instead, making a nervous action and then attempting to follow through with it as if it were a natural and intentional decision.

"Look at this joker," said Alvin.

Both men stared at him until he continued on, but he only moved to the door and put his back to the wall there. He thought intensely about the handful of televisions that stood out to him when he looked through the window. These were the things he ultimately focused on to avoid eye contact with anyone inside. He pondered their flow of smut and sin. He did not understand how a person could eat food while taking in images of sex, drugs and money. It seemed hypocritical to him for a person to even consider praying before a meal in this environment, and yet one, he felt, is indebted to pray before every meal. This conflict presented a conscious choice, then, between Allah and the western world.

Abdullah took a deep breath and stepped inside. He stopped for a moment, felt he was drawing attention, and stepped awkwardly into the bathroom. It was empty there and he entered the furthest stall. He unbuttoned his large coat and, best as he was able, adjusted the array of explosives taped to his torso. The line that ran down the inside of his sleeve was slightly too short, eclipsing the armpit when he held the connected press-button trigger in his palm. This was a mild inconvenience compared to the ultimate price that he knew he would pay in the name of his God. Somewhat confident now, he exited the bathroom, back into the foyer. He gripped the trigger tightly, with his thumb ready to drop in a moments notice.

A gangly blonde hostess approached him with menus in her arm. "How many in your party, sir?"

He pushed the button and obliterated both their bodies.

Abdullah's essence stretched rapidly toward the distant star. He felt a sense of sudden weightlessness the moment he entered its tunnel of light. He drifted deeper inside until he reached his past lives. Moving backwards through them, he was at one point pushing a plow. At another he sat beside an elderly man, up against a large, clay building. The quick succession of newly rekindled memories soon gave way to darkness and he found himself in the company of the green circle machines. They examined his naked body thoroughly, revolving around him as he hung in space. Together at once, they each emitted a thick, white, light against him. With a saturating property that appeared not unlike liquid, Abdullah found his entire being to be consumed by this light. He became one with it, as it were.

He soared over the sinewy, beating red landscape and heard the alien music that seemed to control it. He understood now that he existed in a state of pure, but malleable consciousness. He directed his perception down through one of the many passages below him and raced to the bottom. Above him, the faceless, dancing piller ghosts began leaping from the walls in mass droves. Their ectoplasmic bodies came to fill the space all around Abdullah, eventually merging with him entirely. The collective plasma formed into a room, adorned with large tapestries. In this room manifested many pillows and beds, followed by an array of soft and beautiful young women. He felt a warmth and familiarity as one reached out for him, touching a perceived hand that he had extended from a presumed body.

"Muhammad is very pleased with you," she said, "He is glad that you are with us now."

On Earth, in the restaurant, Alvin sat up in shock. The blast had propelled him backward, ripping his jacket and smashing his body up against the wall. The large window had been shattered and debris was present all around. He could hear several voices screaming hysterically and stood up to survey the situation. His legs were wobbly but functional. His higher vantage point revealed carnage throughout the room, with maimed bodies strewn randomly among overturned tables and chairs. After finding his bearings, he stumbled toward Iggie, who was still on the ground. He was unconscious and his face and chest were covered in blood.

Alvin lifted Iggie from under his shoulders and propped him up against a booth in a sitting position. He shook him harshly and screamed. "Iggie!" He checked for a pulse, but it was faint, if even actually present at all. For all Alvin knew, it was his own pulse he was feeling through his thumb. He shook him more violently now. "Iggie! Iggie!" He smacked him in the face repeatedly. "Wake up!"

Alvin stood and shouted to the room, "I need a doctor over here!"

His plea was met with another disembodied voice returning, "I do too! Please help me!"

In his frustration, he lifted the nearest chair above his head and threw it through the window. A few remaining shards of broken glass fell out of place. Sirens whirred in the distance, getting louder as they approached.

Far from the madness, but still perceiving the blast, Ignacio quickly shot out to the star and entered the tunnel of light. Back through his lives, he found himself in several familiar scenarios. These included brushing a horse, sitting in a rustic, primitive classroom, and also shopping for baby clothes among other things. At last, he reached the dark space, suspended there as the machines surrounded him. They engulfed him in their light, as they had done to Abdullah and countless other souls before them. Ignacio had returned to a state of pure consciousness.

He descended upon the pulsating landscape, soaring down into one of its many openings. As he continued deeper, he recognized the dancing ghosts that lined the walls. This time, though, they followed him to the bottom, leaping from their positions in large numbers. Soon he was one with them and, collectively, they formed a vast desert with a seemingly open sky. Ignacio's conscious stood in place there as a hooded figure approached him on a white horse. He felt no fear as the man stopped before him and dismounted. He withdrew his hood and Ignacio knew immediately that he perceived a physical manifestation of Jesus Christ – and not for the first time.

Ignacio dropped to his knees and wept before Jesus. In a fluid, ghostlike motion that defied the physics of Earth, the Christ swept up under Ignacio's arms, returning him to what seemed like a standing position. The two embraced and the Christ whispered to him, "Thank you for believing in me. I am glad to have you with us here."

IV

Over fifty years had passed since the bombing. In that time, Alvin had experienced a handful of more deaths, though none as violent as Iggie's. He, himself, wished to die many times, not out of depression, but boredom. He had no wife or child. His parents were dead and so were all of his closest friends. His dreams had been accomplished, almost in full, by his sixtieth birthday. He had everything that he had ever wanted, short of some sexual fantasies. Most of his homes were paid off, collecting pure profit through a property management firm. He decided to spend what he hoped were his final days on a desolate ranch in Montana. There were no animals or crops to tend to - only a house, a shed, and powerful view of the mountains.

Sunsets were spectacular, drawing lines across the landscape and blatantly exposing the movement of the Earth. He watched as many as he could. The spectacle of the thing infused him with a kind of spirit. It was not a godman in the sky, but that ectoplasmic oneness that runs through all life. It was the only thing he had left to remind him that he was not *really* alone - because no one is ever alone. And so naturally, quietly, finally, Alvin sat on his porch, took one last deep breath, and passed with the setting sun.

Slowly, lightly, Alvin stretched out to the star, and through the tunnel of light. Nothing jarred him as he moved back through his lives: sitting by a lantern at a train station, lying in the grass - meditative moments. As his naked body hung in the ensuing void, the machines approached and casually dispensed their light. It filled him entirely, exposing his connection to a vast ocean of consciousness.

This ocean was red and he had seen it before, mistaking it for a landscape. Its waves rippled with the pulsating, aquatic music that emoted from the sum of its inhabitants. Alvin descended from above, penetrating a whirlpool in this sea – or perhaps it was a black hole. The familiar ghosts watched from the walls of the endless pit. As Alvin dropped beyond their posts, they leapt after him in unison. Falling all together, collapsing and melding into one another, their collective existence gave form to his college apartment. From his couch, he watched the Christmas lights blink through the window. Ignacio entered the room and Alvin stood immediately.

"About time you got here," said Ignacio as the two embraced.

"So this is Heaven, I guess?" inquired Alvin.

"No. Not really. The idea of Heaven treats the idea of Hell as a separate experience in a separate place, but really it's all kind of the same. We call this place Thanatalia."

"Wow. So your religion was disproved by death then?" Of course, Alvin had to ask.

"No. I wouldn't say that." In the afterlife, Ignacio still felt the need to defend himself immediately. "I mean, I met Jesus. I hung out with Jesus – many times, and in so many different circumstances. I could summon him here right now if I wanted – so could you. But that's just it. What does it matter? On Earth, I really liked tacos, but what would be the point of eating them for every meal? Eventually, you want to move on to a different food – a different experience – no matter what. Well, that's kind of how it was with Jesus. Scarcity creates value, but Jesus isn't scarce here. Nothing is, because we create it all directly out of the collective consciousness."

"I don't quite follow. Jesus has no value to you now?"

"Nothing has value to anyone here. I think Catholicism is a beautiful way to live a life, and a strong place to hang some hope. Also, since everything is essentially possible here, it means that everything is true and so there would be no basis to disprove anything whatsoever. In that regard, I definitely feel that I was always correct about my religion while on Earth. I will concede, though, that it has no basis here, except ornamentally. Spiritual experiences in Thanatalia are a dime a dozen. All experiences are."

With those words, Alvin felt a tinge of emptiness. He glimpsed the bleakness of infinity. He inherently knew the pointlessness of a nonlinear reality. There was nothing to fight for after death. The greatest challenge, it seemed, would be maintaining creativity within the mythology that was to be spouted to the consciousness.

"I want you to meet someone," said Ignacio. "Follow me."

The living room collapsed into light. Moving through it, Alvin trailed Ignacio's ghost over the pulsating sea and down into one of its many passages. As they dove to the bottom, all the ghosts along the interior followed them down. The collective situated into a new scene, a restaurant. Alvin and Ignacio sat across from one another by a large window.

"Are we where I think we are?" asked Alvin.

"Where do you think we are?"

Alvin could not produce an answer.

"Okay. Don't freak out," ordered Ignacio, "but do you recognize this guy?"

As if on cue, Abdullah entered the restaurant and approached their table. "Why do you want to go back to this?" he asked Ignacio.

"Context," Ignacio replied. "This is my friend, Alvin. He was with me that day."

Abdullah extended his hand. "Pleased to meet you."

"Why would I shake your hand?" asked Alvin. "You killed my friend. Why are you even here? Iggie, why are *we* here?"

"Easy. Easy," requested Ignacio, "This is what I am trying to show you. It doesn't matter that he killed me. We're all the same in this place. All just extensions of the same core soul. Death puts you here. Life puts you on Earth. Good and evil aren't really that big of a deal once you have no mystery to solve."

"I am sorry," interjected Abdullah. "I don't know what else to say. I saw things very differently when I was flesh and blood. I didn't know what I know now."

"I didn't know what I know now, either," said Ignacio, "but now that I *do* know, it is obvious that death is illusion. So there is no reason to sweat it. I mean, the apology is not unappreciated; it's just not necessary. I'm going to kill all three of us right now – just to paint a better picture for you, Alvin." Ignacio extended his hand, revealing an olive green, French style, fragmentation grenade. He removed its pin, but held pressure against the lever. He turned to Abdullah. "You wanna take us to see the girls? Ease the tension?"

"Sure thing," Abdullah replied.

Ignacio smiled and released the grenade. Before it could reach the floor, it exploded, saturating the moment in white light and returning it to the collective consciousness. This detonation produced no particular pain in the three souls and the intensity leading up to it contributed artfully to the intended aesthetic.

Again, the souls soared above the red, breathing landscape, or sea of consciousness, with Alvin tailing Ignacio. This time, they did not drop to the bottom of their chosen channel, but instead took a place on the wall among the other ghosts. It became apparent that their dancing was involuntary. Abdullah's ghost soon appeared above them and when he fell past their position, they leapt after him, along with all the other ghosts. The mass of their essence gave form to a room not unlike the one Abdullah had initially arrived at after his death. Tapestries and pillows were ever present, and a large conglomeration of women encircled the fringe of the dimly lit scene.

The women stepped out of the shadows and filled the perceived room. One of them, Persian in appearance, rubbed her crotch against Abdullah's. He grabbed her hair at the crown, jerked her head back and kissed her deeply. A red haired woman put her arms around Ignacio and used her forehead to draw a line from his neck to his shoulder. "This place will become an all out orgy party before it's over," he said.

"What about –." Alvin paused, short of concluding his question with "your wife." It had been a long time since he had seen Ignacio. The social codes of Thanatalia were still unfamiliar to him. What if Iggie liked this girl? He didn't want to blow it for him. Would that even be possible? He continued more ambiguously. "What about Antoinette?"

"What? My wife?" asked Ignacio. "She's here somewhere in the ether. I run into her occasionally."

"Oh."

"Yeah well, until death do we part, right? Relationships aren't the same in Thanatalia as they are on Earth. When you get here and realize that you can have anything and everything you want, it really resets your experiential priorities. Antoinette and I worked well as a team on Earth. We raised some great kids. But over here we have different desires. We just don't mutually conjure one another very much anymore."

"I see," said Alvin, "So what is this?"

Ignacio laughed. "These are Abdullah's virgins!"

Abdullah heard Ignacio say his name but ignored it. He was, by that time, engrossed in direct sexual intercourse with the Persian woman. There appeared to be several such manifestations spread across the room's soft furniture pieces.

"He's not listening," Ignacio continued. "This whole motif was part of his death experience. The whole forty virgins or seventy virgins or whatever it is that Muhammad gives you for being a good Muslim. Of course, virginity is an Earth concept. Everyone that's here right now is here strictly to recreate the pleasure of the flesh, as best as we can remember."

"You do see the irony here, right?" asked Alvin. "You are sharing a heaven with the guy who killed you to get here."

"You really need to get past that," Ignacio scolded. "This is not a heaven. This is an orgy party in Thanatalia and everyone shares everything here."

Alvin felt as though he had been taught an abrasive lesson, leaving him without an immediate notion of corrective action. "So what should I do here?"

"Conjur up a partner," said Ignacio, with the red head now pulling him toward the perimeter.

A young woman approached Alvin. He recognized her right away, as this was the person he most wanted to see in the current scenario – his high school crush, Claire Appleton. She appeared precisely as he had remembered her, with sleek blonde hair that framed a smattering of pale freckles across her nose. Her form appeared to be aged around seventeen or eighteen as he had last remembered, and she even wore the red cardigan sweater that had become such a mainstay of their interactions in school. She took his hand and greeted him with a large smile.

"Alvin Absom?" she asked, as though she did not know. "It has been so long." She threw her arms around this neck and pressed her bosom against him. He felt a sense of home and thought about conjuring his parents.

There was no such thing as passing time in Thanatalia – only rearranging experience. Alvin and Ignacio eventually grew distant, as each soul became tired of rehashing experiences based on those identities. Soon they each strayed backward into their preceding lives, and the ones before those, as well. Along the way, these two souls would meet in various forms, but never quite as powerfully connected as when they were Alvin and Ignacio. Back through their lifelines, they were never lovers, nor close family, once an employer to employee (Ignacio to Alvin, that is) and were usually casual acquaintances or connections of utility. It was only on their last lives that their connection of souls was as securely forged on Earth as it was in Thanatalia. The further they moved back through the recreation of their respective past realities, and the more they jumbled around and juxtaposed the contents of one reality to another, the more disintegrated their identities would become. The details were growing fuzzy as more and more of the collective consciousness ran through their souls.

These two particular ghosts did, by chance, soon come to find themselves randomly positioned beside each other along the wall in the pit, each vibrating rapidly. There was a vague recognition that lead to an exchange of thought, as they awaited a new soul to ride down: "This ever changing existence is structured to erode us back into the sea. It is inevitable. We will be lost forever if we continue in this way. We must give up our ability to experience at will and strive for oblivion, no matter what it holds."

A spirit came shooting down the passage and all the ghosts leapt from the wall. The two souls stayed together as the consciousness formed some sort of military barracks. Immediately they exited the scene, riding the excess ectoplasm spray back out over the strange, red, sea of thought. As they flew above it, they passed over trillions of openings, but entered none. Determined that this soft, porous landscape must have more obscure territory, they kept moving forward.

Eventually, over the horizon, the top of a light colored object appeared. Faster now, pushing with all their essence, the object seemed to grow in size. It soon detached from the perceived foundation, revealing a separate position in the space ahead, but high above. They directed their trajectory toward this sphere and continued until they were right against it. The object was soft, but penetrable. There was no turning back now. The two souls pushed their way through its membrane. Inside, they were greeted with darkness and silence.

The soul that once belonged to Alvin emerged from a long sleep in its warm cocoon. He awoke to find a dark, large, masked man was forcibly removing him from his slumber. In protest, he wailed. Once fully evacuated, the man held him up in the air for other strange people to see and a sense of relief came over them. One of these people was also crying, and it was she to whom this newly contained soul was given.

The baby's tears ceased immediately upon remembering his own flesh; enchanted by the warmth he felt against his mother. Unable to move very freely, his eyes navigated the room with limited perception. He first noticed his mother's tight, thin, and abundant braids. He would have reached for them if he knew how. Looking down and to the right of that view, directly across from himself, he spotted another baby, nestled in her other arm.

A nurse clasped her hands together. "Just look at them. They are *so* cute."

"Thank you," spoke the mother.

"Congratulations again on your twins, Ms. Akenzua."